IT BEGAN WITH *SAVING THE QUEEN*, THEN *STAINED GLASS; WHO'S ON FIRST; MARCO POLO, IF YOU CAN; AND THE STORY OF HENRI TOD.*

NOW BLACKFORD OAKES RETURNS IN HIS SIXTH FASCINATING ADVENTURE OF ESPIONAGE AND INTERNATIONAL INTRIGUE....

SEE YOU LATER ALLIGATOR

"Tense, chilling, unflaggingly lively ... The tales of Blackford Oakes get better and better."
—Edmund Fuller, *The Wall Street Journal*

"Buckley's most successful attempt to shade his fanciful thriller-comedy into more serious matters of love, loyalty and honor." —*Kirkus Reviews*

"Chilling ... action-packed ... Blackford Oakes adventures are addictive." —*B. Dalton Bulletin*

"Buckley brings us face-to-face with the possibilities lurking behind our real headlines."
—*San Francisco Chronicle*

Novels by William F. Buckley, Jr.

SEE YOU LATER ALLIGATOR
THE STORY OF HENRI TOD
MARCO POLO, IF YOU CAN
WHO'S ON FIRST
STAINED GLASS
SAVING THE QUEEN

SEE
YOU
LATER
ALLIGATOR

WILLIAM F. BUCKLEY, JR.

A DELL BOOK

Published by
Dell Publishing Co., Inc.
1 Dag Hammarskjold Plaza
New York, New York 10017

ISBN: 0-440-17682-4

Reprinted by arrangement with Doubleday &
Company, Inc.
Printed in the United States of America
March 1986

10 9 8 7 6 5 4 3 2 1

WFH

For my nieces and nephews:

James Buckley
Pamela Curzon
John Kirkover
Priscilla Langford
William Buckley
Mary Alison
Elizabeth Stanton
Jennifer Wild
Timothy Buckley
Janet Powell

Mary Lee
Aloise Harding
John Joseph Montgomery

Peter Pierce
James Frederick Wiggin
Priscilla Langford
William Frank
David Lane
Andrew Thurston

Cameron Outcalt
Maureen Kimberley
Talbot Lee
Bruce Buckley
Jennifer Outcalt
Susan Bradford

Christopher William
Kathryn Lois
Michael Buckley
Maureen Robbins
Lee Brent
John Claude
Aloise Steiner
Patricia Lee
William Reid
James Wyman

William Huntting
Fergus Reid
Elizabeth Hanna
Claude Langford
John Alois

Patricia Egan
Priscilla Lee
Gerald Ambrose
Ann Steiner
William Buckley

Thomas Jackson
William Buckley
Anne Read
Carol Lawton

SEE
YOU
LATER
ALLIGATOR

One

He'd call Rusk.

No, he wouldn't call Rusk. Yes, he'd better call Rusk. No, dammit, he wouldn't call Rusk.

Yes, he'd better call Rusk, even if the State Department couldn't do anything right. But he'd better call Dillon. After all, Douglas Dillon was the chief of the U.S. delegation. Hell, he's Secretary of the Treasury. It was an economic meeting, down there at Punta del Este, just now, with the economic heads of all the countries of Latin America.

Huh. Bet they could have had a quorum and voted the majority stock of the Swiss banking industry, those buggers, the way they salt it away, or anyhow, that's what the CIA reports, and Dad's always said it's true, and you certainly don't read about a lot of former economic ministers—"Ministros de Economía," not bad, Jack; it wasn't you who had trouble with Spanish at Harvard—of places like Argentina and Mexico going exactly broke after they leave office.

CIA? I wonder. Dick did *stress stress stress the secrecy. Fat chance his meeting will be secret for very long.* "Castro's No. 2 Man Meets/With Presidential Special Assistant. Che Guevara, Cuban Economic Czar, Spends Late Evening/With Richard Goodwin, JFK Speechwriter. They Meet Privately in Montevideo/Reportedly Got On 'Famously.' "

Let's see, did I miss anything? Yeah. "House Committee on Un-American Activities/Issues Subpoena of Goodwin/Aide Pleads Executive Immunity." *Dick said the journalist in on the rendezvous promised he'd keep quiet, and—not bad—the news isn't out yet, and I figure the meeting ended—let me see—oh, it's . . . 11 P.M. When was it 6 A.M. in Montevideo, when their meeting*

*broke up? I suppose I could call the Library of Congress and ask.
Probably would take them two days to come up with the answer. Call
it sixteen hours ago. I think Buenos Aires and Washington are on the
same time zone. So nobody has come out with it yet. But they will, they
will.*

He reached over his desk and depressed a button. "Bring
me a Coca-Cola, please." *Coca-Cola. Cocacolonization, nice. I
wonder who first came up with that? Dick would probably know. He
knows a lot. In fact he knows more than Arthur wishes he knew.* He
smiled. In acknowledgment of the Coca-Cola, the butler
thought; actually, at what he was thinking about professional and academic rivalries, Schlesinger, Goodwin—et al.

*"No disguising the totality of that man's absorption in his cause."
Were those the words Dick Goodwin had used? Something like that.
And true, of course. The executions going on in Cuba right now are
executions of anyone who gets in the way not only of Castro, but of
Che. Funny name, Che. He adopted it when he was backing the
Commies in Guatemala, ten years ago, and now that he's Minister of
Industry instead of Bank Minister—let me see, Ministro del Banco,
sounds good—he can't sign all the bank notes just plain "Che" the
way he did last year. Who says he has no affectations? Would they say
I had affectations if I signed congressional bills "Jack"? Right. And
they would be right in saying so. Anyway, I don't like that kind of
informality. It took me two years before I figured out that Harry
Truman was Harry Truman's real name. I thought he was being
informal and was really Harold Truman. And no middle name. S
stands for S. And who says it shouldn't? It isn't even easy anymore to
remember that Bobby was baptized "Robert."*

*I just don't believe it that the Brazilian diplomat who invited Dick
to that apartment for a "party" for his "friend" just "happened" to
invite Che Guevara. Heap big coincidence, that one. And anyway,
everybody knew that the whole Latin-American gang was trying to
get Che and Dillon to exchange a few words, maybe chip away a little
at the ice of the Bay of Pigs. God, was that nightmare only four
months ago?*

Still. They did meet. No journalists present, just the translators and the bodyguards, Dick said. Why any Cuban would think he needed a bodyguard to protect him from any American beats me after the Bay of Pigs. That was a nice wisecrack Guevara opened with: "I want to thank you for invading our country. It has made a great power out of us and eliminated all resistance to Castro." Well, we had it coming. I like Dick's answer too: "You're welcome. And you can repay the favor by invading Guantánamo." Nice. Smart, Dick, and tough, though maybe just a little too open-minded about certain subjects.

Still. That was a hell of an interesting offer Che Guevara made.

The President yanked a sheet of paper from the stationery drawer, pulled a ballpoint pen from his inside coat pocket, and scratched "1," which he followed by a dash, then "2," through the number "4."

"1. We lift the trade embargo on Cuba.

"2. Cuba agrees from the proceeds of trade with the U.S. to compensate us for the U.S. property confiscated by Castro.

"3. We promise not to make any attempt to invade Cuba or to replace Castro. And,

"4. Castro promises to make no attempt to export his revolution outside the borders of Cuba."

He leaned back in his chair and reflected.

This one is for the CIA. I'll be rid of Dulles in the next couple of months—he damn well should have resigned after the Bay of Pigs, instead of waiting until a few weeks ago to announce his retirement. Bay of Pigs. Bad forecasting. CIA's fault, I say. Don't like the alternative! But then maybe I should have resigned. But why would I want to go and do that? Being President is a lot of fun. Yes, I'll see Dulles. This is a lead we've got to follow up. But not publicly.

"Get me Allen Dulles," he spoke into his telephone, pausing only then to look at his watch.

Oh well, being called at midnight goes with the job. My guess is they really like it. I don't. I'd rather be doing something else at midnight. On the other hand, I'd rather be doing that any time.

"Allen? Come on over, will you—want to talk to you about something."

Two

It had gone well with Sally Partridge. More properly, Sally M. Partridge, Visiting Professor, Facultad de Filosofía y Artes, University of Mexico, known to most of the students as the Summer School. Not all the students were Americans, but most of them were. And serious students, mostly. There was the usual ration of young people there only because they got twitchy when asked, "How did you spend the summer?" and now they could say they had attended the summer school at the University of Mexico, never mind what they did there, or got out of it, or even whether they had learned any Spanish. Half the classes were given in Spanish, and Sally was making a vigorous effort to learn enough about the Spanish language to use it in the formal semesters during the fall and spring, though in her correspondence with the dean it had been specified that she was free to lecture in English, "inasmuch as most of our students who wish to learn about Jane Austen and other early nineteenth-century authors are presumed to be able to follow a lecture delivered in English."

Sally had begun in June, speaking only in English but hoped that by October she would be able to manage the switch. It both pleased her that Blackford had also been studying Spanish, because she could practice with him, and annoyed her, because his German was fluent and hers was not and she liked to think that in academic matters she outpaced him in every discipline, except of course engineering, which was his thing.

"Si, tu puedes venir a visitarme," she wrote now to him in

Berlin, acknowledging his letter, written after a mutual, ninety-day freeze, asking reconciliation. "But enough of the lingo. I have the wing of a house off Insurgentes (that's the big north-south street in Mexico City), three quarters of the way from the center of town to the university. It is owned by a charming couple, both a little daffy—I mean, she is a writer, a mother, a den mother, a best friend, an aunt, uncle, grandmother, godmother. She isn't happy unless she is doing something for me. She knows everybody in Mexico, is utterly impoverished, couldn't care less, and runs a boardinghouse of sorts. You eat with the other guests. On the other hand if you don't want to, they will bring you your food to your own little dining room. A rambling place. Every now and then Mrs. Littlejohn (that's her name) calls a carpenter, who mostly drinks pulque (that is the Mexican drink-for-all-seasons, half gruel, half alcohol) but when he isn't doing that, he is building new rooms for Mrs. Littlejohn. He charges one dollar per day, and completes a room in about two weeks, then Mrs. Littlejohn goes to the Thieves' Market which thrives on Sunday. (Do you like that, Blacky, 'thieves thrive on Sunday'? Or shouldn't thieves thrive at all? Spies thrive, on the other hand. Or at least you used to thrive on spying.) Do you realize I have not seen you for six months? The longest period without seeing you since Yale. Notice, I didn't say 'the longest six months in my life.' That would make things entirely too easy for you, and you don't deserve things being easy for you. Or *do* you, my precious, beautiful, brainy, arrogant, reckless, bloody Cold Warrior? Yes, you can come here for your vacation, provided you do not go communist-hunting at night, though to tell you the absolute truth, Blackford (notice, I called you 'Blackford' just then, which means that I am being very serious), if you promise not to quote me, we could use a little communist depopulation over at the university. I mean, the place is crawling with them. It would be a lot easier for me if I were

British, anything but an American. On the other hand, it's American students who keep the Summer School going.

"Where was I? Yes. Come to Mrs. Littlejohn's and stay in my little wing. I think . . . yes. Mrs. Littlejohn is, about certain matters, *very* formal, so I think you will come as 'Blackford Partridge,' my brother in the foreign service, just completed a tour in Berlin, waiting for reassignment. Oh dear, Blacky, how I long to see you. Cable me and tell me the flight you will be on, and I will meet it in my 1959 bug—same one, the red convertible. Yes, I will. Your Spanish would never get through to the taxi driver, and Calle Calero is not easy to find. Though you could begin by telling the taxi driver to take you to the house of Diego Rivera, they all know where that is, and from there you can find Calle Calero, can't miss Calle Calero. Besides, come to think of it, with your training you could find Calle Calero anywhere, darling, couldn't you? Even if it were painted in invisible ink? Do bring me some invisible ink, dear. I've never handled any, and I am tempted sometimes to write on some student papers my true judgment of them, but this would need to be a deep dark s-e-c-r-e-t, shh!! Am I being silly? I feel silly, even though I am thirty-two years old, a Ph.D. from Yale, and a Visiting Professor of English Literature at the University of Mexico. And what are you? Do they give you invisible promotions? Are you a colonel or something? Or maybe even a general? Have you been secretly decorated by Adenauer? De Gaulle? The Queen? You will find me as bright and beautiful as ever. 'The lenient hand of time did much for her by insensible gradations in the course of every day.' Recognize? Of course not. *Northanger Abbey*, J. Austen, and if *per impossibile*, as you liked to say at Yale, you do, then you can write me back and tell me which word I altered. Good night, Blacky, until the 21st, 22nd, or 23rd. Cable me which day, what airline, what flight number."

Blackford had sat an hour in the Tiergarten, staring at the wall the East Germans had begun to build only six days before. For the first two days it had been merely barbed wire, with here and there concrete stanchions. But the work was progressing—it was pursued doggedly, twenty-four hours a day—and already it was shaping up as a proper wall, unfinished of course, but one could see that its architects envisioned nothing transitory. Blackford wondered briefly whether the Great Wall in China was sturdier than what he was looking at. Longer, yes. But how long would this wall be before the communists were done with it? The logic of a wall separating East from West Berlin presupposed complementary walls, did it not, around the western perimeter of Berlin, to prevent East Germans from seeking freedom from that direction? And another wall, right up the national frontier of East Germany. He read the letter again, a third time, and wondered, and was gladdened that such a spirit as Sally's had not been dampened by his eyewitness account of what had happened in Berlin during the past week. He walked first to the travel bureau at the Hotel Westfalenhof, then to the concierge from whom he took a cable blank. He wrote out: "PARTRIDGE CARE LITTLEJOHN CALERO 32 VILLA OBREGON MEXICO D.F. YOUR BROTHER WHO PINES TO SEE YOU WILL ARRIVE ON AUG 21 EAL 1520. WILL BRING WHAT YOU REQUEST PLUS INVISIBLE PIECE BERLIN WALL. MUCHOS BESOS PARA MI BONITA SALLY COMO AM I DOING?"

Three

The Director came right out with it and said to the President that inasmuch as he was scheduled to retire within a month or two, perhaps it would be better to turn the new project over to his deputy, or perhaps even wait until his successor at the CIA was named. The President declined the opportunity to become sentimental about the impending personnel change, indeed coming as close as he ever did to snapping shut an exchange. "I want *you* to go with it," was all he said, rising from his rocking chair.

And so they had gathered at the little inn in Leesburg— old, picturesque (though the Director had never noticed this about it), and eminently usable, as six discrete cottages came with it, sprawled about on the six-acre lawn, handy for romantic, subversive, or patriotic assignations. Rufus came in at exactly six minutes past ten, and Cecilio Velasco exactly five minutes after that.

The two men knew of each other, but had not met. As usual when the CIA Director's mind was absorbed with business, his manners were perfunctory. "Er, Rufus, this is Velasco, Velasco, Rufus." Rufus stared at the diminutive Spaniard briefly, though unobtrusively. If he had had to do so, he could later in the day, or month, have sketched a faithful likeness of Cecilio Velasco, given a pad of paper, a soft pencil, and instructions or an inclination to do so. Rufus lived resolutely by his own rules, and one of these was that no acquaintance should slide by unphotographed by his mind's eye. "How do you manage to remember the faces of thirty people if you are introduced to thirty people?" Blackford Oakes had once asked him, to which Rufus gave the simple reply, "I am never introduced to thirty people."

Oakes had felt convivial that day, and a little combative, so he pressed on. "Were you never initiated into a club, or fraternity?"

Again Rufus had had an easy time of it. "No," he answered.

"Well," Blackford persevered, "have you never briefed a room with twenty or thirty people in it?"

"Yes," said Rufus.

"Ah-ha then, you old charlatan!" (Blackford was the only man, young or old, who could so address Rufus, and then of course only in private.)

"I have briefed thirty men at one time," Rufus continued, his voice unchanged. "But I did not lay eyes on them, nor they on me. I was in the next room, and I used a microphone."

Blackford gave up.

Rufus, looking at Cecilio Velasco, would have sketched a man in his early sixties, his black hair thinning but still jet black, combed down flat over his skull. The skin, tightly drawn over Semitic features, was faintly yellow, and there were hints of freckles, which became distinct on Velasco's bony hands, the right one open so that he could hold his burning cigarette. He was very small, not more than an inch or two above five feet, his dark blue double-breasted suit buttoned over a vest, notwithstanding the temperature outside, in the nineties. The threadbare little moustache was flecked with white, and the expression on Velasco's face, which Rufus noticed never changed, was one of a kind of civil skepticism, as if to register, "I know that what you are telling me is silly, but I'm willing to pretend it isn't, provided you do not require me to modify the musculature of my face." The Director indicated a chair, and the 120-

pound frame of Cecilio Velasco settled into it, reaching first
for an ashtray which he perched on a left knee that, since it
never flexed, served him as reliably as a coffee table.

Rufus sat opposite in an armchair, his face as usual without expression, his eyes moving systematically about the
cottage's living room, settling finally on the Director, who
was looking old and spoke without the polished gusto Rufus had become used to during twenty years' association.

"The subject, gentlemen, is Cuba," the Director said.
"More exactly, Castro Cuba." Both men were silent.

"Do you know Spanish, Rufus?"

"Not a word."

"It is unlike you to be so imprecise, Rufus. You know at
least one word of every language, including Swahili."

"I know only *Uhuru!* in Swahili."

Allen Dulles did not repress a smile. "Well, may as well
get this part over with. Your generic skills are useful in
every situation, but there is only one very specific reason
why I have brought you in on this assignment. Blackford
Oakes."

Rufus looked up, a hint of curiosity in his face. "I saw
Oakes ten days ago in Berlin."

"I know that. You also know, because you were present,
that Oakes reported on the Berlin Wall directly to the President and the National Security Council in the Situation
Room last month. Well, the President apparently took a
shine to Oakes. This week, he *directed* me—" (the verb was
used with obvious professional resentment; the Director
had nothing against Oakes—well, there was one old score
involving the Russian satellite, but long since forgiven—
but he was not accustomed to being told who on his staff to
put onto a specific assignment. He chose not to dwell on
the irregularity.) "—the President said, 'Who was the
young man who came in and reported to us on the Wall last
month?' Well, there were just the three of us, Rufus, and I
cannot in good conscience call you young, given that you

came out of retirement a year ago. So I mentioned Blackford's name, and he said, 'Give the job to him.' I said that Oakes's professional experience had been in Europe, and it was as if I hadn't spoken. He merely said, 'Yes. Oakes. That was his name. Blackford Oakes. Yes. Get him onto this.' "

"Forgive me, Mr. Director," Cecilio Velasco said, speaking for the first time, his English accented but confident. "Have you and, uh, Mr. Rufus already discussed the problem? I do not know what 'this' refers to."

"I just got here, Velasco," Rufus said, "just five minutes before you. I don't know either."

"Yes, yes," the Director said, rising to bring the coffeepot in from the kitchen stove. The sound of the steam had distracted him. " 'This' has to do with arranging a meeting between Oakes and Che Guevara."

Velasco looked skeptical.

An hour later they knew the details of the meeting two days earlier between Guevara and Richard Goodwin in Montevideo, and the startling proposals put forward by Guevara.

"The President figures that the Sovietization of Cuba is in very high gear. In the past few weeks Castro has nationalized all the schools, introduced the study of Russian into the regular curriculum, forbidden the teaching of religion, deputized the Swiss ambassador to communicate with us, instituted a regular air run to Prague, and shot a lot more people. They are in terrible economic shape, thanks in substantial part to our general embargo. They need the Soviet Union and we figure Russia is already spending at the level of three million dollars per day on Cuba. The President figures Guevara isn't serious when he promises, in exchange for our lifting the embargo, to contain the revolution. The Soviet Union wouldn't be showing the kind of interest it is in Cuba if it knew the Castro people weren't willing to go out and cause trouble in other parts of the hemisphere. But he feels he needs to pin this thing down, and the one thing he can't risk is doing it through regular channels. For one thing, he doesn't trust the State Department at any level. For another, the CIA is supposedly non-partisan: We gather information, and the best cover this side of an actual deal with Castro is information collection. Remember, the Republicans would eat him alive if they thought he was talking with Che Guevara. Let alone smoking his cigars."

"Cigars?" Velasco said, puffing on his cigarette.

"Yes. He showed me. Fancy stuff. A large box, mahogany, inlaid with all kinds of ornate material, with the Cuban seal, and a Cuban flag around the key. The President offered me one, and I took it." He reached into his pocket and pulled out a large cigar, a voluptuous reminder of what had been generally available to American cigar smokers only a year earlier. "Montecristo #1, I'd guess," he said, twirling it about his fingers. "Anyway, he wants a back-channel operation. No one else is to be in on it."

"Not even Goodwin?" Rufus asked.

"That's the President's business. He told me he did not intend to inform 'anybody.' Maybe Goodwin doesn't count as somebody, if you can figure that out."

"And the mission, exactly?" Velasco inquired.

"The mission is to ascertain from Guevara what kind of guarantees he is in a position to make on the matter of keeping hands off the rest of Latin America."

"And then we decide whether to lift the embargo?" Rufus asked.

"And then we decide whether to lift the embargo," the Director echoed.

Four

Although the midday sun in Mexico City in summer brings heat, it does not bring discomfort, at least not for someone arriving from Washington, D.C., where Blackford had spent a sweltering day answering questions that issued from his report on his Berlin operation. His spirits were sluggish and he had taken a few liberties with the narrative, reasoning that what he withheld from the questioning deputy did not directly impinge on the national security. Moreover, Blackford reflected while walking down Pennsylvania Avenue from the safe house to his hotel, his views on the national security were maturing. He was glad he did not have to answer, at this moment, how exactly these views were changing or what were the implications of the change. But he knew at least that formalities engaged him less. (They had never exactly obsessed him, though he acknowledged their importance.) As it happened, the record need not show what exactly Blackford Oakes did the day the Wall went up. He acknowledged it might have been otherwise. If he had been caught. But in fact he hadn't been, so why worry?

He wished only that the night in Washington would hasten by, as the next day he would be with Sally. Toward her his thoughts also were maturing in that he resolved— while acknowledging he had done this several times since leaving college a decade ago—that, really, he would not live without her for very much longer, a resolution reinforced by her letter from Mexico which had somehow changed his perspectives. Though perhaps—he attempted to reason objectively—the realization of the Wall in Berlin, and the

renewed palpability of life on the free side of that wall, had
also done much to affect his spirits. They focused now on
the need to snatch his own life from the rotting carcass of
the political world he had inherited, and to breathe deeply
the free air of the West, resisting the impulse so to involve
himself in the mixed motives of mankind as to develop
chronic melancholia.

On reaching the Hay-Adams Hotel he dialed the number
of Anthony Trust, fetching a recorded answer that "the
party at that number" could be reached at "his New York
number," a referral vague enough to discourage casual
phoners. Blackford knew the New York number and what
code to give the woman who answered, after which he
asked for and promptly got the number at which he could
reach his old schoolmate, who ten years before had re-
cruited him into the Agency. Would Anthony be out to
dinner, he wondered, as he dialed the eleven digits. He had
only, when the phone was picked up, to say, "Anthony?"

"Well I'll be damned if it isn't Blackford Oakes! Yale
1951! Ace fighter pilot! Honors graduate, School of Engineering! Subsequent activities . . . vague. But thought to
be engaged in His Majesty's service—"

"We don't have a Majesty, Trust."

"Oh? How long have you been out of the country, Blackford? Over six months, I happen to know. And I guess you
just don't happen to know that there has been a coup d'état
in America since you went away. We don't have a republic
anymore, though we are all very careful to conceal this. We
have a kingdom! The king is installed in the White House, a
quaint republican relic. He and his queen and the little
prince and princess live there in regal splendor, and they
invite to their court the most distinguished spirits in the
land, who go there and pay tribute and leave frankincense
and myrrh—they do not need any gold, because the king
gets all the revenues from a vast commercial empire
founded by his father, and besides, he has the keys to Fort

Knox, which surrendered without a fight, thereby saving the defenders from the garrotte—"

"Oh shut up, Anthony. Really, you were always bad, but you are becoming an insufferable tight-ass Republican—"

"Please do not make references to just one of those parts of my anatomy that all women swoon over—you know that, Blackford, since once you actually had the privilege of seeing it happen—"

"Anthony. Get your dirty mind off your dirty appetites and concentrate on my dirty appetites. Out of curiosity, is Mabel still around these days?"

"Ah, Mabel. Well, Blackford, you will be happy to learn that Mabel is well and prosperous and that her finishing school is more selective than ever. So selective, in fact, that Mabel's unlisted number is highly restricted, and I don't know that I could take the liberty of giving it to you . . ."

"Anthony, look. I'm tired. I'm going to Mexico on vacation tomorrow. I'll be back in a couple of weeks and then we'll visit."

They chatted for ten minutes.

It was hard to remember when he hadn't known Anthony Trust—an American prefect at Greyburn College, where Blackford had been sent to school when his mother divorced his father and married that genial and endearing Colonel Blimp, Sir Alec Sharkey, who immediately packed Blacky off, age fifteen, to the same school he and his forebears going back a hundred years had attended; where he had found only one other American student, Anthony Trust, witness to the humiliating flogging Blackford had got from the sadist whose avocation was to serve as headmaster of Greyburn College.

Blackford could pick up, from Anthony's guarded talk, some idea of his current preoccupations, even as close familiarity with the work of an artist can cause the student to know what direction the artist is embarked upon after a few brushstrokes. Clearly Anthony was involved with the whole subject of monitoring nuclear tests, the bilateral suspension of which, in the atmosphere, had been and continued to be a high priority of the Kennedy administration. But the hardnoses in Congress, particularly Senator Thomas Dodd, wanted to know more about the verifiability of a freeze than the Executive was willing to let out. All this Anthony communicated in fits and starts, using metaphors and verbal sign language probably no single person other than his oldest friend would have succeeded in piecing together.

"When are you coming back from Mexico?"

"Couple of weeks."

"I'll tell you about it when I see you. Listen, let's spend Labor Day weekend sailing. I've got access to a nice yawl, forty-footer, sails out of Marblehead. We could sail to Nantucket, and on the way, curtsey at Hyannis Port, what do you say?"

"Sounds great, Anthony. I'll call you as soon as I get back."

"Oh and Blackford, about tonight. Do you need me to remind you of Mabel's phone number?"

Blackford hung up, smiling. And concentrating on how to forget Mabel's number. His thoughts were of Sally.

The following afternoon, on Eastern flight 707—unusually empty, Blackford thought, for the month of July—he found himself in random conversation with Elsie, a Mexican-American stewardess who had instantly displayed a curious and imaginative intelligence. She accepted Blackford's invitation to sit with him while he had coffee and a liqueur ("Captain Rickenbacker won't notice. Nor will the other eight people on the plane"). They talked a full hour. First about Theodore White's theatrical introduction to American politics in his big bestseller *The Making of the President, 1960,* a book both Elsie and Blackford had read— "It quite turned my head about JFK," she said, sipping on a

Coca-Cola. To his astonishment, Blackford heard himself saying, "I have met him." Elsie was incredulous, and of course wished to know the circumstances, so that Blackford made up something about a Democratic Party fund-raiser which had been briefly visited by JFK during his campaign. Her delight was manifest, and Blackford thought he might as well take advantage of it, and so added, "What would you do if it were he who was here with you, instead of me?"

What followed consumed a full half hour and led to the subject of James Baldwin, and once again it turned out that both had read his haunting book, *Nobody Knows My Name.* Elsie said that after reading it and searching her innermost soul she had to admit that she harbored certain racial prejudices. "Just the way, I guess, that some people have them against Mexicans." Blackford was suddenly struck by whatever special fragrance exuded from Elsie, and looked quickly about the cabin to find the few passengers ahead of where he was seated either asleep or preoccupied with food, drink, and magazines. Elsie, for the first time, was looking directly into his face, and her voice had dropped. "Do you have such a prejudice against Mexican-Americans?"

Blackford assured her he did not. She asked if, on arriving in Mexico, he was immediately engaged, and he said he was, in every sense of the word, since he would be visiting the woman to whom he was engaged. Elsie said there was a lucky woman living in Mexico, to find someone like Blackford, who "looked so wonderful. Not as wonderful or as beautiful as President Kennedy, but nobody else is like him." Blackford knew he didn't want to think anymore about the fulminations of James Baldwin, or even about the star-striking emanations of Theodore White's early capture of the image of the young man who, only nine or ten years older than Blackford, had been elected President of the United States. And already King Arthur had shed his blessings on this subject, Blackford thought, reasoning that the

mention of no other name could have aroused Elsie to such
heights of appreciation. But if all the time she had been
thinking of JFK, then maybe, after all, he should be thinking about Sally.

It crossed his mind to discuss the encounter with Sally,
later in the day—the sudden platonic infatuation aboard
the plane. At that moment the light at the bulkhead went on
and, sighing, Elsie rose, and he saw her bringing a liqueur
to a passenger who in turn engaged her in conversation. He
closed his eyes and appreciated the soundless air condi-
tioner and wondered how she would look, and what Mexico
City was like.

Five

Sally threaded Blackford through Customs, pleased with herself for having obtained a pass that permitted her to meet the passengers as they disembarked. She was pleased also to show off her Spanish, and Blackford was vocal about being impressed, and noted gratefully that she had not changed in the least in the months that had gone by. She was efficient, and strikingly—visible; she could *never* be anonymous. Not in any respect, Blackford thought. She wore a trim yellow cotton suit, with her little pearl necklace, and the dark blond hair framing her vividly intelligent face. Neither had the perfume changed—any alteration in the scent just behind her left ear would have upset Blackford greatly, as if someone had trifled with the magnetic North Pole. He hugged her, and somewhat to his surprise he felt moisture in his eyes and so he didn't say anything more, merely cleared his throat, and waved more or less inconclusively at an idle porter.

Driving off she chatted, abiding by the convention of not asking in any detail about Blackford's activities, though after scrutinizing him carefully when he had sat down in the passenger seat, she remarked that he looked tired.

"But it's a superficial fatigue," she quickly added, and went on to brief him on the geography of Mexico City, its history, its Brobdingnagian growth—"Do you realize that when Porfirio Díaz was overthrown in 1910 there were 500,000 inhabitants of Mexico City, and the figure is now well over four million, nobody knows exactly how many? Oh that reminds me, don't drink the water"—she narrowly

missed a car that lurched out from a side street—"there are
no traffic lights in the most obvious intersections—no,
don't drink the water, because it's poisoned by the sewage
system. You see, the sewage system is still adequate for only
500,000 people. And don't assume that bottled water is
safe. Bottled water in Mexico City is prepared by running
tap water into a bottle, sealing it, and selling it to you for
two pesos. You have to boil your own water if you want to
be safe, or put halazone in it. Oh dear, we'll have to stop for
a minute, it's going to rain." He helped her to raise the roof
of the Volkswagen. Back in the car she explained that summer was the rainy season. "It rains every day, but only for
about fifteen minutes, and then it's lovely and cool."

And she was right. By the time they had reached Insurgentes and taken the right fork up Altavista it was tangy-
cool, like early September in New England. "We are now in
Villa Obregón, only most of the natives still call it San
Angel Inn. Obregón was shot right over there, and the
statue has his hand in it. Altavista runs right into San Angel
Inn, which is a state-protected monument with a little park
behind it, only maybe it will open up as an inn again, nobody is exactly sure. Oh, over there, that's Diego Rivera's
house. Notice the passageway between the two houses?
Well, he kept his wife in one house, and when he was speaking to her, which was about half the time, they say, he went
to visit her through the passageway. When he was mad at
her, he locked the door."

"When he was mad at her must have been when he
painted his pictures," Blackford commented.

"Yes, he became something of a bore," Sally conceded.
"You would think the United States and God created peon-
age. Come to think of it, I suppose God did. Somebody did,
and Diego Rivera never got over it. Now, watch this. You
turn to the right here—" she turned off Altavista at San
Angel Inn. "And you take your first left—" she turned left.
"And this street," she pointed to the block-long cobble-

stoned street ahead of them, "is Calero. And," she turned
the car sharply to the right, stopped, and honked the horn,
"this is how you get somebody from Mrs. Littlejohn's to
come out and get your bags."

A Mexican in his fifties wearing a yellow shirt and blue
pants materialized, smiled at Sally, and ducked his head
into the car to get the bags from the back seat.

"Don't worry. Manuel will take care of the car. Come and
meet Josephine Littlejohn."

Blackford reflected that his own mother could not have
greeted him more warmly. Tall, gray-haired, her figure entirely amorphous, Josephine Littlejohn addressed Blackford as if his arrival were the high point of her summer. She
led him into the main living room, in which were crowded
rugs and lamps and curios and photographs, and from
which one could go out into the garden from three sides.
Kenneth Littlejohn was reading *The News*, the Mexican daily
paper. A striking, white-haired man in his seventies, six feet
two, angular, his eyes bright, his face seasoned from a lifetime's work as a land surveyor, he rose now to greet his
wife's latest guest.

Josephine Littlejohn had a way of doing more or less
everything simultaneously. She ordered coffee and cake
and extra logs for Sally's suite, instructed a maid in fluent
and execrable Spanish please to take out of his bags and
wash all the señor's dirty clothing, described the book she
was reading, described the book she was writing, announced who would be joining them for dinner, including
one ambassador, one beautiful mosaicist, one bullfighter—
"I don't like bullfighting," Mr. Littlejohn had interjected.
"Maybe I have it wrong, dear. Maybe Juanito is a ballet
dancer, not a bullfighter—I know it's one of the two." "I
don't particularly like the ballet," Mr. Littlejohn said.
"Mostly fags, you know." Josephine Littlejohn beamed and
said to Blackford, "Kenneth is *so* old-fashioned. Pay no
attention to him." This was easy to do since attention could

only really be paid to Mrs. Littlejohn, but then suddenly she ushered them off to the suite. "You must be very tired, Blackford. There is your room, right across the hall from your sister's, and," she opened the shades, "—there. Usually we like to keep the sun out of the sitting room, but you will want to be nice and warm. The fireplace is ready to light whenever you wish. And," she opened the door to the bathroom, "Sally will show you how to work the Rápido. It's an old-fashioned way to get hot water, but what does it matter? All you need to do is to make up your mind a half hour ahead of time when you want to take your bath, and light the kindling. There!" she clasped Blackford's right hand in her own. "You look just alike. The most beautiful pair I have ever seen. I hope you stay all summer. I will see you at seven. We meet for drinks. Oh, yes. Kenneth likes our guests to wear coat and tie. Those are the only rules!" she closed the door.

"Whew!" said Blackford.

"She's marvelous," Sally smiled.

"Anyway, that was good news."

"What was good news?"

"That coat and tie at dinner are the only rules of the house. Or did she mean I also have to wear a coat and tie in bed?"

"Only when you sleep in other people's beds," Sally smiled, drawing him toward her.

At first Blackford had resented the idea of sharing their first evening with a dozen strangers, but a half hour after they had convened for drinks he found himself wholly distracted. Rum and soda was Kenneth Littlejohn's specialty, and he was visibly disappointed when a guest opted for anything else. He literally forced the rum and soda on the bullfighter, insisting that it would permit him to kill three bulls the next Sunday instead of merely two. Josephine managed at once to talk continuously and also to cause all her guests to do the same thing, so that the New York *Times* correspondent started telling a story to the architect only to find himself, halfway through, addressing the ambassador and then delivering the closing lines to the bullfighter, who affected to appreciate the whole thing. Dinner was served on aluminum trays set on foldable aluminum stands in front of each guest, who perched on a couch or chair, while one or two squatted down on the floor, their trays in front of them. Three maids, more or less dressed in (cannibalized) uniforms, kept an apparently endless procession of platters and trays of meats and vegetables and salads and Mexican red wine and sweets in circulation. Blackford and Sally contrived to stay close to each other, and quite suddenly Blackford reflected that he was perfectly relaxed for the first time in many months, and was even emboldened to attempt a few words of Spanish with the mosaicist, who said she would be glad to give Blackford lessons every day, beginning tomorrow, and Blackford replied that he had always wanted to learn how to do mosaics, but Josephine straightened that out, or thought she did, as no one who knew only Spanish was ever quite certain what it was that Josephine Littlejohn had said. Then, almost as suddenly as they had come, the guests left, and Josephine kissed Sally good night, declaring that they must both get a good night's sleep because she knew of the tour Sally had planned for her brother beginning early the next morning. Blackford said good night to both his hosts and followed Sally through the door to their suite.

Kenneth Littlejohn, a rum and soda in his hand, sat in the deep armchair looking absently at what was left of the log fire in the room empty save for Josephine Littlejohn, who was bustling about straightening out chairs.

"Do you know something, Josephine?"

"What, dear?"

"If that boy and that girl are brother and sister, I am Antony and Cleopatra."

"Kenneth, now how can you say anything like that? They are so darling. They wouldn't pull your leg. Did you know that Jane Austen only wrote six books? I've written seven, and I just know it, Kenneth, that this one is going to be published."

Six

It was day three of their holiday and they were staying at the Hotel Victoria in Taxco, high up the cobblestoned streets of the antique silver-mining village saved in the 1920s from architectural plunder by an American silversmith with an aesthetic eye for more than his artistically original silver artifacts. The streets were never widened, nor the roads paved, nor the central square enlarged, nor skyscraper erected. Only the bougainvillea grew with unregulated abandon, along the stone walls that lined so many of the streets, and up the wooden walls and pillars fondling the upper reaches of the two-story open-porched houses, in several of which, around the village square, tourists were served. Here and there in the shadows elderly Mexican peasants and artisans and shopkeepers leaned over their game boards or sipped their tequila. Outside, by the huge sixteenth-century church, an elderly woman fried her tortillas, stuffed them with chicken and beans and onion, and peddled them smilingly for a peso apiece. They climbed up the narrow road from the square to the hotel, not easy work at 5,500 feet of altitude, so that they arrived at the Spanish-style open lobby a little winded, eager for the half-hour snooze before dinner to which they had treated themselves on three consecutive days.

Sally, the room key in her handbag, went directly to their quarters, while Blackford paused at the concierge's bureau to pick up the Mexican daily paper, *The News.* He was interrupted. "You have had three telephone calls from a Mrs. Littlejohn in Mexico City, Señor Partridge." Blackford felt the freeze in his stomach. Only the Duty Officer knew where he was, or rather what his principal address in Mexico was. Blackford decided to use the telephone in the lobby before joining Sally.

He reached Josephine Littlejohn, who told him that a gentleman in Washington had telephoned urgently for Blackford Oakes, and that she assumed of course that he meant Blackford Partridge, that she had not written down the exact itinerary described to her by Sally, so that one after another she had telephoned to hotels in Puebla, and then Cuernavaca, and then Taxco, the three hotels she had recommended to Sally, and finally she had tracked him down. Blackford listened, waiting for his message, which finally came. "Dear, it was a Mr. Longford who called, leaving a number. He said he had some urgent news regarding your mother. I do hope all is well with your mother, dear Blackford, and if there is anything I can do, you must advise me. I know the very best doctors in Mexico, and if she needs some care, she should get down here right away. Where is she now?"

Blackford told her their mother lived in London, and it turned out that Mrs. Littlejohn knew an excellent doctor in London, an old beau of one of her daughters . . .

Finally she was off the line.

Blackford recognized the telephone number. Any message involving the health of his mother was a code to call in immediately. He did this, and was put through to the Deputy Director, who asked where exactly Blackford was.

"Taxco," said Blackford perfunctorily, "—a hundred miles from Mexico City." There was a pause at the other end of the line, and he was asked to hang on. A moment later:

"We've made reservations for you on Eastern Flight #203 departing Mexico City tomorrow at 1405 for D.C. But alternative arrangements may prove preferable, so call in at noon tomorrow from Mexico City. Okay?"

He knew it was probably foolish even to try, but he felt he should at least make the effort. "Sir, is it possible to get someone else? I am—heavily engaged."

"It is impossible, for reasons you'll soon know, even if you will not understand."

He broke the news to her right away, and for a tense hour before dinner she did not speak to him. At dinner in the candlelit outdoor patio overlooking the city and the illuminated church tower he said, "What do you want me to say, Sally? That I don't believe organizations should exist that do not have the right to summon their members in an emergency?"

"I would have predicted you'd come up with an original way of putting it. So that if I object to the Central Intelligence Agency arbitrarily calling you back from the first vacation you have had in one year, I am obliged also to object to the right of Parliament to summon its members for a vote on a declaration of war. In logic it is called the fallacy of division: Government has emergency powers, therefore the Library of Congress, which is an arm of government, has emergency powers . . . Thank you, I reject the ambush. Let's just leave it that we are reminded, once again, of what keeps us apart."

But her mood softened, and soon she was—Sally, dining with him for the last time until they could be reunited; and tenderness overcame her, though she had lost appetite for food, only nibbling the chicken croquettes and the little dumplings and the sherbet. They walked back down to the square, climbed up to Bertha's and took a margarita and listened to the brass band, and then watched the excited children who chased after a man wearing a monk's cassock and cowl and carrying over his head a scaffolding made from plywood with a bull's horns jutting out on top, Roman candles and other fireworks attached to the wooden frames. He would charge like a bull at the little children who darted off screaming and yelling as the firecrackers provided a pyrotechnic spume for the bull's cavortings. "You will be in Washington this time tomorrow," Sally said. Blackford did not look up.

"I expect so."

She studied his profile against the lighted square. In the dark she could see no signs of the little creasings one expects in thirty-five-year-olds. His hair hung over his forehead, glints of blond visible when the fireworks were especially luminous. A drinking straw reached from his lips to the wide rim of his margarita glass. She felt a shiver of longing to keep him with her, to protect him. "Let's go," she said.

"Wait just a minute. The bull is almost out of gas."

Soon it was so, the final firecracker spent; and they left, climbing up the steep road and moving directly to their room. She opened first the shutters, then the shade, and turned off the light. The moon supplied the illumination the fireworks had previously provided, and soon they were in each other's arms and she felt him hug her more tenaciously than ever before, and harder than ever before, yet more tenderly. He moved, then, beginning to alternate practiced and spontaneous actions of his body, bending hers to his and kneading her desire until the spasm came. His hands behind her ears, he could discern her smile, her eyes closed.

"Get kind of winded at 5,500 feet," he said.

"I suppose you're going to tell me you're out of practice."

"Well—how high is Mexico City?"

"Seventy-three hundred feet."

"Well, that's the highest I ever did it—but tonight is something else . . ."

She smiled again. She would flirt with the subject of her Blacky's other lives, but never probe, never probe.

"Why don't we get married?" Blackford said.

"What would be the use of our getting married if you

continued in your present job, which keeps you out of the country half the time?"

"I would need to make arrangements."

"Inside your Agency, or outside it?"

"Whatever. I think we should have a family."

"In due course."

"I don't understand you."

"Then we are on very unequal terms, for I understand you perfectly well."

"Where did you pick up that line?"

"Jane Austen, where else?"

"What comes after that?"

"You're supposed to say: 'Me?—yes; I cannot speak well enough to be unintelligible.' "

"Are you against having children?"

"No. It's just that I am against procreating them."

"Well I'm afraid, Sally, we have here an insuperable problem."

She laughed.

He continued. "I suppose we could always adopt a child. That way you wouldn't need to take any time from your study of the eighteenth century."

"I tell you what, Blacky. Let's do this. Let's agree to marry on June 1, 1964. No matter what."

"No matter even if we don't want to?"

"That's right. No matter if we don't want to."

"What does this mean for our professional lives?"

"It means that we have three years in which to tame those lives. My book will be out and published, you will have contrived a coup d'état in the Kremlin and a restoration of the Romanov dynasty, and we'll just take it from there, and have lots of children."

"And meanwhile?"

"Meanwhile, my darling Blacky, we will simply stay in touch."

"Is this," he slid up between her legs, "what you mean by staying in touch?"

"I call that staying in touch *à outrance.*"

"No French. Except kissing." Later, when she slept, Blackford felt that their relationship was somehow consecrated. They had, so to speak, exchanged vows.

Seven

From the Littlejohns' he called the number in Washington and was told to proceed to the airport. "Before you board, someone will introduce himself. He will ask after your stepfather by name. Follow his instructions."

He told Sally there were no changes in his plans to fly to Washington, and that he desired to go to the airport by taxi.

"Yes," she said. "It's better that way."

They shared a quick lunch with the Littlejohns. Kenneth wanted to know why, if their mother was ill, it fell to Blackford to look after her, rather than to Sally? Blackford decided to demonstrate to Sally the ease with which an experienced agent handled such provocations.

"You never told Kenneth and Josephine about—you and Mother?"

Sally swallowed and said quietly, "No."

"Well, Ken, it's one of those terrible things. Psychiatrists have tackled it, two sisters, a brother, we even got a letter from J. Edgar Hoover."

"What? What?" Kenneth Littlejohn looked up.

"McCarthyism. You lived out of the country during those days, Ken, but McCarthy had all of America in his grip, and he just sowed suspicion, you never saw anything like it. Well, after listening to McCarthy for a year or two Mother became absolutely convinced that Sally is a Soviet agent. And refuses to see her, or even to discuss the matter. She says she expects to see Sally next on the day Sally comes in leading a red brigade and confiscates Mother's house."

Josephine sighed and said she was certain that if she

could spend a few hours with Mrs. Partridge she, Josephine, could *convince* her that Sally was a good, red-blooded American. Blackford said that he would be glad to sponsor the effort. "But not now, not when she's ill. Later."

Kenneth held his peace. And soon Josephine was embracing Blackford, and Blackford embraced Sally, and then Josephine embraced Sally to console her on her brother's departure, and Kenneth felt it would be appropriate if he too embraced Sally to console her. Blackford managed a smile and a fraternal wave when he got into the taxi, and they all stood there, just before the rain began, and waved him goodbye as the 1956 yellow Studebaker taxi drove off, though only after Josephine had negotiated the fare—"in Mexico you must always arrive at an understanding with the taxi drivers," she warned Blackford, blowing him one final kiss.

He was fourth in line to the ticket window at Eastern Airlines when the man approached him.

"Pardon me, Mr. Oakes, but I am a friend of Sir Alec Sharkey, and he asked that you come with me. Here, let me help you with your bags."

The agile little man grabbed the heavier of the two bags with his right hand, transferring his cigarette to his left hand. And said matter-of-factly, "I have canceled your reservation. We'll be driving to an apartment where I hope you will be comfortable until we get things sorted out."

The stranger was a careful driver, though he used primarily a single hand, reserving the other for his cigarette. He indulged nonchalant challengers the right of way except, Blackford noticed, in the two situations when the challenger was being provocative. When that happened, the stranger simply stepped on the accelerator, giving the challenger the obvious option of braking or facing instant death, along with the stranger and, Blackford calculated detachedly, Blackford. The rain had long since stopped, and the vernal freshness was back as they muscled their way across the density of the city toward the Reforma and up onto the Lomas of Chapultepec. "I used to live in Mexico City," the driver said, again betraying his accent, and adding nothing more, as though it was clearly up to Blackford to signal an interest or not in this datum.

Blackford complied. "You were born here?"

"No. I was born in Spain. I came here in 1939, when I was thirty-nine. I left here—let me see—seventeen years ago. The changes are extraordinary, but then there are almost three million more people living in Mexico City than in 1943. It is quite haunting to be back. On the other hand, the Lomas have not changed all that much."

The reference was to the comfortable "lomas" of Chapultepec—the extensive hilly pastures that lay at the northwest end of the palace, and belonged to it when Maximilian and Carlota reigned as emperor and empress, until Maximilian got himself executed. The eight square miles were something like the middle-class suburbs of America, with substantial houses, each one on an acre or more; only in Mexico, unlike Scarsdale, they were all tended by servants. And the homes were lush with summer flowers, like the whole of the Mexican valley.

He drove to a small apartment building, indicated the bags to a porter, nodded his head at the concierge and led Blackford to the elevator, pushing the button for the fourth floor.

The appointments of apartment 4E were what you would expect if you had sent a letter to the local manager of Sears, Roebuck with instructions to decorate a two-bedroom apartment inconspicuously. The pictures on the wall were graphic reproductions of Diego Rivera's paintings which in Mexico are inconspicuous, as giraffes are inconspicuous in giraffe parks.

Blackford, accustomed to the protocols of secret service, merely sat down and waited. It wasn't long. His host had only to draw the shades and light another cigarette. He sat down opposite him.

"I am directed to apologize for breaking into your vacation."

Blackford gave the requisite bow of his head.

"Briefly, I am on the Cuban desk—"

"How is it I didn't run into you last winter and spring?"

"During the preparations for the Bay of Pigs operation in which, I am aware, you were tangentially involved, I was detached on Argentine duty."

His host rose from his chair and, puffing away, ambled nonchalantly toward the bookcase. He rested his left hand, outstretched, in a cavity at the corner of a shelf, its contents beyond Blackford's vision. He wondered, suddenly, what other than books might sit on that shelf.

"I see," Blackford said, reflecting.

True, he had asked by name after Alec Sharkey, Blackford's stepfather. Yet it was just possible. Blackford now had ten years' experience in the Agency and had walked the streets of intelligence and counterintelligence and become prudent. "Do you have a telephone here?"

His host pointed with his right hand to the corner of the room, where a small coffee table was almost hidden by the curtain.

"Over there."

Blackford stood up. Passing him, Blackford lunged quickly, pinioning the stranger's left arm against the shelf. "My friend, I am going to make a telephone call. While I make that call—to ascertain whether you are who you say you are—you will put your arms behind . . . That's right, easy does it . . . which I will tie together." These, Blackford bound with his necktie over the wrists, behind the man's back. "If everything goes well, we will be chatting together comfortably again in about five minutes." Blackford, one hand on the necktie that bound his host, quickly inspected the corner of the shelf. He found a small semiautomatic pistol, probably a .32.

His host smiled, and his blackberry eyes looked benevolently through the two narrowed slits. "There is just one thing, Mr. Oakes. You will have to make it so that I can continue to smoke my cigarette. Otherwise I get very nervous."

"Sit here." Blackford then pulled over the side table, slid the ashtray to the edge nearest his host, took a cigarette from his pocket, lit it, and deposited it so that the man could puff away without using his fingers. He went then to the telephone, got long distance, and whispered a number in Washington. He gave a code, and asked for "Summerville," who came on the line.

"Joe, Blackford. Okay?"

"Yeah. Nobody else sounds like you."

"Just checking. I've got someone here—he hasn't given me a name. I was told someone might grab me at the airport. He gave me the right identifier but I want to make sure—funny-feeling department—I've got the right guy. About five two, tight, sallow skin, little cropped moustache, black hair, chain-smoker—"

"So far so good. Ask him: Who did he lunch with yesterday—no, don't do that. Ask him what he had to eat at lunch yesterday."

Blackford turned to his host-prisoner. "Señor, what did you have for lunch yesterday?"

"Ah, what a question you ask! Food, I never notice food —ah! *Dios mío*, I cannot remember any meal anywhere, not even the meal I was given just before I was to be executed."

"Keep this up, Buster, and the meal just before you were executed will turn out to be whatever you had at lunch."

The man gnashed his teeth and growled, his eyes imploring the ceiling to help his memory. "Please, ask me another question."

"Joe. He says he can't ever remember meals. What else?"

"Ask him who was it who interrupted us during lunch."

Blackford asked the question. His prisoner smiled.

"It was the secretary of the Director, with a message for —for our host."

Blackford relayed the word.

"That's right. That's Cecilio Velasco. Now listen, Blackford. You hearing me? You won't want to be commenting on what I say."

"I hear you."

"Velasco is very special. I rate him right up there with Rufus."

"Okay. Thanks, Joe. Anything more?"

"No. Good luck."

"Thanks."

He walked over to Velasco and untied his hands. "Sorry about that."

Velasco rearranged himself and picked up the cigarette. "Why be sorry? I would be sorry if you had not made some check."

"So where do we go from here?"

"We were talking about Cuba. I am on the Cuban desk. We have an overture. Made directly to the President. He wants it checked out. That means you are going to Cuba, to have a conversation—or perhaps several conversations."

"I'll be damned. It sounds interesting, but why me? I don't know a hell of a lot of Spanish, only just enough to order a meal, that kind of thing."

"You have been selected at the personal instruction of the President."

"What? Why?"

"Apparently you had a meeting with him on the Berlin question. It appears you impressed him. If he has elaborated on his reasons for designating you, I don't have those reasons."

Blackford thought back on that day, only a few weeks ago, in the Situation Room of the White House. He remembered the inquisitive, searching expression on the face of the President as he listened to Blackford's story, the attentive relaxation with which he listened while Blackford was interrogated. And then the decisive way in which he put an end to the drill, nodding to Blackford that he was dismissed, and going on to utter a civility entirely nonexecutive in character—"Thank you very much," or something like that. Rufus had stayed on at the presidential meeting. Perhaps Rufus had been quizzed about him. Curious, the whole thing.

"The President has told the Director he is imposing total security on this mission. He's not telling either State or Defense about it."

"Okay," Blackford said. "So what is it all about?"

Velasco told him the story of the Goodwin meeting at Montevideo. "I have with me two or three hours of reading material on the current situation in Cuba. We are paying a very heavy debt for the Bay of Pigs."

"You mean we are paying a very heavy debt for the failure of the Bay of Pigs."

"The Cubans are united behind Castro."

"And Castro is united behind Moscow."

"But that is why this development is of such great importance. The man you are to talk with is to be Che Guevara himself. As Industry Minister, he recognizes that our economic embargo is doing greater harm to Cuba than the Soviet Union is able to make up for. That is why the President thinks we may have a historic opening; have it quickly, and perhaps in two or three months things can be made to change, notwithstanding the Bay of Pigs. But he has got to find out first whether Guevara is on the level, and second whether he is in a position to guarantee what he promises. That depends on whether he is representing Castro, not merely himself. Or, if he is representing himself, whether he is likely to win over Castro if we decide to go along."

"Why are we meeting in Mexico City?"

"This morning I made an approach to the Cuban ambassador to Mexico who, as it happens, I had previous experience with. It is obviously necessary to advise Guevara that the President is willing to take an exploratory step."

"What did he say?"

"He said, of course, that he would have to clear it with Havana."

"Concretely, clear what?"

"Clear your going to Havana to see Guevara."

"What if he says it can all be done in Washington through some agent. Or in Mexico?"

"It is one of the President's conditions: either his representative—you—will speak with Guevara, or the whole thing is called off."

"And if he says yes?"

"Then we discuss how to get you into Havana."

"What's the most obvious way?"

"Guantánamo."

"I always wanted to see Guantánamo before I died."

"Do you have better ideas?"

"Che Guevara is high on culture. Couldn't I go over as a German rock singer?"

Velasco puffed on his cigarette, and his little cynical smile deepened perceptibly. "If you like, I shall make that suggestion to the ambassador when he calls me."

"Which will be when?"

"Not before ten tonight. They love late hours, as you may know." He rose. "Until then, we are at liberty. I make one recommendation and one request. The first is that you go through the material I have here. That will take you until about seven o'clock. The second is that under no circumstances should you advise anyone in Mexico that you are still here. I would be most happy to take you to dinner, if you would care to join me. We could go over some of the material you have read. Provided, that is, that tomorrow you will not ask me what we ate."

"All right," Blackford said. "But before I start in, I need some exercise, maybe a half hour's run. Any problem in doing that out of here?"

Velasco paused, but only briefly. "No," he said. "No, no problem, I think. We can go down together."

"Hang on," Blackford reached for one of his bags and took out of it a pair of khaki pants, a sweater, and some tennis shoes. In a minute he was changed. As they went down in the elevator Velasco turned the apartment key over to Blackford. "You will be returning well before I do. It is extremely unlikely that the telephone should ring. If it does, please do not answer it."

In the lobby Velasco waved at Blackford and walked over toward his parked car.

Eight

Cecilio Velasco drove back toward Chapultepec Park, then turned to the right, up Asalto Boulevard. He was headed toward Coyoacán. He had known many years ago that if ever he returned to Mexico he would need to go there. Perhaps merely sitting in the car and looking at the site, he would sort out one of the residual confusions he still harbored about his long experience worshipping that awesome god. Or was it simply a morbid desire to revisit the scene of a crime?

A great crime. But then, really, that was one of the questions that continued to vex him, whether it was a "great" crime in other than the conventional sense. The assassination of Leon Trotsky had been "great" in that it had been the center of international attention for weeks, with months, even years, of ripple effect. It had been a great crime in that Trotsky's legion of followers had lost, irretrievably, their leader, who proved irreplaceable. And it was a crime formally defined to take a man's life, inasmuch as Velasco, and Hurtado, and Mercader—it was Mercader who had planted the mountaineer's pick in Trotsky's skull —were hardly engaged in executing a civil commission. The phrase normally used in such situations, Velasco reminded himself as he turned west toward the district of Coyoacán, was "killing an innocent man." But he was no longer certain that such a phrase described what he had engaged in. Trotsky was perhaps—probably—innocent of having committed any capital crime under Mexican law. Was he otherwise innocent?

1922: When at age twenty-two in Barcelona Raúl Carrera was told that he would have to leave the law school because there was now no money, his father having left nothing but the tiny, heavily mortgaged house in which Raúl's five sisters lived with their mother, he was saddened at the prospect of not finishing his law studies. But he was desolate at the prospect of losing touch with those of his companions who, like Raúl, had been inflamed by the great events in the Soviet Union. They had taken, ever since Lenin's April theses, to meeting at least four times a week. At first only three or four of them, but now as many as twelve or fifteen, and the growth was steady, in order to discuss developments in Russia and the opportunities that surrounded them to universalize the great energies they were discovering among the disaffected—however few—with all those Castilian encumbrances, most notably the Christian God and the Bourbon king.

Raúl admitted that he found it most difficult to break with the Catholic Church, to which his mother was passionately devoted. But he recognized that the rupture with old, traditional Spain could not be merely formalistic. He needed not merely to drift away from belief. He needed to disbelieve. To know that man is an accidental chemical-biological concatenation of cells that somehow, along the way, developed a will. And that the great narrative cycle of history was coming to a climax during this very century. Perhaps during the next ten or twenty years. That Lenin was showing his disciples how it could come about, that centuries of class consolidations could be wiped away; the poor would find that the future lay in their hands and that the exploiters and the imperialists were forever bereft of the slaves they were so accustomed to oppressing.

Raúl's earnestness combined with an unusual analytical eloquence, which he exercised in small circles only, and infrequently. He would never think of addressing a large public gathering. He had once been invited to develop

formal forensic and oratorical skills by Beatriz, with whom
he shared his vision, his meals, and his bed. She had offered
to pretend that she was a great crowd—they could just go
off to Blanes, toward the cliffs of the Costa Brava, and there
in the pastoral wilderness where no one could possibly
overhear them Raúl could mount a rock, use a makeshift
lectern, and practice public declamation. Raúl did this
three times, but always he tended to speak as if engaged in a
seminar, and eventually even Beatriz was forced to admit
that the project had failed, that Raúl's golden tongue must
be reserved for exercises more intimate than public ora-
tions.

His companions, especially Antonio Durán, whose se-
niority (he was twenty-four) made him ex officio the leader
of the group, were as torn as Raúl by the news that he
would need to withdraw, and so Durán and three of Raúl's
special friends met on the Monday night before Raúl's
scheduled departure on Friday, the end of the term, to
inquire what might be done. Every semester the cost of
tuition and board came to a thousand pesetas. But however
often they reviewed their collective resources they could
think of no way of coming up with that much money, particularly not by next Friday when the payment for the next
semester was inflexibly due.

They sat about an austere, dilapidated empty classroom
lit by a single bare bulb. It was getting cold—Barcelona
gets fearfully cold in January—as the conversational hub-
bub mounted, and then Rico banged his open palm on the
desk, demanding silence. Rico did not speak often, and so
was presumed to have something worth listening to when
he sought attention. It was also Rico who, of them all, was
the most inventive, as when he had got up the idea of the
anonymous letters alleging that the dean they all hated was
a practicing homosexual, practically a capital offense in
Spain in 1921, thus bringing on the dean's premature retirement.

"I have it! I have it! It not only is no problem, it gives us an opportunity to exercise the revolutionary arts! We will rob a bank."

There was a moment's silence, followed by excited crosstalk. Rico was quite carried away. "By robbing a bank not only can we put Raúl through school, we can begin to finance the revolutionary movement to which we are consecrated. Robbing a bank is an excellent place to start since there is no greater affront to socialism than banks."

"Which bank?" Héctor wanted to know.

"What does it matter which bank, my dear Héctor? They are all the same."

"If it is all the same to the rest of you," Héctor said, "I would like to rob the bank that owns the usurious mortgage on my father's house."

"Which one is that?"

"It is the Banco del Sagrado Corazón, on Calle Marina, near the bullring."

And so the plan was conceived.

Rico, because he had thought up the idea, took charge. He assigned Antonio the job of monitoring the bank's activities from outside the building, minute by minute, from nine in the morning when it opened until one, when it closed down for the midday break, to take note, for instance, how often and when policemen patrolled by and at which hours patronage of the bank was heaviest. It had been resolved to stage the robbery in the morning, and now they had to determine at exactly what hour in the morning. Héctor, who regularly delivered his parents' mortgage payments to the bank, was assigned the job of surveying security arrangements inside the bank, in whose chambers he could find excuses to dawdle by making a mistake in the mortgage vouchers, an innocent mistake but time-consuming to correct.

They would concert their findings the next afternoon. Meanwhile Concho was to lay his hands on firearms.

"Handguns would be preferable," Rico observed gravely, stroking his beard—all four of them wore beards and moustaches, in the style of Lenin—"but if we can't get them, then rifles or, better still, shotguns will do. We need"—he paused, not without a sense of the drama that accompanies armed struggle—"a proletarian arsenal."

On Wednesday, at Antonio's home because his parents were visiting his sick aunt at Santander and the house was empty, they convened to pool their information. Concho began by producing triumphantly, from a large bag, one .32-caliber pistol. "I got this from a policeman's holster while he was taking a crap in the railroad station."

"Did he see you?" Rico asked.

"Yes, but he was in no position to get up and chase me," Concho laughed, with the air of a grand strategist. "Don't worry, he'd never identify me. These beards can be useful." He then brought out of the bag his father's militia rifle and the old family shotgun with which his father shot an occasional rabbit or dove.

Héctor reported that there was an armed guard who sat near the entrance to the bank and occasionally would stroll about; moreover that he deduced from his intensive concentration on the cash teller's window and the movements of the teller that there might be a pistol hidden but within reach of the teller. Antonio reported that he had observed only two policemen going by, always between nine and ten. He reported that the customers were relatively few between ten-thirty and eleven-thirty, after which they began to crowd in again.

It was resolved that Rico, using the pistol, would on the stroke of eleven jab it into the back ribs of the guard and disarm him. At that identical moment Antonio would rush through the door with his shotgun, followed by Héctor with the rifle. Héctor would threaten any bystander who obstructed the operation, while Antonio would aim the shotgun at the chest of the bank teller, demand the money, and scrutinize him carefully lest he reach for a weapon.

"How much money should Antonio demand?" Concho asked. "One thousand pesetas?"

"No, you fool," Rico said. "This is no longer merely an enterprise to pay for Raúl's semester. It is a venture in revolutionary justice. We shall demand all the money."

There was discussion about this, and it was resolved to compromise by taking all the money in the till, but not to risk asking the teller to dip into the reserves in the bank's vaults. "Remember, we have to act quickly," Rico warned. "In and out." Concho would be waiting outside in a getaway car that would be stolen that morning, hardly a problem since half the cars parked for a few blocks past the great square outside had keys in the ignitions. Car theft was virtually unknown in Spain in 1922. They would dispose of the car, and then, moving separately, unite in Antonio's house by three o'clock in the afternoon. Later in the day Héctor would make a deposit with the bursar for the account of Raúl Carrera, and Raúl would be told that an anonymous donor had made it possible for him to continue in school.

It was in high mood that they broke out one of Antonio's father's 1917 gourds of good red wine—"an appropriate color," Concho said, smiling, "to toast the beginning, in Barcelona, of true revolutionary activity." They all resolved to sleep in the same house to anneal their fraternal bonds and consecrate the singularity of the historical occasion. "Perhaps someday," Concho whispered to Rico, who was preparing to sleep on the couch, "this house will be a shrine." Rico nodded solemnly.

The money in a pillowcase gripped in his left hand, the shotgun in his right hand, Antonio ran to the revolving door through which they had moments before entered the bank, but the hard thrust of his elbow into the glass pane

had the effect not of causing the door to turn, but of ruptur-
ing the glass. At that point a shot rang out. The bullet
appeared to go right through Antonio's arm, because he
dropped the shotgun in the shatter of glass. Héctor rushed
to help Antonio but he too found the revolving door ada-
mantly shut. He wrestled with it while Rico, his own pistol
and the guard's in his hands, ran to help his comrades. Now
a second shot rang out, this time penetrating Rico's right
hand, causing him to drop both pistols. Héctor stopped
wrestling with the door after a calm voice rang out from
somewhere high above them. "You. With the rifle. Drop it."

Héctor dropped the gun, and looked over at Rico, who
was thrusting his wrist against his sweater to staunch the
bleeding. Sitting, his back against the revolving door, Antonio only moaned.

The voice had come from behind the balcony on the
second floor, where the offices were. It was the voice of José
Luís Cambray y Echeverría, the sixty-five-year-old president of the Banco del Sagrado Corazón.

It all had been very easy, he later explained to the press,
puffing on his cigar and leaning back in his armchair. The
teller, when accosted by the bandit, had simply put his foot
over a special buzzer. The president, hearing the alarm ring
in his office, depressed a switch that electrically bolted shut
the revolving door. He had then reached for his rifle, con-
veniently situated right by the entrance to his office,
opened the door, surveyed the situation below, aimed one
shot at the fellow with the shotgun, a second shot at the
fellow with the pistol, and was ready with a third shot to
take on the rifleman; but that proved unnecessary, Don
José said, tapping his ashes into the brass cuspidor.

At the trial, Rico, Antonio, and Héctor were given ten
years of hard labor. Concho and Raúl were given five years
as accomplices, never mind that everyone swore that Raúl
had been ignorant of the entire proceeding. After searching Raúl's room and finding all the revolutionary literature,

there simply could be no reasonable doubt of his involvement, the prosecutor had argued. The judge, pronouncing sentence, asked that God should forgive the young brutes, and Raúl's mother, sitting diffidently in the second row, glad for once that her husband was dead, bowed her head and crossed herself.

Raúl and Concho were sent to work on a mountain tunnel designed to penetrate the Iberian Mountains to permit the construction of a highway. During the day, under heavy guard and dressed in distinctive uniform, they would work in the seemingly endless tunnel, hewing rock and pulling out earth, and at night they would be driven by truck to the prison site at Altamira. A routine deprivation of the Altamira prison was the denial of any reading matter whatever. This vexation very nearly drove Raúl out of his mind, and he and Concho arranged to loiter outside a guard's office in the few minutes they had, after work and before their supper, to hear the news over the radio. On the day that Lenin died Raúl felt as though he knew what it must have been that the apostles experienced at Calvary. He swore that he would dedicate himself when he got out to avenging Lenin.

Concho said he did not understand this. "What did Spain do to Lenin that you should avenge Lenin?"

Raúl explained to Concho that he was not well schooled in revolutionary rhetoric. Any defiance of Lenin—and the whole extra-Soviet world had been in defiance of him—was a defiance that needed to be avenged. Indeed, the cruel treatment given to Rico, Héctor, Concho, and Antonio, to say nothing of Raúl who had been entirely innocent, was so to speak a profanation of Lenin who was not only a leader but a prophet. Concho nodded his head. He said he wished Lenin would be avenged, but that in point of fact he had to confess that during the past three years he had found his revolutionary appetite abated, and he wanted most awfully first to spend a night with a woman, second to have a decent meal, and third never again to have anything to do with the police.

"Does that mean," Raúl asked, stroking his clean-shaven chin (the prison authority did not permit beards: "You never know what a beard is hiding," the warden had pronounced), "that you never want to have anything further to do with me either?"

Concho tried evasion. "You were not involved with the police."

"Answer me, Concho. Have you lost your communist faith?"

"Well, no," Concho said. "I'll be glad when the revolution happens. It's just that I don't feel quite as . . . creative about it as I used to. I certainly"—he added this with heavy enthusiasm—"wish you the best of luck."

Raúl knew that but for one factor he would be bitter. That factor, of course, was that Concho had got into this difficulty only because of Raúl. At least that had been the initial impulse behind what had evolved as a comprehensive revolutionary gesture. Although he continued to be friendly with Concho, Raúl Carrera had experienced disillusion.

When he emerged from prison Raúl Carrera was five years older, on the record. But he was much older than his twenty-seven years, and his political faith was wholly matured. At the railroad station in Barcelona he inquired about the fare to Madrid. He owned one hundred pesetas, his dismissal bounty. The fare to Madrid was one hundred and twenty pesetas. He turned then from the station and walked to Calle Carmen and entered the public library, where he asked for the periodicals desk.

He read hungrily the papers for that day, and then the day before that, and then the magazines. The papers, he had noticed excitedly, had made several references to the Communist Party, whose headquarters were of course in

Madrid, which was why he wished to travel there. But then he stumbled on what he had subconsciously hoped to find. It was in *El Standard:* a story about a threatened strike by electrical workers. Their spokesman was Gabriel Ponzillo. And Gabriel Ponzillo was listed as leader of the Electrical Workers Union—and Vice President of the Communist Party of Barcelona.

Raúl Carrera stood up.

The Communist Party of Barcelona!

He looked about him. There was no one in sight. With his fingers he tore out the column from the newspaper, stuck it in his pocket, and walked out, past the great obelisk to Colón, south toward the working district. He went into the Cantina de Milagros, and sat down and asked how much was a liter of red wine, and then put down the seventy-five céntimos on the table. The newspaper column in front of him, he drank the wine, one glass after another, his spirits soaring. The Communist Party of Barcelona!

One hour later, Gabriel Ponzillo was testing the voltage of one of the auxiliary generators in the hot engine room of the principal electrical plant in the Jardín region. A clerk entered the room and, shouting to be heard against the generator's loud whining, repeated that a young man demanded to see him and would not leave the premises until Ponzillo spoke to him.

Ponzillo, a huge man in his late thirties, bearded and sweating in his T-shirt, put down his voltage meter without any change in expression.

"Where is he?"

"This way. Just outside the bursar's office."

Wiping his hands and chest with a towel, Ponzillo came out into the dark. It was after ten, and Ponzillo would be on duty until midnight. He stared at a short, slim young man with straight hair and thin lips and eager eyes.

"What do you want?"

"I want to help you, Señor Ponzillo. I was framed by the

police and have been in prison for five years. I was a law student. I have read all of Lenin and Marx. I wish to join your cause."

Ponzillo paused, and stared down at Raúl. Another plant? he wondered. He said to him, "I live at 322 Calle Hércules. Meet me there at 12:15."

"Tonight?" Raúl pressed.

"Tonight."

Raúl Carrera was there at 12:00, but waited outside, across the street. He saw Ponzillo walk into his own house at 12:10. He waited five minutes and knocked on the door.

Ponzillo had washed, and now, wordlessly, led Raúl into the kitchen. On the table was coarse bread, red wine, and cheese. Ponzillo sat down and began to eat and drink, making no gestures toward Carrera except to point to a kitchen chair where he might sit down, which Carrera didn't do.

"Tell me your story."

Raúl did so, giving also one or two details about the gruesome regimen of prison life. He did not speak of the attrition of Concho's revolutionary stamina.

"All that for robbing a bank?" Ponzillo commented—his mouth was full of bread and cheese, but his eyes were on Raúl.

"No sir. All that—without having robbed a bank."

"Very well. Tomorrow morning we are going to rob a bank. Will you join us?"

Raúl Carrera turned pale. He thought of the 1,825 days at Altamira, of five years of rock hewing, of forty thousand hours without reading material. He wavered, but for only a moment.

"Yes, señor."

Ponzillo pushed his plate of bread and cheese to Raúl's end of the table.

"Sit down, comrade."

Comrade Raúl Carrera rose rapidly in the fledgling hierarchy of the Spanish Communist Party, and because of his special, quiet eloquence was much used in the academies, which were hot with sentiment for the overthrow of the dictatorship backed by the king. In the turbulent years that followed the overthrow of the dictatorship and the abdication of the king, the election of a Popular Front republican government, and the outbreak of the civil war, Carrera was specifically engaged in attempting to win over, or win back, those who had gone to the Trotskyist party or to the Anarcho-Syndicalists. The pressure from Moscow was considerable to discredit the Trotskyists, and by the summer of 1936 when the war came, Raúl Carrera had been trained to identify the Trotskyists as the principal enemy. Without their sundering influence, he reasoned, the communists would grow in power, take over the anarchists, and then simply swallow up the republicans. And after all that had been accomplished, taking on General Francisco Franco should not be so difficult, though he acknowledged that the opposition was increasingly united and that just as the republicans were receiving massive arms support from the Soviet Union, so Franco was receiving shipments of arms from Mussolini and Hitler.

In early April of 1937, Raúl Carrera was advised by Party Secretary José Carrillo that he was wanted in Moscow. He went, of course, with great though subdued excitement. Raúl Carrera, as he grew older, grew quieter; in manner, more nearly clerical than flamboyant. But the ideological fires were well banked.

In Moscow, Carrera was taken to an army barracks which had once been used for junior officers. He was assigned a small room and told that he would be interviewed the following morning by Major Boris Bolgin of the KGB. He spent the late afternoon and evening worshipping at Red Square. It required a two-hour wait in line before he could

get in to view the corpse of Lenin. He reminded himself of
the pledge he had made thirteen years earlier to avenge
Lenin's death. He stared at that pale countenance with the
austere beard, at the black suit and bald head, and but for
the guard who brusquely told him to move along, he'd have
stayed there throughout the night, or for as long a vigil as
was asked of him.

Outside the monument, Carrera wished that he knew
someone who might show him about. He had been studying Russian and could manage to read Russian guidebooks.
Indeed he had proved adept at languages, becoming competent in English and in French. As if drawn by a magnet,
he thought to move toward the university, and so after
studying the subway map he made his calculations, as usual
with exactitude; he emerged at the Omsk station and
walked over toward the Student Union Building.

There on the vast ground floor he saw a number of
posters against the wall on the left: Stalin with a little girl
presenting him flowers on his birthday; Stalin with a peasant, head bowed in reverence as Stalin paternally touches
him on the shoulder; Stalin with the troops cheering him at
an armed forces festival; Stalin dedicating a naval vessel.
Something stirred in Carrera's memory. It was the talk the
year before of Lenin's "Testament," in which the communists were warned against Josef Stalin. But he was satisfied
to believe that this was a forgery, probably composed by
Leon Trotsky, the great enemy of communist unity. He
spotted a studious-looking girl, her head bent over a reading table, the day's paper spread out before her. Perhaps it
was because of the exotic circumstances and the loneliness
that had hit him that Carrera addressed her.

"Excuse me, I am Comrade Raúl Carrera from Spain. I
am here on official business. May I speak with you?"

The girl glanced up, unsmiling, and looked at the slim
young man, a trace of the Moorish in his complexion and

skin. She did not smile, but neither was she clipped in her response.

"Can I help you?"

Raúl wondered whether he should ask the routine questions—How to Get to the Main Book Section, or Where did one go to Get Tickets to the Ballet. Instead he said:

"Would you consent to having a cup of tea or coffee with me?"

Without hesitation she rose, bundled her bag of books into a canvas case, buttoned her rough woolen sweater about her—it was April and chilly, though not cold. She spoke.

"You have a little difficulty with Russian, and I do not speak Spanish. Do you speak German or French?" Raúl answered delightedly that he could speak French and so, conversing in French, they went outdoors. She led him to a little shop a few blocks away frequented primarily by students. The service was cafeteria style; there was a choice of several coarse breads and pastries, sausage, potatoes, carrots, Ukrainian wine, vodka, beer, and tea. Raúl watched to see what his companion would take, intending to follow her example, and was agreeably surprised to see her take some of almost everything available, save the alcoholic drinks. Raúl Carrera took sausage, cheese, and a tenth of vodka.

Three hours later he had refilled his vodka glass three times, and Katia had taken a glass of wine. She was twenty, studying European history and literature, and she intended to pursue her studies and to teach, preferably back in Kiev where her divorced mother lived.

"You can hardly blame my mother. Father was sent to Siberia eight years ago and after three years she didn't hear from him anymore. Dead, I suppose."

She had then waited for a complementary recital by Raúl so that they would advance with knowledge of each other more or less pari passu—"My birthplace is Riga, what is yours?" "It is Barcelona. I was born on January 13, 1900.

When were you born?" "December 1, 1917." That kind of thing. Prudent.

And Raúl complied, while taking care to edit his biography since leaving law school. And she maintained this demand for conversational parity for a full hour when suddenly she found herself free of any suspicion of the intense young Spaniard, whose words were so nicely framed in a French obviously learned at the academy, yet learned with idiomatic finesse.

She began then to speak with some abandon, expressing frustration at the difficulty of getting books on modern French and German authors she wished to read, for instance Thomas Mann. Carrera volunteered to attempt to get those books—"though it is not easy today to 'get' things in Barcelona, but I have a few contacts outside Barcelona." To which Katia had replied, looking rather patronizingly at her companion, never mind that he was old enough to have fathered her, "How would you, assuming you got the books of Thomas Mann, arrange to get them to me, here?"

Raúl said he did not know about the difficulties attendant on these matters, that he had always thought of Thomas Mann as a thoroughly progressive writer, to which she snorted that a progressive writer was defined as someone Stalin happened to approve of on that particular day, and Thomas Mann had said or written something a year ago that had got him proscribed in Soviet Russia. Raúl smiled and said that perhaps the Trotskyists were spreading some of these rumors. At which Katia had got thoroughly impatient, and for a full hour she berated Raúl with the intellectual difficulties of conducting higher studies in a Soviet university. All this without, however, condemning the communist system. Had she done this she would have prompted Raúl, however ruefully, to put an end to the discussion, because he did not engage hospitably in schismatic talk. It was all in the day's work to contend polemically with fascists and liberals, but with fellow communists he felt a theological bond, the bond that made so very conspicuous and outrageous the heresies of Trotsky.

They agreed to let the matter of Thomas Mann rest, and Raúl again offered her a cigarette which again she declined for herself, but this time she requested one for her roommate. She deposited it carefully within the neat folds of a handkerchief in her tan woolen purse.

Raúl noticed her heavy Slavic features, and the warmth and intelligence of her face. She expressed now a curiosity about developments in Spain and, lighting his own cigarette, Raúl Carrera told her about the awful chaos in his own country, while she listened. He felt she wanted to make more pointed comments than the conventional ones she used. But she did not again slip into overdrive, and before long Raúl's words felt desiccated in his mouth. There was a moment's silence, neither of them spoke; then Katia said that she would have to go now as she had a long subway ride ahead of her. Raúl said that was true also of him, but he would be grateful for her address, as he would like to endeavor to send her some books by Thomas Mann. At which she had abruptly risen and hissed that it was all very well for foreigners to undertake to send forbidden books into the Soviet Union, but it was not safe for Soviet citizens to receive those books, could he not understand that simple point?

Raúl Carrera apologized. And he thanked her for being so kind. They shook hands at the eastbound station.

"I am going the other way," Katia said and half smiled, tucking the wool collar of her sweater about her neck. "Goodbye, Raúl."

Carrera received rigorous training by the KGB. Special attention was given to the need to weed out of potentially influential positions in the republican government and army those who might have ties to the Anarcho-Syndicalists or—especially—to the Trotskyists. Already Raúl had had

training in physical defense, and a Catalan physical education instructor sympathetic to the Electrical Workers Union
strike in 1927 had given him training in karate. Considerable time in Moscow was given over to the study of foreign
languages, in particular English, in which Carrera became
fluent. Heavy attention was given to ideological orthodoxy,
and this of course was made difficult with the frequent
changes ordered by Stalin. The shifts had sometimes to do
with the party line—there were changes in emphasis on
industrial development and agricultural development. But
mostly the changes seemed to center on men who had been
heroes of the young Soviet Republic but were now demon-
strated to have been traitors, men like Zinoviev, Kamenev,
Bukharin. Carrera had taught himself to accept the word of
higher authorities in these matters and when it became
known that the word had come down from Stalin himself in
the matter of prosecuting the principal betrayers, Carrera
accepted the verdict dutifully if sadly. Carrera was saddened by diluted loyalties, even as he had been saddened
by Concho, at Altamira.

He was back in Barcelona just after the great uprising
there, the so-called civil war within a civil war that resulted,
finally, in ejecting the Anarcho-Syndicalists from the republican government. Carrera's mission was now specific.
He was to provide information to his superior, Colonel
Glukansk, on the activities of the Trotskyists and their
party, the Partido Obrero de Unificación Marxista (or
P.O.U.M.), with the view to getting as many of their leaders
as possible liquidated, on the grounds of putative treason.
Colonel Glukansk was not given to disquisitive talk, and
told Carrera it was simple: the republican government of
Spain would succeed or not against the fascist forces de-
pending on whether the Social Democrats acquiesced in
the leadership being given by the Communists. But the
Communists could not make common cause with the Trots-

kyists, who served only to undermine the philosophical integrity of the movement.

Late on the hot September afternoon of the following day, a hastily mobilized tribunal whose members were dominated by Colonel Glukansk heard the case against Juanito Lorca, cousin of the poet. The prosecutor, parading up and down the abandoned cow barn on the hillside near Valencia as though it were the supreme courthouse of Spain, inveighed against Lorca, charging that he had been seen at the post office staring at the fascist poster offering a reward for the capture or execution of Captain Diego Brujo, the heroic republican guerrilla fighter who in the previous six months had ambushed a half-dozen fascist columns, capturing a trainload of arms and ammunition.

The very next day, emerging from the house of his betrothed where he slept when in Valencia, Brujo was shot by a *pistolero* who had fired from a speeding car. An accomplice in the front seat next to the driver had snapped a photograph, thus obtaining evidence of Brujo's assassination, obviously needed to collect the fascist reward. The prosecutor then triumphantly produced a deaf-mute who had been walking the street at the critical moment. The prosecutor sat him down on a bale of hay that served as a witness stand and wrote out on a pad of paper, *"Point to the man you saw taking the picture last Monday when Captain Brujo was shot."* The deaf-mute, wearing coat and tie and sweating, pointed to where Lorca was standing, handcuffed. The prosecutor rested his case.

Lorca gave as his defense that indeed he had been at the post office on the day in question—but so had he been in the post office every day of the week, since occasionally a letter from his sister and mother in the south reached him. And yes he had seen the poster, but then he habitually looked at all the posters in the post office; indeed it was from a poster that he had first learned that his cousin, García Lorca, had been shot by the fascists. Far from wanting to kill Captain Brujo, he had great admiration for him, and on the fatal morning was at the other side of town, sound asleep, as he had had watch duty from midnight until four in the morning. Moreover, he owned no camera, had never used a camera, and did not even know how to operate a camera. The major asked sneeringly if he had any witnesses to his story, and Lorca replied that he slept alone. The major and the two captains rose and went to the corner of the barn where they smoked cigarettes for fifteen minutes. They returned to their makeshift seats behind the old door that had been propped up as a table and pronounced Juan Lorca guilty of treason and murder, and sentenced him to death. The two guards who watched over the prisoner knew what to do, walking Lorca back to the end of the barn where the hay was stacked. Lorca demanded to see the regimental commander and began to shout out charges of political persecution. The major told the three riflemen who had stood guard outside to get on with it. The guards refastened Lorca's manacles through the thick wire that bound a hay bale together. The major, putting aside his judicial robes and donning executive dress, gave out the order to fire. After which he walked forward, discharged the ritual pistol shot at the head of the corpse lying on the floor, and walked back to his companions.

"Really, Ramírez," he said to the prosecutor, "can't you come up with something better than a deaf-mute?"

Ramírez, smoking his cigarette, shrugged his shoulders. "It is a question of supply and demand," he said. "The demand is very heavy these days."

He offered Carrera a cigarette, but Carrera declined it. He would report now to Colonel Glukansk that there was one less Trotskyist in the Republican army.

In due course it was all over; General Franco took Madrid and Raúl Carrera, reporting for the last time to Colonel Glukansk at the railroad station in Bilbao, was given an address in Paris. "There you will be equipped for your next mission." Which proved to be to look after not Trotskyists, but Trotsky.

Now, twenty-one years later in Mexico City, Raúl Carrera, though now he was Cecilio Velasco, drove slowly up Calle Morelos, as far as the corner of Calle Paris, where he had stopped that night, inasmuch as they would walk softly the last three blocks to Trotsky's villa, there to give assistance to the executioner—Carrera preferred this word to assassin—Mercader, who had infiltrated the household. They would wait until they saw the light in the room on the first floor turn on and then off again. That meant that in exactly five minutes Mercader would walk out of his door down the hallway, thrust himself into Trotsky's study, and swing down the weapon designed to drive holes into mountain rock. Human skulls, to the mountain climber's ice hammer, are as apples to a nail. In exactly five minutes—Carrera held the stopwatch, and he could hear the heartbeat of Julio on his right and Texco on his left—they would create the disturbance that, if all went according to plan, would distract Trotsky's guards and provide the assassin with the opportunity, the deed done, to slip away.

Cecilio Velasco, after staring at the site, the place where he had helped carry out a spectacular mandate of Josef Stalin, drove back toward the flower market off Chapultepec and then, slowly, past the huge Soviet Embassy. It was now even more massive than when he had known it, had worked in it, during those five years after arriving from Spain. That building—he had parked his car and sat down at the coffeehouse diagonally away from it—had housed his superior, Colonel Igor Ochek. It had also housed the ambassador, Dmitri Oumansky. And Mariya.

He had never liked Colonel Ochek. It wasn't so much that he was ruthless—Colonel Glukansk had got him used to that: a job was a job. There was something extraclinical about Ochek's ruthlessness. Operating in a foreign country not engaged in civil war, the colonel had to proceed more carefully than his counterparts in Spain. Besides, the problem of a Trotskyist party standing directly in the way of the Communists during a military operation wasn't there to dominate his attention.

There were, accordingly, far fewer direct victims—or, better, fewer objects of Colonel Ochek's mission. There was occasionally a matter of discipline within the embassy itself. It was the largest embassy Stalin maintained, during the war years, in Latin America, and it was the headquarters for communist operations throughout the hemisphere, excluding the United States.

Mexico itself was extremely hospitable to the Soviets. General Cárdenas was still president. Cárdenas was a communist-populist at heart—he had endeared himself to the socialist world the year before by expropriating American oil holdings. Mexico was the very special haven for refugees from Spain, and a great many of these were Party. The heaviest concentration of Spanish communists stayed in Mexico City; indeed the heaviest concentration of everything in Mexico was in Mexico City. Ambassador Oumansky was responsible for maintaining discipline among the migrant population of communists and this job, of course, fell most directly on the shoulders of Colonel Ochek.

So that there was nothing like the quotidian executions back in Spain. The foremost objective, during that first year, had been of course to monitor Trotsky's activities. Then there was the abortive expedition, led by the artist David Siqueiros, that had failed to kill Trotsky. Ochek had erupted with rage over such an enterprise's having been undertaken other than under his direct supervision. The cable received from the Kremlin did not disguise the primogenital fury of Stalin. True, Stalin had had to bear the brunt of the international democratic uproar over an attempted assassination carried out by acknowledged communists who were presumably acting on instructions from communist superiors. To face all this—and then to fail! Trotsky, it seemed, had simply hurled himself under his bed. His bed! Safe under his bed against a machine gun! Colonel Ochek's fleshy face writhed in pain.

Trotsky had been the first preoccupation of Igor Ochek. But Raúl Carrera noticed that, in exacting discipline here and there, unlike Glukansk, who had been matter-of-factly concerned with discipline, Ochek took manifest delight in enforcing discipline. Utterly routine requests from subordinates were gleefully rejected. Carrera remembered the day in May when María Socorro had asked permission to take three days off to attend her brother's wedding in Monterrey. Ochek said no. Not, Carrera knew, because he feared that María Socorro, in Monterrey for a few days in festive circumstances, might indiscreetly divulge what slight knowledge she might have had about the extent of the activities of the Soviet Embassy; and not because for three working days she was irreplaceable—there were several secretaries to share her clerical burden. Ochek simply liked to say no. And liked especially to say no when he could experience the distress he had caused.

The pain was not always psychological deprivation. There was young Valerian, the day he was brought in drunk by the police. Inside the embassy he was searched. Ten thousand pesos were found in his coat pocket.

Where had Valerian, whose salary was 250 pesos per month, got hold of ten thousand pesos?

Valerian, brought down now to the cellar quarters of the embassy, was interrogated directly by Ochek. He had answered lamely, persistently, that he had won the money at the state lottery and gone out to celebrate.

Where had he purchased the ticket?

From a street vendor outside the embassy.

What was the ticket number?

He did not remember.

Where did he go to cash the ticket?

To the central office, right by Bellas Artes.

Who had witnessed his cashing the ticket? No one besides the cashier herself.

Had he told anyone in the embassy about his good luck?

No, he had kept it quiet—but he intended to give a big party for his associates. *Had* intended to give a big party for his associates.

Ochek had him taken to what they called the library— "We conduct research there," Ochek, his thick glasses especially prominent when he leered and his eyes narrowed, had chuckled to Carrera when he first came to work. After viewing Valerian's condition when he was carried out, Carrera was grateful that he had never had any business to transact in the library. And then suddenly, unexpectedly, because he long had been accustomed to the style of Bolshevik justice, he had asked himself a question the resonance of which would become haunting. He asked: But *was* Valerian guilty? *Maybe it was exactly as he said it was*—he had bought a winning ticket on the national lottery.

Merely to frame in his mind the question *Was Valerian guilty?* was an invitation to conjugate retrospectively the phrase: Was Valerian guilty? Was . . . A. "guilty"? Was B. "guilty"? Yes, all those men were indeed guilty, guilty of Trotskyism. Oh how much better off the world would be— he had finally put his doubts serviceably to one side—when Trotsky was no longer there to poison the wells.

A month later Mariya was brought in to take the place of Valerian, whose broken body was sent back to Moscow on "suspicion of treasonable relations with foreigners."

Valerian was a cryptographer, but within the KGB there are levels of cryptography and Valerian had handled only the routine work. He had sat for eight hours every day behind a large machine, the protruding center of which berthed a typewriter keyboard of sorts. A large collection of newspapers and periodicals from all over Latin America went through a kind of intelligence assembly line. Four KGB officials would mark those columns or articles they thought would be of interest to KGB–Moscow. Before the arrival of Colonel Ochek it was thought perfectly safe merely to clip and photograph these oddments and send them off in the weekly diplomatic pouch on the military transport plane that ambled up from Buenos Aires to Santiago to Lima, Bogotá, Mexico, Havana, Bermuda, Terceira, Lisbon, Stockholm, and Moscow, carrying diplomatic personnel and mail. Colonel Ochek had ruled that all such matter had henceforward to be encrypted. The material, because it was not of urgent security value, could then proceed as before to go forward to Moscow not by radio code but in the pouch, in those bizarre and theoretically inscrutable taped sequences into which the machine converted Russian.

So that Mariya's job was first to translate the Spanish material into Russian, and then to encrypt it. She was a graduate of the KGB academy, trained in Spanish, English, and cryptography. She had been orphaned during one of the early purges in the thirties and brought up by an older sister who—Raúl would learn all this—resented her younger sister's superior looks. Mariya had attempted to be dutiful and behave inconspicuously, and had worked for eight years, after leaving the academy in Moscow, under the supervision of her sister, who occupied a supervisory position in the KGB. Glinka was her name, and Glinka apparently desired above all things that Mariya should have no social life whatever. And so Mariya worked during the day, and then went home to the apartment where the two sisters lived, and did the housework. Thus it had been until suddenly a Spanish-speaking cryptographer was needed in Mexico.

Mariya was overweight, but Raúl found her very attractive; and already, after only a few months, she seemed to be slimming down—as though the nervous tension caused by her sister's surveillance, now removed, freed her to find distraction other than in food.

Raúl took to sharing his lunch hour with Mariya and they practiced languages together, her English, his Russian. They went one night to the movies at the Cine Chapultepec and saw a rerun of *Gone With the Wind* and were quite dazzled by it. They went then to take a late dinner at the Hotel Géneve, right by the American Embassy, and Mariya drank some wine while Raúl had rum and cigarettes. She spoke of her sister, and of the academy. He spoke of Spain, and of his year in Moscow.

Six months later he asked Mariya if she would marry "an older man—I am forty-four, but I am healthy, and I know how to look after . . . somebody"—he found it hard to use the words modestly, so he went into French, the least secure of Mariya's languages—"somebody . . . *que j'aime.*" She looked at him with a face Raúl had never seen before. What he saw was something he adored. She told him she would marry him tonight if he asked her, that she never wanted to be away from him, not ever. That night they walked in Chapultepec until dawn.

The next day Colonel Ochek was utterly unambiguous on the subject. "The answer," he said in his office to his two subordinates, the short, wry Spaniard and the plump, wholesome Russian who stood stiffly in front of him, "is quite simple. It is No. The KGB does not run a dating service or a marriage bureau here in Mexico. We are engaged in a great revolutionary struggle. I expect you not only to remain unmarried but to see less of each other so that you will not be distracted in your work. Otherwise I shall simply transfer you."

Oh how they had talked about the alternatives, that night at dinner, and about the need to exercise great care. But the central objective was taken for granted. They would marry.

This required clerical footwork inasmuch as, in Mexico, foreigners who work for embassies require employer approval on their applications for a marriage license. But Raúl Carrera had become accustomed to the ways of Mexico, and he surmounted that problem with a mere one hundred pesos. The next problem was to consider living quarters that would not come to the attention of the colonel. They resolved, forlornly, that it would be necessary to continue to maintain their separate apartments. They could not afford a third apartment. They would need to run the risk of visiting each other in their separate abodes, always careful not to arrive, or leave, jointly. And, at work in the embassy, they would affect a gradual alienation from each other. No more joint lunches or shared jollity. Ochek and the general staff must be given the impression that it had been a temporary infatuation.

On the twenty-third of September a magistrate in Villa Obregón issued them a marriage license, and they spent the weekend, beginning at noon on Saturday, in Xochimilco, among the flowers, holding hands, and the two nights in each other's very loving arms.

Carrera was surprised when he was reached by telephone at his home by Colonel Ochek four months later—Ochek seldom telephoned. "You are to meet me in Room 51 of the Hotel del Valle in Cuernavaca at 10 P.M. tomorrow, Tuesday night. You will make no reference, during office hours tomorrow, to our forthcoming meeting. If anyone suggests any meeting with you after hours you are to say that you have made plans to do work in the library and will not be home until very late. Is that clear?"

Carrera said that that was clear.

"There are buses, as you probably know, every hour to Cuernavaca. You should be able to make the six o'clock bus after work, but even if you take the seven o'clock bus, you will arrive in plenty of time to make our engagement."

At exactly ten, Raúl Carrera knocked on the door at the Hotel del Valle. There were three men in the suite, two of them strangers to Carrera. Ochek did not give out their names. He merely pointed to one, then to Carrera: "Carrera," he said. And to the other, the same thing: "Carrera," he said. And then to Carrera, directly: "Sit down."

He deferred now to the first of the two men, younger than Ochek by perhaps ten years. Forty, Carrera guessed. But Ochek referred to him as "General." He was smoking a cigarette, as was the third man.

"Your record shows, Carrera, total fidelity to the Party for a period, now, of over fifteen years."

Carrera nodded.

"We have a most grave commission to execute. You will, I assume, be satisfied of my credentials if I inform you, as I have Colonel Ochek, that the orders I bring were given to me by—Comrade Stalin himself."

The mere mention of the name caused the voice of the general slightly to alter. He cleared his throat. And went on to say that evidence, of an incontrovertible character, had come to the attention of the KGB in Moscow that Ambassador Oumansky was a double agent.

Carrera was astonished. He had seen pictures of the great Oumansky with almost every dignitary in Moscow, including Stalin himself. He was the ganglion of communist activity in the hemisphere. Everything that happened in Latin America happened because Oumansky authorized it to happen, or didn't happen because Oumansky did not authorize it to happen. He had been at least twice to Washington to confer there on matters of common purpose—for instance nazi submarines fishing in Mexican and Caribbean waters. The whole idea of Oumansky as double agent was unimaginable.

The general continued. He was seated now, peering at papers on a desk.

"Your record shows that you received training in Moscow in demolition. Is that correct?"

"Yes, General, that is correct."

"Your instructions are to prepare an explosive force of about ten pounds of dynamite. The decision, you will have gathered, is not to stage a public trial. It would be too demoralizing to too many of the comrades who have trusted the traitor Oumansky."

The traitor Oumansky. Carrera breathed deeply at the force of this apparent oxymoron.

"Do you have the necessary materiel?"

Colonel Ochek interrupted. "General, please. Of course we have access to it."

"Where is it to go?" Carrera asked.

"It is to go in the diplomatic pouch, having been set to explode on reaching eight thousand feet of altitude. The altitude in Mexico City being seven thousand feet, the plane will reach eight thousand feet in approximately three minutes, at which point the bomb will go off."

Carrera did not need more details.

That was Tuesday. On Wednesday after work Carrera, ever so careful to tell Mariya nothing of what it was that would keep him from going to her apartment that night, even as he had not told her why she must not come to him the night before, went to a designated street corner where a car waited. Colonel Ochek was in it, and together they drove to a remote, inconspicuously guarded shed in the Guadalupe area near the railroad station.

It might better have been designated a small armory. Everything anyone could need in the way of explosives. "And all of it made in America," Colonel Ochek said, with a leer. "Useful, in case fragments are picked up."

It was simple enough, as Carrera retained what he had been taught and on several occasions, retreating from General Franco's juggernaut, a bridge or a railroad would need to be bombed, and if the regular people weren't there they would call in Carrera.

Carrera selected one of the wooden boxes, of which there were several in different sizes. This one would have berthed two magnums of champagne. He grouped together thirty-six sticks of dynamite, which would occupy about three quarters of the space within the box. With great care to make the opening smooth, he detached the lid from one end of a soup can, lightly filing the edge to remove abrasive surfaces. He cut with metal shears a thin metal strip ten inches long and just under a half inch wide from the same tin can. And a second piece six inches long. Again, light strokes of a fine file to smooth the surfaces.

He cut cardboard into a disk that would fit snugly inside the can, and clipped out two one-foot sections of insulated light wire, removing the insulation from an inch at either end. With care he applied strips of tape inside the can to strengthen the explosives' insulation. He took the shorter metal strip and bent it in half, rounding the insulated lip of the soup can like a clip. He completed the taping and then, forming a kind of U shape out of the original strip, inserted it into the can seating it across the bottom. He fastened a wire to the outside end of the first metal strip, anchoring it firmly into place. Now the current between the two wires could be made to flow only through the junction of the two strips at the rim of the can.

He blew up a child's round balloon to its full capacity to test it. Letting the air out, he slipped it into the can's center and blew up the balloon until there was enough pressure to press the bent tip of the wire to within a tiny distance of the contact on the can's edge. He had calculated that approximately 1,000 feet higher than the current altitude, air pressure would swell the balloon, bringing together the firing cap's leads. And effecting the explosion.

The bomb finished, Carrera was escorted to within a few blocks of his apartment by Colonel Ochek, who was friendlier to him than he had ever been before. (That often happens, Raúl ruminated, when someone shares with you, however unwillingly, a major secret.) Raúl learned on the car trip home that he would serve yet another function on the following day. He was one of four officials who had personal clerical access to the pouch, both after it arrived—when it was Carrera's responsibility to pull out and distribute material for the KGB section—and when it left, it being Carrera's responsibility to insert material compiled by KGB–Mexico. The pouch, as it was loosely called, was more like an indefinitely expandable canvas sack. Indeed sometimes it was several sacks, as it was frequently used by high officials as conduit for small gifts; Ambassador Oumansky regularly received his caviar in the pouch. Colonel Ochek explained to Carrera that he did not wish the bomb to be placed in the pouch in the embassy, as there was always the possibility that someone else, at the last minute, might desire to put something into the pouch and trip across the lethal parcel. Carrera's instructions were to take with him the office seal, go out to the plane when it was almost ready to board the ambassador, and go to the pouch with his package, advising the plane orderly that Colonel Ochek had neglected to enclose a mechanical specimen he wished analyzed in Soviet laboratories. "It will be routine," Ochek said, reassuringly.

And so it was. The diplomatic pass to go through Mexican Immigration to the aircraft was handed to him, on examination of his identification tags. Inside the C-47 transport Carrera turned to the compartment where the pouches of the various embassies were regularly placed, and exchanged an amenity with the orderly, identifying himself. The orderly asked if Carrera needed help. No, Carrera had said, the package was light. The Mexican pouch was, understandably, on top of the heap. Carrera broke the seal, inserted his package, and resealed it with the hand press he carried in his pocket, which he had also shown to the orderly.

He left the plane then and headed toward the little group of embassy officials off at the windowed enclosure on the other side of Immigration. They were expected to show up whenever the ambassador flew away, or when he arrived from abroad. Carrera surrendered the temporary pass, entered the room with his fellow officials and waited. Not for long. The ambassador and his wife emerged from the diplomatic door of the Immigration room and strode out to the aircraft, waving at the goodbye party in the enclosure. Carrera noted ruefully that three staff members were accompanying Oumansky.

And then his heart stopped.

For a moment it was as though he had been blinded by snow. Everything was white except for barely discernible movements of photonegative skeletons climbing up a companionway. The last person to climb into the aircraft before the door shut was Mariya Pleshkoff. Mariya Carrera.

Carrera gave out a shout and threw himself against his startled companions in a race for the Immigration corridor. The propellers were now revving up and it was hard over their noise to hear exactly what he was saying, something on the order of his having to get to the airplane. An Immigration supervisor grabbed the little man by his lapel but Carrera felled him with a karate chop. With that a halfdozen Mexican officials dived at him and held him down on the floor and he heard the airplane engine's noise, as the plane taxied out to the runway, recede. He struggled with all his might, shouting to be released.

And then, abruptly, he was quiet. The rudimentary human engine that speaks of survival had choked off his voice. *You cannot stop the plane. If you shout out that there is a bomb in it you will be liquidated by the KGB. And it will not stop the plane.* He lay there, face down, two Mexicans holding down one arm, two Mexicans the other, three more on his legs. Several minutes went by as they waited for the police. He asked in a quiet voice if he might rise, and was cautiously permitted to do so.

"I am sorry," he said. The official he had floored was still brushing himself off, and his subordinates looked to him for instructions. Should they hold him until the police arrived? "Forgive me, sir," Carrera addressed him. "I was in great distress, and wished to wave to my wife who is on that airplane."

It was then that their attention was caught by the surrounding cries. The word reached them in moments. The Russian diplomatic plane! Exploded! Right over *there!* Just to the left of Popo. Could see it plain as day! A burst of flame! *¡Jesús, María y José, qué barbaridad!*

His chest heaving with pain, Carrera managed in the confusion to rush out to his car and drive to the office. There was already a crowd on the street. A dozen reporters, trying to get in to interview the deputy, or anybody; cameramen were arriving. Carrera fought his way through the crowd and was admitted by the guard into the building. He walked to his office and spotted, right away, on his typewriter a sealed envelope with his name written in her hand. He tore it open. "My darling. This is indiscreet, but I had to risk it. Believe it or not exactly half an hour ago Colonel Ochek told me I was to accompany the ambassador back to Moscow in case I could be of any service to him. No time even to go home and pack. But don't worry. He said he would make certain that I wasn't detained but would return with the ambassador within one week. It will be unbearable without you. Oh my darling, how much I love you. M."

Mechanically, Raúl Carrera put the letter in his pocket. He opened the door to his office a mere crack. By just standing there and looking through the slit he could see officials coming and going into the office of Colonel Ochek down the hall, opposite. This went on at a hectic pace for two hours, slowly lessening until, at about seven, Carrera reasoned that Ochek was alone, or very nearly alone.

He walked across the hall and opened the door. Ochek's secretary, Anna, was in the outer office, bent over her typewriter. She looked up, muttered "What a day!" and went back to her furious typing. Raúl Carrera walked over to the door of the private office, opened it, and closed it behind him. Ochek was seated at his desk, telephone in hand. When he saw Carrera he hesitated, then dived for a drawer. Too late. Carrera thrust two stiff fingers into Ochek's eyes. His scream was short-lived because the chop at the neck brought him prostrate. And then, summoning all the power in his 120-pound body, Carrera kicked Ochek in the temple; and knew, as he turned to walk out, that he was walking away from a dead man. Anna sat frozen at her typewriter.

"What is going on?" she asked hoarsely.

Carrera looked at her, said nothing, and walked out, using the back exit.

He never did return to his apartment, reasoning that it would be many days, weeks maybe, before Mexican security gave up waiting for him. He couldn't even remember exactly how it was that he made his way to San Antonio, or why, or how long the trip took. Arriving there and adopting the name Cecilio Velasco, he put his services as a clerk-translator to immediate use in huge Fort Sam Houston, groaning with Mexican-American recruits who did not know English, in a city greatly in need of white-collar workers to replace those who had been drafted.

He worked quietly in San Antonio, living in a one-room apartment, seeing no one but grieving and following the foreign news.

The war ended, he found that he had qualified for U.S. citizenship which he proceeded to take out, paying more than routine attention to his pledge (hand raised) to defend the Constitution of the United States. When Czech Radio

reported that Jan Masaryk had killed himself in Prague—
thrown himself out the window of the foreign office, just
like that, pity—before the day was over, the press, and
indeed the entire world, were on to what quickly was called
the "Czechoslovakian coup."

Cecilio Velasco stared down at the San Antonio *Express*'s
front-page picture of Jan Masaryk. He cut the picture and
accompanying story out of the paper and folded them into
his pocket.

He drove then to Fort Sam, but not to the War Department Personnel Center where he worked, but to the main
administration building opposite the huge parade ground,
named several years before in honor of General Arthur
MacArthur. He walked into the building and asked the
receptionist for the office number of General McIver, head
of the Intelligence Division of the 4th Army. He went to the
office and there told the receptionist he needed to see the
general, identifying himself with his Fort Sam badge, on a
personal matter. A half hour later he was in the office of the
general, who looked up at the slim, taut man in his late
forties, and then said, "What can I do for you?"

"My name is Cecilio Velasco," he said. "And I wish to
work for the United States Government. I was formerly a
major in the KGB."

The general told Velasco to sit down.

Nine

*Mac and Dulles weren't so hot on the idea of my meeting personally
with Oakes, but so they didn't think it was such a hot idea and so I
did, so what? There's no reason why my National Security Adviser
and my Director of the Central Intelligence Agency should know
more about these things than I do. Besides—*the President rang
the buzzer. "Get me a Coke, would you please?"—*besides, if
you're not the President of the United States you can't, let's face it,
realize what talking directly to the President does to some people. Just
to be talking to you. I mean, I didn't realize what it meant until it
happened to me. But you pick these things up.*

He rose from his desk and walked over to the rocking
chair, scooping up the afternoon's Washington *Star* from
the coffee table. But although he spread the paper out on
his lap, he didn't read it. He continued to think . . .

*It's going to have an effect not only on Oakes but on Che Guevara,
my seeing him personally. Interesting guy, cool, self-assured. If I
hadn't gone to Harvard, he might have made me feel ill at ease.
Bulldog bulldog bow wow wow. I like giving young people I trust big
jobs. I didn't get Allen's permission to select Bobby for Attorney
General or Ted Sorensen over here. I size people up fast. So did
Alexander and Napoleon, come to think of it.*

*I like the way he keeps the issues distinct: we don't like those Cuban
communist bastards, and it would help if we could derail them, but
that doesn't mean we can't accomplish more by being civil to them.
I'm not asking Oakes to seduce any Cuban. Huh. I wonder if there's
a Cuban he couldn't seduce? I wish Castro were a she.*

*Castro a she! Boy, he'd love that, with the macho business they've
got going there.*

I made it plain to Oakes: We don't like them, but we're ready to deal with them. The terms are guaranteed hands off the rest of Latin America, including any deals with the Russians on Latin America. Quid pro quo: we end our economic boycott within three months. Recognize them somewhere down the line. When? Oakes wanted to know. Naïve. "When" is a political question. When the American people are in the mood for diplomatic recognition . . .

That was funny, the way Allen Dulles kept saying to Oakes, "Don't promise them anything with a timetable attached to it." He said it three times. Twice too many times. Why should he be making that point? Anyway, I don't see anything totally wrong about a timetable. You can always change a timetable. I'd like to change the timetable for Haile Selassie's visit to maybe 1981. No, I won't be President in 1981. Unless the "Irish Mafia," as they're calling it in the gossip-critical press, can manage to repeal the 23rd Amendment. Let me see, 1964 2nd term, 1968 third term, 1972 fourth term—I'd pass FDR. Don't think Arthur would like that, but he could write a longer book about me, which would be good. No. On second thought I think Arthur's books are quite long enough. 1976 fifth term, 1980 sixth term. Yup. Great idea. "The President would be happy to see you in 1981, during his sixth term. Moreover, Your Majesty, you are absolutely unique in this respect, and of course in so many other respects, because only you are the Lion of Judah, and we'd appreciate it if you didn't spread the word: You are the only chief of state the President has invited over for a state visit in his sixth term."

Oh hell.

He picked up the newspaper and read the AP account of Khrushchev's speech at the opening session of the Soviet Communist Party Congress.

Rusk was right this morning. That was a clear retreat on Berlin. They've got their Berlin Wall so now they're easing up on the business of a deadline for a treaty with East Berlin. We'll win on that one. We don't need to let them forget the Wall is there—to keep those poor buggers from clawing their way out of the Workers' Paradise.

And so now Khrushchev is going to detonate a 50-megaton bomb. Five million tons. Or is that 50 million tons? Let me see: mega means a thousand, right? So fifty times a thousand is—fifty thousand, that

*can't be right. Mega must mean a million. Then fifty megatons would
be fifty million. Right? Right. Head of the class, Jack. Why did God
give us hydrogen bombs and communists at the same time? What the
hell, while I'm at it, why did God give us Everett Dirksen?*

But Khrushchev speaking six and one half hours! *I don't think
I've ever heard anybody speak for one and one half hours, not even
Hubert. Nice joke at the Al Smith Dinner a couple of years ago:
"What comes after a speech by Senator Humphrey on Saturday
night? Sunday." Well, maybe Hubert. But six and one half hours!
What does the audience do for six and one half hours? What if they
have to pee? Castro's the same way. Over four hours at the UN. Well,
at the UN they deserve it. That's what I call massive retaliation,
Castro speaking four and a half hours at the UN. But six and a half
hours. I think maybe that says something about the differences between them and us. They don't mind being bored. Hate to admit it,
but that's probably a key to their success: they don't mind getting
bored.*

*No, I'm glad I saw Oakes. It won't hurt that he can tell Guevara
he was in here with me, won't hurt at all. Boy, if this works . . .
That dumb thing we did in April, trying to take Cuba away from
Castro. A half-assed operation, and I was responsible, I don't deny it.
But if we now manage to castrate Castro . . . (I like that). He's
making a lot of militant noises, sounds as if he was sucking Lenin's
tit.*

*But Dick Goodwin gave it to me straight. Guevara says they're
willing to make that exchange. We'll see.*

He picked up the paper again.

Ten

He descended from the naval cargo vessel and though it was October, it was hot. He was traveling as a civil servant, assigned to duty at the control center. Most of the passengers on board were civilian personnel returning for duty at the Guantánamo Naval Base after leave. A few were going to Cuba for the first time. Several of the younger passengers, couples and a few unmarried, made social advances in the course of the three-day journey from Norfolk, Virginia, but retreated after a while, finding the tall, handsome "John Gleason" polite but unresponsive. One woman, the chaplain's wife, persisted at dinner, asking what exactly Mr. Gleason was going to do in Guantánamo? Blackford smiled and said he would be the happiest of all to know exactly what was expected of him, that it had not been specified other than that he would presumably be used to make recommendations to the corps of engineers, since he was himself an engineer.

"Castro threatened again last week to kick us out of Guantánamo," the woman observed, reaching across Blackford for another roll.

"I saw that," Blackford said, adding nothing at all.

"Well, what do you think we would do if they tried?"

"I guess we would resist them, don't you think?"

"Damned right, we would resist them," the base athletic director said from across the table. He reduced his voice to a theatrical whisper. "Provided the Kennedy gang can find their, excuse me ma'am, *cojones.*"

There ensued the fiftieth postmortem on the Bay of Pigs

that Blackford had heard since last April. He affected to be interested in the conversation, but managed to convey that he was not really interested in the controversy. When his opinion was asked, he was exhilarated by his masterful evasiveness. "That's a very interesting point. I wish I knew all the facts." That worked, except that the athletic director thereupon volunteered to give him all the facts. After which Blackford tried out, "You certainly are convincing. I see things in a fresh light. What do *you* think about that, chaplain?"

Later, strolling the deck, he wondered at his maturity. Not that, ten years earlier, he couldn't have maintained the equivalent of silence. But ten years earlier he'd have seethed at displays of ignorance, or indifference, or insouciance. Now he heard and he reacted, but his reactions were primarily reflective.

He let his mind travel back among the characters he had known, he had experienced, in his ten years; and he wondered yet again that the world could contain such purposive evil. He thought of the great bomb Khrushchev had just detonated, and of the haunting mystery that such a weapon could materialize in such hands. He then felt the same urge he had felt a half-dozen times during those ten years, the same thing he had felt that summer in Maine at camp on the afternoon he had run off without permission to swim among the breakers. He was only twelve and was certain that he was going to drown when the current began to draw him slowly but ineluctably out to sea. There was nobody about to whom he could shout, and he had come close to despairing. Suddenly he found a reserve of determination. Reason and patience fused. He calculated that he could not make headway against the current by swimming directly at the shore. And so he changed direction, swimming now obliquely toward the shore, saving his energy, and his life.

That reserve was still there, and that night he felt it. It

told him that fifty megatons was not an argument, that it had no powers to validate, let alone sanctify, the evil against which he contended; he, a single soldier. A soldier who, the day before yesterday, was brought, through the Cabinet Room, into the Oval Office to talk to his commander-in-chief, in the presence of just two other men, the head of the whole intelligence establishment and the President's national security adviser. He was engaged—he thought this could easily sound pompous, and so if ever it became appropriate to refer back to that meeting, he'd find another way to put it: he was on a presidential mission. The results of that mission could mean completely different lives for a great many people. Castro's Cuba, smack in American home waters; on the map it looks like South America's crown. He smiled—Senator Joe McCarthy would have termed it "a dagger at the jugular vein of our nation." He'd have been right.

How much of Blackford's success, or lack of it, would depend on his own skills? Any? Does one *argue* with a Che Guevara, he wondered? Does Che Guevara argue with Fidel Castro? In fact, Che Guevara had talked for three hours with Richard Goodwin, so it wasn't that he was particularly laconic when communicating privately with Western officials. But thank God for Cecilio Velasco.

It had been three days, in Mexico, before the Cuban ambassador had called in Cecilio with the word that Yes, Che Guevara would receive the presidential emissary, and Yes, he could bring his own interpreter, if such was the self-effacing designation Cecilio Velasco chose to give himself. During those seventy-two hours Blackford had labored more intensively than ever before on any single project to learn more Spanish, and to master, to the extent that an outsider could, developments in Cuba.

By the end of the period he and Cecilio Velasco had become friends, and on the last night Cecilio had told him his story, told him about Mariya. He was dry-eyed when he came to the part about Mariya's boarding the airplane, and about finding the note she had left for him on his typewriter. But, Blackford noticed, he had not lit a cigarette, and his hand clenched his rum and soda, but he did not drink from the glass.

"What happened to the colonel?"

"Ochek?"

"You didn't mention his name. The KGB colonel. Your boss. The one who . . . gave the orders to . . . Mrs. Carrera."

Velasco reached for a cigarette.

"His name was Ochek. Ochek was the victim of a purge. My last purge."

The word having been given to Washington, it was left for the Cuban ambassador in Mexico to work out details with Velasco. This took another exasperating three days. They would both enter Castro's Cuba via Guantánamo, but separately. The necessary credentials would be given out by the ambassador, there in Cuba. But for this he demanded to see the President's emissary, and to photograph him. This in turn required clearance from Washington, which took another two days because the Agency decided that Oakes's name should not be used, but that on the other hand the Cubans should not be lied to: the ambassador was accordingly informed that no fingerprints of the emissary would be given, and that a passport should be issued. Exchanges with Havana had already designated the operation as *Proyecto Caimán*—Operation Alligator—so that, after tedious exchanges, it was resolved to issue a passport in the name of "John Caiman."

There had been no small talk between the Cuban ambassador and Cecilio Velasco. Security was desired as much by Che Guevara as by John Kennedy. So, late on Thursday afternoon, Velasco and Blackford met with the ambassador in a room in the embassy. A photographer appeared and took pictures. A technician took Velasco's fingerprints. The ambassador spoke occasionally in Spanish with Velasco, some of which Blackford understood. The ambassador suddenly offered coffee or tea, by his standards practically a proposal of marriage. Both declined, and fifteen minutes later they walked out with two Cuban passports, on each of which was written out, "THE BEARER OF THIS PASSPORT IS UNDER THE SPECIAL PROTECTION OF COMANDANTE ERNESTO CHE GUEVARA AND IS TRAVELING TO CUBA ON OFFICIAL BUSINESS." They were instructed that on their arrival in Guantánamo they were to call up the *Jefe de Coordinación*, Colonel Roberto Silva. Colonel Silva was in charge of the administrative center through which Cubans and Americans had such contact as it was necessary to have. They were to inform Colonel Silva that *Proyecto Caimán* was under way, and that Caimán and his interpreter would present themselves at the Northeast Gate border crossing at 10 P.M. on October 4, 1961, "expecting to meet with their escort."

"You will be taken to Havana." The ambassador rose, extending his hand to Velasco and nodding to Blackford.

Blackford carried his canvas bag and his portable typewriter ashore. He looked about him, as he descended the hot gangway, to ascertain whether any one of that sea of faces there to welcome individual passengers might be there for him. Otherwise he had only an office number, and a telephone. And then he spotted what seemed like an endless stream of cigarette smoke coming from someone in the middle of the welcomers, and when it cleared, of course there was little Cecilio Velasco. The smile on his face seemed less cynical. He groped his way through the crowd and grabbed the bag from Blackford, who resisted him. They settled, finally, on Velasco's carrying the tiny typewriter. They walked, Velasco directing, to a car, and got in, first taking off their jackets.

"It is good to see you, Blackford."

"It is good to see you, Cecilio. You have been here two days. Flight okay?"

"Oh. Funny. *Curioso.* From the air you cannot tell that Guantánamo Bay is filled with free people and all the rest of the island is filled with not-free people."

"They don't make different thermals. Not in this world . . . Have you wondered in which category we fall? Four hours from now, I figure," Blackford looked at his watch, "we'll be—over there."

"El Proyecto Caimán comienza."

"Right. We begin. Good luck."

"Good luck."

Eleven

They were met at the border crossing by a bearded major who greeted them economically and told them to get into the car—he pointed to it, the one with the parking lights on. The driver got out and opened the trunk. Blackford and Velasco deposited their luggage in it. The major now pointed to the back seat, himself taking the seat next to the driver. They proceeded in silence to Santiago Airport.

"Will we be flying tonight?" Velasco asked.

"Yes," the major answered simply. "Tonight."

When they reached the guardhouse at the airfield the major got out and talked to the sentry. Evidently more was needed, because the sentry used the telephone, bending over the dim light in the sentry box to read from the major's identification card. He walked out, flashed a light into the back seat, and returned to the telephone. Finally he pointed his flashlight in the general direction of a remote hangar alongside which several planes squatted, their silhouettes only just discernible. The major reentered the car and gave instructions to the driver.

Blackford looked at his watch. It was nearly midnight. The evening had brought no relief from the damp heat and he was perspiring when he pulled out his bags and followed the flashlight beam to the companionway of a DC-3 on which was painted *Fuerza Aérea Cubana*. The configuration was that of a regular passenger plane, and Blackford surmised that it had probably been purchased from Eastern Airlines, or whoever, before the economic lid had closed down the year before.

There was only a single pilot. The major, his job done,

withdrew without any valedictory, and in a few moments they were airborne.

"We are flying right over the Sierra Maestra," Velasco said. "Here was where Castro fought, and won Cuba."

Won Cuba, Blackford thought. *Was that the best way to put it?* He looked out through the porthole, but it was basically black, except for scattered lights here and there. The steward offered them coffee from a thermos. Blackford tasted it and guessed it had been made that morning. Early that morning. He took the yellow-brown sugar and stirred the liquid. There was no milk. "I wonder if they'll take us by the Bay of Pigs?"

"Let us just hope," Velasco said, declining the invitation to romantic historical thoughts, "that the one pilot is healthy."

Blackford turned to him. "I was a pilot in the Air Force, Cecilio. Don't worry."

"Could you fly this plane?"

"Yes. I'd have to do a little on-the-spot research. But you wouldn't get killed."

"Could you find Havana?"

"Depends what kind of instrumentation they have up there. I assume so. I could certainly find Miami. This thing goes 180 mph. So, another half hour from Havana to Miami—"

"They would shoot the plane down."

"I agree. So let's let it stay on course. PRESIDENTIAL ENVOY/HIJACKS CUBAN DC-3/RECEIVES MEDAL OF FREEDOM. I'll wait until I hijack a plane with Castro in it."

Cecilio Velasco reached into his pocket and drew out his rosary. "I will pray for both of us." He smiled, closed his eyes, and began to finger the beads on his flat stomach.

Blackford resolved to pursue the paperback *¿Quién Mató a Roger Ackroyd?*, by Agatha Christie. He reached over his head for the light and clicked it on, but it didn't work. He tried the light over Cecilio's head; it didn't work either. He rang the buzzer for the steward, but heard no sound. He rose, went forward and found the steward asleep in the bulwark seat.

He returned to his own seat and said to Cecilio, "Wake me when we get to wherever they're taking us."

They did not know the name of the field where they landed, almost three hours later, but could tell it was not the principal airport. Again the heat hit them and again there was the waiting car and the escort officer, Major "Joe" Bustamente—"my friends call me 'Joe,' like 'Joe Louis.'" His English was flawless, his tone of voice conspiratorial, his manner courteous, his face, of course, bearded. In hangar-light, Blackford could not make out his age.

"I am your escort officer, Señor Caimán," he addressed Blackford, "and will be with you throughout your stay."

He sat next to the driver, but unlike their earlier escort, he spoke to his passengers almost without ceasing as they drove toward their destination. He was obviously proud of his English, and grateful for the opportunity to exhibit it.

They would occupy a suite of rooms, what was once a beach cottage at El Comodoro Hotel, they learned. An orderly would cook their meals, and a guard would be at the door. They would be hearing "in the next few days" when exactly Comandante Guevara would see them.

Blackford nudged Velasco in the ribs. He did not like the sound of "the next few days." Hardly consistent with his being yanked back from Taxco and Sally, to take just one minor factor it was inconsistent with.

They would be free to swim at the beach, provided they did not swim out of sight of the guard and followed his instructions. If they needed to speak with Major Bustamente they would ask the guard for the telephone, which he would plug in, although it might be "a little while" before the telephone connections could be made. He would give them information "later on" as to what provisions, exactly, had been made for them to communicate with "your principals"—the arrangements had not yet been completed.

The car was elderly and arthritic, the city streets full of holes, the ride shaky and hot, and Blackford was beginning to feel tired and uncomfortable and just a little irritated, though he had no plausible complaint, not yet.

What had once been a decorative knee-high wall, painted white, still stood, disheveled now, around the cottage situated along with three or four others a stone's throw from the eight-story hotel that looked, in the post-midnight hours, as though it were permanently asleep, save that a few lights shone from here and there; burglar-alarm lighting, Blackford called it. Blackford could smell and hear, but not see—the night was very dark—the ocean.

He picked up his bags for the fourth time and took them through the little hallway into a pleasantly large living room which, though once a tourist's home-away-from-home, had evidently metamorphosed into a kind of military officer's utilitarian quarters; and then again into quarters for a diplomatic delegation. An effort had been made to return to it a little color, but one saw the army-khaki couch covers extending down behind the floral chintz hastily sewn over it. A lampshade on the desk sat with the merchandiser's cellophane wrapping still covering it. There was a colored reproduction of an oil painting of Fidel Castro on one wall, and on another a poster-sized photograph of Fidel signing land reform decrees. Blackford wandered into the kitchen and opened the refrigerator door. Inside the small unit there was a case of (Russian) beer, a bottle of rum, another of vodka, some fruit, some odd cans of this and that. He closed his wrist around one of the beer cans. Only just cooler than room temperature. "Joe" was talking in Spanish to the orderly. And now he turned to his guests. "Well, Señor Caimán, Manuel here will look after you, and I will be in touch with you, either personally or by messenger. He smiled, stepped back a foot, and raised his hand in a salute at once self-mocking and friendly.

"Good night, señores."

Velasco poured out two glasses of rum and poked about, without success, for something to mix it with, settling finally for tap water. They sat down on the couches and Blackford told Manuel they needed nothing more from him, that he was to go to bed. Manuel disappeared into a room beyond the kitchen, closing the back door.

Blackford withdrew a small portable radio from his bag and turned it on, fetching up a pronounced Congo beat from a go-go all-night Havana station.

Without exchanging a word, the two men began the search. They found the first microphone behind Castro's picture, appropriately enough just on the other side of his left ear; a second under the desk lamp, a third behind the couch, just under the slipcover; yet another nestling in a compartment carved out for it behind the headboard in the larger of the two bedrooms.

Blackford spoke out, in Spanish. This was an opportune moment for it. He didn't feel he had time to consult Cecilio to straighten out his diction, so he said only, in unexcited tones into one of the surreptitious mikes: "*Uds. no tienen derecho de, de—interferir—en conversaciones entre representantes de jefes de estados.*" Having thus advertised to the monitors that they had no right to intercept conversations of representatives of a chief of state—which admonition, Blackford thought, would confirm any latent suspicions of his amateur standing—he proceeded to cut the connections, one by one, with his scissors.

Blackford addressed Velasco for the first time. "I guess that's the lot, though we can't be sure. It's times like these I wish we could speak in Swahili."

They sat now, relaxed, more or less opposite each other on the couches—Cecilio Velasco trim, upright; Blackford slouching, his feet on the coffee table.

He was attempting to complete, in his mind, the portrait of Ernesto Che Guevara, about whom he had read so much during the past ten days. A pointillist painting, it would need to be, though on a single point—that Che Guevara, Castro's philosophical mentor, adviser, brother-in-arms, hated the United States—there would be no ambiguity.

Velasco whispered, "Do you think it's all right now to speak?"

"There are certain things I wouldn't say. But most of what we'd probably want to be saying right now it wouldn't much matter if they heard."

Blackford sipped his drink and then said in a quiet voice, "There's something going on here I don't like. And I don't mean what I don't like that's going on is Castro's revolution . . . How does this particular reception compare with those you've—"

Cecilio Velasco raised his index finger to his lips.

"Sorry," Blackford flushed. Great effort had been made, beginning many years earlier, to wipe out any trace of Raúl Carrera, the Spanish communist from Barcelona. Cecilio Velasco, by official record, was an apolitical Spaniard who had fled the civil war and settled, as a bachelor, in America, doing clerical work and translation for the 4th Army in San Antonio. He would not logically be asked about other paradiplomatic experiences. According to the plan, Operation Alligator would be terminated before his fingerprints were paired with thirty-year-old records in Moscow. The identity and profession of Blackford the Cubans were expected to know, or discern eventually. "So what?" Blackford had commented, vexed at the delay that had resulted from the Agency's refusal to permit him to use his own name. "They treat all Americans as if they were members of CIA."

Cecilio rose from his chair and sat down next to Blackford, putting the portable radio and the loud music between them. He spoke too softly for his voice to be picked up by any microphone they might have missed.

"There is nothing yet here that surprises me." Blackford finished his rum and said nothing.

Blackford slept fitfully. He woke at four and scratched out a letter to Sally. At some point they would have access to a pouch.

He went into the kitchen and ate an orange, absentmindedly biting into the peel.

He looked at his watch.

Nearly five.

He had slept just over one hour.

He went to the front door and knocked on it. It was, of course, locked. The guard, his hand on his holster, responded, opening the door. Blackford tried out his Spanish again.

"*Se puede nadar en esta hora?*"

No, the guard shook his head quietly. No swimming at this hour. Blackford bowed his head in acknowledgment of a performance on the whole civil; he closed the door, and the guard relocked it. He went to his bag in the bedroom and fished out an eyeshade against the rising sun, went to his bed, and woke up, sweating, at noon.

Lunch was served. Beans and a fish of sorts and hard bread and a caramel paste. They ate pretty much in silence.

"Do you swim?" he asked Velasco.

"No, but I will accompany you."

Blackford put on his trunks and grabbed a towel. They knocked on the front door and this time the guard nodded and followed them to the beach, fifty yards away. There were no other swimmers. To the west Blackford could see at a distance what appeared to be fishing boats, clustered about what must have been a concrete commercial pier. A few soldiers in uniform loitered about the hotel on the

other side, far enough away to give Blackford a sense of
privacy. A sense of isolation was more accurate.

The water was warm, yet refreshing, and Blackford swam
first idly then, in a conscious bid for exercise, vigorously.
On his second lap Velasco waved to him. "The guard says
you are swimming too far away; you must shorten your laps
by one half." Blackford complied.

He returned and asked Manuel whether Joe Bustamente
had called. Negative. He then asked the guard to call Major
Bustamente. The guard replied that he did not yet have the
telephone, that he had only a little receiver that could not
initiate signals.

Blackford beckoned to Velasco to walk back toward the
beach where they could talk with confidence that they were
not being overheard.

"These bastards are in a real hurry."

"The tempo is slow in Cuba, Blackford. Besides, they
may be trying to make a point."

Blackford had endured many tedious situations. But always they had been, if not exactly of his own making, of his
own abiding. One time, in Berlin, he and a companion had
needed to go over written profiles of a dozen suspects per
day, tediously exploring the possibility that each might be
the person they needed to lay their fingers on, and that had
gone on for three maddening months. But their schedule
had been their own. Indeed, the work arrangements were
their own. They were free whenever they chose to roam the
streets and brothels of Berlin; to telephone to America or
wherever, using due discretion of course. The situation in
Cuba was very different.

And hot. Horribly, enervatingly hot. No air conditioning,
needless to say.

Blackford had packed six detective stories in Spanish and
a Spanish-English dictionary and—for this he thanked God
for the forethought—a paperback containing the ten trage-
dies of Shakespeare. So he spent the afternoon with

Hercule Poirot, tracking down the butler or whoever or whomever, as Agatha Christie would have put it, and the early evening with King Lear; had dinner (just this side of inedible), drank more rum than he normally would have, did some push-ups, and asked Velasco what he was thinking about. Velasco replied that he did not need so many stimulants; he had with him Gironella's *Los Cipreses Creen en Dios*, and a great many cartons of cigarettes, and a Bible. He sat quietly on one of the couches and read.

That next day was Sunday, and in the afternoon Blackford once again attempted to get the guard to summon Bustamente. *"Cuando viene tu compañero, mándele comunicar con* Major—how do you say 'Major,' Cecilio? I'm telling him to get his relief guard to go to a phone and call Joe—*el Mayor Bustamente, por teléfono, que viene aquí a vernos, muy importante, muy urgente."* The guard only nodded, and replied that their orders were to wait until Major Bustamente was in touch with them.

By lunchtime on Monday, Blackford Oakes was angry. Again he summoned Velasco to come away, toward the beach, so that they could talk freely.

"If we were mercenaries or even just plain agents working on some common proposition, you might not be surprised by this. But we are here at *Guevara's* invitation and I am carrying messages from the *President* of the United States."

"We know that," Velasco said, squinting his eyes in the sun, an arm resting on the trunk of a palm tree. "And they know that."

"What are you suggesting?"

"That they wish to condition you."

Blackford thought long and hard about the situation that afternoon and his thought went to the psychology of imprisonment. He happened in his Shakespeare on a passage from *King Richard II* in Pomfret Castle jail. He read with fascination the passage in which King Richard expressed at once the impossibility of thinking, and his determination to do so. "I cannot do it; yet I'll hammer it out./My brain I'll prove the female to my soul,/My soul the father; and these two beget/A generation of still-breeding thoughts,/And these same thoughts people this little world,/In humours like the people of this world,/For no thought is contented." And he understood the bitter despair of the later lines of the soliloquy: "whate'er I be,/Nor I nor any man that but man is/With nothing shall be pleased, till he be eased/With being nothing." He felt as nothing, powerless, churning, yet incapable of thought.

On Monday night Manuel served pork, which was intended as roast pork, and they finished the vodka.

On Tuesday he woke perspiring in bed. It was very hot, he remarked to Cecilio, who agreed, although he wore, as usual, shirt and tie. Blackford wore only his undershorts and a T-shirt, and he swam for almost an hour. The batteries on the radio were suddenly dead and he asked Manuel to get more. He was told that would be difficult because there was a great scarcity in Cuba "because of the American blockade." Well, he recalled that King Richard remembered, had said, that prisoners have no need for music. The day was endless.

That night when Cecilio offered him a drink, as usual at about six, Blackford declined it. Cecilio looked up. "You must not reject the simple distractions," pouring himself a generous rum and walking over to the water pitcher. Blackford, stretching out on the couch, asked Cecilio whether he had ever read Chekhov's tale of the young lawyer who had accepted a two-million-ruble challenge that he could live voluntarily in solitary confinement for fifteen years without ever letting himself out.

No, said Cecilio. And did he?

The rules, Blackford said, were that he could have anything he called for, and he proceeded to conjugate all the pleasures of the flesh. For a while it was women, for a while wine; and then came a brooding introspection. And, finally, the slow ascendancy of his spirit to supremacy over his body, and then he wanted only his books and his thoughts.

"Did he make it the fifteen years?"

Five minutes before the time was up, Blackford told Cecilio, moments before his old adversary would be ruined by having to pay the challenge money, the lawyer walked out of his cloister, thereby revealing the true philosopher's indifference to the things of this world. Blackford winked at Cecilio:

"You see, I am trying to compress fifteen years' experience into—into what? Will they keep us here for fifteen days? Is that possible? In any case, no more booze for me until we get out of here. And *you*, Cecilio, should take this opportunity to give up smoking. It will clear your lungs and the air you and, incidentally, I, breathe."

Velasco half smiled, lit a cigarette, and said that long ago he had smoked because it calmed him to smoke and in any case he had become addicted. But now, he said, he would not stop smoking merely because it is supposed that to smoke is to shorten life. No more stop that cause of biological attrition than cause the clock to stop. There was no reason for him, he said, to live forever.

"Maybe not forever, Cecilio, but long enough to see this mission through and get back. I have a very important engagement in 1964 and at this rate I worry about being late for it."

It was Thursday. They had made no further mention of the tedium. Thursday was another hot day.

On Friday morning Manuel advised them at breakfast that he had been told to notify Sr. Caimán that Major Bustamente would be here to confer with them at two o'clock.

At a quarter to two Blackford carefully shaved and put on a fresh shirt laundered by Manuel, who also pressed, as best he could manage, a pair of khaki pants. Blackford sat on one of the couches, a book on his lap. He could not forbear, at 2:30, to signal to Manuel, whose eye he caught in the kitchen, to come over to him. Blackford did not wish to shout out his question, possibly into a furtive microphone.

Manuel approached and Blackford asked him, quietly, "Did you say the major was coming at two o'clock?"

Manuel nodded. *"Sí señor, sí señor. A las dos. Parece que viene tarde."*

Cecilio, sitting opposite, said in English, "They are often late."

Blackford said nothing.

He arrived just before four, with an unsmiling aide. Blackford remained in his chair, reading, as he had instructed Cecilio to do. He looked up at Bustamente, saying nothing.

The anticipated rhythm broken, Bustamente stopped, stood more or less at attention, and smiled. "Ah, good afternoon, Señor Caimán. I hope you—and your interpreter"—it came to Major Bustamente as a genial afterthought to acknowledge the existence of subordinates—"have been comfortable. I am instructed to advise you that Comandante Che Guevara will call on you at two o'clock in the morning."

Blackford raised his eyes to Bustamente's. "Please advise Comandante Guevara that at two in the morning I shall be asleep. I retire just before midnight. And I rise at seven."

"Joe" Bustamente did not, there and then, know what to say. He spoke rapidly in Spanish, in whispers, with his companion. Blackford resumed reading.

"Sir, you must understand that Comandante Guevara is a very busy man."

"I shall be glad to report that to the President."

Again conferences. This time Blackford spoke again.

"Oh, and Major Bustamente, this being Friday, I have decided that if negotiations with Comandante Guevara are not under way by noon on Sunday, I shall conclude that your government has no interest in pursuing the questions initiated by Comandante Guevara to the President's representative in August. Kindly arrange, in that event, to have me and Mr. Velasco taken back to Guantánamo on Sunday afternoon."

With that Blackford turned again to his book—*Diez Pequeños Indios*, by Agatha Christie. Bustamente cleared his throat and, with his companion, walked out the door.

Twelve

Aleksei I. Adzhubei had toured Latin America and, before returning to Moscow, would spend time with President Kennedy at Hyannis Port, the first exclusive interview ever granted to a foreign newsman. All this was still secret when Adzhubei arrived in Havana, where he was given full honors, beginning when he descended from the Soviet transport. He was, after all, the editor of *Izvestia*, the national newspaper of the Soviet Union. And it was widely expected that he would one day be elected a member of the Central Committee. And then on top of all of that, Adzhubei was the son-in-law of Nikita Khrushchev.

So the flags flew in the suddenly brisk October breeze, and the distinguished visitor drove in Castro's own car to the national palace, beginning a ten-day visit.

There was the luncheon. Not the long state dinner that was planned for the end of Adzhubei's trip. A more modest affair, featuring Fidel, Che Guevara, President Osvaldo Dorticós, and Interior Minister Ramiro Valdés. When Castro got up to toast his guest before the hundred or so Cuban officials, together with the first echelon from the Soviet Embassy, President Dorticós slipped his left hand down under the table, and with his right hand manipulated his versatile Swiss watch to the stopwatch mode, depressing the GO button. He did not share the secrets of what he called "Dorticós's Law of Speech Duration" with many friends, indeed with only two not counting his wife, but having listened to Fidel Castro speak perhaps five hundred times during the past three years he knew the Comandante's habits. It went (this was *very* secret) as follows:

If the Comandante speaks for more than one minute, he will not speak for less than five.

If he speaks for more than five minutes, he will not speak for less than thirty.

If he speaks for more than thirty minutes, he will not speak for less than one hour.

And if he speaks for more than one hour, he will not speak for less than two hours.

Castro said how welcome was the latest visitor from the Soviet Union, that he came from a long line of distinguished friends of the people of Cuba beginning with Deputy Premier Minister Mikoyan who had visited all of Cuba in 1960 [Dorticós stole a glance at the second hand: 75 seconds], but that this was not the occasion in which to do other than to wish Comrade Adzhubei a wonderful visit in this beautiful country, that when he returned from his trip, on parts of which Fidel himself would be accompanying him, there would be a festive occasion [two minutes] and that he counseled Adzhubei in particular to experience the sense of freedom of the people of Cuba, liberated now from the fascist imperialism of the Yanqui era, which the imperialists had attempted yet again in April by military force to visit on Cuba but which had been bravely rebuffed by the Cuban people!

Fidel raised his glass and toasted his guest. He had spoken for five minutes.

Adzhubei rose, a tall, thin man, rather academic in manner. It occurred to him that this was not the moment to discuss the barbaric shortcomings of the American President who would be giving him an exclusive interview a few weeks hence, so he spoke instead about the brilliance of the Soviet example, and then about the light that irradiated from this great island of Cuba all over Latin America, which would surely soon experience similar progressive—he

started to say "revolutions" but again thought better of it—
"demarches," but none would stand so conspicuously in
the history of progress in the western hemisphere as that of
Cuba. (Much applause.) Meanwhile he wished to relay the
most cordial regards of the man all Russia hailed as leader,
to whose daughter he had the honor to be married. (Much
applause.)

There were no other toasts, and Castro was preparing to
bid Adzhubei goodbye for the time being when Adzhubei's
interpreter whispered something to Fidel's interpreter.
Castro looked puzzled for just a moment, but chewing on
his cigar he waved his hand to part the milling crowd, and
putting his arm over the shoulder of Adzhubei led him off,
back to the car, with instructions to his aide to take them to
the presidential office.

Adzhubei, seated in the sanctum sanctorum, declined the
offer of coffee and said that he had taken the liberty of
asking for a totally private meeting right away because he
had received only two days before, while in Mexico, confir-
mation, direct from Chairman Khrushchev, of what he had
been briefed to report to Fidel Castro. Before leaving Moscow it had seemed quite certain, but now it was confirmed:

The United States was bent on a fresh military expedition
against Cuba.

It would come in the late spring or summer. And this one
would be unambiguously a U.S. military operation, not a
ragtag affair involving a few thousand refugees. The objective was to replace the Castro government with a colonialist
Yanqui-dominated government.

Castro's expression did not change as his interpreter
spoke out the words, though he puffed more vigorously on
his cigar.

Adzhubei went on at some length describing the prodi-
gies of Soviet intelligence, the high secrecy that was being
attached to the invasion plan in the United States. And—his

voice was dramatic—the proposal he was now authorized by his father-in-law to make to Fidel Castro. He leaned back in his chair, and lapsed now into a whisper.

"We are prepared to give you a defensive strategic capability."

"Are you talking about missiles?" Castro bit on his cigar. Adzhubei closed his eyes. "The same."

"What is the Yanquis' timetable?"

"We have not yet ascertained exactly, as I say. The expectation is that they are thinking in terms of next spring."

"Surely not on the anniversary of the Bay of Pigs," Castro spit out his cigar cud.

Adzhubei smiled. He wished Castro to know that he appreciated the jocularity of the suggestion. "We would not expect that they would celebrate *that* anniversary, Comrade Castro."

Castro stood up, and cursed. "There would appear to be little alternative than to welcome the Soviet offer."

"There is seldom an alternative to assuring one's survival."

"What would be the, er, surrounding conditions?"

"You understand, surely, that the missiles would need to be installed and manned by Soviet personnel, and that Soviet officials would of course be totally in charge of security in all matters having to do with their installation. There would need to be total secrecy in the matter."

"There is never total secrecy in respect of any matter."

"You have not been trained by my father-in-law."

"I will need to think over the implications of all of this."

"It is for that reason that I wished to make you the offer at the outset of my visit to your inspiring country. In two weeks when we confer for the final time you can let me have your consolidated reaction, which I shall report to my father-in-law on my return. After visiting with President Kennedy." He confided to Castro his secret rendezvous later on in the month.

"Be sure to give Mr. Kennedy my regards," Castro said, rising.

Thirteen

At eight on Sunday morning Blackford walked out onto the beach as usual. The guard, who had become accustomed to the daily drill, had taken to lugging his own canvas chair from the porch of the beach cottage, together with his portable radio and of course his carbine, to about twenty yards inland from where Blackford and Velasco sat. Cecilio Velasco knew that Blackford took the opportunity of distancing himself from the cottage in order to talk with him where there was no chance of their being overheard, so he also took a chair, which he would place on the sand away from that of the guard, sitting down on it with his book until the swim was over. When Cecilio was outdoors in the sun he removed his tie, and if the sun was especially hot he would drape a towel over his head. Blackford no longer bothered with swimming trunks. At the water's edge he dropped his undershorts and walked into the water.

He swam out, conscious of the boundary the guard had set. Swimming on his back he could see no one at all on either side of him save, at a distance, the usual cluster of fishing boats. He swam lazily, describing a slow circle. He plunged then and swam underwater until his breath gave out. At the surface he then swam with ferocious energy toward the beach, arriving just slightly short of breath. He walked up out of the water and picked up the towel he had dropped with his underwear, dried himself, and put on his shorts.

"Know what?" he said to Velasco, drying his hair, still laced with blond, with the towel, his skin almost uniformly tanned, "I expect that sometime this morning we will meet with Che Guevara."

"I hope you are right. Your deadline is this afternoon."

"We aren't well situated to impose deadlines. But—what the hell. We'll see." They sat for a while in the sun, Blackford on the sand. There was never any hurry.

Together they walked back to the cottage, followed by the guard. Blackford walked into his bathroom and took a freshwater shower. He was in it, absentmindedly, for several minutes, and was shaken out of his reverie by Cecilio Velasco who drew back the shower curtain and whispered, "He's here."

Blackford dried himself, put on trousers, shoes, and a shirt, and walked out into the living room.

Velasco was standing there, in conversation with Comandante Guevara and a woman. No one else was in the room, but Blackford could see instantly, through the windows leading out to the beach, that what had been a single guard was now a half-dozen men.

Blackford extended his hand. "Comandante Guevara."

Che answered in Spanish, introducing his "colleague." Cecilio translated. "This, Mr. Caimán, is my colleague who because she speaks English also serves as my interpreter. This is Catalina Urrutia."

Blackford bowed his head but did not extend his hand. "Señorita."

"You may call her Catalina. And you may call me Che." Comandante Guevara was slighter than Blackford had imagined, weighing perhaps 160 pounds, five feet nine or ten inches tall. He wore his traditional beret and army fatigues. His regular facial posture was that of the half smile. And he directed his remarks to Catalina, closing his eyes during her translation into English as though evaluating its correctness. And indeed he understood much English, even as Blackford understood much Spanish.

"We have a lot to discuss, Mr. Caimán."

"A pity we could not have begun earlier."

"Ah, yes. I seem always to be behind. I am certainly behind in the matter of rebuilding the economy of Cuba. You are not exactly behind in your efforts to prevent this from happening." Catalina interpreted for Che, Cecilio for Blackford.

"It occurs to me that I am the host in this cottage," Blackford said. "Do you wish to proceed here in this sitting room?"

"Why not?" said Che, sitting down at one end of one of the chairs, indicating to Catalina that she should sit down next to him. Blackford sat down opposite in the single chair, Cecilio in the remaining single chair. They composed a triangle.

"You have a message for me, Mr. Caimán?—May I call you, simply, Caimán? We are very informal in socialist countries."

"I've noticed," said Blackford. "Yes, of course, Caimán is fine. And yes, I do have a message"—Blackford would not avail himself of the egalitarian invitation to address the Minister of Industry as "Che." But neither did he wish to appear to snub the invitation to familiarity. So he used nothing. This was made easier by the presence of a translator as intermediary. "I begin by conveying to you the greetings of the President of my country, who has instructed me to explore with you the suggestions you outlined to Mr. Goodwin in August in Montevideo."

Che Guevara drew on his cigar. "Ah, yes. Well, Mr. Caimán, it is of course sensible that we attempt to define what it is that furthers interests we have in common. I do not disguise, any more than I did in my conversation with Mr. Goodwin—a charming fellow, by the way. A pity his education at Harvard was so incomplete; he'd have made a good socialist." It was easier for Blackford to suppress his inclination to a riposte, given that Che's wisecrack came in framed by Catalina, and hence arrived a little attenuated.

Her American accent was faintly Southern, her English entirely fluent. Blackford deduced that she had probably gone to school in Florida, or somewhere in the South. Her complexion was tan, her eyes hazel brown, her teeth white, her hair austerely arranged, tied loosely behind her head in a bun. She wore a braided gold necklace supporting a surrealistic little hammer and sickle. Her warm voice was without emotion, except that the words came in bursts, lending, no doubt unconsciously, dramatic effect to the sequence of thought. Her eyes were on Che when he spoke, on Blackford when she translated.

Che continued by describing the necessary growing pains of a country that clearly needed to end its dependence on sugar, clearly needed to industrialize and to widen its markets, but obviously had difficulty in doing so during an economic season in which the United States was denying it such basic needs as dollars, spare parts, and all those other things "which you have in such prodigious quantity. Your law now says something on the order of, 'No ship bound for Cuba can leave from an American port. No ship leaving Cuba can land at an American port. No goods made in America may be sold directly to Cuba, or indirectly to any country or company that intends to transship those goods to Cuba.' Out of curiosity, Mr. Caimán, how much do you suppose you spent on your effort last April to invade my country?"

Caimán thought it important quickly to establish a mature relationship with the legendary Cuban luminary.

"Not enough," he responded.

Che's eyes brightened. Clearly he enjoyed combative relations. "Ah, so you have no regrets about last April?"

"No regrets you would welcome hearing about."

"Ah, then, so you wish you had succeeded in toppling Fidel and in reestablishing Yankee imperialism over the Cuban people?"

Blackford rose. "Look, Comandante—"

"Che."

"Look . . . Che—I am here representing the President. My own views are immaterial. I am charged to hear your views in precise detail on whether arrangements might be made—"

"But *I* am interested in your views. Do you object to my having them? Did the President forbid you to express your own views?"

"No, sir—"

"No, Che."

"No . . . Che. The President did not forbid me to do anything. But the President obviously does not expect that I should waste your time with the recounting of my own views—"

"Ah but Caimán, you do not have, not yet anyway, the authority to decide what it is that wastes *my* time. I am the sole judge of the question in two senses. First, I decide whether what I desire to talk about is a waste of my time; second, I decide whether I choose to waste my time."

Blackford thought what-the-hell, he may as well let it out. "It is also up to you to decide whether to waste *my* time."

Che was clearly delighted, and rose from the chair and spoke as if in monologue, scarcely giving Catalina the time to keep up with him.

"Ah, how slow we are to lose our imperial habits. So you come to this country, having failed to conquer it militarily. You come, to be sure, as the result of an initiative taken by me. But that initiative was in response to your own initiative: your attempt to close down the economy of the Cuban people, to make our socialist revolution unworkable. Then when you arrive you expect immediate attention! Immediate attention! As though you were ringing a bell for a waiter to bring you a drink of rum and a prostitute." He pointed to the bedroom. "I wonder how many Cuban women were fucked in there by American tourists in the ten years after this hotel was built? And not by handsome athletes like you but by bloated bibulous capitalists. Poor Caimán. Had to wait for *one—whole—week!* I waited two years in the Sierra Maestra before we could liberate the Cuban people from your puppet Batista. And circumstances were far less pleasant than your own. I did not have a daily swim in the ocean—"

Blackford, seated downwind from Che, knew what intimates of Che—ex-intimates, some of whose diaries he had read—had meant about Che's casual personal hygiene. Che Guevara clearly did not go in for regular bathing.

"—and your royal presence here has perhaps met with less than the attention you would expect to have from a backward nation?"

"Comandante—Che. Please, let's not. I confess that I am everything you know me to be, and perhaps even a lot more. I confess I am not in sympathy with socialism let alone the kind of socialism being introduced into your country, and I also confess that my impression has been—and perhaps this is due to a misunderstanding of my superiors—that you were anxious to get on with it, I mean the business of an exchange of positions. It is obvious, under the circumstances, that it was . . . disappointing not to make contact with you more quickly."

"Ah, make contact more quickly. Yes. *'Disappointing'* "—he spoke the word in English. "Do you know that there is not an exact Spanish translation for that word? It is a distinctively English, meiotic expression. As in, 'I was disappointed to have to sanction the military invasion of Cuba.' I am sure that those words will appear, more or less in that form, in the memoirs of President Kennedy when he has left office. 'Disappointed.' Well, I am disappointed that the United States uses its economic muscle, its military muscle having proved insufficient, to frustrate the socialization of Cuba. But you will not succeed, my dear Caimán, you will not succeed, because we are in tune with history and you are not. You are merely engaged in backward efforts to shore up a dying order . . ."

Blackford thought quickly. What should he do? He had not, in ten years, faced anything on the order of the current situation. Several times, in those ten years, he had been forced to feign sympathy for views he held in profound contempt. That was relatively easy—so to speak, professionally easy, as if his fraternity at Yale had given him the assignment of penetrating the Harvard cheerleading team; in such situations, you shout out your enthusiasm for the other side.

This was different. His identity, his affiliations, his loyalties, were well known to the professionals in the enemy camp, quite probably Che Guevara among them. But he could hardly risk his mission by entering with spirit into a dialectic with the man whom it was his job to bring around to concrete negotiations.

Blackford waited until Che had come to a coda, and then blurted out: "Che. Do I understand you to be saying to me that you resent any effort by me to keep the subject confined to the matters formally on the table, namely the proposals you made to Mr. Goodwin in August?"

"I consider it not only impolite but antisocial, not only antisocial but directly belligerent for you, Caimán, in my country, to decline to discuss with me, in terms I find agreeable and suitable, the differences between your country and my country. Exactly how we approach the direct subject at hand is something which, in my judgment, it is within my authority to determine. If I wish to approach it other than in purely conventional ways, I feel I have that prerogative. If you decline to accept that prerogative you are free to do so. You are, indeed, always free to leave Cuba. Oh yes, let us get that absolutely straight from the outset. You have merely to snap your fingers"—Che snapped his own to reinforce his point—"and you have my word for it that a plane will be put at your disposal to return you to Guantánamo. But as long as you elect to remain here, you will abide by my modes of exchange. By my way of doing things. Is that agreeable?"

Blackford thought for a moment how exactly to frame his reply. "Che," he said, "there is no alternative than to proceed as you see fit. But I must report back to Washington whether you are still interested in the initiatives you put forward in Montevideo—"

"Oh fuck Montevideo, Caimán. Of course I am still interested. Otherwise why would I be wasting my time in this endless conversation with you?"

"Che, it was my point, some time back, that our conversations do not need to be endless."

Che smiled. "Ah, you are a trained dialectician, I can see that. Tell me, have you read Whitehead? Alfred North Whitehead?"

Great God, Blackford thought. He knew Che Guevara was renowned for his academic curiosity. He did not know it extended to the author of *Principia Mathematica*. "I have not read Whitehead, señor."

"Well I have. And he made it a point to say that a culture expresses its planted axioms by its mode of analysis. You are, as your sociologists put it, achievement-oriented. Accordingly you structure your approaches with exclusive reference to what you consider the subject at hand. Well, those of us who are free of such cultural deadweight can understand more about the totality of man. So that if I choose to speak with you with what you disdain as indirection you are not to permit yourself to believe that I am indifferent to the reasons for our meeting. But our meeting, if it is to prove productive, has got to produce an understanding. And that understanding is not something to be put abstractly onto a piece of paper. It is to mean that we have achieved—an understanding. But how can there be an understanding"— he stressed the word, repeating it twice—"*un acuerdo, un acuerdo*—between parties that do not know each other?"

Again Che, who had sat down, as intermittently he did, rose. But this time to say that it had got warm and that he was attracted to the idea of a swim. He turned to Catalina and asked if she would like to swim. She shook her head. He then acknowledged, for the first time, the existence of Cecilio Velasco and asked if he cared to swim. Velasco said, "No thank you, Comandante." Che raised his eyebrows, mutely extending the invitation to Blackford. Who responded intuitively, "Of course I would like to swim."

"You remain here," Che said to Catalina, "as I shall swim naked, in the fashion of Mr. Caimán here. Velasco, you may accompany us to interpret. Although I do not expect to do very much talking while in the water."

Blackford walked into the bathroom and took two towels, giving one to Che. Che led the way through the door. Instinctively six bodyguards, to the leader of which Che had uttered a few words, poised themselves for orders. On receiving them they separated, three walking out toward the beach in one direction, three in the opposite direction, until they were separated by about one hundred yards. Che, paying them no attention, tossed his cigar into the sand and said, "Come along, Caimán. As you know, the ocean here is wonderful, now that it is cleansed of American tourist skin oil."

"I guess it's fair to say I am not an American tourist," Blackford said. And added, "Do socialists use suntan oil?"

"Socialists," Che replied, squinting his eyes against the hard rays of the sun overhead, "normally do not have time to worry about the *appearance* of their skin. They worry about their skin."

They had approached the water, and Che opened his fatigues and dropped them on the sand. He wore no underclothes. He took off his beret and walked toward the water. "Come along, Caimán. It will cleanse your sins. Though perhaps not. It is a small ocean."

Fourteen

Adzhubei stood up when he entered the room, never mind that it was his own father-in-law.

"Sit down," Khrushchev said offhandedly. He was distracted and Adzhubei knew that in such situations it was best simply to wait. In due course Khrushchev would speak out. He always did.

"Well, don't you want to know how it went?"

"Of course, Nikita Sergeyevich. But I did not wish to press you. Was my . . . testimony all right?"

"As far as it went, yes, it was very good. The problem was Shelepin. Knew it would be. Professional problem."

"You mean, that the KGB hadn't come up with it?"

"Worse than that. He denies it. He says he positively doubts Kennedy is going back into Cuba."

"What did you do?"

Khrushchev chortled. "I can be pretty mean, you know, young fellow," he said to the editor of *Izvestia,* of all people, "I said to him, 'Aleksandr Nikolayevich, if "our sources" are so reliable on these matters, how is it that you didn't give us a few weeks' warning of the U.S. invasion of Cuba in April?'

"He didn't like that," Khrushchev chortled. "But then I didn't intend for him to like it. And then I went on and reminded him that in the interview I gave Sulzberger a few weeks ago, I said that if the United States were to invade Cuba and Cuba were to ask for our help, Cuba would not find us deaf to her entreaty. That's on the record."

"Did that turn him around?"

"By all the gods—assuming there are any gods—no.

Quite the opposite. Shelepin said that by making that statement I had simply reinforced Kennedy in his determination not to sponsor another military operation against Cuba."

"To which you replied?"

"I said, 'Look here, Aleksandr Nikolayevich, there are five hundred thousand Cubans in the United States and they are everywhere. They are in government. Soon they will be in Congress. Their sources of intelligence on such matters are bound to be better than our own, and this is hardly a criticism of you'—I can be soft as a dove's ass, you know, Aleksei"; Aleksei nodded knowingly—"'it is simply *what one would expect.* And remember, there will be congressional elections in the United States in the fall of 1962 and the Republicans will make a great deal of it if Cuba is still socialist. Especially if our plans mature . . .' Gromyko was useful at this point because he reported that the American press and the voters are putting great pressure on the government to do something about Castro. So I went on; I told them that it would greatly set back the best thing that has happened to the Soviet Union since the war—namely, Castro—if we were to deny him what he asked for."

"Was it then that you mentioned—"

"Quiet. Let me tell it my own way. I don't mind reminding you, Aleksei, that I am renowned as a raconteur. I said then that of course we would need to step up the flow of conventional arms to Cuba. But I did not think that was enough."

"Did that do it?"

"There was a pause, and Malinovsky then broke in. 'Are you suggesting,' our renowned defense minister asked me, 'are you suggesting, Nikita Sergeyevich, that we send nuclear missiles?'

"I said to him, 'Rodion Yaklovich, to begin with, it wasn't *me* who suggested this. It was *Castro. He* asked for them. I had instructed Adzhubei not to reveal this to you gentlemen just now, when he came into the room to give you personally the report on Castro's conversation, because I thought we should give full attention *first* to what it is that Castro says the United States is planning, and only *then* to what we must do about it. But yes, Castro asked Adzhubei to request what Castro called "strategic defensive missiles." A very good term that, don't you think so, Rodion Yaklovich? I'm glad to see that you do. Well, that is what Castro asked for, and I am recommending that under certain conditions we agree to his request.'

" 'What are those conditions?' Malinovsky wanted to know.

" 'They are 1) Total secrecy of installation, 2) The job must be done exclusively by Russians, 3) Those who man the missiles will be Russians, who take orders only from Russia, 4) The territory in which the missiles reside must be ceded to the Soviet Union.'

"Malinovsky exclaimed, 'He agreed to that?'

" 'Absolutely,' I said."

Adzhubei registered his alarm. "But Nikita Sergeyevich, nothing of the sort was touched on in Havana—"

"Never mind, never mind. Just forget what you said. While we're at it, I do not expect you to reveal your role in this ever to anyone, that is obvious. But I want our missiles in the American theater. We are surrounded here by hostile missiles. Oh, I said all of this at the meeting, you can bet your apple harvest on that. I said to them, 'The Soviet Union faces missiles in West Germany, in France, in Great Britain, in Italy and, soon now, in China. Meanwhile the United States is surrounded by Canadians, Mexicans, and Indians—' "

"Castro is not an Indian."

"Never mind what Castro is, the point I am making is that he has no bombs. At least not yet. I don't mean—obviously—that Castro is going to get nuclear bombs, but that *we* will have nuclear bombs in Cuba. And that will change the geopolitical structure of the struggle for the world."

"Did you tell them that?"

Khrushchev shouted now. "Of *course* I told them that, you idiot! Because it is true! And that is the point we need to get across, that *we want missiles in Cuba under our control.* And now we have reason to place them there, though of course this must be done furtively. They must be in place before the United States is on to them."

"Did you discuss what the United States would do when it finds out?"

"I said the United States would not be in a position to do *anything* about them. You do not talk back to thermonuclear missiles. You simply accept them, as we needed to accept them in NATO."

"What about the . . . invasion?"

"That is important. Malinovsky raised that point exactly. What good would the missiles do if not in place in time to abort the invasion? I asked him for an estimate of how long deployment would take, and he said six months. Our diplomatic mission in that case, I said to them, is to use whatever means we have of delaying the American invasion for at least six months. Remember, I told them, we don't know that it is scheduled for sooner than six months from now. But there are ways—Aleksandr Nikolayevich, you are a master, after all, of this—by which we can affect policy: force on the Americans postponements, delays, that kind of thing. We can have a prominent American complain that a fresh invasion is being prepared, and do this at a time extremely inconvenient to the American administration. But then I said—they say I am a clever old fox, Aleksei—"

"You are indeed a clever old fox, Nikita Sergeyevich."

"And then I said, 'And of course, our ends are brilliantly served if simultaneously we abort the American invasion and succeed in deploying our missiles in Cuba. They will then be there as brooding instruments behind all our fu-

ture policies.' " He laughed quietly at first. Then uproariously, rising from his seat and throwing his arms around his
son-in-law.

"The project will be under way. You will see!"

Fifteen

Blackford had told Che after their swim that the time had come to file a report to Washington and Che had said fine. How did Blackford desire to proceed to do this?

Blackford said that the Cuban ambassador in Mexico had assured Velasco that if Oakes stayed on in Havana long enough to require communication with Washington, it would be "arranged" that he could do so by means satisfactory to Oakes. Well, Oakes was asking, what means had been arranged?

Che said he hadn't given it any thought, but why not let Oakes write a message, seal it, and the Cubans would deliver it to the Base Commander at Guantánamo?

Blackford had said, "Che, you must be kidding. Give my report to the President to one of *your* messengers to deliver to Guantánamo? I am a professional intelligence officer, as you let slip you knew a half hour ago."

Che managed to look as though he had hurt feelings. As though he would look at Blackford's private messages! Did Blackford have an alternative proposal?

Blackford said he would think about it, and by the way, he would appreciate the guard's being told that when Oakes needed Major Bustamente to talk to, Bustamente would show up.

"*De acuerdo,*" Che had said—Okay—picking up his briefcase and heading out toward his bodyguards clustered outdoors, the strong sea breeze blowing on their shaggy beards. Guevara turned at the door.

"*Hasta luego, Caimán.*"

"See you later, alligator." Cecilio Velasco quietly interpreted the phrase Comandante Guevara had used. He wondered whether Che knew that that parade of syllables, in English, came out droll.

"Some character," Blackford said to Velasco as the sun was setting. And then, his finger raised to his lips, he motioned to Velasco and out they went, the guard trailing as usual, toward the beach. From the south a storm was coming, low gray-black clouds contaminating the virginal sky above, still blue to the north. The hard winds came suddenly and it began to blow. "A goddam bore," Blackford said. "Looks like we'll have to try to talk back in the cottage. Yes, he is a character. But there's something appealing in there. He is anything but a cookie-cutter Commie. I don't know what he was up to all last week, keeping us waiting, but I have a feeling he wants something and wants it badly, and is laying the groundwork carefully. Let's get out of the rain."

They trotted back to the cottage. Blackford pulled out his typewriter and wrote: "To The Director, CIA, Eyes Only from Blackford Oakes, Havana." The message was economical:

HE KEPT US WAITING A FULL WEEK BUT SPENT TWO HOURS TODAY. HE SAYS YES HE IS STILL INTERESTED IN PROPOSALS BUT HE WISHES TO DISCUSS THEM IN HIS OWN WAY IN HIS OWN TIME. IT IS TOO EARLY FOR ME TO ARRIVE AT ANY JUDGMENT ON EITHER OF THE TWO QUESTIONS: WILL HE PLAY/CAN HE PLAY. NOT ANTICIPATING PROLONGED STAY, NO ARRANGEMENTS WERE MADE FOR REGULAR COMMUNICATIONS. I'LL PROPOSE USE OF SWISS EMBASSY AND WILL SEND VELASCO THERE EVERY DAY OR TWO TO CHECK FOR MESSAGES FROM YOU. STOP. OAKES.

He took the sheet from his typewriter and showed it to Velasco, who read it and nodded his head. "There is nothing to add."

Blackford informed the guard he desired to see Major

Bustamente. He found Alejandro's attitude—he was the four-to-midnight guard, heavily bureaucratic in manner, the kind who likes to look at both sides of a sheet of blank paper—significantly changed since Che Guevara's visitation. Alejandro reached into his pocket and turned toward a wooden locker, sitting now, for the first time, on the veranda outside the house. He unlocked a padlock and pulled out a telephone with a jack. He brought the phone into the living room and connected it. He then telephoned a number and asked for Major Bustamente, who came on the line. There was a rapid conversation, and then the guard extended the phone to Blackford.

"Ah, Major Bustamente. How nice to be able to talk with you."

"I am Joe. What can I do for you, Señor Caimán?"

"I want to send a communication to Washington and to use the Swiss Embassy for that purpose. This will require that Mr. Velasco talk with the Swiss ambassador. That will require that someone from your office take Mr. Velasco to the Swiss Embassy, having previously made an appointment. Mr. Velasco can then talk with the Swiss code clerk, and arrangements will be made. Now, can you set up that appointment for ten o'clock tomorrow?"

Bustamente said he would have to check with higher authority, but that he supposed this would be all right. The guard would inform them at breakfast time.

Breakfast time. A full thirteen hours away. Or rather, an un-full thirteen hours away. Agatha was palling. Even Shakespeare did not soothe Blackford's restlessness, and there was no music to soothe the savage breast. Blackford slumped down on the couch and said, Yes, he would have a drink of rum with Velasco, it was okay now to break his fast. Outside the wind howled and the rain fell heavily. Blackford felt a touch of moisture on the nape of his neck but paid no attention to it. Then a drop fell on the page his eye had arrived at in *Asesino en el Orient Express*. He looked up.

The roof was leaking. He dragged the couch to one side. Velasco looked at Blackford and winked purposively.

Velasco stripped off his outer clothing and, dressed only in his shorts, went to the guard, huddled under the little porch roof in a raincoat.

"I am going up there to fix a leak," Velasco shouted into the wind and rain.

Alejandro nodded, while gripping the collar of his raincoat tighter about his neck. Velasco grabbed the telephone locker and hauled it to where the eave of the cottage was lowest. He stood the locker on its end and stepped up on it. He could grab the corner of the roof. With his foot on a trestle that had once led flowers up from a flower box, he bounded up onto the roof. He proceeded to conduct a systematic search for radio wiring. On the back slope of the house, near the southern end, he found the tiny aerial, connected, presumably, to the three microphones they had disabled on first entering the cottage. He disassembled the aerial. If there was a fourth, undiscovered microphone in the cottage, it would not now transmit via *that* antenna. He then pounded with his fist over where he thought the leak was and received from Blackford a rat-tat-tat indicating he should move a little more to the right . . . There. Just there. He removed one of his socks and stuffed it under the suspected shingle, this with some shouting, primarily for the benefit of Alejandro, and came down, very wet, the little antenna hidden under his arm. He returned from the bathroom a few moments later, dry. "I think we can talk now, if we talk quietly." And they did this, although with discretion when certain subjects were approached.

The next morning there was first a message from Major Bustamente: that the Swiss ambassador would receive Velasco there at eleven, that Major Bustamente would arrive to conduct Velasco at 10:45. And then a letter addressed to Blackford. Velasco reached for it.

"Wait a minute, Cecilio. My Spanish is beginning to shape up. Let me see what I can do with it and then I'll give up."

He read it slowly, and then said, "It's an invitation. Have a look."

Cecilio gave an extemporaneous translation, never quite satisfactory. " 'Dear Mr. Caimán'—the Mr. is crossed out. 'I would be . . . very happy to take you on a tour of our . . . handsome capital city . . . *arrancado de*—wrested from the hands of the exploiters if you will not be . . . *avergonzado* . . . ashamed by it all but you . . . appear to be young and strong. Please advise me through the medium of . . . via Major Bustamente if this . . . suits your convenience in which case you and your interpreter should be ready at *approximately* two. Please fix upon—Please notice that I have said approximately . . . so that you will not be capricious —be annoyed with me if I am five minutes late.' It's signed 'Che.' "

Blackford went to his typewriter: "Dear Comandante Che: Reluctant as I am to leave my Walden Pond, I can console myself that, in your hands, we can pursue our mission, which of course includes your familiarization course in the horrors of capitalism. We shall expect you at approximately two. Caimán." He showed it to Velasco, put it in an envelope, addressed it to Guevara, and left it on the table, to give to Bustamente when he arrived.

The Swiss ambassador, Guy de Keller, greeted Velasco courteously and efficiently. "Do you have credentials, Mr. Velasco?"

Velasco produced his passport. "Only this. We are here on a mission. You can corroborate this by making an inquiry directed to this number"—Velasco scratched out the frequency in the 14 megahertz band. M. de Keller took the piece of paper, depressed a button on his telephone console, and directed his secretary to send in the radio operator. When the elderly technician appeared, Velasco was surprised that he spoke to the ambassador in Spanish. The ambassador handed him the sheet of paper on which Velasco had set down the data. "Verify an Okay-to-Transmit on Mr. Cecilio Velasco."

"Desde luego, Excelencia."

Velasco noticed the Castilian "excelen-thia." The radio operator was clearly from Spain.

During the interval, M. de Keller sounded like a roundup of world news. It was a convenient way to fill the time without engaging his visitor in conversation neither of them desired. Khrushchev had exploded his 50-megaton bomb and now there was talk of exploding a 100-megaton bomb . . . Khrushchev had also announced that he would not restrict his nuclear testing to the atmosphere. He said that nuclear tests would only be ended on the basis of "total disarmament." President Kennedy meanwhile had rejected the proposal of President Sukarno of Indonesia that a fresh summit conference with Khrushchev should be held. "It's too soon after the Berlin Wall," M. de Keller soliloquized. President Kennedy had assured South Vietnam that the United States would aid it in its defense against intensified guerrilla campaigns launched by the communist Vietcong forces. "And quite right," said M. de Keller. The communists had meanwhile seized border areas in Laos. The President had been asked whether U.S. troops might go to Vietnam, and had replied that his verdict on that question would have to await a report from General Maxwell Taylor, whom he was sending to Vietnam in order to conduct a reconnaissance. But General Taylor had said that he would not recommend United States troops "unless absolutely necessary." On the other hand, said the ambassador, the Washington *Post* had carried a story on October 7 that the Administration had definitely decided to send U.S. combat and training formations to communist-threatened areas of Southeast Asia as required. This was denied by a State

Department press officer. But reports from SEATO nations were to the effect that the U.S. had made "definite commitments" to military intervention and communicated that decision at the alliance's military advisers' meeting in Bangkok last week . . . In about fifteen minutes his phone rang. De Keller listened, and said, *"Bueno.*

"You are cleared for transmission, Mr. Velasco. Now if you will give the message directly to the operator he will use the United States code, which we regularly use by arrangement with the Cuban Government and have been doing ever since we took over responsibility for official Cuba–U.S. transmissions. It is secure, and, besides, is changed every two weeks."

It occurred to Velasco suddenly to ask whether the operator was secure, but he swallowed the words as a clear affront on Swiss professionalism.

The ambassador led him to a room on the third floor. He opened the door into the office of Pedro Nogales, whom he now introduced to Cecilio Velasco. In Spanish he instructed Nogales to oblige Mr. Velasco, who was in Havana on official U.S.–Cuban business.

Velasco took the typewritten letter from his coat pocket and gave it to Nogales. "I do not know English," Nogales said, "but that does not matter. The one perquisite of the operator is that all he needs to do is get the individual letters right! The message will be received in Washington within five minutes." Velasco thanked him and told him he would be coming by every day or so to receive messages from the same source to which he was directing this message. Nogales said he was glad to oblige. They shook hands, and Velasco left.

Within twenty minutes Velasco, who on the brief ride had looked about greedily on the bustling streets of Havana, was back in his eremitical cottage.

In one hour Che Guevara sat with Catalina, studying a

Xerox sheet. He said to her, pronouncing the English words, "What exactly does it mean, 'Will he play . . . Can he play'?"

Catalina explained.

Sixteen

At the ending of the meeting of the National Security Council, the President signaled to his new intelligence chief to stay behind. After the others had left the Situation Room the President said, "Congratulations, John. I assume it was you who got Castro excommunicated. The outside world never fully realizes what we Catholics can accomplish when we put our minds to it."

McCone laughed. "Yes, nice break. It will help in Latin America. I got to say, Mr. President, that was an incredibly dumb thing Castro did, deporting one hundred and thirty-five priests and putting some bishops in jail. I don't understand why the Commies do things they simply don't *need* to do."

"John, if you had said that to the Senate committee, you would never have been confirmed. A totalitarian does things because he feels a compulsion to do things that stick it"—the President made the appropriate gesture with the middle finger of his right hand—"to the other side, even to their icons. You can't believe in both Christ and Castro, so clamp down on the people who prefer God."

"There are other ways of accomplishing the same thing without torturing priests. But—with due reservation over taking pleasure in the threat to anyone's immortal soul—it was a great break for us."

"Is the USIA playing it up?"

"Mr. President! You wouldn't ask the Director of the CIA what the USIA was up to? We don't monitor the USIA. That would be against the spirit of the law."

"I can't imagine it would break any spirit of any law I ever heard of if you called Ed Murrow and asked him if he was playing up the excommunication of Castro in broadcasts to Latin America."

"*Fiat voluntas tua.*"

"What's that?"

"Evidently something they didn't teach you at Choate." Kennedy gave his little chuckle. "You mackerel-snappers will never forgive those of your fellow communicants who weren't forced to study Latin."

"Those of us who were forced to study our Latin were told to forgive everyone everything—*sicut et nos dimittimus debitoribus nostris.* I meant, Thy will be done. I'll check on the USIA."

"Good. But what I really meant to ask you was, what in the *hell* is going on with that whole Guevara-Oakes business? Bring me up to date."

"The nut of it is that Che Guevara continues to be very much taken by pretty much the same deal he described to Goodwin. Oakes suspects that Guevara is out of sympathy with the day-to-day march by Castro into the hands of Khrushchev. Guevara is very frank with Oakes, but Oakes says he can't tell exactly whether Che is just letting off steam. And Oakes reports that there never was a more convinced communist with a small 'c.' Apparently Guevara even argues with Castro. It seems to me Cuba has gone pretty far with Moscow to take the kind of turn Guevara described to Goodwin."

"Any chance of Guevara's coming out on top?"

"No. There's no chance of anybody other than Castro holding down the number one spot. Only Castro has whatever it is he has."

"Charisma. Did you know I have charisma too? Jackie says the *Ladies' Home Journal* says I have charisma."

"Of course. Isn't that why the CIA provides a secret subsidy to the *Ladies' Home Journal?*"

The President chuckled again. "So if the deal plays, it's got to get Castro's backing. Are you saying it's impossible to get that backing?"

"No. Just that it's going to be hard to do. It's inconceivable Guevara would spend this much time on the whole thing except that he thinks there's a chance it might fly. It would be the great diplomatic accomplishment of the decade if we would succeed in repatriating Cuba into the hemisphere. We could tolerate a socialist Cuba. Not a communist Cuba."

"When you say we can't 'tolerate' a communist Cuba, do you have any plans for preventing a communist Cuba, which is exactly what is shaping up right now?"

"Beyond the Guevara plan there is nothing on the table. Should there be?"

"Hell yes. If you say it's intolerable, then we can't tolerate it, right? So either say it's tolerable after all, or tell me what we're going to do to keep it from happening. What's supposed to happen when popes anathematize somebody?"

"He goes up in smoke."

"Good. Get good Pope John please to anathematize Castro." The President rose, nodded his head and, scratch pad in hand, went out of the room. "See you later, John."

Seventeen

Che Guevara was dressed exactly as he had been the day before, indeed probably in the same set of fatigues, Blackford thought, consulting his reservoir of information about him. Catalina, on the other hand, wore a skirt instead of yesterday's pants: khaki-colored, to be sure, but well-fitting, and her white cotton shirt was braided with colored thread rising from waistline to schoolboy collar. Her hair looked freshly washed, and there was a touch of rose lipstick on her full lips. Blackford had wondered what kind of a vehicle Che would drive up in. It (or they) would need to be large enough for the two principals, the two interpreters, and however many others traveled with Che.

It turned out to be a Volkswagen bus. Or, rather, two; the bus behind them conveying the bodyguards. The day, benefiting from yesterday's storm, was cooler, and Che Guevara was talkative.

He began by conceding immediately that the cars on Havana's streets were neither numerous nor new. "We imported a few of your cars in 1960. Nothing since then. We have twenty thousand cars in Cuba that need American spare parts. We cannibalize and meet with some success. But I do not pretend it would not be helpful to be able to import parts if you lifted your imperialist embargo."

Blackford was elated that Che had actually got back on track, consenting to talk on the subject that had prompted their meeting. He took him up immediately.

"That's one of the things we're here to—" But Che cut him off. "Over there," he said, pointing to a cluster of buildings standing around a green quadrangle, boys and girls in blue cotton uniforms ambling about, an impromptu soccer game going on at one end, "is the Colegio San Juan. I mean, that *used* to be the Colegio San Juan. We have renamed it. It is now the Colegio Ciro Redondo. In honor of Ciro Redondo. Do you know who he was?"

"Of course."

Che Guevara stopped, and turned his head inquisitively toward Blackford.

"Well then, tell me. Who was Ciro Redondo?"

Blackford half smiled, then closed his eyes in mock agony of concentration. He was seated on the right of the bus, by the window. A narrow aisle separated him from the seat opposite, occupied by Che. Behind Blackford was Cecilio, attending to his duties as interpreter, and behind Che sat Catalina doing the same thing for her principal. Blackford paused a tantalizing second, as if Che had called his bluff. And just as Che was about to exclaim on the subject of imperialist hypocrisy, Blackford said, "Ciro Redondo, the founder of the 26th of July Movement in Artemisa; one of the twelve survivors of the *Granma* expedition; a skillful young military commander who was killed fighting alongside you, Che, in November 1957 at Tocio; elevated posthumously to the rank of major."

Che Guevara was at once impressed and disappointed. He looked hard at Blackford and whispered in Spanish to Catalina, something Velasco was not supposed to overhear. Blackford would find out later whether Che had succeeded.

"Anyway—at Colegio Ciro Redondo we have now the sons and the daughters of the poor. Before the revolution it was a preparatory school run by religious bigots for the sons of the rich."

For the hell of it Blackford said, "Where do the sons of the rich go to school now?"

"Eton, Winchester, Groton, and Hotchkiss."

Che is paying me back (Blackford attempted not to reward the riposte with a grin) for knowing about Ciro Redondo.

They were driving down Avenida Marianao, through what had obviously been a middle-class neighborhood. At first Blackford made no mention of the long lines outside the food stores, but his failing to note the lines finally itself became conspicuous. So: "There are many people in line. Shortages?"

"Not only shortages. There is rationing. And I expect you knew that. Any Yanqui who knows about Ciro Redondo, who has been dead for four years, knows we have had rationing for two months." Blackford said nothing. And then decided that, once again, he would try to draw attention to the agenda.

"What will your sugar production be this year?"

"We don't need American spare parts for our sugar production."

"But how would you expect to pay for imported American goods?"

"We have, under socialism, cooperative ventures. There is no profit motive anymore, and for that reason we will be able to compete in world markets."

"Uh-huh."

"What does that mean, Uh-huh?" The Spanish version was heavily accented, and Che's caricature added further flavor. "It means you do not believe me?"

"Che. I really don't think we ought to get into that. The question is whether the United States will lift the embargo, and on what conditions. Not *how* you are going to pay for what you import. Not only are you expected to pay, you told Goodwin in Montevideo you would even be willing to compensate American owners for confiscated properties out of the profits of your trade with us."

"Wait! Quiet for a moment!" Che commanded. "There you see a two-thousand-bed hospital under construction. It will be a great complex—hospital, medical college, research facilities. Of course these things cost money . . ." He paused, peering out the window of the bus.

"Ah yes, profits with which to pay the Yanquis, a problem. But a problem we propose to face up to. As you know, I have embarked Cuba on a program of industrialization. Cuba has been too long dependent on sugar. That will end, believe me. And that will end"—he had raised his voice— "whether the United States does or does not lift its embargo."

"The United States is right here in the bus, willing to hear your proposals. For instance, how would you guarantee noninterference in the politics of governments in Latin America?"

"How would *we* guarantee it?" He puffed on his cigar, then flicked the stub out the window. "That is a silly question. There is no way we can 'guarantee' that our neighbors will not see the light. By the same token, presumably *you* would be free to reimpose *your* embargo if we were caught explicitly violating our promise. But you cannot expect us to help to repress revolutionary movements in Latin America, can you?"

Blackford thought the moment right to be tough. "Che, we are well situated to monitor the difference between indigenous revolutionary movements, and others that are —might be—cultivated."

"How, 'cultivated'?"

"We would not want Radio Havana preaching revolution. That would need to be a part of the agreement. And no Cuban economic credits could go out to revolutionary movements. And obviously no Cuban arms. *Comprehensive neutrality.*"

"Why should we be neutral since you are not neutral?"

"Because, Che, as of the moment, Cuba has"—he needed to be careful here—"become so heavily dependent on the Soviet Union that it is in the nature of things that interference by Cuba in the affairs of any Latin-American country becomes a Soviet operation. We would be no more concerned about the spread of Cuban socialism than we are by the spread of Ghanese socialism in Africa if it were not Moscow-oriented. I guess I ought to say that our concern would be platonic if it were just indigenous socialism."

Surprisingly, Che said nothing. Neither about what Blackford had just finished saying nor about the Paseo del Prado, a broad street with palm trees and every few blocks a statue to—Blackford guessed—somebody heroic, though Castro-Cuban revisionism was running behind, and no doubt some of the equestrian bronze figures he passed had been sentenced to be court-martialed before the external pantheon of the new Cuba was regularized.

Occasionally there was a store, but most of these were closed; the others as ever characterized by people waiting to enter them, some of them reading books while standing in line, Blackford noticed.

Guevara suddenly pepped up. "We are coming now into Colón. And Zanja. They are very spirited parts of the city. The bohemian sections, where there is very much life. Much music, much gaiety. But with it, of course, many of the bad habits bred by capitalism." He pointed to the numerous bars and cafés they passed by, and to larger establishments—nightclubs, perhaps. Brothels. Blackford drew a deep breath.

"This is where Operation P took place?"

"What do you know about Operation P?" Guevara puffed on his cigar, blowing it directly into Blackford's face. *Protest Operation P, you Yanqui bastard, he was challenging him, and fuck you.* Blackford had to wait a second or two so as not to choke on the cigar smoke. He went on calmly, "I am referring to the night a couple of months ago when the police descended on Colón and on Zanja and rounded up the prostitutes and the pimps and the homosexuals. And herded them into prisons and detention centers, and made them dress in uniforms with a huge 'P' in back. 'P' for 'pederast, prostitute, pimp.' "

"Scum of the earth," Guevara spat out the window.

"Do you intend to execute the homosexuals?"

"No," he said curtly. "El Comandante"—Che's very first reference to Castro, Blackford noted—"has decided to send them to rehabilitation centers."

"And the pimps?"

"They will be—they are being—executed."

"And the prostitutes?"

"Prostitution is now forbidden."

"As it is forbidden in Russia?"

"I have been to Russia, Caimán. There are no prostitutes in Russia."

Blackford thought it wise to let it go; go along with the fiction that communism had eliminated paid sex. Almost let it go. "As there is no alcoholism."

"That is a cultural problem. The Russians have always had that problem. Peter the Great complained about it."

Blackford said nothing.

They drove in silence through Zanja, and in due course Guevara resumed describing the parts of Havana they traversed. But his narrative had somehow become routinized, though from time to time he would pass along an animadversion about how-it-used-to-be under the Yanqui-backed Batista government, with all the corruption, and the sloth, the bribery, the repression. Blackford said nothing, but he felt he must ask the crucial question, touch on it . . .

"Che, is Premier Castro encouraging our exchange?"

Che drew on his fresh cigar. He whispered to Catalina and again Blackford could not tell whether Cecilio could overhear it. To Blackford Che said, "Fidel Castro is the undisputed leader of the Cuban revolution. I would not undertake anything that would damage it. Or him." Again Che was pensive for a few moments.

But by the time they had come to the harbor he was again

aroused, and told of plans to nationalize the fishing industry and make it more efficient. "There are great resources out there," he said pointing to the ocean. "All of Cuba could subsist on the fish that die of old age."

Blackford counted eight cargo ships in the crowded, oily harbor, half of them Russian, the other half of Panamanian or Costa Rican registry. Around the northeast end of the harbor he was shown the most resplendent of the prerevolutionary beaches. "All these residences," Che said proudly, "are inhabited now by the workers."

"And the big houses?"

"They are occupied by the cadre." Pause. "Fidel ordered many of his associates, and many of the men and women with . . . heavy responsibilities to occupy them." Pause. "I myself live in an apartment. But that is a matter of personal choice. Fidel does not tell me where to live."

"Of course."

And they were back, the two buses driving up to the front entrance of their cottage, which Blackford and Cecilio now regularly referred to as the Walden-Hilton.

The bodyguards milled about awkwardly, at a distance of no more than twenty yards. Blackford spoke:

"We are most obliged to you, Che. That was a most interesting tour. Would you care to come in? We can offer you only a rum or a vodka."

"I don't drink."

"Yes, I guess I knew that. We also have coffee and tea, and whatever else Manuel can concoct that you might want?"

"No. Not today." Afterthought: "Thank you."

"When will we meet again?"

"I must go over your comments today and think about them. Tomorrow, no. Tuesday, perhaps."

"Might it be possible for Velasco and me to go out again tomorrow? Perhaps with Major Bustamente?"

"What would you want to see?"

"Perhaps visit the museum, the library; perhaps to lunch out, somewhere not conspicuous, perhaps the Floridita."

"You have a good knowledge of Havana. Did you fly a U-2 over the city before arriving?"

"No. I helped with the invasion, and we needed to put together a tourist guide for the conquistadores. I mean, for the imperialist conquistadores."

Che cocked his head, as he looked at Blackford in concentration. There was, once again, one of his short pauses. Blackford had gambled, but apparently he had won.

"You may go—with Bustamente—wherever you like. I mean, Caimán, wherever you like *within reason.*"

"You are very hospitable. I will need to send another message to Washington tomorrow. Perhaps before the tour. May I urge you to move expeditiously at our meeting on Tuesday on the matters central to my . . . mission? Which is," Blackford said this deferentially, "after all, to implement your own suggestions of last August."

Che nodded his head. *"Hasta luego, Caimán."*

Eighteen

That night Blackford instituted a new social convention at the Walden-Hilton. "I can't imagine why I didn't think of this before," he said to Cecilio as he lifted the round aluminum table from the veranda over his shoulders, two of its legs jutting out, one each over his shoulders, his left hand dragging the chair along the beach. Cecilio carried his own chair, and with his right hand a basket with the ice, the canned fruit juice, and the bottle of rum. Alejandro, although he had become energetically amiable after Che Guevara's second visit, did not volunteer to help with the logistics of the CIA's Happy Hour on the Beautiful Downtown Beach of Havana. He obliged by coming to a halt and settling down a good five yards before the usual twenty-yard interval, leaving them perfectly secure for freewheeling talk.

The chairs dug in, never mind the rickety angles caused by the sand. The table on which the two glasses, ice, and cans were laid out sank home, finding the bedrock. The drinks poured, they sat and talked about Che Guevara and the afternoon's experience. "Did you," Blackford wanted first of all to know, "catch any of the comments whispered by Guevara to Catalina?"

"No," said Cecilio, looking down at the sand. "He—he spoke too—softly and whatever little bits I could almost hear were in a kind of private code between them."

"I was afraid so. A pity. It would be nice to know what his perspective is right now."

"You asked him the crucial question"—Cecilio pried the subject away from what Guevara had said to Catalina—"the question about Castro, and what *his* position is toward our negotiations."

"You noticed his reply? If I were a Philadelphia lawyer, I'd be a little suspicious. He said he would never do 'anything' to hurt Castro. Okay, so he is negotiating in effect with the President of the United States on a deal which, if the deal is brought off, he, Che, is certain will 'help' Castro. But that doesn't mean, does it, that Castro *knows* about the negotiations?

"Second point: He said he would never do anything that Fidel would not approve of. Well, that doesn't tell us, right away—does it?—that Castro has approved the outline of the deal? What it tells us is that Che won't end up doing anything Castro disapproves of. Well, he's hardly in a position to do anything Castro disapproves of, is he? Castro would not necessarily 'disapprove' of his talking to us, on the understanding that nothing that comes out of these discussions is binding on Castro. So, Che may be reasoning: I have on my own initiative undertaken negotiations, the successful resolution of which would in my judgment help Cuba and be approved of by Castro.

"And that," said Blackford, raising his glass, "is not the same as saying, 'I am talking to you on orders of Fidel Castro to discuss a deal the outlines of which Fidel Castro has approved.'" Blackford brought his glass to his lips. "Let us, Cecilio," he said in mock gravity, "toast to the beauty of Euclidean analysis."

Cecilio, flicking his cigarette out to sea, said, "The Spanish are not greatly moved by Euclidean logic. Euclidean logic does not add up to Christianity. Fidel Castro is a failed Christian. He is not a logician. Why would he want to hurt his people as much as he has done?"

"Because he can only exercise the kind of power he wants to exercise by assuming absolute power, and you can't do that without getting in the people's way."

"There are other ways to exercise power. Francisco

Franco has all the power he needs. No one can threaten
Francisco Franco. But life under Franco is tolerable—if you
do not try to unseat him."

"But Franco does not have absolute power. And Fidel
Castro insists on absolute power."

"Then why would he negotiate at all with the United
States?"

"It does not dilute his power, does it, to negotiate? If he
gets what he wants? . . . Anyway, you must go again to the
Swiss Embassy tomorrow, but this time with a detailed
cable. McCone knows all of us have reservations about
Guevara. Let him in on our thinking. If it's okay with you,
Cecilio, I'll leave out your sunburst that Castro is, really, a
Christian by temperament, and therefore not logical."

"Perhaps you should not send the cable at all at this
point, Blackford. Wouldn't it be better to communicate
after we are more sure than we are now?"

Blackford admired the two or three early stars that appeared around them. They seemed to have energized a soft
wind in happy celebration of the stellar legions' incipient
liberation from darkness. He paused to consider Cecilio's
point, and wondered that he could not get at its analytical
root.

"No, I think they should have our thoughts on this right
away. We can give them our modified thinking as it develops. After all, we have a perfectly secure channel."

Cecilio said nothing.

After dinner, Velasco took from the coffee table several
of the magazines he had bought at a kiosk during their
afternoon tour and told Blackford he intended to go to bed
early, and would retreat now to his room. Blackford was
rummaging in his portable library in his suitcase, and came
up with a slender volume in hand.

"Before you go," he said reading the title of his new
book, "what is *La Ratonera?*"

" '*La ratonera*' is the mousetrap."

"Oh. Sure. That's the Agatha Christie that's been playing in London for something like ten years. Actually I saw it once. But it doesn't matter—I don't remember the plot. Good night, Cecilio."

In his room Velasco lay on his bed, smoking. By the time he had put out his third cigarette he knew what he would do. "God help me," he whispered as he heard Blackford's typewriter tapping out the cable for the next day. All-important, until it was well over, for Blackford not to know. If it didn't work out—especially if he was caught—Blackford must be ignorant of the circumstances. Moreover, Blackford might not approve. And in some matters, never mind that Velasco was subordinate on this mission to Blackford, he felt more experienced. He set his alarm for six. Blackford regularly rose at about seven to take his run along the beach.

At six Velasco went into the living room. He reached into the jacket pocket of Blackford's light gabardine jacket and, as he expected he would, came on Blackford's typewritten cable. It contained all the political and formal speculation he had ventilated the evening before on the beach.

He put it back, put a fresh sheet of paper into the typewriter, and began to hunt and peck. A few minutes later Blackford appeared, wearing pajama bottoms and yawning, "What gets you up at this hour, and what are you doing on the typewriter?"

"A letter to an old friend in San Antonio. I'll ask the Swiss ambassador to send it in the pouch to Switzerland and mail it from there. Sorry it woke you."

"Doesn't matter. Did you know, Cecilio, that the detective—his name was Trotter—wasn't really a detective but was—get this—the *murderer!* They tell you that, in London after ten years of *The Mousetrap*—it'll probably run twenty years—they figure every American tourist is bound to see it. So if a taxi driver feels you haven't tipped him enough, he'll say to you as he drops you off at the theater, 'By the way, guv'nor, the detective is really the killer. Don't let Trotter fool you.'"

Velasco laughed and turned back to the typewriter. He wrote, after the usual designation code, "GUEVARA AND TRANSLATOR TOOK ME AND VELASCO ON INTERESTING TOUR OF CITY. MANY WAITING LINES, OBVIOUS SCARCITIES OF ALL GOODS. GUEVARA SEVERAL TIMES ADVERTED TO THE DAMAGE DONE BY THE BLOCKADE, BUT NO SPECIFIC PROGRESS BEING MADE ON NEGOTIATIONS. HE SAYS HE CANNOT SEE US TODAY, MONDAY, BUT WILL ATTEMPT MEETING ON TUESDAY SO THAT NEXT COMMUNICATION WILL PROBABLY BE ON WEDNESDAY. OAKES." He folded the sheet of paper and put it in an envelope in his pocket.

After breakfast Joe Bustamente arrived, as ever with good cheer. He asked if Velasco was ready. Velasco said he was, and turned to Blackford for the cable. Blackford reached into his jacket over the chair, picked out the envelope and handed it to Velasco, who put on his blue cotton jacket, like those most Cubans wore these days, ever since Castro had mounted his "blue" campaign, emulating Mao's green. He had asked Alejandro, last week, to buy him one. He walked out the door.

In Ambassador de Keller's office he bowed and was shown a chair while the ambassador gave his instructions over the telephone to his secretary. "It won't be a minute, Señor Velasco."

"No trouble at all," Velasco said. "Do you mind if I smoke?"

"Certainly not," said de Keller, lighting up his own cigarette.

"Forgive me if I ask you," Velasco said, "but there may be a need to send a further message later on today. What are the hours when transmission is possible?"

"You mean when Pedro Nogales is here?"

"Yes."

"We shut down between twelve and two. Nogales goes home for lunch. He lives nearby."

"And after that?"

"He is here from two until six. In an emergency we can call him over. Or, the deputy knows how to use the codes. You can always leave your messages for transmission after Nogales comes in."

"My principal does not like that practice."

"Well then, you are perfectly welcome to wait here until Nogales arrives," said the ambassador, with the air of everybody-has-his-own-peculiar-habits.

There was a knock. It was Nogales, who greeted Velasco and asked whether he should merely take his message.

"Thank you," Velasco smiled at the ambassador. "I shall accompany you."

In the intelligence community questions are not asked about other people's security habits.

In the code office, Velasco reached into his pocket and pulled out the envelope with his own bland, uninformative message, and handed it to Nogales. While he opened the envelope Velasco's eyes moved as he concentrated on the office, looking for whatever it was that years of training had taught him to register, even as a magnetometer measures magnetic intensities. He spotted the papers on the desk.

"Excuse me, Señor Nogales. It suddenly occurs to me there is a sentence that needs to be added to the communication. Might I have it back?"

"Certainly."

Velasco inclined in the direction of the desk, then paused, in a posture that clearly solicited permission to proceed.

"By all means," Nogales said. "Sit down, use the desk."

Velasco nodded his thanks, placed the ersatz message in front of him and crouched over it, pen in hand. It was a matter of seconds. An electrical utility bill sat there on top of the heap. Mailed to Pedro Nogales, Apartamento 8A,

Séptima Avenida No. 81, Miramar, Habana. To the cable he
added, "ON THE OTHER HAND HE IS UNPREDICTABLE SO
YOU MAY HEAR AGAIN BEFORE THAT."

He thanked Nogales, left the embassy, and was returned
by Bustamente to the cottage. Blackford was at the beach,
the guard as usual sitting behind him with his improvised
parasol.

Now! Velasco said to himself. He scratched out a note.
"Blackford: Am making the rounds. Cover for me as necessary—I am theoretically in my room. Will be back sometime
early afternoon." He grabbed from his briefcase what appeared to be an antique letter opener in a velvet case. That
and his map of Havana. He ascertained that the guard was
still at the beach, his back to the cottage, and walked nonchalantly out, back toward the driveway and then away from
the beach, through the hotel property, to Primera Avenida.
He would take no pleasure in executing a double agent,
though he supposed that if people deserved to die, double
agents should head the list. But he could not countenance
continuing interception of their cables to Washington. Nor
initiate a protest to Che Guevara that could only be sub-
stantiated by revealing that he had overheard Guevara's
own private conversations with his aide. There was only
this one way to go, and it was a way in which he had, under
other auspices, been trained. He flagged a taxi and gave
him an address.

Séptima Avenida ran through a middle-class residential
area, a street so narrow the sun never really got at it. Velasco sauntered toward that end of it that edged, a few
blocks farther down, into the beginning of the diplomatic
district. The end through which Pedro Nogales would naturally come to on his way to his lunch. The end through
which he would pass to return to his office. It was exactly
noon. Either it must be done now, or else after Nogales's
lunch. Velasco's practiced eye looked at the half block be-

fore the entrance to No. 81. There was a fruit stand. A liquor stall.

No good. He walked hastily into the apartment building. There was very little light. The elevator was of the antique kind, enclosed by glass and brass grillwork that had not been polished in years. Not exactly private, but then from inside the elevator one could see up one floor if there were others waiting to step into it. He looked up the elevator shaft, and at the old sundial-style indicator registering the floor at which the elevator nestled. There were ten floors.

Cecilio Velasco made up his mind. He walked up to the eighth floor, studying the building's configuration. To the left of the elevator, in every case, was apartment A. Ahead of it, Apartment B. To the right, Apartment C. Behind it, Apartments D and E. He stopped outside Apartment D on the eighth floor, took out a notepad and bent over it, as if writing a note to leave outside the door of someone not home. Cigarette in his mouth, hat tilted over his face, he waited.

He calculated that it would be very soon. He would be deterred only if two people stepped out of the elevator together. At thirteen minutes past the hour he saw the elevator cable rising. He stared down through the grilled grate. The elevator stopped two or three floors below. Good. One less possibility of extra traffic. It resumed its rise and it was between the seventh and eighth landings when Velasco could see that the elevator carried a single passenger.

Pedro Nogales stepped out of the car and turned left toward 8A.

At the moment Velasco approached him from behind, the doors of 8B and 8C suddenly swung open. Out of 8C a six-year-old boy was led by his mother, laughing and singing, to 8B, which had somehow burst out in song: "Happy birthday to you, happy birthday to you . . ." There was the sound of a piano and of a dozen children's voices singing out their congratulations to Bobito.

Pedro Nogales, his key already in the doorlock, turned his head toward the jubilation. Velasco struck. A combination he had been taught in Barcelona and had—he was not so calloused as to forget exactly how often he had summarily executed—six times used, that had never failed him. The quick pile driver's chop with the hard edge of his left hand across the upper temple, while his right hand drove the razor-edged letter opener up through the rib cage into the heart.

There was not a sound, merely the collapse of a few score pounds of flesh. The mother ushering in her child was momentarily distracted by the disorder in front of 8A, but the welcomes shouted from 8B recaptured her attention, to say nothing of Bobito's, who kept puffing into his paper blow-out. Velasco leaned over the fallen figure, as though administering first aid, for the few seconds required as her concentration went back to the birthday party and she shut the door behind her. Leaving the body slumped on the floor, he entered the elevator, burying his face in a newspaper. The elevator stopped at the third floor, but Velasco continued reading, in doing so becoming undistinguishable from a hundred thousand Cubans who could not be distracted from their preoccupation with *Revolución*, the jaunty, exuberant tabloid edited by the renowned friend of Fidel, Carlos Franqui, veteran of Sierra Maestra.

Outdoors, Velasco walked down Séptima Avenida, and two blocks away found a taxi. He gave an address ten minutes' walk from the Walden-Hilton. He approached the cottage with caution. He was relieved to see that Blackford was sitting in a chair on the beach, Alejandro behind him in the blazing sun, his carbine on his lap. Velasco slipped into the cottage, got into his formal beach clothes (baggy short pants, a T-shirt, and a kimono of sorts). Magazine in hand, he walked casually toward the beach and sat down on the sand by Blackford.

"Gee, Cecilio, it is so nice to see you. Are you entirely over your awful seizure?"

Cecilio performed like a trained seal.

"Yes, thank you Blackford. It must have been something I ate. Absolutely terrible. But I think it is out of my system. Thank you for the trouble you took." His statement was a clear interrogatory.

"After I saw your note," Blackford lowered his voice, though it was not really necessary, "I went to the door of your bedroom and though it was obviously hard for you to talk, sitting in the can, I made out to Manuel that you were alive. I then went to the beach every fifteen minutes and stayed there for fifteen minutes, before walking back to catch up on your 'condition.' It was necessary for me to speak rather loudly to you from the living room. Almost had to shout, but at least I established that you were among the living. Then back to the beach—so damn hot in the cottage. Good old Alejandro walked right back to the beach with me every time. It meant access to the cottage for fifteen minutes out of every half hour, to give the impression I was looking after you, fifteen minutes on the beach to give you a chance to slip in, Manuel having taken his usual afternoon off. Figured that would be useful. You son of a bitch, what in the hell have you been up to?"

"I'll tell you when it makes sense to tell you," Cecilio said, lighting up a cigarette. "Meanwhile, if I may suggest it, I think it would be appropriate to call in Major Bustamente on the grounds that you have another message to send in to our principals."

Blackford turned and looked at Cecilio, sitting on the beach chain-smoking, his beachwear so totally, preposterously unsuitable. He suddenly understood. As plainly as though he had been given it all in words of one syllable.

He said, as if talking into a KGB loudspeaker, "I am glad

you reminded me. I have supplementary thoughts I should add to this morning's message.''

They walked together in silence back to the cottage, dragging their effects behind them in the sand. They no longer bothered to bring back the beach chairs, as they now referred to them, and Alejandro seemed content to let them stay there in the broiling sun, just this side of the high tide, so that they would not float out to sea.

Nineteen

Joe Bustamente was the last cheerful thing Cecilio Velasco
saw on that Tuesday afternoon. Joe arrived at the Walden-
Hilton the soul of good cheer to take Velasco once again to
the Swiss Embassy. On the way he chatted that Washington
must be ever so obliged at being kept so current on the
matters Sr. Caimán was engaged in, whatever those matters
were—"Joe keeps his mind on the things Joe is told to keep
his mind on," Bustamente said, smiling. And anyway, was
Mr. Velasco feeling better, after the seizure Manuel, the
cook, had told Bustamente Velasco had suffered that morning? What on earth could it have been, since the water at
the hotel was crystal-clear; indeed Havana had never had
any trouble with its water, in particular now that the imperialists had been . . . invited to return to the United States,
no offense intended. What on earth could it have been?
Velasco said he was still feeling a little bit weak, but that he
had suffered from a weak stomach "ever since getting ty-
phoid as a boy in Spain"; he had learned to control it, and
now he would drink only bottled water—no offense intended on the subject of Cuban water—but water and soup,
and perhaps a little boiled chicken, and he would be a new
man tomorrow, etc., etc.

At the embassy Bustamente was surprised to find, there
in the enclosure outside the entrance, a corporal's guard of
soldiers and plainclothesmen—Castro's plainclothesmen
of course wore fatigues, but without insignia. Velasco
seemed unperturbed. He walked through the informal bar-
ricade, explaining that he had an appointment with the
ambassador, not exactly correct, but he could say that he

had been invited by the ambassador to come by any time before six o'clock if he had any cables to send out. When the door was opened, he saw three guards in the hallway. Again paying them no heed he asked for the ambassador. Instead of being taken directly to his office as before, he was taken to a waiting room and told to wait. The commotion was quite general, and Velasco affected, finally, to be disturbed, and quietly inquired of the receptionist whether M. de Keller was all right.

"The ambassador is quite well, thank you," she said. "Pedro Nogales is not. Pedro Nogales is dead."

"Dead?" Velasco's face was solemn, his eyes questioning. "But I was with him here this morning! He seemed so well. Heart attack?"

The receptionist, a middle-aged lady with a heavy German accent, began to whisper something, but then saw the door to the ambassador's office opening and said nothing. Guy de Keller appeared outside the door to his office and signaled to Velasco to come in.

"I just heard," Velasco exclaimed. "Mr. Nogales . . ."

"Murdered." Guy de Keller sat down heavily at his desk, motioning Velasco to sit down. "Murdered. Right outside the door of his apartment."

"Murdered! Did they catch him?"

"No. The police—the G-2—are asking a great many questions. It is not clear to me why the G-2 are involved. No doubt because Nogales was involved in diplomatic work. The G-2 can be very conscientious, you have to hand them that. I have never been troubled here in transacting official diplomatic business. Of course, my burden has been greatly increased since I have had to attend to United States business. But no, they tell me they have leads, and that they are certain to apprehend the culprit. But everyone is searching for a motive."

"Was he married?"

"In a manner of speaking. I make it a point not to inquire

into these things—I mean, after the normal security checks. He is—he was—a widower, but he has kept company with a lady who lived with him. I have never met her."

"If it is not too painful, what exactly happened?"

"I know only that shortly after noon—I think I told you—yes, I did, didn't I?" the ambassador looked up, then resumed, "Pedro went regularly home for his lunch. It is only a half-dozen blocks from here. Anyway, there was a children's party, and traffic between the two adjacent apartments, and one of the children saw this—body. The mother rang the bell of his apartment, and Nogales's—lady—came out, and screamed. They called an ambulance. But he was dead."

"Why, then, 'murdered'?"

"Because, Mr. Velasco, there was a knife wound that had pierced his heart."

"Dios mío de la vida!" Velasco relapsed into Spanish. "I am so very sorry . . . But, sir, I must kindly ask that—was it your deputy, you said? The gentleman who can work the codes?—I must ask, inasmuch as this is important official business, that you be good enough to permit me to consult with him on the matter of a cable . . ."

Guy de Keller sighed, and picked up his telephone. In German he relayed his request, and in a few moments a young man whom he introduced as Beathe Jutzeler walked in, looking harried. Jutzeler spoke to Velasco in Spanish and told him to follow him into the code room.

Velasco did so, and the door having closed, he gave the code number and pulled out of his pocket the cable Blackford had written that morning, on which he had typed a fresh introductory sentence, FURTHER TO THE CABLE OF THIS A.M. "Sir, I am embarrassed to ask this question, but can we assume that, the commotion notwithstanding, this cable will go out with normal security arrangements?" Velasco was tempted further to ask whether abnormal security arrangements might not be more appropriate.

"Of course," Jutzeler said, extending his hand for the cable. "And, as ever, this piece of paper will be shredded after it has been dispatched. Good day, Mr. Velasco."

"Good day, Mr. Jutzeler. And permit me to express my sympathy over the loss of your . . . colleague."

"Thank you."

He made his way back through the soldiery and signaled to Bustamente, who was talking in excited gestures with a lieutenant.

In the jeep, on the way to the cottage, Bustamente spouted incessantly, repeating mostly details Velasco had heard from the ambassador. "We live in a violent world, Mr. Velasco."

"We do indeed," Velasco sighed deeply, under the crushing impact of Joe's profundity.

In his office, the Deputy Minister of the Interior, Nemesio García Naranjo, stormed up and down. From his desk, behind which was a huge picture of Fidel Castro, to the opposite end of the room where the large bay window overlooked a square. There were three men in the room, seated on an assortment of chairs; all of them were, like García Naranjo, bearded. They were in their thirties and forties, senior officials.

"Goddamndest thing. Middle of the day. Middle of Havana. Middle of a most *extraordinarily* useful career. Months it took to get him in there. And one month—*one month*—after Nogales gets installed in the Swiss Embassy, where he might have been useful to us in such matters as how many cuckoo clocks Switzerland plans to export this year, the embassy takes on the whole business of traffic to the United States! Granted most of the traffic is ours. But then the nuggets! Nuggets! Washington asking the Swiss to hold messages for a dozen Cubans. Counterrevolutionaries they are! They were, I mean. Nogales dead. How? Who? You have your orders. Every counterrevolutionary who had any contact with the Swiss Embassy during the past four months. Round them up. Bring them in. C-o-a-x them into cooperating with us. Who was the last outsider to use the Nogales facility?"

"Sir, that was the American, the Spanish-American, one Cecilio Velasco, the man who brought the cable that Nogales made available yesterday to Comandante Che. There was a second cable this morning, also made available to Comandante Che. The last service Nogales performed for us. How much do we know about Cecilio Velasco?"

"Velasco is here under the special protection of Comandante Che. We do not need to know more than exactly that about him." García Naranjo looked out the window.

"Has Comandante Che been informed?"

"I have an appointment with him at the Industry Ministry in one half hour." He looked at his watch. At exactly that moment the door swung open. García Naranjo very nearly shouted out his indignation at being thus disturbed. *Nobody* entered the office of Nemesio García Naranjo without his permission . . .

In came General Espinosa, grim-faced. He said nothing, wheeling about to make way for the man he was escorting.

Comandante Che Guevara.

Everyone rose to his feet. Guevara did not motion them to sit down. He walked to García Naranjo's desk and, without a word, sat down. No one spoke.

"Where was Cecilio Velasco at noon today?"

García Naranjo said that Bustamente had, as usual, driven Velasco back to the cottage after the morning cable had been filed.

"I did not ask you where he was at 10:30 this morning. I asked you where he was at noon."

García Naranjo said he was presumably in the cottage, under guard.

Che Guevara spat into the wastebasket. "Find out where

he was at noon. You are rounding up the friends of the counterrevolutionaries we recently liquidated?"

"Yes, Comandante."

"You will attempt to replace the Swiss code clerk with a suitable substitute?"

"Of course, Comandante. We are preparing a list—a very short list—for the consideration of the ambassador."

"It might be appropriate to advise the ambassador that we hold him partly responsible."

"How exactly shall we phrase that, Comandante?"

"Pedro Nogales was a Cuban citizen engaged in delicate work. It greatly harms the reputation of Cuba that a diplomatic servant should be murdered. The Swiss ambassador should accept some responsibility for not providing proper . . . security."

García Naranjo knew better than to press the question of just how this would be communicated to Guy de Keller, an experienced diplomat who had held posts in Ghana, Ireland, and elsewhere and was presumably familiar with security responsibilities.

Guevara lifted his hand and said to García Naranjo, "Clear the room."

The general and the three aides left the room hurriedly.

"I have a hunch," Guevara said. "Velasco did it."

"But Comandante, how could he have known?"

"I have an idea how he might have found out about Nogales, but it is not relevant. Dig out what you can." He paused, speaking now to himself. "Bloody clever. Goddamned plucky. You have to admire it, if it's so." And then, picking up his voice, "What do we have on Velasco? Background?"

"Not much, Comandante."

"Get our people in Moscow and in Madrid to make inquiries."

"But sir, what more do we need to know? After all, he is a CIA operative. He is—the enemy."

"I want to know more. I like to know what I can about my enemies." Guevara pulled out a cigar and lit it. He thought. And smiled. In due course he noticed that García Naranjo was still standing. He motioned him to sit down, and resumed smoking. Suddenly he got up.

"Get on with it, García Naranjo. And report to me tomorrow. And tell Ramiro to call me when he gets back from Santiago. Tomorrow I shall be spending some time with Caimán. And Señor Velasco."

Twenty

It was just after midnight, a time Fidel Castro enjoyed. To spend with his intimates (defined as those who had known him for a long time and who saw him frequently, rather than as those who know a man well and give advice and friendship), but also to spend with others whose company, for a variety of reasons, he might desire. Diplomats he deigned to see (few, infrequently) were often summoned to meet him at that late hour, and even later. But today it was just his brother Raúl, Che Guevara, and Osvaldo Dorticós, nominally the President of Cuba. On the table in the study at the apartment on Calle Once in the Vedado district, the most inconspicuous of his three regular residences and the smallest, was carbonated water, ice, rum, fruit, and cakes. Castro was absentmindedly chewing on a cake and drinking from a soda-water bottle. The others were chatting. They had known Fidel Castro in every circumstance, in the days since, on December 2, 1956, the vessel *Granma* had arrived from Mexico with eighty-two young men determined to liberate Cuba from the dictator Fulgencio Batista. Twelve had survived that awful, seasick voyage and the subsequent ambushes, and there had begun the renowned and triumphant saga of Sierra Maestra. Twelve survivors of the *Granma*. One or two had died in battle, one or two before Castro's own firing squads, one or two were in prison. But all had known Fidel in circumstances of almost connubial intimacy, one consequence being that though they were blindly loyal to him, they were not in the least overawed by him. They spoke to him using the familiar voice, and argued with him; argued with him until it became clear that he had made a decision. After that, the arguing stopped. So that it was not in the least unusual that until Fidel chose to address them, they should be chattering among themselves (or to him), not especially mindful of his dominating presence. But now, the cake finished, Fidel Castro lit a cigar and said, in such a voice as to bring instant silence, "Very well then, Che. Let us have a report on what you call *Proyecto Caimán.* How does that all go?"

Guevara had prepared himself carefully for what he knew would be a difficult session.

"Fidel, Caimán is very anxious to bring the discussions to a more formal level."

"Ah-hah. It is clear to me why that is so, is it not to you, Che?"

"What is on your mind, Fidel?"

"Kennedy knows that we are getting from the Soviet Union increasing supplies of the kind we especially need. And Kennedy knows that there is much lack of sympathy in Latin America with his policies toward us, especially since the Bay of Pigs. So he is anxious to negotiate with us while he has the advantage. But every week that goes by, that advantage diminishes as we get the time to reorder our economic house and get aid from the Soviet Union."

"Fidel, I see exactly what you mean. But I do not see what is the purpose of neglecting to establish how far exactly it is that Kennedy is willing to go. Why not see his whole deck, how he will play?"

"Che, we are committed to the Soviet Union. The home of international socialism, for one thing. You know that as well as I do. Indeed you have lectured me on the subject. And Raúl here can put anyone to sleep talking about it—"

"I was not talking about where our sympathies lie, Fidel, but what kind of a deal we could succeed, even hypothetically, in making."

"We *know*," said Fidel, tapping his cigar on a large ashtray, "that great events are unfolding. The United States is

planning a military operation against us. The Soviet Union
will make of that operation a total farce! A total farce. Not
only will it be a farce, the politics of the hemisphere will
change. Change forever. The Yanqui colossus will be something we read about in the history books. Because its great
nuclear firepower will be neutralized by"—he liked this
image, which he had picked up from Adzhubei on
Adzhubei's second visit—"a 746-mile-long aircraft carrier
anchored just off the United States, with enough missiles to
reduce its principal cities to ashes. A carrier called Cuba.
Jesus Mary and Joseph, to think I shall live to see that day!"

Dorticós spoke. "You forget one important thing, Fidel,
which is that we need to forestall the invasion until the
missiles are emplaced—"

"And that exactly is where your friend Sr. Caimán comes
in, Che." Fidel was now speaking earnestly, with those
charismatic accents that worked as well with two or three
people as addressing a million. "Every device we can use to
delay the American military operation brings closer the day
of deployment. They began, in Moscow, by saying it would
take six months. It will be more than that. The first antiaircraft missiles should be in place by June or July. I have only
recently learned that the interval between their emplacement and the emplacement of the offensive missiles has
been greatly reduced by feats of Soviet engineering. By
September, Cuba shall be forever impregnable." Fidel had
slid into the declamatory mode.

"Now *that*" he wheeled his torso around to Che Guevara,
"means that any encouragement we give to Caimán, relayed to Washington, might have the effect of postponing
their attack. That is a reason why you must on the one hand
delay Caimán, since we have no intention of concluding any
pact with the gringos, and on the other hand you must
make him feel he is making progress so that, in Washington,
they will continue to feel that there is a possibility of—an
Understanding. We are not dealing with very bright people,

Che, remember that. Bright people would not have launched the Bay of Pigs."

"Now easy, Fidel, easy. While you are at it, bear in mind that even very dumb people are not going to sit around and let the Soviet Union place nuclear missiles on their front porch."

"They will not detect those missiles until it is too late."

"I grant that *possibility*. But you must also grant the *possibility* that they *will* detect them. Missiles come rather large, you know."

"A military question; a security question; a question of Soviet know-how." Fidel puffed on his cigar—little puffs, which meant he had switched gears from his ruminative, philosophical mood to a mood more combative. "We do not need at this point to go over the precautions being taken, do we?"

"Except insofar as they have a bearing on what we *are* talking about. My point is that it is in the interest of the Cuban revolution—in your interest, Fidel—that we should vigorously pursue every possibility. I mean, without closing the door, at the outset, to the *possibility* that under certain circumstances we might have to move in one direction rather than another—"

"Bullshit," said Raúl Castro.

"Ah, good evening, Raúl. You have been taking elocution lessons."

Fidel suppressed a smile. "Raúl is right, Che. It is inconceivable we should ever make a deal with the United States. But that does not alter the tenor of what we are concerned with. Which is that you must put on the greatest private show on earth. I give you considerable liberty to improvise —gestures of good faith, that sort of thing. We will, of course, advise General Malinovsky what we are up to. But always, *always* bear in mind this: There are exactly five men in Cuba who know about the missiles. Four of them are in this room. The other is Ramiro Valdés. The Cuban military thinks we are dealing exclusively with antiaircraft weapons, ground-to-air weapons—'SAM' missiles, they are calling them in Russia. They will continue to believe that until the great unveiling. That great unveiling must come," he pounded his fist on the table, "and you will help to make it come. Take Caimán under your wing. Give him a good time. Make him feel he is progressing. Shall we consider the subject closed? We have other matters to deal with."

Castro wanted to know why Che's most recent projections on sugar production were so abysmally low, why there was no coffee in Cuba, why there were no oranges in Cuba, and he wanted to know from Raúl what was it exactly that was going on in Camagüey—why hadn't the pocket of counterrevolutionary resistance been wiped out? Did he, Fidel, need to don his Sierra Maestra fatigues and go back into military work to show Raúl how to dispel a few dozen guerrillas? And Dorticós should consider a state visit to Mexico—you can't overemphasize the importance of Mexico. They've been terrific and have reacted in exactly the right way to the April invasion and subsequent events. Had he told them that he had decided to cancel Easter? It would no longer be a holiday, even as Christmas was no longer a holiday. In fact, he was considering canceling Sunday as a regular day off, as Mao Tse-tung had done. Mao is probably the wisest of them all as a *pure* Marxist theorist. It was a great tragedy that Mao and Khrushchev had fought; it was of course fitting that admiration for Mao should be expressed only discreetly, given Cuba's special relation with Khrushchev, but the more Fidel read about the requirements of introducing socialism, the greater his admiration for Mao. He would give some more thought to the Sunday business—naturally there would be a lot of opposition to it —but he especially enjoyed the thought of how the Vatican would react. Henry VIII had retaliated against his excommunication by founding Protestantism, and perhaps he,

Fidel, would retaliate against his excommunication by eliminating Sunday.

"You will be known as Fidel the Sunday-killer," Che ventured. Eventually the meeting broke up, sometime after four.

Twenty-one

Wednesday was another of those awful, long days, leavened only by Joe Bustamente's "surprise package" of six flashlight batteries, which activated Blackford's radio. They listened to the station in Miami for much of the day, and at night they were able to hear, though the reception was wobbly, a station in New York. The Soviet Union, Blackford was especially interested in hearing, had come up with some formula or other (there had been static) on the German question that was conciliatory in not asking the United States to cede rights of access to West Berlin.

A United Nations tribunal reported that the protracted inquiry revealed that Patrice Lumumba had in fact been murdered—by Katanga President Moise Tshombe. ("Notice how they call it 'murder'?" Blackford turned to Velasco. "All *Lumumba* ever did was make war against Tshombe.") And General Taylor had returned from his investigative mission in South Vietnam, reporting that he was confident that the South Vietnamese had sufficient resources to defend themselves against the communists. Both the New York and the Miami stations had carried the subsequent statement of President Kennedy, relayed to the press by his press secretary Pierre Salinger. The President's message, issued on the sixth anniversary of Vietnam's Independence Day, pledged that "the United States is determined to help Vietnam preserve its independence, protect its people against communist assassins, and build a better life." Blackford tucked that one away in his memory. It might prove useful under the relentless inquisitions of Guevara and his jibes about Western and capitalist irresolution.

But another news item he almost regretted hearing. A New York *Times* scoop. One Mariano Faget, identified as a secret police official for twenty years for Fulgencio Batista, had been employed by the U.S. Immigration and Naturalization Service to "interrogate Cuban refugees passing through the Opa-Locka detention center near Miami." His job, the announcer said, was to "weed out" Castro agents, and his last post under Batista had been that of "Director of the Bureau of Repression of Communist Activities." Blackford looked over at Velasco.

Velasco beat him to it. *"Mierda,"* he said.

"Ugh," Blackford said. "Some Americans can be so goddam dumb." And added, "Anyway, you would think that anyone who had been in charge of suppressing communism in Cuba would have a hard time establishing his credentials as competent to do anything."

And so another day swimming and reading. Blackford had started his penultimate Agatha Christie, *Testigo del Cargo.* He knew that *testigo* meant *witness.*

"What's *cargo,* Cecilio?"

"How is it used?"

"Testigo del cargo."

"Witness for the prosecution."

"Have you ever read it? The book? Agatha? Agatha Christie?"

"No, but I would be suspicious of the witness."

"Good point," Blackford said, and began reading. After a while he wrote a letter to Sally, reminding her that a couple of years down the line they were scheduled to be married, and on second thought, might they advance the date, to be married on Saturday? "You could get a friendly Mexican jet to bring you to me, no? I would then tell you where I am; what do you say, Señora Professor?", and remembered to attempt to devise a faster means of getting it to her than through Switzerland.

Manuel came back into the living room, en route to the

kitchen and his own quarters. The orderly was looking very much the worse for wear. Two police officers had come into the cottage during lunch and summoned Manuel outside to talk to him. He returned to apologize to Blackford that he had been called to give testimony at a police station and would not be able therefore to finish serving lunch. "Never mind," Blackford had said.

And now, three hours later, Manuel was looking disheveled and frightened. He spoke not a word, merely going to the kitchen and beginning to wash the lunch dishes.

"I can guess what he was questioned about," Blackford said, keeping his voice low.

"Oh?"

"Your wretched stomachache. You remember, the one you nearly died from yesterday? I hope our friend Manuel doesn't become a *testigo de cargo*."

"You do worry so sometimes, Blackford," Cecilio said, seated, and resuming his reading.

The following morning Bustamente delivered a letter. It was from Che Guevara. He would pick Blackford up at two. Velasco was to stay behind, for reasons Che would explain that afternoon. Blackford would be gone "for several days, in connection with Sr. Caimán's mission," and so should bring along whatever he might need. "You may bring along your Agatha Christie collection, if you like."

Blackford was inclined to reply there and then that no, he would not travel without Velasco, who was his aide as well as his interpreter, and whose presence had been specifically authorized by the Cubans. Cecilio proposed that they listen, instead, to the reasons Che Guevara would give for not taking him along, deferring a decision until then.

"Catch that 'you can bring your Agatha Christie' business. What's he trying to demonstrate, that they've been through our bags? Why?"

"I don't know. There is a lot I don't know about Comandante Guevara."

Joe Bustamente had been waiting, as the Comandante
had requested a reply from Sr. Caimán.

Blackford went to the typewriter: "Dear Che: I am here
on official business together with Cecilio Velasco. I see no
reason why I should be separated from him. Whatever reason you have for not taking him with us will need to be
compelling. I'll look for you at 2 P.M.—Caimán."

Guevara arrived at two-forty. It no longer made much
difference, since punctuality was not expected.

Che Guevara was unchanged, in dress and in manner. He
sat down on the couch, pointed to Manuel who was in the
kitchen, and signaled him to go outside. He wanted to be
alone with the CIA. Catalina was dressed in slacks and
wore, like Che, a beret, except that hers was red. Her voice,
when she was engaged in translating, was mechanical.
When she was herself speaking to Che it was vivid and
mellifluous.

Che announced that he had discussed the entire project
with Fidel Castro the night before last and had been authorized, indeed encouraged, to proceed with the negotiations. But in order to do this, Che said, he needed to give
Blackford some idea of what the march from Sierra Maestra
had been like. And not merely for sentimental reasons. He
wished for Blackford to see the actual circumstances of
guerrilla warmaking, concerning which, Che said, he had
written a manual. An objective reason was for Blackford to
know what it was that other progressive socialists in other
Latin-American countries might resolve to do, and what
were the difficulties in isolating such guerrillas, or in establishing whether they were in fact being aided by the Cuban
Government, "which, if our understanding goes into effect,
we would pledge not to do."

Blackford said he was perfectly willing to accompany

Che, but what was the difficulty in bringing along Cecilio Velasco?

"Oh, that. Very simple. We shall be traveling a great deal by helicopter. I wish I could report that we have as many helicopters as we would like to have. But we shall have to do with one, and that model, the Bell 47-J, holds only four people." Che pantomimed a pilot at the controls of a helicopter, together with the pilot's slow turn of his head, from far left to far right, looking out of the cockpit window for traffic. Then he lifted the index finger of his left hand and pointed to it with his right hand. Then to himself with the middle finger. Then to Blackford with the third. And, finally, to Catalina with his little finger. "That makes four.

"But there is something else," Che added quickly, "a second reason. I spoke to Mr. Goodwin about compensation. I desire for Mr. Velasco to spend some time with our accountants. It will take a while to put together the papers evaluating the assets we have . . . seized. The American assets, you understand. There will obviously need then to be a trip back to Washington—you, Caimán, and Velasco—to go over the figures, as well as the other matters we shall be discussing. Velasco, then, is needed here, in Havana. As for translation, Catalina is perfectly responsible. Beside that, she is a lieutenant in our military intelligence organization we now call 'Jiménez'—borrowed, my dear Caimán, from your term G-men—and she will from time to time conduct directly some of the conversations if, for instance, I am suddenly needed back in Havana.

"So," he said, rising, "you say you are in a hurry to get started. So am I. Shall we get started?"

"I wish to confer with Velasco," Blackford said.

Che bowed, extended his right arm operatically to Catalina, as though to escort her to a ball, and the two went outside and mingled with the bodyguards.

Blackford sat down. "What do you think, Cecilio?"

"I think there is a design in everything that comes from

Che Guevara. No, not quite everything. He is a fluent and orthodox ideologue, but he can be impulsive. I suspect there is a plan in separating us."

"Yeah. On the other hand it is true that the Bell holds only four people . . ."

"Frankly, Blackford, I don't think we are in a position to say no. He is, after all, the second most important man in Cuba. And what he is asking is not unreasonable."

"Do you know anything about company balance sheets?"

"I am not an accountant. But it will not be hard to note down the difference between Cuban evaluations and American evaluations. Differences that will simply have to be negotiated."

"Hm." Blackford harbored a dark thought: Velasco, and his stomach illness. And his disappearance on Tuesday. He thought it wiser not to say anything about it.

"Tell you what. In moments like these you get minor concessions. Why don't I tell Che that life in the Walden-Hilton is too damn claustrophobic and that you would like to be able to get about the city when you're not doing your paperwork?"

"That would be pleasant."

Blackford went to the door and hailed the Comandante, as he was careful to call him in the presence of any Cuban other than Catalina.

Che and Catalina came in.

"Okay, Che, but on behalf of my comrade I would like to make a simple request."

"Name it."

"It is very confining in this cottage day after day. I hope you will permit Velasco, when he is not here going over the financial documents, or wherever you plan to do the paperwork, to stretch his legs. Walk about the city of Havana?"

"I think that can be arranged," said Che. "I know Mr. Velasco likes to walk about the city. I mean, I should have guessed it. It is very Spanish."

The icicle had done its work. The quick dislodging note about the peripatetic habits of the Spanish attenuated the impact of it. But Velasco now knew. Knew, at least, that he was a suspect. He merely puffed again at his cigarette, sitting on the arm of the sofa methodically translating Blackford's words; difficult, when their subject was himself. He wondered whether Blackford, whom he had labored to shield from direct knowledge of what his mission had been on Tuesday, had caught Guevara's guarded insinuation. He would not open the subject up by asking him.

"Yes," Che continued. "But of course for security reasons there will need to be an escort. I shall advise Bustamente that he is to be at the personal disposal of Mr. Velasco and to take him everywhere it is authorized for him to go. Some parts of Havana are not designed for guided tours for CIA agents."

Blackford went into his bedroom and was back in a moment with a canvas bag. "Might I need a typewriter?"

"We will have them, as required," Che answered.

"Okay. Let's go."

Blackford turned to Velasco, who extended his hand and said to him softly in Spanish, "*Hasta luego, Caimán.*" Blackford shook Velasco's hand with unusual firmness, looking the aging Spaniard directly in the eye. Velasco looked up at Oakes as he might have done to his son. For a very brief moment they were frozen in a posture that was nevertheless almost kinetic; quickly Velasco disengaged to reach over to the ashtray, to retrieve the burning cigarette to his lips; and everything now was normal again, as Blackford walked out and gave his bag to the orderly who reached for it.

Twenty-two

At the airfield there was considerable formality when Comandante Che Guevara, Minister of Industry, hero of Cuba and of revolutionary Latin America, intellectual godfather of the revolution (as the men of letters thought of him), came in on his jeep, the forward jeep full of his bodyguards. What appeared to be a squadron of pilots in training stood at attention and in formation. Che climbed out of the back of the jeep and walked by them, stopping to chat with one or two, who clicked their heels, English-style. He came back to the jeep and nodded to the driver, who advanced to a waiting DC-3. He motioned to Blackford to climb aboard. It might have been the same plane as the one that had brought him and Velasco from Santiago a fortnight ago. On impulse Blackford walked two seats aft and clicked on the overhead light for the aisle seat. It didn't work.

He looked over at Che, as if to ask whether he was expected to occupy any particular seat. Che told him to sit where he was, which he did. Che sat diagonally across, one seat forward. Catalina was across the aisle from him, directly in front of Blackford. About as close as they could come to an equilateral triangle, though when the engines were turned on conversation was difficult. Che gave up trying but only for about a half hour, at which point they were comfortably airborne.

Blackford noticed that the plane was dipping down from its cruising altitude. Down it came to a thousand feet or so above the ground. With his right foot Che reached out and banged on the pilot's compartment door (Blackford noticed that when Che was aboard there were two pilots, not just one). The copilot came aft quickly. "Go down lower. Go to three hundred feet."

They were skidding now over stubby-looking green fields with tiny red-brown figures dotted about them like cayenne pepper sprinkled over green ears of corn. "Look," Che Guevara said. "Just keep looking."

It wasn't clear to Blackford, at first, what it was he was supposed to be focusing on. The number of workers? The scarcity of mechanical aids? He concentrated his eyes, searching out the anomaly presumably there. And suddenly he noticed what it was. They were traveling at 180 miles per hour, and ten minutes had gone by with absolutely no discernible change in what he saw. He looked up at Che. "No, no. Keep looking," Che said.

He did so. They passed over Matanzas, and Cárdenas (he had been given what must have been an old tourist map, because the legends were written in English). He calculated now that they were over Quemado de Güines. On to Sagua la Grande. The pilot moved inland now; still the fields of sugarcane, everywhere sugarcane and sugarcane workers. He became almost dizzy, and finally closed his eyes.

Eventually the airplane pulled up—but only to conform to landing pattern protocols. They put down at Camagüey. It had been over one hour and a half. Nothing but sugarcane fields.

A jeep was waiting. "Bring your bag," Catalina said to Blackford, Che having walked down the companionway. She carried, over her left shoulder, a sizable army pouch, and, stepping out of the plane, she put on her dark glasses against the sun in the west opposite, came down the steps, and got into the jeep.

Away they went, followed by a single jeep with three soldiers and a tall radio antenna. The driver took them over roads that were progressively cruder. The pot-holed pavement stopped and the road was now a brownish clay; and always, on both sides, the sugarcane. It evolved finally into what was nothing more than a passageway hacked out of the cane forest.

They reached a village. Several dozen houses, all of them smoking through the chimneys, or such was the impression. The odor was not of tobacco. It was pungent, acrid. Che said, "They are burning dried cane stalks. They cook with it, and when at night it is cool, keep warm with it. They harvest the sugar, eat the sugar, burn the sugar, coat their rooftops with sugar—though if you tasted it, you would find that it has in common with what you are accustomed to only its sweetness. It is coarse and sticky. We have no refineries, such as are required to prettify the sugar used by the stockholders."

"My impression was that most of the sugar was owned by Cubans."

"Great tracts of it were, repeat were, owned by Cubans. But much of it was also owned by the Yanquis, and the big rum makers. They own none of it now, not one hectare. All the sugar is owned by the people."

"By the people who harvest the sugar?"

"By the people."

Che walked into a ramshackle general store. Its drabness was its principal feature. It seemed to flaunt its drabness. All the products for sale appeared to be of the same basic color, between middle yellow and middle brown, dirty brown. The rum bottles were unmarked. There were two splintered round tables, three or four rough wooden chairs surrounding each of them. At one, two men were seated, drinking silently. Che sat down at the other table with his party. He went unrecognized, but his manner carried authority. Besides, there was the jeep outside with the armed men. The distance between the two tables was measured in inches.

"*Oye viejo*," Che said, motioning his head toward the elder of the two men, perhaps forty. "Do you always stop working this early?"

At first the quiet translation of Catalina for Blackford's benefit was generally distracting, but he gradually realized he really did not need her most of the time, the language having, under the intense pressures of the past few months, begun to beckon to him its cozy and regular rhythms and penetrable constructions, and indeed Blackford found the language marvelously hospitable to sincere postulants. He put his hand down on Catalina's knee. "When I don't understand," he whispered into her ear, "I'll signal you like this, okay? Otherwise it means I'm getting the drift." She nodded, again inconspicuously, so as not to interrupt the colloquy.

"You think five o'clock is early to stop working, General, if you begin working at five in the morning?"

"How could you start working at five in the morning when there is no light at five in the morning?"

"We make our own light, General. The children. They burn the old stalks every twenty meters right down the road, right down the road as far as you can see, General."

"How old are the children who do this, *viejo?*"

"My son is eight. He is one of them."

"And how long have you been working the sugar?"

"Since I was eight."

"How old are you now?"

"Twenty-eight."

Blackford was startled, training his eyes on the concentrations of wizened skin surrounding the—young—man's eyes.

"When do you stop working?"

He laughed, and shared the joke with his companion. "Things are a little different now, General, though we never know exactly what is going on from one day to the next day, so many changes are being made, but we do not stop working until the harvest is completed. Then we stop working until the time to sow for the new harvest. That means six months."

"So then, every year you get six months of vacation?"

This brought a laugh almost contumacious. "A 'vacation' we call it now, do we? Until Castro we got no pay during those six months. You try, General, intending no disrespect, to take six months' vacation without pay if you have no money and no savings and no other work. The six months' vacation means six months of lying in the sun eating sugar for breakfast, *merienda*, lunch, and supper. Now we get pay for those six months. But what good is pay? There is no more coffee now. *No more coffee* now, General. No more coffee in all of Cuba, the radio says, isn't that what you also heard?" he nudged his companion and raised his rum glass to his lips.

"Do you read, *viejo?*"

"Read what?"

"Do you know how to read?"

"A little, you know, like Drink Coca-Cola, Long Live Castro"—his companion quietly dug his elbow into his talkative friend's side; he should be careful, talking that way to uniformed strangers. "But not anything else. What is there to read? But my wife reads, and I know how to say my prayers by heart."

"Does your eight-year-old boy know how to read?"

"The new government schools at Ciego de Avila are making all the children come to learn how to read. It is orders directly from the Comandante. My son will know how to read. Maybe he will know how to read a map that takes him away from the sugar."

Che rose. His face was grave.

It was for this man that he fought. He fought for the socialism that would free this man.

He said nothing to Blackford, and they walked to a house at the other end of the village, a shade stouter than the others. Here, Blackford discovered, they would spend the night. It was not an inn, merely the house where visitors stayed when they came in from neighboring regions to attend a baptism, wedding, or funeral. There were two guest bedrooms, each with a double bed. Che indicated instantly that he would sleep in the living room, so Catalina took her pouch into one room and Blackford his bag into the other. Opposite his door was a deep sink and a mirror. The sink could obviously be used to wash one's face or one's clothes. In his room the sheets were sere but clean. There was a chair and a lamp, and an old dresser. He was hot and wondered about a shower. He opened the door and knocked on Catalina's door, alongside.

"Sí?"

"It's me. Is there a shower, do you know?"

"I do not know. I do not regularly frequent this inn. Why don't you ask Señora Ortiz? Do you know the word for shower? It is *regadera*. The word for bathtub is *tina*. Good luck. And oh, Caimán, please let me know what you find out."

He walked downstairs. Che was nowhere about. He found Señora Ortiz in the kitchen.

"Dispense Ud., señora. Hay regadera? Hay tina?"

He was pleased that she manifestly grasped his question, because she walked out of the back door of the kitchen signaling him to follow her. At the side of the house was a tubular iron protrusion. A few feet away, a pump. She worked the pump for a few minutes, then, stretching out her hand, pulled down on a rusty chain. Water dropped from an overhead sprinkler. Señora Ortiz nodded her head and went back to the kitchen. "There is a towel in your room," she called back.

The dinner was beans and rice and—a specialty for her guests from a hidden supply—some strong coffee, into which Señora Ortiz automatically put a half cup of sugar. She apologized that there was no fruit. "Not for many months have we had fruit," she said.

Che Guevara, after dinner, said only this to Blackford

before taking up his book, a biography of Stendhal: "You must not imagine, if some of the people such as you saw today revolt against the system elsewhere in Latin America, that Fidel Castro has pushed a particular button."

Blackford asked Catalina if she cared to go out for a walk. She readily agreed, and in due course they found themselves at the general store, occupying the same table as before dinner. They talked into the evening, drinking rum sparingly. She would speak in English, sometimes lapsing into Spanish. And Blackford attempted some Spanish, though not with the confidence to which he was entitled, she told him, given his increasing and impressive familiarity with the language.

They talked about Ciego de Avila and life there, and how it might hope to change under Castro. Neither of them sought to make a point. Catalina asked him if it would break the rules if he told her something about his background, and he said that probably a great deal was known about his background back at headquarters, but that beyond his being an agent of the intelligence arm of the United States, what kind of thing did she want to know? And she said she would like to know whether he liked to read, if so what; would like to know if he listened to music, if so what; would like to know if he believed in God, if so why. They left the little cantina-store at midnight, and then only because the owner told them he was shutting down.

Twenty-three

The airplane took them, the following day, to Santiago. The arrival there of Comandante Guevara was a big event, and either Che had consented to address a political rally at the instigation of the local comisionado or else Guevara had initiated the idea.

It was scheduled for twelve o'clock, at the baseball stadium. The plane touched down at 10:30 and Che told Blackford that while he conferred with the City Council, Catalina would take charge of Blackford for a few hours. He was welcome, if he chose, to attend the political rally. Meanwhile he would be taken to a hotel, and was free to do as he liked.

What he liked was first to take a hot bath, then to have a look at the city that had played so important a role during the revolution. But by the time they got to the hotel, went to their rooms and bathed, they needed to go straight to the stadium, Blackford having told Catalina he was anxious to attend the rally.

The stadium was not full—"the meeting was called on short notice," Catalina explained, "and it is not possible for all the surrounding workers to come in." But it was a lively crowd of over ten thousand, and there was a military band playing with gusto via great amplification. There was much gaiety among the crowd, men and women and young people of all ages, dressed mostly in whites, yellows, and khakis, with touches of the colors that were harder for Castro to suppress in remote Santiago than in Havana (he had proscribed, in a recent edict, the practice of color-thread-ing women's white cotton shirts, having read about and admired the uniformity of dress under Mao).

By Cuban standards the ceremonies began promptly, at about 12:35, and there was first an extensive welcoming speech by the mayor. After that a young orator, aged perhaps sixteen, was presented. He had won the oratorical prize at school, and although Blackford had difficulty following him, and it was not easy for Catalina to translate at the pell-mell rate of his delivery, Blackford gathered that it was mostly an encomium to Fidel Castro. Then, changing gears into a hostile mode, the young man threw himself into his oration, fiercely denouncing this and denouncing that in a long anaphoral litany that began, each phrase, with *"Abajo!"*: *Down with* imperialism! *Down with* Yanqui militarism! *Down with* a great many other things—Blackford lost count. But then the upbeat: a testimonial, especially minted for the occasion, to the great Comandante Che Guevara. The crowd cheered for at least five minutes before Che was able to use the microphone.

His oratorical style was quiet, by contrast with that of the young man who introduced him. Very, very quiet by contrast with the recordings Blackford had listened to of Fidel Castro.

Quiet but intensely magnetic. The crowd was silent, never breaking out into spastic cheers and yells as the voice of Che Guevara spun forth its fervent, hypnotic message—more complex, perhaps, than an audience one third illiterate could readily comprehend, but the spell was cast and when, after a half hour, he was finished, he got great applause. Not the same kind of rapturous applause associated with Fidel Castro, but the applause of men and women who had been soberly but profoundly moved.

A children's parade followed, then the Cuban national anthem, *"Al Combate Corred Bayameses"*; and then the mayor again, this time apparently telling the crowd it must not move until their special guest had been provided for. A column of three freshly painted jeeps drove in to the stadium and stopped, their motors still running, by the speakers' platform. Che descended, boarding the middle jeep with the mayor while various dignitaries and guards occupied the first and the third. Then, on a signal from a captain carrying a walkie-talkie, the caravan moved out, the crowd more or less cheering but absorbed primarily with the business of getting out of the stadium. In fact they were restless. There had been nothing passed about to eat or drink during the two hours that had gone by, and they were hungry and thirsty.

Certainly Blackford was. "Where to, Catalina?" he asked. "I would settle for a hot dog. I mean a tamale."

"Tamales are what one eats in Mexico and Texas. Mostly Texas."

"How do you know that?"

"Because I often ate them while I was at the University of Texas in Austin. They call that food Tex-Mex. It is, by the way, very good. In Cuba we do have tamales, but what you want is probably a frita."

"Well what do you say we go to where they have some fritas? I'll treat."

She smiled, and pointed to the jeep (my second home, Blackford thought). They were driven to what appeared to be an office building, but on the top floor was a club for military men and senior civil officials. The cafeteria fare was abundant, providing fish and meats and vegetables and fruit, as well as beer, wine, and something that looked a pale orange, against which Catalina warned. "That is a Soviet orangeade. Goats get sick on it."

They sat down and soon Che came in, and the twenty or thirty officers eating stirred, as if wondering whether to rise to attention. Che, with a wave, put them at ease. He turned to the mayor and said goodbye with terminal inflections and, at this point entirely unencumbered, plunked himself down with Blackford and Catalina.

"Did you understand the speeches?" he asked, his mouth soon full of cheese and crackers.

"Not word for word, but I think I got the gist. You didn't, by any chance, divulge the terms of the agreement we are supposed to be forging?"

Che laughed. "Ah, always you want to get on with it, don't you."

"That is my assignment."

"We would want a limit on the size of United States military missions to countries in Latin America," Che Guevara said casually, placing a slice of ham on a piece of bread.

Blackford drew back. Che kept on eating. He had just made the first formal demand in respect of a hypothetical U.S.–Cuban agreement that Blackford had heard in two weeks' pursuit of the subject. Che's offer (was it an offer? Blackford wondered) was clearly unacceptable.

"Che"—Blackford attempted to speak calmly, and decided to imitate his adversary by putting some guacamole on a saltine and nibbling away at it more or less as he spoke —"we're not here to discuss what the United States contracts to do in Latin America except as far as Cuban–U.S. relations are concerned. If sometime in the future we are asked to send a large military mission to Ecuador or wherever and we agree to do so, what has that got to do with what we're discussing?"

"Well just write that down, Caimán. I don't want you to forget it."

"I won't forget it, Che."

With great speed he changed the subject. "We are going on a trip by helicopter. Right after lunch. You will see the Sierra Maestra, and know something of the conditions of guerrilla warfare. The areas we were in are not so different, in fact they are not different at all, from what they were when we first got here on the *Granma*." And then Che began to talk—about that memorable voyage, about the absence on board of well-qualified seamen, about the storms, the wretched seasickness, about coming up on a stretch of land different from what they had thought they were headed toward, about the ambushes by Batista's men and the deaths, and their struggle, traveling often just two or perhaps three together—even one—to reach various rallying points. "Always Fidel was there, and Frank País, and we learned what it is to make war against the oppressor class from the countryside. That is the key, the countryside. Mao knew that." Che Guevara's eyes were bright, but he was not lost in any reverie. He was simply being the effective host, communicating to the CIA agent Caimán, whose real name Che Guevara had temporarily forgotten, something of the excitement of twelve desperate idealists with a providential light shining down on their fortunes from overhead, taking on a dictator who had forty thousand men under arms. Blackford commented only that it must all indeed have been very exciting. "There is no doubting that what you accomplished is legendary."

The helicopter let them down on a field near the village of La Plata. "This was one of the first villages we came to control," Che said as they walked toward it. Children and a few herdsmen tending goats, pigs, and sheep stopped to look at the helicopter, even though they had become tolerably familiar with helicopters, but they ignored the three figures that stepped out of it. A few recognized Comandante Che and waved at him, but did not seem to take his appearance as in any way phenomenal; no more would they have taken as entirely unexpected the appearance of Fidel Castro. These were mountain people, and the passions of the hot country were not, in them, so easily stimulated.

At La Plata there was a memorial building. It had been erected on the site of the hut Fidel had used as a headquarters, off and on, for five months during 1957 and 1958. To it had been taken such world celebrities as Anastas

Mikoyan, Jean-Paul Sartre, Simone de Beauvoir, and Pablo Neruda. It had several guest rooms and a permanent staff of a half-dozen Cubans charged with looking after it and, on those very special occasions, its very special visitors.

They were given rooms. Che told Blackford he would take him on a walk. To Catalina he said that the ground was rough, that perhaps he and Blackford could manage to communicate with each other with their pooled knowledge of each other's languages if she desired to stay at the guest house.

In Spanish Catalina spoke very sharply to Che. Blackford caught something to the effect that women are every something something something as men and he damned well had something something every reason to know this. She spoke stormily and censoriously, and Che was visibly cowed. So the three of them set out.

The air was cool at the high altitude, and Che led them first down a tiny trail—rocky, clammy, weedy, wet. The rains fell copiously, and often, on the Sierra Maestra. They found it necessary to hang on to limbs or small tree trunks to keep from sliding uncontrollably down the barely discernible trail, maintained by the occasional shepherds who used it, at an angle of incline surprisingly steep. "This is difficult to do even as we are doing it," Che commented. "You can imagine how it is to come down this trail with a rifle and supplies. I must have used this trail one hundred times during those early months in 1957."

He stopped suddenly. At a distance of about two hundred yards Blackford could make out a traversing dirt road, only just wide enough for a car to chug along it.

"This spot is special for me," Che said, sitting down on the ground, Catalina beside him, Blackford standing, one hand on the branch of a ceiba tree, his heels dug in to maintain his balance. "This was my first time. It was here that, as the French say, I was *défloré*. It was a lone sentry. There were only a half dozen of them patrolling this road between Niquero and La Plata, each of them with a walkie-talkie—and oh how badly we wanted those radios because our communications system was, well, it was nothing. Fidel had said to us, Get the radios. And he said, If in order to get the radios you need to kill the soldiers, by all means do so.

"I had just reached this point, and I saw the sentry"—he pointed to the little road visible through the trees, perhaps a hundred-foot stretch of it. "He was walking very slowly, in fact he had paused and was just standing there, smoking a cigarette, and I knew the moment had come, so I sat down. Exactly where I am right now. Exactly here." He raised his left arm, opening his hand into a crotch as if cradling the fore end of a rifle. He cocked his head over, closed his left eye, and raised his right hand, trigger finger extended. "I got him in my telescopic sight. The cross hairs I placed first in the center of his head, but thought better of it—too risky, might miss, better to aim for his chest, a broader target. The moment came to squeeze the trigger. It did not come to me automatically. I had to will it. I did. I learned that one has to will a revolution. It is only because we willed it that we won Cuba." He continued sitting for a moment.

Blackford said nothing, but nothing was expected of him. Che got up and continued the descent, and now the trail moved laterally and it was possible to walk without struggling against gravity. "We would patrol these little lanes, and recruit our volunteers, and make friends with the villagers, who would give us supplies. In return, we gave them our protection. Before long we were effectively in charge. First of a small area, then of a larger area. It was only then that the military operations began, like El Hombrito and Mar Verde.

"Now, my dear Caimán, you see it is not guaranteed that guerrillas will succeed. But the Cuban example is much admired by a great many lean and hungry men and women who thirst for social justice. And how can you, or President Kennedy, expect that such uprisings will not occur? And when they do, are you going to come to the conclusion that they were engineered by Fidel Castro?"

This was not the ideal ambience in which to draw fine lines, Blackford thought. Perhaps that night, perhaps after supper . . . Indeed it had grown, suddenly, quite dark. Catalina was the first to remark on it. "Che, we must be a good three kilometers from La Plata. It will be black in twenty minutes."

Che smiled as he lit a little cigar. "I do not need light to find my way across this range. Follow me first," he said to Catalina, "and when you can no longer see me, follow my cigar glow." They ambled, and then climbed, and then groped their way back, finally, to the cottage, where a Major Hernández was waiting anxiously to give Comandante Guevara a most urgent message. He flashed a light so that Che could read it there and then. He did so, and said in Spanish to the major's aide, "Go inside and bring my brief-case. Leave my bag." He spoke then to Catalina in rapid-fire Spanish. And then, through Catalina, to Blackford.

"It is important. Fidel wants to see me. I will be in Havana by midnight and will see him then, and I will be back here tomorrow. Catalina will take care of you."

Five minutes later, Comandante Che Guevara was airborne in his helicopter. A half hour after that, Blackford and Catalina were eating dinner in the memorial building, sitting side by side at a table designed to promote a view through the large plate-glass window Castro had ordered built to view the valley, seen by him so furtively for so long, where for so long the enemy was in control and men were killed, day after day.

"I am required to admit that it is a remarkable story," Blackford said.

"Which has not ended," said Catalina.

"No, it has not ended," Blackford said. And to himself he began, for the first time, to wonder: In objective fact, was Che Guevara a friend of the Cuban people?

For the second night in a row he and Catalina sat alone, talking, and drinking now the cold beer that sat in such copious quantity in the large silver container of ice that had been left after dinner to one side of the table. They spoke more directly than the night before about the revolution, and about its aims. Blackford dared to touch on his reservations. And Catalina did as much, her reservations having nothing to do with socialism but much to do with Sovietization, as she put it, but always in Spanish, *sovietización*, the word's formation lending itself so readily to the orderly processes by which some words begin first as simple nouns, then stretch forward into a verb, leap past the gerund into metastasis. Soviet, sovietize, sovietization. It was happening to Cuba, she whispered, and Che is aware of it. That, she said, is why he is so anxious, so anxious about this— initiative with you. But he cannot move faster than Fidel will allow him to move. So much depends on—your patience. And the patience of—her eyes were open wide—our President. "You see," Catalina smiled, "actually I am technically an American, because I was born in Texas. My father was at Fort Sam Houston taking training. But my loyalty is to Cuba, my parents' birthplace."

Blackford said "our" President would be as patient as he was permitted to be.

They went upstairs. There was a moment of hesitation as they parted to go to their respective bedrooms. Just a moment. And Blackford went on to his bed, excited in mind and body.

Twenty-four

They breakfasted together, and talked vaguely about what they would do pending Che's return. "We covered all that is especially interesting in the area yesterday," Catalina said. "I mean, there are a hundred thousand hectares of the same sort of thing on the Sierra Maestra, or maybe a million hectares—I'm not good at that kind of thing. But to make it interesting to go farther on other trails, you'd need to have someone along who had been there on the campaign. And there are not many left. Or . . . available."

"You are referring to Huber Matos?"

"Yes. A name we do not mention. He is a nonperson. It was a very quick journey, from revolutionary hero and boss of Camagüey—to his resignation—to charges of treason—to twenty years in prison."

"What exactly was the charge against him?"

"It was exactly that, treason. Raúl wanted him executed. Fidel thought about it, thought about it quite a long while in fact, and decided he should be sentenced instead to twenty years."

"Why?"

"Fidel Castro never says why. He simply decides. He is not particularly oracular or melodramatic about it—I mean when he's talking to the inner circle, Che tells me—he just decides, and that is it. He does not like the growing prominence of any of his confederates, and Huber Matos as the military and civil head of Camagüey was growing in prestige and resisting some of Havana's orders, for instance to get on with the executions. So he resigned. Nobody resigns from Castro's legions."

"But isn't Che big, in the sense you say Castro does not like people around him to grow big?"

"Che Guevara is an institution. He is also an Argentine. More even than Castro, he is the Latin-American symbol of radical socialism. It would not be easy to do away with Che, or to do without him. But who knows, one of these days?"

"And Raúl?"

"Raúl is the original Stalinist. Sometimes I think even Fidel is afraid of him. To eliminate Raúl would require direct, Mafia-style skulduggery. You could not haul him up in court and accuse him of treason. Cubans are not much given to fratricide. But you watch, you watch. Not only will Fidel prevail, but Raúl, little by little, will become less prominent."

"Does Che actively oppose what you persist in calling *sovietización?*"

"Not openly. And he recognizes the continuing military threat from the United States, and he knows that that requires defensive armament. But as Minister of Industry above all he needs what only the Soviets are sending us right now."

"What's that?"

"Everything. I mean, everything they can spare. Raw materials, mostly. And some dollars. These are precious, because with them Che can buy from Canada, and Europe, and Latin America." Catalina forced herself to smile. "Your imperialist dollar is very much in demand. You smile. So were the gold pieces of the Caesars. Dollars buy food. They also buy explosives. And drugs. And invasions of Cuba."

"Churchill had a more amiable way of putting that, Catalina, when he was fighting the nazis. He said to us, 'Give us the tools and we will do the job.' The fighting at the Bay of Pigs was done by Cubans."

"And obviously there weren't enough of them."

"It would be interesting to know what would be the vote for Castro in the event of free elections."

Catalina was silent. "Castro has been very popular ever since you invaded our country."

"Presumably less so with people he has imprisoned. Or, for that matter, shot. And then there are others, no? Who have lost, or are losing, the same freedoms they lost under Batista? And resenting it?"

Catalina got up from the bench with her coffee cup and went to the coffee urn on the side table.

"Has this trip taught you nothing? What are the freedoms those sugarcane workers have enjoyed? It is always so easy to isolate this poet or that philosopher or that editorial writer who has lost his freedom to stand in the way of a revolution designed to help not so much individual poets but five million peasant families."

"Shall we knock it off?"

"If you like."

"It's the Soviet angle, and only that, that you care about?"

"There is hardly any point in winning a revolution against the United States and its puppet dictators and then turning over the country to the Soviet Union. That has not happened, but that is exactly what threatens."

Major Hernández walked into the living room of the guest house, removing his hat. He spoke to Catalina, and Blackford understood what he said, or most of it. Che Guevara would not in fact be back today, not until tomorrow. The major had been directed to escort them on a helicopter trip. Hernández turned and walked out.

"Where?" Blackford asked Catalina.

"I am not absolutely certain. I'll find out. I expect we will be seeing where the *Granma* landed, and something of the itinerary of the 26th of July men during those early months. It will be interesting—I haven't made such a trip myself—if that is what is in store for us."

It was indeed such a trip, another ride in the helicopter, gliding over the mountain ranges of the Sierra Maestra toward the southern shore of the long, eel-shaped island and out over the water. Heeling the helicopter over to give them a better view through the cockpit window, Major Hernández pointed out, just below, three naval ships: destroyers, in formation, heading toward the island. "American destroyers," Hernández said over the propeller noise. "Going to Guantánamo." If he needed to parachute home any time soon, Blackford mused, this would clearly be the place.

They saw it all. Well, not exactly all, because "all" could not be seen from a helicopter. "All" meant days and nights in jungles and mountains, fighting mosquitoes and snakes and hunger and Batista's soldiers. You cannot get an overview of a twenty-five-month-long struggle, Blackford thought, from a helicopter, useful though it was. He saw the beach, the famous Playa Colorada where the *Granma* let off its bedraggled and thoroughly incompetent graduate-student revolutionaries, and then the foothills where more than three quarters of them were killed. Blackford would not impugn the heroism that had taken place in the area over which the little helicopter flew.

They stopped at Holguín for a brief lunch served up by the mess hall that fed the four dozen air force personnel stationed there, and Blackford shut his eyes wondering how much of what he was at that moment experiencing was different from what it would have been five years ago under Batista, and just exactly how.

Major Hernández asked Blackford, Would he be interested in seeing a collective citrus plantation begun at the orders of Che Guevara? Mostly to be polite, Blackford said Yes, knowing just the kind of thing he would be seeing. Which was what he saw. He could not gauge exactly the spirit of the workers—whether they thought themselves engaged in a great communal enterprise, whether they were better off than before, whether, for them, Castro was a godsend or simply another caudillo with unconventional ideas. Suddenly he thought to ask:

"Where do they go to church?"

The Director de Producción greeted the query apprehensively, consulting in rapid Spanish with Major Hernández. Priests had gone to jail, some had been exiled, religious festivals were outlawed. But churchgoing had not been prohibited, and the director was inadequately briefed on exactly the formula that was appropriate in addressing Sr. Caimán, who had been introduced simply as "an American guest of Comandante Guevara." He had all along supposed that no guest of Comandante Guevara would be less than enthusiastic about anything Comandante Guevara had instigated, but the question was troubling because in fact no funds had been provided for the construction of a church. Would Major Hernández wish this to be divulged, or was there, well, an evasive way of putting it? Blackford was developing an ear for even quite rapid Spanish, and he got the drift of his host's problem.

Major Hernández was clipped in his reply. "A church has not been constructed yet. A priest comes in and says Mass in the recreation room." He returned to a discussion of quotas, and how they had all been exceeded every month for the past five months. Somehow the religious question had chilled the discussion, and soon they were back in the helicopter, and, by five, back at the memorial building in La Plata.

They had been hot and dusty, though the mountain air quickly cooled them. Inside the guest house, Catalina suggested they dine at seven.

In his room, Blackford bathed, and was surprised to find on the shelf in his bathroom, where he had laid out his razor and toothbrush, a bottle of cologne. Had it been there the night before, without his noticing it? Unlikely, he thought, though he didn't remember for sure. He did not use cologne, but he opened the bottle with curiosity, squirted a few drops on the back of his left hand and lifted it to his nose. For an insane moment he hallucinated that he was in Paris, at a bordello. In Paris at a bordello! Was he going mad?

He went to his bed and lay down on it and closed his eyes, attempting to define the political configuration of the past week. He decided he would need to go back to Washington. He had learned a great deal, but in learning as much as he had he knew that what he needed to know most profoundly was eluding him. He needed from Washington official guidance. Needed, also, an update on what the CIA had learned from its own regular sources during the past month. For instance, about the Cuban economy, and the extent of the flow of Russian economic aid.

His mind turned to Catalina. University of Texas. Born in San Antonio and schooled in Austin. Yet thoroughly Cuban, thoroughly the Castroite, whatever her reservations about the Soviet Union. Was she a *tricoteuse* in the making? Would she shed those traces of liberalism—worrying, for instance, about the Russian bear—that, at this high-strung moment in Cuban-American relations, caused her to worry about *sovietización*? Was she a mistress of Comandante Che? There was so little that was sensual, he thought, about the Castro revolution. Operation P, to eliminate the prostitutes. Even the nationalization of the indigenous little kiosks. The public frowning on the Cuban dance-all-night fiestas. Were there still links, unbreakable, to her experiences at that oasis of liberalism in Texas, the University at Austin, whose undergraduates had voted, he recalled from something or other, in overwhelming majority for Kennedy, against Nixon? How was it that she had caused to stir so throbbingly those juices in him, not abnormal in a bachelor in his middle thirties; but normal biological impulses he managed, in most professional relations, to contain?

Was Che's absence preplanned? Was he getting from Catalina more than she was getting from him? But what could she, in fact, get from Blackford, other than that which was officially known, namely that the President of the United States was acting on an initiative of Guevara made last August?

He meditated on her mind, and then lazily allowed his curiosity to extend to her body, fastidiously garbed whether she was wearing skirts, pants, or sportswear. He permitted this to go on until he knew he had to force his mind to other things, and this he could not manage in the privacy of his own room, so he got up quickly, put on a fresh pair of khaki pants and a sport shirt, and pulled out of his suitcase a sweater he had never thought, while sweating in Havana, he would need. But now he was glad for the warmth. And then, although it was not yet seven, he opened his door and went down to the large luxurious living room, inside from the glass-fronted dining room, and looked at the bookcase, but could not find a *novela policiaca* by Agatha Christie. He settled for *The Major Speeches of Fidel Castro, January 1959–March 1959*, and began to read them. Fidel Castro was talking about freedom and orderly government and the promise of free elections. Blackford sighed. His Spanish was still so primitive, he was under the illusion he was reading John Stuart Mill. And then Catalina came down the stairs.

She was wearing a light lavender dress and high heels, and a tiny pearl necklace, and as she joined him, coincidental with the arrival of a white-jacketed waiter with a tray of daiquiris, she leaned her head forward just that suggestive little bit that demands a social kiss on the forehead, which he gave her, and he smelled the cologne.

They sat down and were served their drinks, with Mariquitas, fried green banana chips, the Cuban equivalent of Fritos. "You are looking very lovely tonight, Catalina," he said.

"That is the kind of thing they would say in Texas," she answered.

"What's so bad about Texas?" Blackford wanted to know. "They beat the Mexicans, didn't they, and colonized great stretches of America that had once been Mexican territory?"

"Yes," she said, raising her glass to her lips. "Santa Ana was no Fidel Castro."

They lay, three hours later, in bed. During the overtures under the sheets she had begun to giggle, and then laughed softly, and rebuked the moon's invasion of their privacy. She said that when, briefly after Operation P, she had been made to serve as an interrogator in the large schoolhouse that had been taken over as an administrative center, an aging madame was ushered into her little classroom who in her younger years, she whispered to Catalina, had been the prize lady of the Cuban streets. "I used to charge *one hundred dollars,*" she said. "And that was way back. In 1950! Imagine *one hundred dollars in 1950!*" Catalina had merely continued, asking the stipulated questions and filling out the form, as required: she had been warned by the colonel that bribery would almost certainly be attempted, by the pimps especially. Arcadia was not a pimp, but she was not without resources, and she had said to Catalina that in exchange for gentle treatment in the questionnaire (gentle treatment would diminish her rank from madame to mere prostitute, prostitutes receiving lesser punishments) she, Arcadia, would agree to tell Catalina what were one or two of the special arts she had perfected in her long career, "which will turn your lover into your slave, adoring you forever, for the great, the unique pleasure you give him."

Greatly to her surprise, Catalina said as she fondled her lover, she had impulsively told Arcadia to go ahead, to tell her—no one else was in the room—which she proceeded to do, most graphically.

"Would you like me to do what Arcadia taught?"

"That depends."

"On what?" she giggled.

"On whether I shall become your slave, as Arcadia said. On how many men have you tried Arcadia's magic?"

"Oh," Catalina giggled, "maybe just one, or two. Three, not more."

"Well?"

"Well what?" Catalina was stroking him now . . .

"Well, did they become your slaves?"

"Well, let me think. Hmm. Yes as to . . . one. Yes as to . . . two. The third was shot, so I didn't have a chance to find out."

"Well, how can I risk it, becoming your slave?"

"You are much more beautiful than they, so perhaps you will escape becoming my slave. Why don't you take a chance?"

He laughed, and kissed her. And she proceeded to initiate him in the arcadian mysteries, with delirious effect.

Later they lay together, silently. Blackford told her she was very beautiful and very loving. He undertook to name all the beautiful parts of her full body in Spanish, starting with her brown hair—*cabello color de café, muy fino, muy bonito*—and working down, slowly, until his vocabulary ran out, just where he desired to praise her most, and he cursed the limitations of Agatha Christie. After an interval Blackford rose and reached about for the light dressing gown he had in his suitcase. He did not want to turn on the light, so he dragged the suitcase into the moonlight, found it, and put it on.

"Where are you going?"

"To bring my slavemaster something to drink."

"Bring me a cold beer."

"Very well."

"It will be where it was last night."

He descended the stairs. The dim lights in the large

living room were still lit, but no one stirred. With the beers he rose again, and gave her a glass, sitting down in the chair beside the bed.

"Are you a Mata Hari?"

"What is a Mata Hari?"

"Oh my God. And you are a graduate of the University of Texas. Or claim to be. And you do not know who Mata Hari was?"

"Come on, who was she?"

"Let me see, where shall we start. Do you know who Cleopatra was?"

"Caimán, tell me who Mata Hari was or I shall have you shot."

"You can't do that."

"Why not?"

"President Kennedy would invade you."

"I bet he wouldn't invade me if I taught him Arcadia's secrets."

"Aha. Good point. Although that is precisely why he would want to invade you. I'll throw that in."

"Throw that in what?"

"In the package I am negotiating with Comandante Che. On top of the other Cuban concessions, you throw in Arcadia for the President."

"Who was Mata Hari?"

"Mata Hari was a very famous spy during World War I. Maybe I shouldn't say she was very famous, if you never even heard of her. Let's say she used to be famous, and thirty-five-year-olds like myself know who she was. She vamped important French officials, and got secrets from them which she gave to the Germans."

"What does that have to do with me?"

"Nothing. I hope."

"You haven't told me any secrets. Yet. Won't you tell me just one secret, in return for Arcadia?"

Blackford got up and slid into bed again. "All right, I'll

tell you something nobody else knows. Not even Mr. Velasco. Not even President Kennedy. Not even the head of the CIA. Not even Che Guevara."

"What?" she laughed.

"I am going back to Washington."

"When? For how long?"

"As soon as I can. Of course I intend to come back to Havana. And Che, as you know, has made it clear he wants me here. But then we are all at the mercy of Fidel, are we not?"

"Yes," she said. "But do not underestimate Che Guevara. Other people have."

"And they are all dead?"

"Not all of them. Arcadia is just fine."

"Viva," he said, invading her anew, "Arcadia."

"Viva Arcadia, my dear Caimán."

Twenty-five

Blackford was not entirely surprised when, just after breakfast the following morning, Major Hernández advised them that, unhappily, Comandante Guevara had radioed that he was delayed further, indeed that he could not even be sure he would be free to be with them on the following day, that he was held up in Havana on important national business and he recommended that Caimán fly back to Havana. Major Hernández said that the message emphasized that "there would be plenty for Sr. Caimán to do in Havana."

"Major, are you in a position to communicate directly with Comandante Guevara?"

"I can certainly get a message to him, and would expect a reply by radio here, or by telephone at Santiago."

"All right, here's what you're to do. Radio the Comandante and tell him that Mr. Caiman needs to return to Washington. Ask him kindly to make whatever arrangements are necessary to pass through the Northeast Gate at Guantánamo. You take us on the helicopter to the Santiago base and arrange to have someone there take me to Guantánamo. Either the base commander or his representative can tell me after we land there what arrangements have been made."

Catalina relayed all of this, and Major Hernández's head nodded as he took notes. He knew the voice of authority, and assumed in any case that Comandante Che's special guest would not be asking for something the Comandante would not readily provide.

"And oh yes, Major Hernández. In your radio report, kindly instruct the Havana office that I shall need to speak, from Santiago, by telephone with my assistant, Señor Velasco. Major Joe Bustamente is in charge of Mr. Velasco, who is staying at El Comodoro. A telephone can be plugged in to him, and he should be advised to expect my call."

In twenty minutes they were packed and in the helicopter, the blades swirled and it began a grudging rise. A hundred yards up, the pilot tilted the aircraft on its side and Blackford looked down at the village with the conspicuous guest house at the edge of it. He wondered whether, at Yenan, Mao Tse-tung had set up something comparable. The spot from which he had set out to capture China. Probably. Professor Karl Wittfogel had written about the "megalomania of the aging despot." Self-commemoration is popular among tyrants. And ex-presidents are not altogether immune.

It was an hour's ride and Blackford was surprised, on being taken to the headquarters of the base, to find that the commanding officer had already received a reply from Havana. It was, first, a clearance to be driven to Guantánamo. Then a message that a telephone call to Mr. Velasco would be put through any time.

"And finally, Sr. Caimán, the Comandante desires to speak to you himself over the telephone."

"Now?"

"I have two numbers. If it is convenient for you to speak to him now, he advises me he will be at one of those numbers. Would you care to take my office? I will stay here. You need merely pick up the telephone that rings."

Blackford turned to Catalina. "Explain to him we'll need an extension phone for your interpreting." This she relayed, and it was arranged that the secretary's telephone could come in on the same line.

Five minutes later Blackford was interrupted from his study of the huge detailed air map of Cuba behind the commander's desk by the telephone's ringing. He picked it up. He heard Catalina, sitting at the desk outside, say over her line, "He's coming to the telephone." And then the voice of Che Guevara:

"Caimán, how are you?"

"I am well, Comandante. I am sorry you were not here to complete our tour. But I think I picked up some of what you wished me to learn."

"Why is it that you need to go back to Washington?"

"I need to get the feel of things there. It has been weeks since this enterprise began, and we have not made much headway."

"You are not doubting the seriousness of my interest, Caimán?"

"No. But the idea of this agreement is to get on with things before certain other things—you will understand me, I know—become irreversible. I need to know what kind of tempo is okay back there, and that's not the kind of thing you can get from a cable."

"I understand. I simply did not want to think that you were discouraged by the delays. Cubans always delay. It is their—our—nature. When do you expect to return?"

"I would hope within a week. Now listen: It may be that they will want some specific answers in Washington before I return. If that is the case, I will communicate with the Swiss ambassador, and he can reach Velasco without any problem, right?"

"Of course."

"And Velasco, is he making progress on the evaluations?"

"Ah, alas, Caimán, not yet, not yet. You see, Señor Velasco had an accident."

Blackford stiffened. He felt a pang in his stomach. He spoke slowly.

"What kind of an accident?"

"Well, three men who were friends of the code clerk at the Swiss Embassy—I forget his name, the one who was killed—were stupid enough to suspect that your friend Velasco was the killer, even though they had been told that that was impossible, that Mr. Velasco was at your cottage during that whole period, nursing a bad stomach. Anyway, they grabbed him on the street two days ago, at a moment when Joe Bustamente was momentarily distracted, took him into a building, and gave him—I am afraid to say—a most severe beating. But then," Blackford could hear Che sigh over the telephone, "I guess all we should say is that he was lucky he wasn't killed."

Blackford felt the sweat on his brow. He could manage only to say, "Is he all right?"

"Oh, he will be quite all right. In about a week. About when you get back. They are taking very good care of him at the hospital."

This Blackford knew he had to say, and he did what he could to resonate indignation. "And the fucking bully-boys?"

"Ah, they will be most severely dealt with, leave that to me."

"Can I talk with Velasco?"

"I am afraid not. Not for a few days. His jaw, you see, is wired, but the stitches, I am told, will be removed in three or four days . . . Well, as you gringos say, Caimán, Godspeed, and I will welcome you back on your mission. The Swiss ambassador will know how to reach my office. A word now, if I may, with Catalina. *Hasta luego, Caimán.*"

Twenty-six

At Guantánamo, after Washington had been consulted, Blackford was put on a naval plane that went cautiously out to sea ten miles, then turned east until it was twenty-five miles past the eastern point of Cuba, and then headed, having given Castro Cuba a berth several times wider than international law requires, for Miami. There Blackford caught a commercial plane to Washington. For several hours he was tormented by the thought of Velasco. But ten years' professional experience tamped down his turbulence, and he found himself predominantly grateful—that Velasco had not been simply shot. After all, he was apparently guilty not only of eliminating a very useful Cuban mole. He was guilty of murder. Murder was illegal even under Batista.

He was forced, finally and fondly, to grin. He was prepared to bet that Velasco was doing the same thing, assuming he could do so, athwart all that wiring in his jaw. Velasco owed his life to his having been in Cuba under the auspices of an understanding between Che Guevara and the President of the United States. It was that simple. He wondered —though the curiosity here was entirely professional— what Che would have done if he had been able to *prove* that Velasco was guilty. And, he suspected, Che Guevara, in doing what he had done to Velasco, in the way he did it, had been communicating to Blackford Oakes. Along the lines of: *Do not play with me, Caimán.* At the same time he expected that Guevara was understanding and, again professionally, admiring of what Velasco had done. It was, after all, hardly in the spirit of the general Guevara-Goodwin-Kennedy-

Oakes agreement that copies of Blackford's private communications to the White House and the Director of the CIA should be passed on to Guevara.

Although it was November, it wasn't cold in Washington. Still, he could almost feel the winter straining to assert itself. He went directly to Georgetown, to an address he had got over the telephone in Miami, and rang the bell. The door was opened by Rufus.

Blackford knew that Rufus was made chronically uncomfortable by any sign whatever of sentiment, and Blackford consciously abused him when, perhaps once a year, he embraced him with a bear hug. But it happened that he felt that way about him. And Rufus, though he would never permit himself to show it, was always happiest when working with Blackford; content, also, in his company.

"The Director will be here any minute now. Do you want to start in? No, let's wait. How are you? Sit down, Blackford."

"Well, among other things I'm anxious to know what's been going on. You can imagine how much news I was able to pick up in Cuba. There's a lot I understand now about the Cuban revolution. What's happening on the international front?"

Rufus told him that he would find the last several issues of *Time* magazine in his bedroom, and, of course, Blackford's beloved *National Review*. That as far as Cuba was concerned, the exchanges continued: the hostility of Castro for the United States was pronounced, and his ardor for things Soviet seemed to grow. David Lawrence had got hold of a State Department document and published its content in his newspaper column in the *Herald Tribune*. And he got it right. It said there were over three hundred Russian and Czech military technicians in Cuba.

"How did State know that?"

"From us. We're not without assets in Cuba, as you know. Even though you don't know who they are. And won't."

"I've got a report for you on that, by the way. If a lot of our assets to whom you were communicating via the Swiss ambassador have been strangely silent, you will know why when I'm through briefing you."

Rufus paused. And then went on. "At the OAS conference of foreign ministers at Punta del Este just a couple of weeks ago we picked up word that as many as one hundred MIG fighters may be in Cuba right now and that a lot more of that kind of thing is coming in. The *National Observer*—and I don't know where *they* got this—reported that twenty-five to thirty Soviet-bloc vessels per month are steaming into Havana bringing arms."

"So things are warming up?"

"That's what makes the success of your mission increasingly improbable."

It was at this point that the Director came in.

And it was two hours after that that Rufus and Blackford went out for a late dinner, talking as old friends and confederates. And then, the next morning, the Director called Blackford's number at the safe house and told him he would be picked up by a driver at 11:52, that he was to accompany the driver, who would say only, "Good morning. It is warm for November."

Between 12:05 and 12:55 Blackford was in the Situation Room of the White House with the Director, Rufus, the National Security Adviser, and the President.

After Blackford and Rufus had left the White House with the National Security Adviser the President was silent, rocking back and forth in his chair. He didn't feel like talking, but he wanted the Director to stay in the room. The Director caught the mood and said nothing, leafing through a notebook. Finally the President spoke.

"What've we got to lose? Maybe we should—just slightly —deinstitutionalize the thing. You know what I mean?"

"Withdraw the presidential mandate?"

"Can't go that far, I shouldn't think. That would torpedo the whole thing. We'd lose Guevara."

Again he stopped and thought. Then stood up.

"Send him back. We'll figure out something. Maybe have it both ways. That's the best way, it seems to me, having it both ways. Let me think about it. Anyway, go ahead and send him back. Wait a few days—never a bad idea. But let's plan to have him back in Havana in, say, one week. That Velasco thing is fascinating. Bobby will like that."

"The Attorney General knows?"

"The Attorney General knows everything. Shouldn't an Attorney General know everything? After all, John, he may have to prosecute you over this business, one of these days. That would be an awful shame, with your fine record. I'll slip him the word, if that happens, to find a nice, low-security penitentiary for you, John. With a private chapel." He waved his hand at him. "Let's agree. Top top security on this business."

"Yes, Mr. President."

"Good day, John."

Most awfully long day this has been, with conferences, God how many conferences you need to have around this place, though I like very much the conference that plotted a very long trip away from Washington for Lyndon. God, Washington is a reposeful place without Lyndon underfoot. Reposeful place—What a stuffy phrase. Wonder, come to think of it, if the word "reposeful" exists. Well, if I use it, it will exist ex officio. Call the Librarian of Congress, whatshisname, tell him: From now on, reposeful is a word. That comes from the highest quarters. What are the highest quarters? Well, the highest quarters are so high, ma'am, we can't identify them. But take my word for it, the word reposeful now exists, highest quarters..

Oakes has a real case on Guevara. Wonder what he's like. What's going on there, between him and Castro? Could they really just be raising the ante? It's possible. I like Oakes's suggestion about the shopping list. Nice idea—ask Che what exactly he would want from us if the big deal went through. *Interesting. Oakes never lets you doubt he knows where the authority is but he does his own thinking. I like that.*

I'll let it go forward. But careful at this end. That's the problem. Give Oakes "authority" to go ahead and explore his hunch. But at this end what we don't want is a Read All About It/JFK Secret Commission to Castro to Discuss Economic Aid and Full Recognition —maybe ten minutes after Castro has dynamited the Panama Canal or something. It's a question of making that rug under Oakes's feet real slippery. I gotta have a little tug-line. Just in case.

Wonder if Oakes has any extracurricular interests in Havana. I mean, it wouldn't be normal if he didn't have. At thirty-whatever he is, he couldn't have sown all his wild oats. I bet he manufactures them faster than our GNP growth, which reminds me, Dillon wants that nudged a bit, why not? Next November isn't the ideal time to find us in a recession. Bright fellow, Dillon.

Hell yes, let Oakes go, see what happens. But we'll see. We'll see-ee/In Glo-cca Mor--ra. No, that's not how it goes. But it is reposeful. We'll see-ee/In Glocca Mor--ra.

Twenty-seven

Blackford's route to Havana took him, as before, through Guantánamo, but he flew rather than going by boat as that idiot at Operations had specified on the first passage. The same old aircraft took him to Havana, but this time he arrived in the late afternoon, and found his heart beating as the driver approached the Walden-Hilton. He did not bother to take his own bag out of the jeep—the driver could damn well bring it in. He was dogtrotting when he got around to the back of the cottage, and on spotting Alejandro his spirits soared. If Alejandro was there, so would Cecilio be there. He shook Alejandro's hand and went in. The sitting room was empty. He went to Velasco's bedroom and knocked.

"*Pase.*"

Velasco was lying in bed, propped up on two pillows. His face broke into as wide a smile as his damaged muscles could manage. Blackford went to the bed and grabbed Velasco's hand, lifting his lit cigarette out of Velasco's mouth and perching it on the ashtray. He took the bedside lamp and trained it on Velasco's face. The bruises were everywhere, but they were mending, had become brownish in color with striations of blue. The left eye was fully open, the right eye still half closed. Blackford reached for a chair and drew it to the bedside.

"They gave it to you, eh, Cecilio?"

Velasco pointed to the portable radio on the bedside table. Blackford flicked it on, fished out a local chachacha station, turned up the volume, came closer to Velasco and lowered his voice. "Is the rest of you as bad as your face?"

Velasco managed his smile, and lowered the sheet to his waist. They hadn't neglected his body. Blackford pointed to the crotch. "There too?"

"There especially."

Blackford sighed. "I guess you're going to have to go a little easier on the next code clerk. Which reminds me, I wonder whether de Keller got himself another mole?"

"I think I was able to see to that."

"How?"

"Before they got me, I was able to contact one of our— assets. Someone I happened to know. Gave him the word— to get to de Keller and tell him Nogales had been done in by a resistance Cuban who had discovered Nogales was a double agent. De Keller raised hell, apparently Berne raised hell. They've insisted on sending an old-timer right from Berne to take over the communications job. Nogales's successor will be okay."

"Well, that's good. We're going to be using that link a lot, I'd guess, in the next few days, or weeks, or months, or however long this damn thing is going to take. Can you walk?"

"Yes. Slowly."

"Well, good, *viejo*. It's cocktail time and I think we ought to resume our convention and have our drinks on the beach. Come to think of it, I could use a swim."

He helped Cecilio Velasco up, brought him his bathrobe, put on his own after getting into his swimming trunks. He wondered whether it would be possible to transport to the beach in a single trip two chairs, a bottle of rum, a can of orange juice, ice, a towel, the radio, and Velasco. But he gave up. He went with Velasco and a single chair to the beachfront, then returned for the second chair, the radio, and the refreshments. Alejandro kept his distance and Blackford poured the drinks, dived into the sea, came back, sat down, and told Velasco everything that had happened.

Twenty-eight

It was July.

Blackford Oakes had kept count. He had been with Ernesto "Che" Guevara thirty-five times during the nine-month negotiation. Sometimes the meetings were brief, at the cottage. Sometimes he traveled with Che. ("I find I have most spare time when I am away from Havana. We can talk without interruption in the evenings, and sometimes in the late afternoons.") Blackford had accepted the custom that Velasco would stay on in Havana, but always Catalina was with them, as interpreter when Blackford and Che did not understand each other but, increasingly, also as collaborator.

And sometimes they met elsewhere in Havana, at one of Che's many offices. On such occasions there was usually a specialist or two at hand to help with what was turning out to be almost endless paperwork. Late in April, in part for the hell of it, in part to make it easier to get about, Blackford grew a beard. His Nordic eyes and features and the strains of blond in his hair had made him conspicuously a foreigner. When his beard was full he found he could walk about, as often as not, without attracting attention. He was not surprised that on Day 4, Che had commented that Caimán was evidently a postulant revolutionary, but that his beard had a long way to travel before he might consider himself baptized into socialism. But on Day 14 Che suggested that perhaps a religious ceremony was now appropriate, to which Blackford had replied that he did not attend black masses, causing Che to reply that he did not attend masses whether black or white or technicolored.

"What do you call those things they do in front of Lenin's tomb?" Blackford asked. "Orgies," said Che, cutting off the exchange.

He was given freedom of movement, but always with an escort. Joe Bustamente was his constant companion. But Bustamente was a worldly man, and when Blackford visited with Catalina would discreetly disappear at the door of the apartment house, inquiring approximately when Blackford would be ready to return to the cottage, which as often as not was the following morning. Blackford kept Joe supplied with fresh ten-dollar bills "to buy presents for your children." Always, on the next day, Blackford would receive two penciled letters of thanks on lined paper in childish hand. These rituals were unaffected by Velasco's quietly informing Blackford one day that in fact Joe Bustamente had no children. What it meant, of course, was that in fact Blackford had the freedom of the city, provided he chose to confine it to walking the thirty-block distance to Catalina's apartment on Calle Línea. He was careful not to abuse this. When he visited with Catalina he stayed in her apartment until he was ready to return to the cottage, with Joe waiting in the lobby.

The paperwork began when, shortly after his return from Washington, Blackford asked Che to come forward with a list of the purchases the "Cuban Acuerdo"—as they had settled on calling the proposed accords—would anticipate. How many tractors, spare parts, generators—the whole bit. Blackford had been gratified to see the light in the eye of the Minister of Industry at the very thought of such a shopping list.

It took two weeks before a working list was drawn up. Then another two weeks on the matter of financing. Che had asked whether payment in the form of sugar futures would be satisfactory, and all of this bounced about. From the Director there were cables reflecting the reactions of the President: pleased that work was being done, steadily more impatient at the slowness of the negotiations. And, as was to be expected, as Che desired more and more assurances at the economic level, Washington wanted more and harder assurances on the character of the projected shift away from Moscow. Such a shift, as the weeks went by, during which Soviet-Cuban relations became more ardent every hour, appeared more and more remote.

Here Che tended to confine himself to elaborating the inhibitions the Castro government might find acceptable in the matter of ideological evangelizing in the rest of Latin America. Once again, in early May, Blackford traveled to Washington. Again he met with the President, who stressed his growing skepticism. But Blackford was passionate in his insistence on the sincerity of Che Guevara, and the CIA had no reports to the effect that Che's intimacy with or influence on Castro was in any way strained. The President asked Blackford how in the hell Che could continue these talks in the face of mounting Soviet military involvement in Cuba, to which Blackford replied that it was simply too much to hope for that Castro would turn down any offers of Soviet weaponry, any more than Nasser would turn these down, but that their importation into Cuba was no reason to turn down a Cuban Acuerdo, provided the weapons were defensive.

And, always, there was the question that tended to put the quietus on further discussion—namely, What was there to lose?

"I mean, Mr. President, apart from my own time?" Kennedy had liked that. "Oakes's *time!*" he remarked to the Director. "He treats it like a fucking national asset. On the other hand, that's probably exactly what it is."

The blow came little more than one month later. On the first of July.

Joe Bustamente informed Blackford that a cable awaited him at the Swiss Embassy. Blackford sent Velasco there, as he had been doing with some regularity, two or three times a week.

An hour later Velasco was back. He entered the sitting room where Blackford was going over figures on existing Cuban "diplomatic" representation in Latin-American countries. Velasco put the cable in front of Blackford. It read:

"THE DECISION HAS BEEN MADE TO TERMINATE EXISTING OPERATION. YOU AND VELASCO SHOULD RETURN TO WASHINGTON IMMEDIATELY. MCCONE."

Blackford shot up from his chair. He looked down at Velasco. "But *why? Why?* What in the *hell,* as of July first, makes everything we've been slaving over suddenly pointless? . . ." He stood up and closed his eyes. Then, "Let's go to the beach."

They took out their chairs and for the thousandth time Alejandro, reading the tabloid *Hoy* and his collection of comic books, could be seen sitting on his beach chair, carbine on his lap, the conventional twenty-five yards behind the two men on the beach chairs: the little, spare Spaniard in his sixties wearing the wide-brimmed sun hat he had begun to use in March as the sun got hotter, his torso protected by shirts, bandanas, and towels, his chair a couple of feet from that on which the tall, tanned, finely proportioned American, with his blond beard, sat, his legs stretched out, his toes playing with the sand.

They talked more than usual. At one point, in speculating on the motives of the President, Blackford conceded, "Of course, Cecilio, getting so little news we can't know what the political pressures are. Maybe he's afraid of the political effect of its getting out that he has a little delegation in Havana talking recognition and aid—that's what they'd call it—to Castro." The speculation went on. But when they came in for lunch there was nothing said, and both men ate sparingly, without appetite. Then, listlessly, as he stirred his coffee Blackford said suddenly that he must see Guevara.

Bustamente was called, the telephone plugged in. Blackford dialed the requisite number. His Spanish was, by now, serviceable, and he spoke in Spanish with the woman at headquarters who answered, by now familiar with him. "Rosaria, it is Caimán. I must see the Comandante. There or here. This is very urgent."

Che Guevara was there at six.

Blackford had debated whether to show him the actual text of the cable, decided against doing so, and said simply that he had been called back to Washington, that the operation was terminated.

"But why?" Guevara asked.

"I do not know."

"Did they not say?"

"No. On the other hand, Che, we can do our own surmising: We are approaching the anniversary of your initiative to Goodwin on the Cuban Acuerdo. All that has definitely happened during this past year is an increasing intimacy at every level between your government and the Soviet Union."

"But isn't that all the more reason to work out the Acuerdo, to try to refine it? To try a truly spectacular demarche?"

They talked on for almost an hour, but nothing was said that changed significantly the inflections of the initial exchange.

Finally Che Guevara said that he requested only that Blackford should delay his departure for two days. Castro was touring the eastern provinces but was scheduled back in Havana the next evening. Che would talk with him then, and report the results to Blackford. "We could," he paused, tugging on his little beard, "without any difficulty find that, for just two days, there was, unfortunately, no airplane standing by to fly you to Guantánamo." He winked. Blackford smiled, shaking his head over it all. He found himself colluding with Ernesto Che Guevara in a dissimulation aimed to deceive his own government. The thought amused him.

He turned to Velasco first and read the expression on his face. And then said to Che, "Okay."

Adding immediately, "Okay, this is Sunday, right? Fidel or no, we will meet on Tuesday morning?"

"Certainly on Tuesday morning. Not inconceivably on Monday evening, if I can confer with Fidel before his usual conference hour. Be sure to stay here tomorrow evening." He got up to go. But turned, as he approached the door.

"And don't worry about Catalina. I will explain to her why you cannot visit with her on Monday night." Che Guevara smiled and did his informal salute, touching his beret.

"*Hasta luego, Caimán.*"

Twenty-nine

Che Guevara communicated in a single sentence what the American, Caimán, had been told by Washington, and over the telephone Castro instructed Che to round up Valdés, Raúl, and Dorticós—still the only Cubans privy to the ultimate nature of ongoing arrangements with the Soviet Union—for a conference at midnight on Monday.

Castro, seated at the head of the table but this time in his secret suite in the Habana-Libre Hilton, beckoned to his aide to shut the doors and prevent anyone else from coming in. He looked tired, having orated a total of seven hours that day at three political rallies, but he ate heartily from the fruit bowl, and then some bread and cheese with a tall glass of red wine. He lit his cigar and turned to Che.

"I would guess this means the American invasion is scheduled, wouldn't you? The Soviets have still not been able to advise us exactly when it is to be launched, but it is clear that it will come before their November elections, and now there are reports being published in Washington and New York about equipment coming in here from the Soviet Union. Wouldn't you, if you were Kennedy, choose this moment to strike?"

Raúl spoke before Che could do so, spoke in ferocious accents. "With what we have ready right now, Fidel, it will be a bloody encounter, and lots of gringos will be eaten up by my guns before they establish anything like a beachhead."

"Raúl, we are not here to underrate the Cuban military. But it is just this clear: Until we get the big weapons, we are vulnerable. If the United States decides to treat Cuba as it treated—Okinawa, then Cuba will be conquered. Our job is exactly what we defined it to be last January: to keep the Americans stalled until we get the missiles here. *That* will be the end of the United States threat. Now, Che: Do you have any ideas on how to get Caimán to persuade Washington to put the Cuban Acuerdo back on the agenda?"

"I suppose we could offer them a major concession."

"Like what?"

Che thought. "We have—as you know—small military missions at our embassies in Mexico and in Guatemala. I suppose we could recall them, making a significant noninterventionist gesture. That might be something."

Raúl again: "But would the Russians understand?"

"Obviously we could communicate to the proper party in the Kremlin what our motivation was," Castro said, a little impatiently. He thought, and puffed: "Not bad, not bad. The 'withdrawal' could be arranged to get more foreign notice than local notice, am I right?"

Valdés said there was no longer any reason to give it *any* local notice, if that was the Comandante's decision. "The press and the radio are in absolutely sound hands, and Carlos Franqui's *Revolución* is about the only paper we worry about. But even there, I think arrangements can be made . . ."

"You're not to harm Franqui," Castro said.

"Don't harm him then," Raúl said about the editor—a communist, but not reliable; "just kick his ass out of the country."

"Franqui is a problem I will face at another time," Castro said. And to Valdés, "No, it does not matter, Ramiro, if it receives *some* publicity. I could go on television and say that it was merely a reconsolidation—something of the sort." And then to Guevara, "But would that be enough to influence Washington?"

"I shouldn't think it would be enough to deter the invasion if the plans are firm to get on with it. Nor is it likely that the United States will cancel or not cancel an invasion merely because they have two agents in Cuba who might get hurt. I have no reason to believe that Caimán has any idea there's an invasion scheduled. I myself am not one hundred percent convinced that such an invasion is scheduled."

"Are you doubting the word of Khrushchev's own son-in-law, reporting what Soviet Intelligence has absolutely established?" Raúl asked.

"Soviet Intelligence can be wrong, Raúl. I do believe we should play for time until those missiles arrive. But I also think we should push on the American front, and that before we see their final proposals we're going to have to move beyond this paperwork business and make a few concrete gestures. Like the Mexican-Guatemalan military mission recall, and maybe one or two others."

"Like what?" Fidel asked.

"Why not ask them?"

"Ask them what?"

"Ask them, through Caimán, to suggest a gesture of some sort, more or less as earnest money."

"What kind of a gesture?" Fidel Castro's voice was demanding now.

"I would precisely leave it to them to think of one. We shouldn't be ridiculous about it. Obviously they are not going to suggest that we suspend diplomatic relations with the Soviet Union, or that you get Raúl here to inaugurate a Havana branch of the National Association of Manufacturers. But let *them* think of something. That will take time. And *we* can then take time thinking about *their* request. Look, if the idea is to keep them on the hook, let's keep them on the hook. Meanwhile, my commission doesn't have to be suspended, not until we see what kind of a deal they would actually be willing to make if we pushed them as hard as we could."

"The kind of deal they are willing to make," said Raúl,

looking at his brother rather than at Che, "is to hand Cuba back to the capitalists and the gringos and then maybe they will forgive us."

"I assumed you wanted a serious analysis of the question, Fidel."

Castro leaned back in his chair and puffed on his cigar. "What are your thoughts, Osvaldo?"

"I would be guided in this by your instincts, Fidel."

"Ramiro?"

"I would agree. But it can't be overemphasized that any apparent concessions we make must be explained, before we go public with them, to Moscow."

"Of course," Raúl said.

"Of course," Dorticós said.

"Very well then," Castro said. "Let's hear from Raúl on exactly what it is that is now fully installed, and what the exact dates will be for the missiles to arrive."

"But Fidel," Che interjected. "I am meeting with the American, Caimán, tomorrow morning. What am I to tell him?"

"Tell him we are very disappointed, that we have truly been looking for a way to have better relations. Go ahead on both your ideas. The one on Mexico and Guatemala. And the one about a 'gesture' of a kind Washington comes up with. Only, of course, coordinate with Dorticós. Moscow must have word of this before Washington."

Che turned to Dorticós. "That means you will have to get word tonight to Moscow."

"Done," said the President of Cuba.

Thirty

The next morning, after Che Guevara had left, Blackford was elated. He went to his typewriter and paused in attempting to contract as tightly as possible the text Velasco would take to the Swiss Embassy. In a half hour he had batted out 750 words. He read them aloud to Velasco. The final sentence of his cable read: "GIVEN ALL THE ABOVE I RESPECTFULLY REQUEST THAT YOU AUTHORIZE A CONTINUATION OF CURRENT MISSION. AWAITING YOUR REPLY. CAIMAN."

He felt exuberant when Velasco came back from the embassy, the cable dispatched, and suggested to Velasco that they invite Catalina to lunch with them and go out someplace, perhaps for a picnic. "We could put together something here—Manuel can come up with something—and on the way here Catalina can go to the commissary and get a bottle of wine."

Velasco smiled. "I'll stay here. I am very happy with my book, now that our paperwork is suddenly suspended. You and Catalina go alone."

"You sure?"

"I'm very very sure. Besides, if Washington reacts quickly, I am free to go to the Swiss Embassy."

Every now and again everything seems to work, as it did that day. Catalina was at her office. She was instantly and utterly enthusiastic about knocking off for the rest of the day, and she collaborated with Blackford with the gusto of a sophomore planning to go to a fraternity ball. She arranged to get an official dispensation to the effect that Joe

Bustamente would not need to accompany them, she volunteered to get all the food and drink ("It will be my surprise"), reminding him that, after all, her office was next door to the commissary (Why did Caimán think I elected to situate my office where it is?). And at one-thirty she was there, not even in a jeep but in a 1958 Oldsmobile ("I borrowed it from Fidel. He said to keep it as long as I wanted"), and she knew of a totally private beach ("It is generally used only for political executions, so I declared that no one was to be shot today") and that therefore he should bring swimming trunks ("On the other hand, why should we bother with bathing suits? Just bring a towel. And some cologne. Or have you used it up?").

They drove down the Vía Blanca thirty kilometers on what must, by Cuban standards, have passed for a superhighway. Catalina drove fast, and with skill. There was virtually no traffic on the road, until they hit a column of heavy military vehicles, presumably Russian, lugging great supplies of military goods, or perhaps building materials. It depressed them to have to cut their speed down to the military's 60 kph, which for a full ten minutes they had to do, until Catalina spotted a long stretch of road without contrary traffic, at which point she raced past the convoy. Absentmindedly Blackford counted: eighteen trucks, driven by white-skinned men in uniform. Certainly Russian, he supposed.

By two-thirty they had arrived, having taken a side lane that had obviously once been private. It led to the beach, past a huge mansion. She had a key to the beach house, entered it, and directed Blackford to pull a small table outdoors. To the table, under a palm tree, she brought out her feast, making several trips to the parked car. Lobsters, and Swedish crackers and caviar and onions, cold chicken and fresh carrot salad, and chocolates, and white wine. And a portable radio, tuned to the least jingoistic music on the band.

They ate, and talked, and then took off their clothes and ran into the surf and ducked each other and, under the water, ran their hands over each other's bodies, and went then into the bathhouse and coupled, con brio, and Blackford thought that politics could be romantic, especially when the prospects perceptibly heightened for affecting great events peaceably.

They slept, and the sun now was low, its light shimmering in through the palm leaves to the bed. They woke together and she said, in Spanish, that this had been a wonderful afternoon, and he said yes, it had been a wonderful afternoon, and added that he wished his Spanish could be more poetic. She replied that he might begin by using the familiar mood with her, given that he was otherwise extremely familiar with her, and he said that English was really a far more useful language inasmuch as English didn't distinguish between a formal and an informal mode of address—"Everybody is just 'you' in English."

"What about 'thee' and 'thou'?" she countered, and he said that was just for when you addressed God and King Arthur and she said that socialists didn't believe in either God or King Arthur, and he said that he would not ask her to reflect on this declaration when they met in the next world, and she said that the next world could not possibly be as much fun as this world was—"This afternoon."

"Why just this afternoon?"

"Because all afternoons are not like this one."

"Have you spoken to Che today?"

"Yes," she replied.

"Did he tell you what is going on?"

"Yes," she said.

He got up, went out to the beach table, and came back with his shorts on and sat down in an easy chair opposite her. Responding to this formality, she drew a towel over her body.

"What do you think?" he asked her.

"I was pleased."

"Pleased by what?"

"Pleased by what I learned about Fidel's reaction. It was very different from Raúl's reaction."

"I don't suppose you would care to elaborate on that?"

"No. But I am not sure I could, in any case. Everybody knows that Raúl is the most—dogmatic."

"Why does dogma demand eternal hostility between us?"

"It's funny you should say that when a year and a half ago you backed an invasion of Cuba."

Blackford didn't reply.

"Do you think we have a chance?"

"On Operation Acuerdo?"

"Yes."

"I think so. Do you know something?"

"What?"

"I trust Che. He is all screwed up about some very basic things. But I like him."

"I like you."

He leaned over, and they kissed. "We must go. There may be something waiting for me at the—" he almost used the Velasco-Oakes vernacular, but corrected himself—"at the Caimán-Hilton."

"Let's hope so."

They drove back at half the speed, and she let him off at the cottage, and they kissed again, lingeringly.

Alejandro nodded at Caimán perfunctorily.

In the sitting room, Velasco greeted him once again with a sheet of paper. It read, "EARLIER DECISION IS FINAL. RETURN IMMEDIATELY. MCCONE."

Thirty-one

Some people don't know what a toast is, for God's sake. Come to think of it, it rather goes with his name. Carlos Julio Arosemena Monroy. (He had spent a good five minutes that morning just memorizing the name.) *Eleven syllables. John Fitzgerald Kennedy, 1-2-3-4-5-6-7. That's moderation for you. Carlos Julio Arosemena Monroy, President of Ecuador. If he, JFK, ever gave a toast that long they'd cart him off to Walter Reed, and LBJ (ugh) would take over. Of course, be reasonable. The whole thing was being translated, which doubled its length. The* longueur *of the thing, as Jackie would put it. He wondered whether translations of nothing sound longer than translations of something? Here he is talking about "major changes" in the "social and economic structures" of the smaller countries. Would it sound shorter if he said that on reconsideration he thinks the military were right in forcing Ecuador to break relations with Castro last April? He had a feeling it would.*

That Oakes guy is something. Poor McCone. But he was right to talk to me about it. Had to call off that whole Che Guevara thing after that last speech by Ken Keating. Old Senator Keating charging that my administration is "indifferent" to the military buildup of Cuba.

Wonder where in the hell he gets his figures? McCone says Keating's estimates of Soviet military shipments are more than double the CIA's. Keating must be full of baloney, but you can't just say that to a senator. Still, to have a mission out there month after month after month, that does not make sense. And if the Republicans get wind of it, wow. Kennedy Emissary Plotting Recognition and Economic Aid to Castro While Dictator Develops Fortress Cuba Courtesy of Moscow. . . . No, it doesn't make sense to run that risk. Do you think so? Carlos Julio Arosemena Monroy?

The President of the United States had a half smile of
admiration and concentration on his face as the President
of Ecuador cleared his throat and continued his toast.

*So we tell Oakes to come on back and the next day he appeals,
wants us to think it over, we say no, next day he asks for a leave of
absence. McCone wires him back, Permission denied, and Oakes
cables back that he requests leave of absence without pay as he intends
—get that, "intends"—to remain in Cuba as the personal guest of
Che Guevara who has extended an invitation, and in the event he
comes up with something he thinks of interest to the United States,
may he use the Swiss facilities? Well, sure. But McCone was right to
advise Che Guevara formally, through the Swiss, that Oakes wasn't
on assignment from me anymore. If Oakes manages to persuade Che
Guevara to overthrow Castro, kick out the Russians, and make a
deal with us, I'll be glad to give our 007 the handsomest secret medal
we give to our secret agents. Either Guevara is just having us on—
using Oakes—or else there's a power struggle going on in Cuba. The
more power struggles in Cuba the better. Yes indeed, that was a very
searching point you just made, Carlos Julio Arosemena Monroy. I
must nod my head a little more often. But now that Oakes is discredited. No, not discredited. That's the wrong word. Now that he no
longer has official status, what can Che hope to use him for? Is he
getting information from Oakes that Castro needs? But Oakes doesn't
know what our secrets concerning Cuba are. Funny. I kind of like his
style, don't you, Carlos Julio Arosemena Monroy?*

The President smiled broadly, and applauded a patriotic
obbligato in the speech.

*Maybe I'll take up just that one point with McCone: Does Oakes
know anything we care about? And still another point. Now that he's
an official guest of Che Guevara, maybe we can slip in there some stuff
that would be useful for us to slip in. If Oakes insists on going to bed
with Guevara, maybe we can give him a case of crabs. Wonder if
McCone has a pill that gives crabs? If not I must remember in the
next State of the Union to request an appropriation for a crab-pill, a
crab-pill bill. Come on, Mr. President, Carlos Julio Arosemena*

Monroy. He's about to finish. What comes now, the Pledge of Allegiance?

"That was a truly beautiful, moving toast, Mrs. Arosemena Monroy." The President gave the first lady his arm, and they led the company to the East Room for coffee and brandy.

Thirty-two

Velasco had three times offered to stay in Cuba. Blackford said no, no, no. He didn't intend to ruin Velasco's career. He didn't put it that way to him, he just said that it made no sense anymore, given that the detailed official mission was terminated, and that he would now be living—elsewhere. They had received a conciliatory cable from McCone advising that the facilities of the Swiss Embassy would continue to be available to Blackford, but that Velasco should return.

"My Spanish has got pretty good now. And anyway, when I'm with Guevara Catalina will always be there for when I get stuck."

And so Velasco had packed his bag, and Joe Bustamente drove them both to the same airport he had met them at in October of the year before. There was little left to say when Blackford walked with Velasco to the companionway of the old DC-3.

"I will pray for you every day, Blackford. And be careful. *Do not trust Guevara.*" And, under his breath, he added, "Or Catalina." There was an awkward moment. And then Blackford threw his arms around the little Spaniard, and Velasco's tears flowed. That hadn't happened to him since that day in Mexico in January of 1945. Velasco turned sharply and stepped up the companionway. He did not look back when the door closed, and the aircraft revved up its engines.

The next six weeks were alternately frustrating and exhilarating. Blackford lived with Catalina and she became for all intents and purposes his confederate. She was given

leave from her regular duties and pursued much of the
work Velasco had been pursuing. On a typical morning she
would leave the living room they had transformed into an
office to wrest from this official or that the lists and the
supplements. More systematic than Blackford, she kept a
formal ledger. It contained, on odd pages, "Cuban Concessions," on even pages, "U.S. Concessions." The even
pages ran a good bit longer than the odd pages. The list of
U.S. goods the Cubans desired had now reached a figure
the working value of which (pending tomorrow's addition:
every day, it seemed, another item was added) was something on the order of eight or nine hundred million dollars.
"We may as well think a billion," Blackford said after the
addition in mid-September of "24 crop-dusting light aircraft."

The Cuban Concessions list, while shorter, at the constant prodding of Blackford and now Catalina was increasingly specific. In many conversations Catalina would reas-
sert her faith in the socialist alternative. But increasingly as
she talked of it she would talk of a vision very different from
what lay about her. And the encroachments of the Soviet
Union she particularly resented; in this she was, Blackford
thought and hoped, particularly influenced by Che Guevara, whose anxiety to avoid the complete subordination of
Cuban communism to the Soviet Union had prompted the
endless mission.

So that it became emphatic, in their ledger. There would
be no military missions attached to any Cuban Embassy in
any Latin-American country. Only defensive weapons sent
by the Soviet Union would be received. Where there was
ambiguity about the purpose or use of a projected or hypothetical military machine, a board was to pass judgment on
whether, at the margin, it was defensive or offensive. Whis-
key-class submarines, for example: Che argued that submarines, particularly those whose range and firepower were
limited, should be classified as defensive. Blackford de-

murred. The board that might make the decision would be made up of three representatives from neutral nations, even as three nations were then supervising the implementation of the Laos treaty.

There was a three-day wrangle on what it was that constituted a "neutral" nation, Che Guevara insisting that, for instance, Sweden would not qualify because although it was not a member of NATO, Sweden was "clearly" a "Western power." On the other hand, he said, Ghana was notoriously neutral. "Cut it out, Che, Nkrumah has been kissing communist ass for three years."

And so the days went by, but the ledger was growing in specificity. And then one day Che said:

"Of course, Guantánamo will need to be returned to Cuba."

Blackford said that he doubted this would be a political possibility even if President Kennedy were satisfied that a fair exchange had been worked out. "I can't," Blackford said, "go to the Swiss Embassy and send a telegram to McCone and say, 'By the way, is it okay if we give up Guantánamo Bay?' He might wire back, 'Sure. If they will give us back the Platt Amendment.'" The Platt Amendment, rescinded in 1934, was the Cuban equivalent of "Remember the Alamo" for Texans. Enacted after the conquest of Cuba in which Theodore Roosevelt became prominent, it authorized U.S. intervention in Cuba in perpetuity whenever Washington held that Cuba was not behaving.

One evening in early October Che stayed on after a working session and had dinner with Catalina and Blackford. He had been suffering acutely from his chronic asthma, and was having problems in breathing normally. He spoke distractedly about this and that, about his reverence for Ho Chi Minh, about the military-industrial complex in the United States. And suddenly he asked, bluntly: Was the United States preparing to invade Cuba?

"Not that I know of," Blackford said, peeling his mango.

"If it were planned, would you know about it?"

"Not necessarily."

"I should confess to you, Caimán, that when your mission was deactivated in July, we surmised"—he left the "we" unspecified—"that Mr. Kennedy was ready to launch an invasion. Such things are planned in America, are they not, with some reference to congressional elections?"

"In democratic countries, Che, with which you have had limited experience, elections do mean a good deal because the idea is to formulate policies that appeal to the people. But you should know this: The United States is no longer an imperialist power. We gave the Philippines their freedom and walked out of a half-dozen countries we had taken over after the war. There aren't six Americans alive who want to take over Cuba for the sake of taking over Cuba—"

Che interrupted him. "There are a lot more than six Americans who would like to invade Cuba right now."

"I don't deny that. But that is so only for one reason, and that is that Castro appears to be forming irreversible ties with the Soviet Union and no country has ever done that and then gone on to reestablish its own sovereignty, with the exception of Yugoslavia and China. What we want is a Cuba independent of the Soviet Union. And then you can be as free to undertake your own domestic policies as Papa Doc is in Haiti."

Che tilted his head to one side and, to ease asthmatic pressure, sniffed on an inhaler. He said, "You may be surprised, but I substantially agree with you."

"I am *not* surprised. It's been a long time since it became pretty clear to me that you've been pushing a set of proposals very different from the kind of thing others around Castro want. The question is, What does Castro want? Right?"

Che rose and lit a cigar. He looked down at his cigar case: "I should give these up. Especially when the asthma is raging. Yes, Castro is the supreme leader. But that is to say something a little bit less than that he can move in absolutely any direction he desires. That isn't true even of Khrushchev. I think that when he feels safe against an invasion from the United States he will be more reasonable."

"But how can he ever feel 'safe' unless we go forward with the Acuerdo? Castro's Cuba is not about to become a superpower."

Catalina got up rather brusquely, collected the coffee cups, and disappeared into the kitchen.

"No, certainly not a superpower with nuclear weapons, if that's what you mean. But we are much stronger today than we were one year ago."

"So are we. We have crushing power. And the idea is, or ought to be, to keep us from using it against you, and to keep you from becoming so provocative that there is no alternative for us than to use it."

"Are you telling me, then, that if the Acuerdo does not go through, you will invade us?"

"No. Only that it doesn't make sense to encourage relations between Cuba and the United States to deteriorate. If you will think back to a glacial age ago in Montevideo, that exactly was the point *you* advanced to Goodwin."

Che put out his cigar. "Ah well, we can only try to make progress. If I could tell Fidel that the Americans were willing to give up Guantánamo, that might be the crucial consideration. Perhaps you should think of getting some reaction from Washington on this point. Are you willing to do that?"

"Sure. But unless that was told to Washington in context of"—he held up Catalina's ledger—"the list of Cuban reciprocal concessions, they would take away my citizenship."

"I will make you a Cuban in that case. And you can then be an American-Cuban. Like Catalina"—he called out to her—"Do you like the idea, Catalina?" She didn't reply. "I will think about that, and then maybe you can send the Guantánamo cable."

"Take care of your asthma, Che. Why don't you take a trip to Lourdes?"

He laughed. "Both Lourdes and I would lose our reputations." He put on his beret. *"Hasta luego, Caimán."*

Blackford sat back on the couch and called out to Catalina. Once again, she didn't reply. He got up and walked into the kitchen. It was empty. He went then to the bedroom and knocked softly.

"Come in." Her voice was preternaturally quiet.

She was seated on the edge of the bed, looking out at the bright moonlit night.

"Catalina, what is the matter?"

He approached her. Her features were set grimly. She did not turn her face to him. "I can't go on. No, that's not right. I could go on. I don't intend to go on."

"What are you talking about?"

"The time has come to tell you. No. To show you. But you will have to come with me in the car."

He caught the deadly seriousness in her voice and resolved to do exactly as she asked. He went into the closet and took a light sweater from the shelf. "It is getting chilly. You'd better wear something too." She put on a light jacket, and together they walked down three flights of stairs, out of the apartment, and outdoors where, in the little parking lot on the right, her jeep sat.

They drove for almost an hour. Out of Vedado, up the Vía Blanca, over the Almendares River, past Miramar. The moon's fullness bathed the exposed part of the island in light, and it was only after they reached the beach at Santa Fe that Blackford, looking back, lost sight of the lights of Havana.

She came upon a road on which was posted a large sign, TERRENO DEL PUEBLO—ENTRADA PROHIBIDA. There was visible a guard in a sentry post, reading from a dim light. Catalina drove past about a kilometer, turned off the lights, and slid the car under the protective covering of a large ceiba tree. "From here we will need to walk. Try to be quiet."

She led him in the direction of a small cluster of lights a kilometer or so away. The area was wooded, but the path was clear. The trees' shadows hid their own, and Catalina walked toward what seemed a vast hangar. At one end it was dark, at the other, opposite, were some lights. "We'll see if there is a door at this end," Catalina said, pointing to the dark side. "When I was here last week I was taken through the other door."

There was a door. Locked.

She took him by the hand and under the shadow of the great hangar they moved toward the opposite end. At the corner of the building she stopped, looked, and listened. There was no sound coming from the illuminated office twenty yards across the road. The night watchman was either asleep or making his rounds. Catalina held her breath and whispered, "Come!" Just around the corner was the door to the hangar. She rushed to it, momentarily exposed in the moonlight. The door was open. She walked quickly through it, leading Blackford by the hand. She shut the door, opened her purse, took out a flashlight. She shed its light on the floor, again drawing Blackford along until they had walked, he calculated, a third of the length of the hangar. She stopped then, and pointed the ray of light above her.

On two huge cradle mounts was a 50-foot-long white object, torpedo-shaped. She swept the room with her light. The object was one of four in the hangar. Blackford drew in his breath. "Do you know what we're looking at?"

"Yes," Catalina said. "A Russian medium-range ballistic missile capable of carrying a medium payload of about a megaton a distance of twelve hundred miles."

"My God!" And then he hissed, *"Let's get out of here."*

Again she turned the flashlight toward the concrete floor

to guide them, and when they reached the door turned it off
completely. She opened the door a crack and again looked
and listened. They rounded the corner quickly, into the
safety of the hangar's shadow. And then back across the
forest toward the car. They missed it and were confused
whether to turn left or turn right. "It's safer to walk in a
direction away from the sentry," Blackford said. They did
so and, quietly, came on the car within a few minutes.

For a while, driving slowly, careful not to arouse attention of a police patrol, they headed back to Havana, the
moon still bright, the shadows along the road still black, the
air warm but no longer hot, the odor of the forest green
and tangy. Blackford was silent. Then he spoke.

"How did you know it was there?"

"Because last week Che made a scene at a meeting with
Raúl, after I reported what you told me about Washington.
About Washington's getting itchy—about the scale of Rus-
sian arms imports. Che demanded to know whether the
Russian missiles had actually arrived. When Raúl said yes,
the first batch were already here, Che demanded to lay eyes
on them. Raúl said all right. And Che just brought me along
—Raúl didn't raise any objection. I guess he knew if he had,
Che would have made a scene."

"Then Che has known—"

"The whole time."

"And all of this business *all the time* on the Acuerdo was a
ruse?"

"Not the whole time. He did hope to sell the Acuerdo to
Castro, even up to a month or so back. But no longer.
That's why I couldn't stand to hear him when he was talking
to you tonight, the things he said that now weren't so.
Especially he knew the Acuerdo wouldn't go after last Mon-
day, when he actually *saw* the missiles. That's why I wanted
you actually to see them: that is the effect seeing them has.
Last Monday he knew that Fidel wasn't actually afraid of an

American invasion anymore. The Acuerdo was dead from the moment the missiles actually arrived."

"Then why continue our discussions?"

"Because they want Washington to have the impression that there is still a possibility of an Acuerdo. Until the missiles are in place—mounted, with their warheads on. At that point Castro figures he is permanently secure. At that point, I calculate the Russians figure Washington will take orders from Russia."

"And when will that be?"

"Raúl told Che about ten days."

"You know what I must do, Catalina?"

"Yes. And I want you to do it. That's why I brought you here, for God's sake. I didn't join the socialist revolution to take orders from Moscow and maybe help start a nuclear war. We must go quickly to the Swiss Embassy."

"It is three in the morning."

"That hardly matters. I'll stay parked outside and make sure they let you in. You deliver the message"—Catalina had been calm, was speaking now excitedly—"then *don't leave the embassy.* A patrol officer might spot you, pick you up. I will drive by"—she looked down at her watch—"at exactly . . . let's say three-thirty and pick you up. Does that give you enough time?"

"If it doesn't, drive off and come back exactly one half hour later."

The streets were nearly empty as they approached the city. An occasional car, once in a while a bus carrying night workers to or from late shifts. Their route took them by Havana Bay, and at the commercial wharf there was much activity. One large wharf was tightly cordoned off by military policemen. Coming down the Malecón, Catalina was waved to a side street to be out of the way of the unloading, on twin lorries, of what Blackford now assumed was another missile. The streets approaching the embassy were again almost empty.

When they reached the embassy she dimmed the headlights, pulled up outside the iron gates and, after Blackford had sprung out, waited to make sure that someone would wake up, emerge, and let him in.

The spotlight blinded Blackford just as he reached for the buzzer. A second searchlight was thrust at the face of Catalina. Four men, two with pistols drawn, a third with a machine gun, finger on the trigger. The fourth, carrying the walkie-talkie, barked out their orders. Blackford was thrust into the back of the second car, the pistol in his ribs motioning the direction he was to take. Catalina was thrust, handcuffed, into the back of her jeep by the second *pistolero* and the man with the tommy gun. The fourth, the man with the radio, got into the driver's seat of Catalina's car and gunned the motor. His voice was heard as the car eased forward:

"You think Joe Bustamente is just a joke, Sr. Caimán." The voice was all acid.

The cars proceeded in sequence to La Cabaña. There was some quick paperwork done at the adjutant's desk, a few words exchanged. Catalina was led off down one hallway, Blackford down another. A cell door opened and Joe Bustamente shoved him inside, locking the door with a triumphant thud.

Blackford could detect from the darkness through the high little window that the moon had spent its course. He found the cot, got down on his knees, and prayed for divine help. He rose much later and lay down on the cot. His sleep was drugged from fatigue, tormented by his incommunicable knowledge of catastrophe impending.

Thirty-three

Nikita Sergeyevich Khrushchev was jubilant. The day's news had brought reports of angry denials by several contenders for reelection in the American political campaign that President Kennedy had been anything less than absolutely observant of all relevant developments on the Cuban front. One senator was quoted in the *Christian Science Monitor* as saying that the very idea that the Soviet Union was going to stick its neck out by sending arms to Cuba on such a scale as would make Cuba a threat to "Republican yachtsmen floating about Caribbean waters" was an indication of how hungry the Republican military-industrial complex was for "one of those blustering, breast-beating confrontations with the Soviet Union" that could lead to war.

Khrushchev patted his son-in-law on the back, reached for an hourglass sitting on Aleksei's desk in his study at his home, turned it upside down and said, "Aleksei, imagine that hourglass representing not one hour but one month. In exactly one month, the politics of the world will have changed. Now the Americans will know what it is like to have their own Berlin at *their* doorstep. And anything *we* then choose to do to West Berlin—why, that will be like sliding downhill on a virgin breast! You know that expression? Ukraine. Not the kind of thing you would pick up reading *Izvestia*. Does *Izvestia have* to be so boring? I suppose so, otherwise I would send you to Gulag, if *Izvestia* were more interesting. But then I would not do that to the husband of my dear Rada. I don't know, maybe it would cool you off. I must ask Rada whether you need cooling off. Or maybe you need a little"—he laughed uproariously—

" 'heating up' in bed! In that case I could send you to be our ambassador to Ghana. Lovely, the weather in Ghana, as Pasternak has no doubt said in one of his interminable poems. How is that tall jellyfish? Unhappy, I hope. Like everybody in his novels—which I *do not* read. Say something else unpleasant about him in *Izvestia.* If I had time I would write it myself."

Aleksei chortled, sort of, and said that indeed the Chairman seemed about to pull off one of the greatest political upsets in history. "If only they do not find out about it."

"Find out about it? The CIA, my dear Aleksei, is incompetent. I told Castro—actually, it was you who told him—that there was no substantial risk in going ahead with our design, so careful we would be—we have been—with security arrangements and camouflage. Their weekly U-2 flights haven't spotted anything. We'd hear about it if they had. And Castro believed us; he has faith in us, and quite right. Che Guevara was not so sanguine, but Guevara—I don't know. Guevara is in so many ways what Lenin called a 'sectarian.' On the one hand he wants revolutions all over the world, on the other hand he is naïve enough to think that every revolution can run itself without any direction from us. Hah. Can you imagine even *our* revolution managing on its own? You need leadership. Enterprise. Did you know, when I was at school I was named the 'most enterprising' student in the class? In the first place they will not find out about the missiles; in the second place when they do it will be too late. And then!"—he nodded his head when offered more vodka—"and then we will say, with great calm, with great solemnity we will say, 'What was that you were "demanding" about Berlin? And demanding about the testing in the atmosphere? Oh yes, and speaking of demands, we want to talk to you about your missiles in Turkey.' Oh I can *see* the expression in that young matinee idol's face. We will say, 'What was that again about your "demands"?' " The Chairman laughed, and gulped down his drink.

Aleksei said he thought a diversionary maneuver might be in order, something that would distract the attention of the Kennedy White House, get the political candidates with Cuba on the brain to lay off.

"Like what?"

"Perhaps something aggressive about Berlin? There are several theaters in which the Soviet presence could be reinforced, no, Nikita Sergeyevich?"

Khrushchev pondered the question. "No, I do not think anything aggressive is desirable, not at this moment. Although it might distract attention, it might have the effect of mobilizing Kennedy's—his hostility. Actually, he *can* be tough, never mind the impression I had at Vienna, where I cremated him, dear Aleksei, *cremated* him with my arguments, but I told you that. Ho-ho—ask Adlai Stevenson if John Fitzgerald Kennedy can't be tough! Besides, to be truculent now, this close to the American elections, runs the risk of encouraging blasts of bravado.

"No. I think maybe a speech, or even better a letter. Something soothing. Perhaps even directed at all the talk about the Soviet arming of Cuba.

"Good idea. I'll personally reassure him everything going to Cuba is purely defensive. And then, when the day comes and they find out, we can use that *wonderful* phrase of Castro's—a winner, Castro, provided I don't have to sit through too many of his speeches; mine are bad enough—that in fact all we sent to Cuba were 'strategic defensive missiles.' Yes. I love that. Draft me a letter to Kennedy, Aleksei. Take your time. If I have it by noon tomorrow that will be soon enough.

"And now," he said, getting up, "I will join my wife and your wife, and perhaps we shall have another toast to the birthday of my grandson. I do hope he will not grow up looking like you, Aleksei. Even though I like you personally, you are really—quite ugly to look at. You must have something else, to appeal to Rada. On the other hand, I haven't *seen* that something else. Ho-ho!

"Well, let's go and pay some attention to the ladies."

Thirty-four

Some courtroom. There were three judges, sitting roughly as judges at a military court-martial would sit, behind a single table. On the left, Raúl Castro. In the center, Osvaldo Dorticós. On the right, Ernesto Che Guevara. None had on the costumes in which, however studiously casual in cut, they frequently appeared on formal occasions. They wore instead their fatigues, though Raúl Castro had something that smacked of insignia on the lapel of his shirt, and Dorticós had a blathering of red and yellow over his shirt collar. Presumably whatever it was that indicated that he was the President of the Cuban Republic. Che Guevara wore only his fatigues.

A few feet diagonally to the left of Raúl was a card table, a white cloth covering it. On it was a pile of disordered papers. There Ramiro Valdés sat—Minister of the Interior, and, on this occasion, state prosecutor.

A few feet removed from the prosecutor sat Catalina. She was dressed in yellow prison garb, an amorphous robe that reached down halfway between knee and ankle. Her hair was disordered, her complexion pale. Her hands lay on her lap, handcuffed. Opposite her, on the right side, sat Blackford Oakes. The military policemen had brought them into the room, fetid with cigar smoke, sat them down on their chairs, and left. Almost immediately the prosecutor and the judges had entered from a door at the far end. Blackford estimated that the room was about the size of the living room-dining room of the Walden-Hilton. There was a single window, the shade drawn.

It would hardly have mattered, since it was after ten at

night. He had been led out of his prison cell by Major Joe Bustamente and driven to wherever they now were—a residential house, it seemed. When led, handcuffed, into the comfortably furnished room outside the court chamber, he had seen Catalina, already arrived, standing in her handcuffs. They had not spoken, had hardly time to speak, as they were instantly led into the inner chamber.

Valdés rose. He began by saying that inasmuch as the matter at hand involved the highest considerations of state security, no one else would be present during the proceedings, which in any event were proceedings the factual background of which was established beyond any question of bourgeois cavil. He looked up at the tribunal and said:

"Gentlemen, excellencies, as Minister of the Interior I am in charge of state security, and I level against the defendants here the charge of high treason."

He then proceeded, for whose benefit Blackford could not imagine, to say that just twenty-four hours earlier—"indeed on this very day, just after midnight"—the defendant Cátalina Urrutia Sánchez had conspired with an agent of the American CIA, knowing that to do so was to violate the most explicit laws of Cuban security, for the purpose of divulging a secret that bore most directly on the security of the state. That woman, he said pointing to Catalina without looking at her face, led the CIA agent to a military installation and revealed to him the nature of Cuba's most confidential defensive weapons. Happily, a conscientious Cuban patriot assigned to follow the movements of the American agent had followed them, at a safe distance, to their remote destination, had done so undetected by them, had with great resourcefulness radioed with his walkie-talkie to the State Security Office, which had instantly got into touch with the prosecutor himself, who had given orders to reinforce Major Bustamente, which orders had resulted in a military vehicle's being dispatched from the military installation to follow the traitor and the spy as they returned to Havana, and to abort what had obviously been a treasonable attempt to communicate Cuba's military secrets to the American imperialists, which attempt had been foiled by the resourceful and ingenious behavior of Major Bustamente and three other Cuban patriots, acting under the close radio supervision of—well, himself.

I demand, he said, that she be given the sentence of death.

He turned, then, to Blackford Oakes.

This spy, he said, who was invited to Cuba by Comandante Guevara to explore possible matters of mutual convenience between the United States and Cuba had so far exceeded his commission, both as a representative of the government in Washington and as a guest of Comandante Guevara, that even his own government had canceled his commission, and moreover had done so over two months ago. Notwithstanding, and prevailing on the good nature of Comandante Guevara, he had feigned a sincere interest in the independence and security of Cuba while secretly maneuvering to penetrate Cuban defenses. He had been guilty of enticing the defendant Catalina Urrutia into acts of treachery, had conspired with her to deceive Comandante Guevara, a great hero of the revolution—"Forgive me, Comandante Guevara, if it embarrasses you if I speak thus of your historical reputation"—and had suborned her—"One can only guess how many imperialist dollars have been paid to her either directly, or through her parents, who live with other Cuban traitors in Miami"—into colluding with him in an attempt to subvert Cuban defensive precautions. Although he was here in the first instance under the protection of Comandante Guevara, that protection had lapsed at the moment that his diplomatic mission was ended. Under the circumstances, the prosecutor said, *he is no more than a foreign spy*—"out of uniform!" These words he very nearly shouted. (Blackford dazedly wondered whether he could remember exactly when last he actually had worn a uniform. Sometime in the late spring of 1945, after returning from a fighter mission over Germany.) As for this American, who goes appropriately by the name of Caimán, his real name"—the prosecutor needed to consult a paper on his desk for a moment— "is Blackford Ohks, and it is known about him from friendly sources in the Soviet Union that he has a protracted international record of attempting to thwart the popular revolutionary will." As regards Blackford Ohks, he, the prosecutor, demanded that he also receive the death sentence, *as is appropriate for any spy caught in an act of espionage against the Cuban people.*

He sat down.

President Dorticós spoke. His words were enunciated in studied humdrum, as if he were calling for a cup of coffee.

"As to the defendant Urrutia, do you have anything to say?"

Catalina looked perplexed. She spoke softly, "Am I supposed to stand?"

"You may remain seated," the President said.

"I have always backed the 26th of July Movement," she said. "I do not see that movement, which stressed the independence of Cuba, represented here."

"Is that all, Defendant Urrutia?"

Catalina opened her mouth as if to say more. But then, slowly, she closed it. And, very slowly, looking down at her handcuffs, shook her head.

"And the defendant Ohks. Have you understood the charges leveled against you?"

Blackford nodded his head.

"Do you have anything to say?"

Blackford cleared his throat. No point, he figured, in not making the old college try. "I demand to see the Swiss ambassador, the Honorable Guy de Keller, who, by agreement with the Cuban Government and the government of my own country, has undertaken to expedite such affairs as claim the joint attention of our two countries." Blackford had not quite got this right in Spanish, and, spontaneously, Catalina spoke out the necessary correction.

"Request denied. There are no legal representatives in Cuba for foreign spies. You have no diplomatic credentials in Cuba, Sr. Ohks. Do you have anything else to say?"

Blackford thought for a moment.

"Señorita Catalina took me last night to where she did only because I told her that Comandante Guevara had told me, while she was in the kitchen and we were still at the dinner table—he had dined with us—that I should ask Catalina to take me to a military site the better to understand what I needed to know in order to pursue my attempts at negotiation. I lied to her. She understood herself to be acting on Comandante Guevara's orders. All she can be blamed for is for believing in my own—deception."

Catalina, experiencing difficulties of several orders, transmitted the exact meaning in Spanish of what Blackford had said.

The prosecutor rose in all his fury. "This is a contemptible effort to shield the defendant—whore! Yes, gentlemen, that is the primary role Catalina Urrutia has been playing for many weeks. She is nothing more than a Mata Hari."

Che Guevara raised his voice. "We are not, Mr. Prosecutor, engaged in a theological trial. The Inquisition is not a part of our revolutionary heritage."

Valdés paused, wondering whether a polemic with Che Guevara was indicated. He decided against it. "What you are hearing, honorable judges, is nothing more than the routine sentimentalities of protective lovers detected in treason. *I demand, sirs, that you pronounce a verdict.*"

President Dorticós rose and gestured to his fellow judges to retire to their antechamber for consultation.

The door closed, and Valdés was left alone with his papers. He did not turn his face to the defendants. Blackford spoke to Catalina in English, hoping that Valdés knew no English. He decided to begin by asking exactly that question. He spoke as rapidly as he could, using circumlocution and obliquity.

"Does our friend in charge of the proceedings follow what I say in my own language?"

"No," she replied. "He speaks not at all in that language."

"Will our friend on the court protect you?"

"I honestly do not know. He made no attempt to reach me during the day."

"I will attempt to raise holy hell. I can't tell you that I am very hopeful about it. But I will make a speech after the sentences are handed down. My guess is they'll give us prison terms. I'll demand this, demand the other, give indications that if I am not heard from in a day or two inquiries will be initiated in you-know-where, that sort of thing, and that perhaps those inquiries will themselves initiate the kind of surveillance that will reveal what they are up to. Of course all of that is better said alone, to our friend, than to the entire court. Would you guess he will be visiting either of us privately, perhaps right after the verdict?"

"Again I don't know. He may be in a little hot water himself. After all, he just routinely brought me along when —when—the younger brother of the Big Chief took him out to . . . that secret installation a week ago."

"Is it likely our friend will try to cover for himself by voting stiffly? Twenty-years-in-the-clink kind of thing?"

"Your guess is as good as mine. At this point you probably know him about as well as I do."

But at this point the prosecutor decided that for all he knew, supplementary subversion was going on under his very eyes. He turned and ordered, *"Silencio!"* They obeyed.

And, in the silence, they found that raised voices from the judicial antechamber could be heard through the door, however indistinctly. There was, for Catalina, the indisputable accents of Raúl Castro in high dudgeon. Blackford recognized the metallic voice of President Dorticós and, of course, the argumentative, seductive, provocative sound of Che Guevara. But there was a fourth voice. It came first to Catalina whose it was, and, not much later, to Blackford. Fidel Castro was in that room. Which meant that the verdict of the judges would be the verdict of Fidel.

The door opened, and President Dorticós led the three judges back to the long table, where they took their seats.

The prosecutor rose.

"Your excellencies. As regards the defendant Urrutia, have you reached a verdict?"

The President replied, "We have."

Following judicial procedure, the prosecutor turned toward Raúl Castro. "Comandante Castro, your verdict?"

"Guilty."

"Your recommended sentence?"

"Death. By firing squad."

The prosecutor, visibly unshaken, turned to Dorticós. "Mr. President: Your verdict?"

"Guilty."

"Your recommended sentence?"

"Death by firing squad."

The prosecutor was animated. "And Comandante Guevara, your verdict?"

"Guilty."

"Your recommended sentence?"

Blackford drew his breath. In the silence, it was audible. Che Guevara did not hesitate. "Death by firing squad."

It was all repeated for the defendant, Blackford Oakes. Guilty, firing squad. Guilty, firing squad. Guilty—Che Guevara treated himself to a leisurely puff on his cigar before answering: "Death, by firing squad."

Thirty-five

The hilltop prison to which they were taken, arriving after midnight, was El Príncipe, perhaps a half hour away from central Havana. Again they were logged in, and this time led to adjacent cells. After taking off their handcuffs outside their cells, the guard permitted Blackford to press Catalina's hand on her way into her cell. In his own cell, Blackford looked about and was glad to see that there was electric light. A single overhead bulb, but unlike the night before, it was possible to see. There was a little desk, with a pad of paper and a pencil, and three volumes of Castro's speeches and a life of Lenin. There was no way to communicate with Catalina. The walls between the cells were too thick even to attempt the basic prisoners' code, the rat-tat-tat by which gradually one learns to break down the alphabet. A process, Blackford reflected ruefully, that in any case takes longer to learn than they probably had to live.

In the morning he heard his cell door open. It was a captain attached to the Ministry of the Interior. He advised Sr. Ohks that an appeal would automatically be made on his behalf, and that it would probably be acted upon that very day. If his sentence was commuted, he would be taken to more permanent prison quarters . . . Short pause.

"If not, what?"

"If not, the sentence will be carried out at dawn tomorrow."

Blackford thought wildly.

"I have a communication for Comandante Guevara. Extremely urgent and extremely important. He will be very disturbed if he does not have it, or if there is any effort made by any other person to read its contents."

"Where is the message?"

"I have not yet written it out. I request the help of Señorita Catalina Urrutia to render it in proper Spanish."

The young captain paused to consider the request.

"As I say, Comandante Guevara will be *extremely* interested in what I propose," Blackford repeated himself.

"Very well."

He called to the guard, and in a moment Catalina was brought in. The captain said, "I shall return in fifteen minutes."

"Make that twenty minutes. Remember, translation is necessary."

The moment he was gone, Catalina, looking pale, asked, "Did they tell you about the one-day appeal? And the execution tomorrow?"

"Yes."

"What do you have in mind?"

"Take this dictation and translate it." He handed her the pad and pencil.

"To Comandante Che Guevara.

"Our relationship has been at two levels. The first was one that governed while we both hoped to work out an Acuerdo that would have prevented the current crisis."

"Slow down, Caimán."

"The second is at the level of enemies—" Blackford slowed down. "I of your system, you of mine. We have graduated to the second relationship, which is hostile. I do not ask you to suppose that I am now appealing to our first relationship in making the following proposal.

"It is this: that I give you information of vital interest to Cuba, in return for a commutation of sentences for Catalina and me. I will give you this information only in a face-to-face conference with you, orally. If you agree that the information I give you is significant, you will spare my life, and commit me to a jail until the moment when you reveal, or the Americans discover, your missiles. I will then be given safe conduct to Guantánamo Bay. If you do *not* believe the information I give you to be that valuable, you are free to proceed with my execution.

"The only cost you will then have run is a commutation for Catalina, which your government will decree in any case —i.e., no matter what value you attach to the secrets I will divulge. My agreeing to meet with you requires that you hand us that commutation instrument for Catalina at the outset of our meeting." Catalina looked up at him, but the tone of his voice kept her from interrupting.

"I should like to add, without invoking the other relationship, that I continue to trust you. If you acquiesce in this proposal, I am satisfied that you will not betray us."

"How do you want to sign it?"

"Sign it Caimán. That's how he thinks of me."

Che read the message from Caimán carefully, and thought. In Castro's presence, the day before, Raúl had screamed at Guevara over his indiscretion in taking Catalina with them to the missile site. For the first time, in front of both men, Che had been on the defensive. In every preceding situation when Raúl had got out of hand, Che had treated him, as often as not in front of Fidel, with withering condescension. Che knew his own prestige and his own value. Moreover he had always been faithful to Fidel, executing the leader's orders with dispatch even if he had expressed disagreement with Castro's judgment. Che Guevara had an immense prestige throughout the revolutionary world; he knew it, and Castro knew it. He was a philosopher as well as a soldier. He had lent such philosophical breadth as Castro's evolutionary communism had been able to achieve. Che had several times pointed out that many of the self-same communists now in Castro's court, for instance Carlos Rafael Rodríguez, had from the beginning backed the infamous Batista and actively opposed Castro's 26th of July Movement. On all these occasions Fidel had not merely permitted what others present might have interpreted as an act of condescension, he had visibly and sometimes even audibly encouraged it. Raúl, in point of fact, had been something of a problem for Fidel himself, and it was easier all the way around for Che to administer occasional deflations of his brother than for Fidel to have to do so.

But yesterday had been different. In plain fact, taking Catalina to the missile site had been a mistake which came close to being disastrous, never mind the plausibility of what he had done. One's translator and aide one comes to think of as an extension of oneself. Fidel, after all, pronounced regularly in his dining room, in front of the house servants, on any number of delicate national questions. So that Che had, this time around, suffered with silence Raúl's excoriation of Che's "stupidity." But when this charge graduated to Che's "near treasonable stupidity" his blood boiled and he shot back. "I was wrong in taking along Catalina, Raúl. But if my stupidity approached treason, why did not your stupidity approach treason in permitting Catalina to come with us? I admit to *my* mistake in taking her; do you admit to *your* mistake in permitting her to come along? You could have said, 'No—you, Che, must come by yourself.' *You* are the Minister of the Armed Forces. Do *I* therefore deserve all the blame?"

Fidel, sitting with his cigar, had interrupted the howl of his brother by snapping, simply, decisively, "Che has a point."

Che's willingness, at the trial that evening, to acquiesce in the sentence of death had been formal expiation for his mistake. He had not even argued with Fidel in the antechamber when Fidel said he desired the death sentence for both, immediately.

Che thought more about Caimán's letter and then made

his decision. He called Castro and simply told him that he was on his way to see him on very urgent business, and where did his leader choose to meet? Answer: At Cojímar. Che arrived at one o'clock: after lunch for Che, before lunch for Fidel.

Fidel listened.

Did Che think Caimán had information that might be really useful? He assumed, for instance, that Che had already interrogated him on the matter of the invasion?

"Of course. And of course he said not only that he knew of no such thing, but that he was very surprised at hearing the allegation that any such thing was planned."

"Is he the type who would give you secrets to spare his life?"

"That's the principal problem. No, he is not such a type. I must assume he is trying to get the girl off. But in order to get her off, he might give us useful information."

"The clock is running very fast now. The only thing we would need to fear is an invasion if it came within the next two weeks. The KGB and our own people have not been very useful about exact dates, but if in fact a massive strike were within two weeks of taking place, you would think— no?—that we would have heard *something*?"

"I would."

"There is, of course, the obvious solution. Hear what he has to say, then shoot them both."

"No, Fidel."

"Yes, I expected you would say that." Castro half smiled. "But you would have no objections to shooting him if his information was less than extremely illuminating?"

"None whatsoever."

Fidel thought for a while. "He didn't take the precaution of asking what, in place of a commuted sentence, we would still be free to mete out to the girl." He laughed.

"No. I was rather surprised by that. There is nothing in

the proposed contract that would prevent us from giving her a life sentence."

"We do not give out life sentences in Cuba, Che."

"Of course. I forgot about that progressive aspect of our penology. We could give her twenty years."

Che went on, rising from his chair. "Here would be one way to do it that is attractive philosophically—"

"You always get philosophical, and philosophy bores me. I mean, except Marx's and Lenin's philosophy."

It was Che's turn to laugh, but he pursued his point. "Why not do this: If the information he gives us is truly useful, we let him go to Guantánamo—*after* our D-Day, when he cannot hurt us. And we give the girl a light sentence. If his information is not useful, we shoot him and give the girl twenty years."

"Why not?" Fidel said. "If that is your recommendation."

Che smiled inwardly. Fidel often ratified difficult decisions by recording that they had originated as someone else's suggestion. Che knew what was expected of him:

"In that case, I will proceed with"—he put the slightest emphasis on the possessive—"my suggestion."

Castro nodded.

Che was almost out of the door when Fidel spoke again. "One thing. Let us first deny the appeals—let them think they will die tomorrow. That will put them in better shape for your conference. Schedule it some hours later."

"*Bueno, Comandante.*"

At six o'clock the captain from the Ministry of the Interior arrived at Blackford's cell door. Though the message was hardly so complicated as to need reading, he nevertheless did read it, from a piece of paper he took from his pocket.

" 'The appeal from the sentence of death by Blackford Ohks is herewith denied. S/Osvaldo Dorticós.' " The captain added that any reasonable requests would be granted for Sr. Ohks's final evening, and that a representative of the superintendent of El Príncipe would be there shortly to hear from him.

"Did you deliver my note to Comandante Guevara?"

"I did."

"He had no reaction?"

"I do not know. I gave it to his personal secretary and left."

"What is the appeals verdict on Catalina Urrutia?"

"Her appeal has also been denied."

"Has she been told yet?"

"Yes. Good night, Sr. Ohks. I shall . . . be a witness tomorrow, so I shall not say *adiós.*"

"Then *hasta luego,*" Blackford Oakes replied, dully.

At 7 P.M. the huge bearded assistant to the superintendent came in, and Blackford noticed with wry amusement that he read out his questions from a printed form on a clipboard.

"Does the condemned man *[el condenado]* desire to see a priest or a minister?"

"Yes." The assistant made a notation on the form.

"Does the *condenado* desire anything unusual from the kitchen?"

"*Anything* unusual from your kitchen."

(No comment.) "Does the *condenado* desire any alcoholic beverage? He may have a total of eight ounces of rum. He may have them all tonight, all tomorrow before he is summoned, or half tonight and half tomorrow."

"All tonight."

"Does the *condenado* have sufficient writing materials for anything he desires dispatched upon his decedence *[decedencia]*?"

"I will need more paper, and I would appreciate the use of a ballpoint pen."

"Does the condemned understand that any correspondence is subject to passage by Cuban security censors?"

"I understand I have no rights."

(No comment.) "Does the condemned have any other
requests?"

"Yes. I would like to visit with the Señorita Urrutia."

"I shall inquire as to whether or not that will be possible.
Buenas noches."

Odd, the strength of convention. To wish a "good" night
to someone scheduled for execution on the following
morning.

Blackford went to the desk and began a letter to Sally.

He was still writing at eight when the door opened and a
tray was brought in. Chicken and beans and rice, and about
eight jiggers of rum.

"*Gracias,*" he said to the guard.

"*Para servirle.*"

Another of those conventions. *Para servirle.* Rough translation: Anything to make you happy.

He nibbled at the chicken, and had drunk half the rum
when the door opened again and the captain from the
Ministry of the Interior, manifestly surprised by it all, said:

"We have instructions to take you to a . . ."—he had
mistakenly begun to give the site of the appointment,
thought better of it, and continued—"place, for a meeting
ordered by the High Command."

Oh my God, Blackford thought. Here it is. He had
thought of nothing else since dictating the letter than what
it was he would confide to Che Guevara. But his heart
leaped with life. He had saved Catalina. He had better make
the point absolutely certain.

"I go nowhere without Señorita Urrutia."

"She is listed on the order to go with you. She is waiting
in the corridor."

Blackford looked back at the cell. His worldly goods, at

that moment, added up to his unfinished letter to Sally and the clothes he had on. He followed the captain out the door.

Catalina said nothing, but her eyes were wild with hope as she looked up at Blackford. They were led to a military truck and seated in the back, facing each other. The grilled hatch door was then locked. Each had a guard seated to one side; in front, shielded by a steel bulwark relieved only by a high, small barred window, was the captain, seated next to the driver. The truck moved to the prison gates, which were raised after a brief transaction between the captain and the sentry. Soon, on the highway, they were tooling along at eighty kilometers per hour.

Catalina spoke. "It will be Che, obviously."

"I can only imagine."

"Are you prepared?"

"As much as I can ever be."

"I owe you my life."

"I was a horse's ass this morning."

"What do you mean?"

"I neglected to specify for you anything other than the commutation of your death sentence."

"Believe me, I never thought of it."

"I didn't either. But anyway, if we can 'trust' Che, to use the word you and I exchanged on a certain beach six weeks ago, at least you will not be shot tomorrow. You will not be shot at all."

The truck slowed down. Blackford stretched his head and peered through the small window that gave him visual access, across the driver's compartment, to the road. There was another truck there, flashing a policeman's red light. The two guards stiffened and took their pistols out of their holsters. When their own truck had come to a full stop, ten meters from the flashing light, Blackford saw the captain step down and an elderly, slight, bearded man wearing a colonel's insignia walk out of the truck ahead, a clipboard in hand.

They conferred, the red light still oscillating, causing the two officers alternately to disappear from view and then to emerge as animated red statues, apparently engaged in calm discussion.

The captain paused, and then directed the colonel to his own truck. Blackford heard the captain say, "They are in the rear quarters, with the guards."

The colonel responded, "I must ascertain their identity —my orders, Captain."

The captain led him around with his flashlight and un-locked the grilled door at the back of his truck.

He flashed the light inside, at the two guards and the two prisoners. The colonel, situated behind the captain, sud-denly beamed his own much more powerful light at the staring faces of the four occupants. With his right hand he fired first into the head of the captain, then with a bullet each at the heads of the two guards, who slumped down. Simultaneously, from the back of the truck in front a rifle cracked, a bullet piercing the head of the driver.

"Come along," the colonel hissed.

Catalina and Blackford jumped from the truck into the cavity at the back of the police truck.

"*Quick!*" the colonel said.

Two armed men in fatigue uniforms jumped in beside them. The colonel went to the front beside the driver and the truck sped off, though not at such speed as would arouse suspicion. Several minutes went by.

Catalina: "Should we talk?"

"Yes, unless our friends here tell us to be quiet. Talk in English, of course. I think it would be wise if we did not address them at all."

"What a . . . I mean . . . what an . . ."

"Operation. That was something. But we don't know

what . . ."—it was Blackford's turn to be rattled—"what it means . . ."

Catalina's face was barely visible, by the moon, still strong, its rays collected, strengthened, focused in the light that passed through the window's prism. Her expression was of wonder and relief and exuberance.

"I tell you, Blackford, it is—" she must not use a word the guards would recognize "—it is . . . the man you and I said we trusted, on the beach. I think he has delivered us."

"Funny way of doing that, Catalina. Four Cuban officials were killed five minutes ago. By—the-man-we-trusted?"

They were off the main road, approaching the lights of a small seaside town. The truck drove, with unhurried deliberation, along the main street to the outskirts, where there were fishing wharves. Next to one of them the truck stopped.

The door behind them was opened. There was no flashlight this time, merely the bearded colonel, who said, "Follow me."

They descended, and the colonel told them to wait. He went up to where the two silent men were, extended his hand and said huskily, *Dios les bendiga, compañeros.*

He had evidently already said good night to the driver, because he beckoned to Blackford and Catalina to follow him, which they did. They walked along a wharf toward the end. There was a fishing trawler there, perhaps thirty-five feet long and twelve feet wide.

"Step down," the colonel said.

Within five minutes the boat's captain had the vessel under way. The diesel pushed it along at seven knots. Blackford looked up, from force of habit as an old fighter pilot, and located the north star. He was not surprised that it lay in front of the little boat. The moon, still bright, made silver the pathway out of the harbor. One or two fishing boats, their running lights on, passed them to starboard. Their own vessel was unlit. The captain was at the wheel.

Catalina and Blackford sat on the starboard side of the little cockpit. Opposite them the colonel.

He said in Spanish, "I don't care what your rules are about lights, skipper. This is the longest I have been without a cigarette in forty-five years."

He struck a match and, behind the beard, Blackford discerned the features of Cecilio Velasco.

Thirty-six

Che Guevara had decided to meet with Caimán at the military intelligence headquarters of the Jiménez. There he could have instant access to all Cuban records and personnel and could check out without delay anything Caimán said to him that could be verified—or discredited. He waited, having assumed the prisoners would arrive just before ten o'clock. At ten-fifteen he became anxious. At ten-thirty, quietly desperate.

He radioed an aide and told him to call military and civilian police and ask if there had been any sign of an incapacitated truck between El Príncipe and central Havana. That, specifically, he was looking for a military truck carrying two prisoners and four officials. Another aide was told to call the military prison to establish whether they had left on schedule.

He rapped his knuckles on the table, puffed on his cigar, and suffered an attack of asthma. He pulled out his inhaler and a bottle of pills, swallowing two without water. It was after eleven that a report came from a police motorcyclist that an apparently empty truck had been spotted off the Vía Blanca. Moments later the aide reported excitedly: "There are four bodies in the truck. All shot through the head."

"Identifications?"

"The police are reporting in by radio. They appear to be government officials. Do you wish the names?"

"No!" Guevara said, pausing for an agonized moment at the humiliation that lay before him. "Get me Comandante Valdés."

Every accessible resource of a heavily militarized totalitarian society was mobilized that night before midnight had struck. Patrols were sent out scouring the roads in every direction from Havana. Beyond advising the network that an American man, age about thirty-five, and a Cuban woman, also about thirty-five, were two of the quarries, not much could be said. They might be with two resistance guerrillas, they might be with four, they might conceivably be with eight.

The missiles! Che thought. Valdés had taken the precaution, two nights ago, of guarding the Swiss Embassy so that no one could enter without scrupulous investigation. Suddenly he thought: the commercial telephone! Beginning a few months ago an order had gone out to expedite instead of to encumber outgoing and incoming calls. They were, to be sure, all monitored, and almost all were calls from Cubans in the United States to grandchildren, or sons, or in-laws. Suddenly it occurred to Che that conceivably Caimán might have reached out for a commercial telephone and had the good fortune to get through to the United States without the usual six-to-eight-hour wait.

It required a single telephone call to cancel all overseas service until further notice.

And then, Che thought, there was the sea. Obviously the resistance movement that had engineered the escape would at least consider that possibility.

A small boat. God knows enough of them had left Cuba, landing in Florida, even though that ass of an "admiral" that Fidel likes, never mind his manifest incompetence, insisted that his patrol boats brought in the overwhelming majority of those vermin.

Another telephone call, rousing the admiral from his bed.

Che had ascertained that they had left the prison at nine. The ambush would have taken place roughly between nine-fifteen and nine-thirty. There was no way of telling which of the hundred tiny ports along the north coast of Cuba the guerrillas had headed for, if they were gone to sea. But it was reasonable to suppose that they would go out no farther than, say, fifty kilometers from Havana, the area in which the concentration of boats was heaviest.

Probably not a speedboat, since these were difficult to commandeer, were always conspicuous, and were in any case unreliable in a sea. Probably they went for a sailboat. Or a fishing boat—these Fidel had nationalized so that there were at hand rosters of them, where they were supposed to be, etc. That would be another telephone call.

Where was he? Yes, 10:30 embarkation, let's suppose. Traveling, say, at ten knots maximum. Fifteen nautical miles north of Cuba at midnight, 25 miles at 1 A.M. 35 miles at 2 A.M., 45 miles at 3 A.M., 55 miles at 4 A.M., 65 at 5—what time was dawn?

He screamed out at an aide: "When is dawn tomorrow, *quick?*" The aide rushed to that morning's paper: 6:16. Twilight, one half hour before that. He would send army aircraft. They would describe an arc north of the island, from two hundred kilometers east of Havana to two hundred kilometers west. They would go out seventy miles—seven-ninths of the way to Florida—way beyond the distance they could legally detain traffic, but the hell with that. Six coast guard cutters would head instantly to that arc—six into four hundred, approximately sixty kilometers apart—and they would listen for reports from the aircraft. Any boat, *any boat* detected heading north would be stopped and searched.

Two more telephone calls.

He stopped. An awful thought. "Get me the Admiralty communications chief. Instantly. Wake him up if you have to."

"There is always a communications official on duty, Comandante, at the naval base."

"Get me him."

In a few minutes he was talking to a young man obviously awed at the presence, over the telephone, of Comandante Guevara.

"What would be the typical radio equipment of a small fishing boat?"

"Ship-to-shore, Comandante?"

"What other kind is there, for God's sake."

"Ship-to-ship, Comandante."

"What kind do they mostly have?"

"A ship-to-shore radio usually has, also, facilities for ship-to-ship."

"What is the range?"

"That depends, Comandante, on the wattage of the set."

"Well what is the wattage of the average set?"

"Anywhere from eighteen to fifty, Comandante."

"What is the range of the eighteen-watt set?"

"It depends on climatic conditions, and on the time of day."

Che sensed that with this young man he would need to be very specific.

"Could an eighteen-watt set reach Miami from Havana?"

"Not very likely, Comandante."

"How close would he have to be to Miami before reaching Miami?"

"It depends on climatic conditions, and on the time of day."

Che reached into his pocket and gulped down two more pills. "Assuming existing conditions, what would be your estimate?"

"There is a lot of luck, Comandante, involved in such matters. Atmospheric conditions, for instance."

Che gritted his teeth. "What would be the chances, eighty kilometers from Miami, of a ship's signal reaching Miami at, say, 3 A.M.?"

"They might get through, they might not get through, Comandante. I would hesitate to give you the odds."

Che Guevara slammed down the telephone. He asked one aide if he had got through to the admiral. The answer was that yes, he had; the admiral had understood the Comandante's instruction and had instantly issued orders to the coast guard vessels, but given the hour of the night there might be a delay of as much as two or three hours before the coast guard vessels, other than the two already on duty, would be seabound.

"You told him it was a state emergency?"

"Yes, Comandante."

"And the air force?"

"We could not reach Comandante Portillo, but I got through to his adjutant and he told me the orders would go out instantly."

"Did he say when the planes would be airborne?"

"He said, Comandante, that there would be no point in getting them into the air before twilight, since the moonlight is almost gone now, but that they could easily monitor the arc you described by four-thirty."

Che sat back. He heaved under the pressure of the asthma. He ordered the oxygen tank brought from his car. He breathed deeply from it, his mind constantly skating about the one question remaining, which had shrouded every moment, even while he was talking over the telephone.

Should he call Fidel?

He dreaded even the thought; the thought, however, would not go away. Che Guevara had written *Guerrilla Warfare*, a missal on guerrilla tactics, a heavy book which he knew would earn him great recognition as a revolutionary tactician. In that book, drawing from his experience in the Sierra Maestra, he had stressed the usefulness of small, light, mobile enterprises. This, of course, would be exactly the moment when Fidel would ask him what in the hell Che had been up to, bringing two important prisoners of state in one lousy truck with only four personnel. He would

answer that that was the way he—and Fidel—and Camilo
Cienfuegos and Frank País and Juan Almeida had always
operated, that theirs was not a Maginot Line-type operation, that four armed guards had always been deemed sufficient to bring two unarmed prisoners from anywhere to
anywhere . . .

How much easier it would be to call him in the morning,
tell him that guerrillistas had ambushed the truck with Caimán and the girl, that they had got away, but that they had
been apprehended on Highway X on route to Y, or at sea,
en route to Florida.

Would he then say, *"Why didn't you call me?"*

Che reasoned that if he had the prisoners at hand, that
question would quickly reduce to a matter of protocol. If he
did not have the prisoners at hand, violations of protocol
would be the least he would have to worry about.

He rang. "Bring me some tea."

He would stay exactly where he was. Ideally situated.
Main office of Cuban Intelligence: of the Jiménez.

Until he heard from the land patrols. Or the sea patrols.
Or the ocean patrols.

Or from Fidel.

He reached into his shoulder bag and brought out a copy
of the poems of García Lorca.

Thirty-seven

Blackford, Catalina, and Velasco sat in the *Aguila*'s utilitarian little saloon, below. It was illuminated by two low-burning kerosene lamps hanging on gimbals so that they appeared steady, imperturbable, in seas rocky now, as they plodded into northerly winds gusting at over twenty knots. They could barely discern the shape of the captain at the wheel, through the top third of the companionway hatch, through which they let in air.

"You'd have to be less than a hundred yards away to see this light," Blackford said. And turned to Velasco.

"Cecilio, you're the goddamnedest son of a bitch in the whole world. I think if the struggle for the West is won it will be because you left the losing side to join the winning side, and you turned the fucking tables. I've got to have the story, where the hell have you been, what the hell you've been doing the last six weeks. But first, let's calm down."

Velasco maintained himself on the windward settee by bracing his leg on the steel stanchion that ran up the after end of the little dining table. "There is a lot to think about very quickly, Blackford. We are at least eleven hours from Florida."

"Right. And when we run into the Gulf Stream, with this northerly, it's going to be rough."

"Where is the Gulf Stream?" Cecilio asked.

"It runs about thirty miles wide, northbound into the wind, beginning just outside Florida. It snakes northeast around the Keys, which is where we'll find it. We should hit it between seven and eight. There is a lot we need to do before then. Well, not a lot, but enough. We've got to get through to Washington."

"Blackford, any radio messages will be picked up by Havana. They would then find us in a minute."

"We can't use the radio yet, I agree. Not yet. What do we have on board?"

"A Raytheon, twenty-five watts."

"It's in working order?"

"It would be more accurate to say that it sometimes works, I have gathered from the captain."

"Now listen, Cecilio, here is why we have to use it at some point if there is ever any question about our getting through. The Soviets have installed missiles in Cuba."

Catalina clarified: "Medium and intermediate-range missiles."

"The intermediates travel twenty-six hundred miles. The medium-rangers, twelve hundred miles."

Velasco's eyes closed nearly shut. "Are you *certain,* Blackford?"

Blackford pointed to his own eyes. "I have seen them. Thanks to Catalina. That is why you found us in jail, instead of at the Tropicana."

"It is mad."

"That's the whole point. So mad, my guess is there isn't anybody in Washington has any idea of it. Otherwise there'd have been action. We've got to get them the word. The best way to get them the word is to use a commercial pay phone in Key West.

"Let's think, now: If we use the radio, the Cubans will pick up the signal on RDF and home in on us. If we were *certain* we could get through to an operator right away, we could wait until the last minute before they came in on us and then radio. But if this Raytheon is like a few others I've experienced, it might take anywhere up to fifteen minutes to get through, and we might not get through at all. Though at least it'll be early enough not to be competing against too much other ship radio traffic." He turned to Velasco. "Ask the captain, Cecilio, what kind of range he's had with the radio."

Velasco returned from the cockpit to say, "He says sometimes he has reached as far as Matanzas."

"How far is that?"

"A hundred and twenty kilometers."

"He says 'sometimes.' Ask him, at the safe end, what range can he count on?"

Velasco went up again and came back to say, "Fifty kilometers. Thirty miles."

"Thirty miles. About when we hit the Gulf Stream—7 A.M." He got up and, hanging on tightly to the guardrail, made his rolling way to the little chart table and flicked on the red overhead light. He studied the chart carefully and returned to the seat.

"I'd say this: Let's think in terms of radio at 7 A.M. If they haven't spotted us by then, we'll continue to guard radio silence. It's pretty unlikely they'd attempt to board us when we're as close as thirty miles from the U.S. On the other hand, if there are any signs of action, we'll have to go for broke on the radio wherever we are. Now let's, before we do anything else, get exactly right how this model works. Are you familiar with it, Cecilio?"

"The captain checked me out on it yesterday."

"Well, let's not put it off. It's been a relaxing day. We may as well get to work."

For a full half hour, both men hanging tight to the guardrail, they diddled with the equipment, doing everything except broadcasting. They could now operate it in the dark, if they had to. Blackford left the set on standby. "We'll let it keep warm."

"Where's the radio telephone guide?"

Velasco fished it out and Blackford pored over it. At Key West, Miami, and Lauderdale, marine operators guarded telephone channels. "Obviously our first go should be at Key West—Miami is a hundred miles farther away, though probably their receivers are more powerful—and then hope like hell for Miami if Key West doesn't pick us up. A reserve we can flash to is MAYDAY on the emergency channel. At that point, if we've gotten no action, Cecilio, ¿Quién sabe?"

Catalina, her body very nearly upright at the end of the settee, had fallen asleep. Not easy to do, given the rolling seas.

Blackford got up and, maneuvering her comatose legs, stretched her out gently on the settee, which was not quite long enough for her to extend out on, so he put two life cushions under her legs, lifting her feet against the wooden bulwark. He fastened the bunk straps around her. She would not, now, be tossed onto the cabin sole if one of those rolls, coming now every few minutes, tilted the vessel into an angle that overcame the serene gravitational inertia of a body lying on a level surface.

"Who will you call?" Cecilio asked.

"I've got to think that out. Help me. Most obvious: Duty Officer, CIA. We both know that telephone number. But God knows who will answer. Presumably he wouldn't dismiss it as a nuthouse call, but who knows." Blackford paused. "I think maybe the better first number to try would be Trust's—he is an old friend, a professional colleague. This is Sunday, and I know his home number in New York. The third number—if Trust doesn't answer, and CIA bombs—is the home telephone number of McCone. Dammit, I have it, in code, in my logbook, which resides, happily and uselessly, in my suitcase at Catalina's. Do you by any chance have the number, Cecilio?"

"No. Anyway, it wouldn't work."

"What do you mean?"

"He is off on a three-week honeymoon."

"Come on! Not that I am against three-week honeymoons—Sally and I had a three-day preliminary honeymoon before you so rudely brought me in from Taxco."

"So then, what?"

"Well, the alternative at that point is—maybe not obvious, but indicated. We call 202-456-1414."

"What number is that?"

"The White House. Probably they wouldn't put me through to *El Presidente*. But those operators are something else. They would put me through to somebody. And the point is just: get the message through."

Blackford thought it prudent to reduce to writing, in priority, all the contingent alternatives. The numbers to call. The first, the second, the third. Preceded by the channel to importune first, second, third, All Ships At Sea—that kind of thing.

He was very tired, and he found his mind refractory in the matter of setting down exactly the priority of objectives. Ideally the President (or the Deputy Director of the CIA, since McCone was out of town) would be told the salient part of their message: that the Cubans had nuclear missiles, prepared to be armed.

What priority ultimately attached to the secrecy of the communication? Suppose that Walter Cronkite, on vacation in a sailboat, overheard the transmission, aborted his vacation, and went on the air to say that he had caught a communication to the effect that the Cubans had, etc., etc., etc. This would deprive the White House of time for deliberating the nature of their response to the Soviet-Cuban threat, but wasn't that risk infinitely preferable to not getting the message through at all?

Blackford forced himself to record, in the log, exactly what would be done, (a), (b), (c), in the event of a) suspicious attention to the *Aguila* by airplane; b) suspicious attention to the *Aguila* by patrol vessel; c) outright assault on *Aguila* by airplane; d) outright assault on *Aguila* by patrol vessel. In this contingency he made two subdivisions: one, an attempt to sink the *Aguila* by gunfire or whatever, and two, an attempt to board the *Aguila*. He wrote out corresponding radio and other activity for every contingency. He read these out to Velasco, who made two suggestions, both useful. Who would be on the radio? Who on the wheel? What would the helmsman do? In what circumstances?

It was after two in the morning. The wind retained its Force 7 velocity; the *Aguila* absorbed the beating but with considerable physical discomfort to its passengers.

"Cecilio, I've got to go and relieve the captain. What is his name?"

"Eduardo."

"Resistance fighter? Mercenary?"

"The latter."

"Quick background."

"Sixty-five. His ship was nationalized by Che in that last edict. Very bitter. Income way down. I propositioned him after one of my friends said he was a likely collaborator."

"Money?"

"Yes. A lot. Fifty thousand dollars if he delivers us to Miami."

"Did you have a chance to size him up? Family problems?"

"That's the good news. No children. Wife died two years ago. He is convinced that if the doctor she had used for thirty years had been around she'd have made it. But the doctor had been shot. Because he had also been the doctor of Batista's wife, and had volunteered to look after the wounded Cubans on the beach at the Bay of Pigs."

"Well. Doesn't sound as if Eduardo would turn around and go home at the first sight of a Cuban patrol. Would hardly do him much good. I'd like to be there at *his* court-martial in front of Ramiro Valdés, Osvaldo Dorticós, and Che Guevara."

"I want to hear about that."

"Any firearms on board?"

Velasco smiled around the cigarette in his mouth. "One .22-caliber rifle. And even that had to be sneaked on board at the last minute. The resistance gentlemen who brought us here declined to part with their guns."

"I was hoping you would say, 'Six hand grenades and two Ak-17's'—what is that complicated Spanish word for machine guns?"

"*Ametralladoras.*"

"Right . . . One .22, and that's it?"

Velasco puffed on his cigarette. "There are the makings, here and there, of some nuisance weapons. There is kerosene, there are rags, there is a rather sophisticated inventory of distress flares. Put it this way: there isn't anything that would keep a well-stocked patrol vessel out of our way for very long."

Blackford reflected. "Let's have a quick drink, *compañero.*"

Velasco's face brightened. He reached over the prostrate body of Catalina to a locker, opened it, and brought out a bottle of rum. Grappling with the seas he tossed the bottle to Blackford and walked his way, clutching the guardrail, to a locker opposite the chart table, which disgorged two coffee cups. He tried at first to hold a cup steady, while Blackford poured.

"That doesn't work at sea," Blackford said, reaching for one cup. Bracing one foot against the table leg between the two saloon couches, he managed to pour a few jiggers into the first cup and jerkily to convey it to Velasco. He took the second cup, did the same, and returned the bottle. Velasco wedged it into the galley-locker. They looked at each other.

"To you, Cecilio. My thanks."

"To you, *amigo. Para servirle.*"

They drained their drinks. "Okay, let's go. Foul-weather gear?"

Velasco stood and made his way to the standing locker on the starboard side of the companionway, opened it, and fished out two sou'westers. He tossed one at Blackford, who said, "I'll relieve the skipper. You go forward and get some sleep. I'll call you if there's any reason to call you."

Cecilio smiled his half smile, visible and then invisible against the shifting illumination of the kerosene lamp by the chart table. "I will have no problem in staying awake. My problem would be in trying to sleep."

"Okay," said Blackford appreciatively.

They donned their gear and climbed up into the howl. It wasn't cold, but it was blowing hard, and the spray of the pounding boat reached back into the cockpit more or less continuously, sometimes as little needles of salt water, sometimes as great tumblerfuls.

"I have come to relieve you, Eduardo," Blackford had to speak loudly against the engine noise. He thought to add his thanks, but decided the moment inappropriate, and the circumstances conceivably dangerous. This was, theoretically, a commercial venture by Eduardo. "You had better go below, grab some cheese or whatever, and try to get a little rest. Mr. Velasco and I will take over. What is your course?"

"Until we hit the Gulf Stream, Zero Three Zero. After that we'll need to compensate. Are you familiar with boats, señor?"

"Yes. We can make the Gulf Stream calculations as late as 6 A.M. Do you have a radio direction finder?"

"*Sí, señor.*"

"Where is it?"

Eduardo pointed to a locker under the chart table. "I put in new batteries yesterday."

Blackford said he would check for drift on the course to Key West at four, and every hour after that.

Eduardo said, Good sailing, in monotone, and made his way below, sliding the overhead hatch back to let himself down, then closing it again and raising the bulkhead to the companionway to its two-thirds level.

"Call if you need me. At eighteen hundred rpm we would be doing eight knots normally. In these seas we will be doing under seven knots."

"Thanks," Blackford said at the wheel, lifting his hood over his head. "Eduardo," he called out.

The captain looked up through the bulkhead aperture.

"Can I borrow your cap?" Blackford asked him.

Eduardo tossed it to Cecilio, who handed it to Blackford. It helped deflect the spray.

Blackford had beckoned to Cecilio to come closer, so that they could converse over the engine noise. He did so happily, though his sacrifices were minor and major. He lost the windward protection of the canvas dodger, which shielded him, though only in part, from some of the spray. The major problem was his cigarette. There was no longer any way of keeping it lit.

"What did you do when I left you?"

"Do you really need to know, Blackford?"

"No. But I want to know."

"Very well. After Castro's DC-3 let me off at Guantánamo, I was ushered through the gate, the usual business. Two hours later, after leaving a note for the commandant that I had a sick Spanish-Cuban relative I had decided to look after before returning to the States, I went back the way I came, gave the usual signals, and told the guard, who had seen me only two hours earlier, that apparently my car was late, but that didn't matter, I would wait, as I had been instructed to do, at the village tavern. No problem, as it turned out."

"And then?"

"I made my way back to Havana. I had done the scouting, and I had pesos and dollars, plenty of them. Once in Havana I met with one of our assets."

"One of the people you knew during the Bay of Pigs business?"

"Yes. He is very well placed. In fact he told me that the day after I left you, reports had come in from the KGB on my activities in Spain and Mexico. That must have confused them. But the scene was quiet because, after all, I was supposedly back in America."

"And then?"

"I organized a quiet watch to keep track of you."

"Where did you stay?"

"In a room in the apartment house opposite Catalina's."

"God."

"I had help. Very encouraging. Castro thinks that the Camagüey guerrillas were all liquidated. That is three quarters true. There are remains, and many live in Havana."

"Did you see me go out that night—Thursday night—with Catalina?"

"Yes. But there wasn't time to follow you. I had access to a car and driver who had very well-placed papers, but getting him would have taken a half hour. So I made some calculations. I waited in my apartment, and I had one of my friends, in a truck, waiting opposite the Swiss Embassy. He reported to me your arrest.

"The problem then was to locate you. My collaborator watching the Swiss Embassy did not have a car, so he couldn't follow the military. So I figured the likeliest way to find you was to keep eyes on Che Guevara. That was not so difficult. When you left the Swiss Embassy with Catalina, under guard, and headed away, we didn't know where. Then we were lucky."

"How?"

"I called your pal Rosaria at headquarters the next morning, just like old times. I told her that the Comandante had asked to see me on the Caimán question. If she had frozen I'd have hung up, backed away. But she said first 'hello,' and then that Caimán had been detained at El Príncipe prison and would appear at a judicial proceeding with the Comandante at ten o'clock that night.

"We followed the military van to El Príncipe. We prepared a guerrilla strike for the next morning—for this morning—after we learned of the death sentence. Then, watching the entrance to El Príncipe, we saw the military truck drive up. One of my friends—he is very good at that sort of thing—made friends with the driver. Told my man he'd be there 'until they brought out the American.' I got the word in my truck, and substituted the ambush for the guerrilla action—which, my dear Blackford, I deceive you not, would have involved a stolen helicopter. My duties were greatly simplified. At one point I had sixteen men prepared. We did it with four—"

Blackford pointed: "What's that?"

Velasco strained to see in the direction Blackford was looking. He could not focus on whatever it was.

"I forgot to bring up the binocs. Do you know where they are?"

Velasco clambered below and returned with them. He took the wheel and handed them to Blackford, who looked two points to port and stared for a full two minutes.

"No problem. Merchant vessel, I'd guess. I can see his green running light, and he is headed well east of our course."

Blackford peered about him. The waves had reached five to eight feet, and the boat's way was sluggish, up against the heightening headwinds. The vessel continued to plod down on the water, as if expressing punctuated resentment over the helmsman's headstrong course. "I'd be tempted to head for the Bahamas in this wind," Blackford called out. To himself he muttered, "If there weren't other considerations to worry about . . ."

And, relaxing again, he returned to the interrupted narrative: "A helicopter. God almighty, Cecilio!"

"Perhaps you forget I had a great deal of contact with Cuba only eighteen months ago. I have my friends there."

"But not every friend has a helicopter."

"I have to admit that the pilot who was prepared to go to the air force base—to Ciudad Libertad—and simply step into a helicopter and fly it off as he used to do routinely was not the most self-assured man I ever met. He had not flown a helicopter in two years. But he had been in prison for two years; and that turns out to be very good substitute training. He amused himself in solitary, he told me, by imagining emergency situations in a helicopter and training his mind—he did this hour after hour, day after day—on just how he would cope with them."

"Don't give me too many details now, because it's a strain to hear. But tell me, what was the plan?"

"Orthodox. I saw variations in Spain. Huge diversion outside the gates. They used dive bombers. We planned to enter the helicopter with two machine gunners. A lot of dead men, but two live prisoners. Anyway, that was the plot."

"And then?"

"Simple. A run for Key West at low altitude. Surprise was essential. Executions are scheduled for 6 A.M. That isn't an hour at which Cuban fighters are quickly summoned. And remember, today is Sunday. By helicopter we'd have had you in Key West in fifty minutes."

"I guess right now I wish you had hung on to that helicopter."

"*That* was emergency action. A hundred things could have gone wrong. One well-aimed shot at the pilot at Ciudad Libertad, for instance."

"How strong is the resistance, Cecilio?"

"Only just about strong enough to attempt to rescue two prisoners."

"It's that bad?"

"I spent much time with the Resistance, Blackford. Castro broke their back at Camagüey. There are many left. But they become fewer day by day. Maybe you will be glad to know, Blackford, that since the unfortunate death of the poor radio operator, Nogales, the rate at which Castro has detected Resistance members has slowed. Slowed considerably. Still—I must go below and have a cigarette, Blackford—still, the freedom fighters are few. I do not know exactly how many. But today's exercise was, well, very—ingratiating. Is that the right word?"

"It will do," Blackford said, turning the wheel to avoid head-to-head confrontation with a huge oncoming wave. "Go get your cigarette, *compañero*."

And so Velasco went below. But stayed there much longer than it takes to smoke a cigarette; even two cigarettes. At one point Blackford simply concluded that Cecilio had succumbed to fatigue. But then he saw the shadow moving about in the way of the two dim lights.

It had got cold, and Blackford remembered his light sweater below. One hand on the wheel, he stretched toward the companionway bulkhead.

"Cecilio?"

There was a shuffle below. Cecilio had been sitting over the chart table.

"Yes, Blackford."

"On the settee, somewhere, is a sweater. Could you hand it to me?"

The sweater was thrust through the open part of the companionway. Ducking under the dodger, leaving the wheel unattended for a moment, Blackford took off the jacket of his sou'wester and pulled the sweater over his body. The sou'wester back on, he went to the wheel and made the minor adjustment necessary to resume course, and his mind turned to navigation, and to the radio direction finder. He looked at his watch. It was four. He called again to Cecilio. "I'd better check the RDF. Will you take the wheel for a bit?"

"In a moment, Blackford."

The moment turned out to be ten minutes. Velasco finally emerged, cigarette in his mouth. It was twilight, and the gray seas were now clearly visible. The skies were less than cloudy, more than merely misty. Visibility was perhaps five miles.

"Stick to 0-3-0 degrees," Blackford gave his relief the conventional instructions. "I'll give you a correction after I've got a bearing. When I call out *Mark,* make a note of your bearing."

Below, Blackford pulled out the five-pound RDF, sat it down on the chart table, aligned it to the boat's long axis, turned it on and quickly consulted his log, where he had written down the primary radio beacon numbers in that area. The signal from Key West had a range of up to 100 miles. He found, and brought in, the signal three separate times, bracketing the null, and shouting out: *Mark!* each time he fastened on it. He got the ship's headings from Cecilio: 0-3-5. 0-2-8. 0-3-2. He made his calculations, turned off the instrument, lowered the cockpit bulkhead and climbed back into the cockpit.

"We've been set to the east. Not surprising. Alter the course to 0-2-2 degrees." North-northeast was only a few compass points from where they could expect to see the sun through the mist, coming up off the starboard bow. When it came, it gladdened them. Now they experienced its psychological warmth. Soon they would feel its physical warmth. That was when they heard the airplane.

Each man looked up.

It was flying at about three thousand feet of altitude, headed in their direction. It began a descent, directly toward them. It looked for a moment almost like a fighter diving at a target.

"Grab the wheel!" Blackford shouted.

He dived below, shouted to Eduardo and Catalina to get up, and turned on the radio full volume. He flipped from channel to channel, hoping to stumble over the line the airplane overhead was using. He heard only static.

"Eduardo. Relieve Velasco. Send him down here."

To Velasco: "Were you able to spot any identification on the plane?"

"Yes. Cuban Air Force."

"Okay. Then the orders evidently aren't as simple as to drop a bomb or release a torpedo and simply sink us. They're probably not happy at the prospect of doing that kind of thing fifty miles from Key West. But we've got to assume they've given our position to Cuban patrols." Blackford paused for a moment. And then, to Cecilio, "Tell Eduardo to keep scanning the horizon. Catalina, put something on"—he pointed to the hanging locker "—and go forward with the binoculars. Keep looking for any signs of a boat headed our way. Or for any boat."

Without a word she reacted. In two minutes, foul-weather gear on, she had bounded to the cockpit and crawled forward, against the wind and seas, to the foredeck. In another two minutes she had returned. Through the hatch opening she shouted, "No good up there. Too much spray. I can monitor better—see better—from the cockpit."

"Okay," Blackford said. And to Velasco, "Remove that hatch cover. We don't need to shield the lights anymore."

He itched with the anxiety he had publicly discussed a few hours earlier.

Should he attempt a radio communication? He decided to share his quandary.

"Cecilio. Do we have *any* doubt that they now know where we are?"

"No, Blackford. They know where we are."

"It follows that to use the radio isn't going to do us any harm as far as identifying our position is concerned. Though it's true that if they hear us trying to get through to Washington, and if there's time to stop us, the fighter may be ordered to sink us. What the hell. Let's use the goddam thing and try to get a connection."

It was just after five-thirty. His contingency log spoke at him his premeditated decision to call first, if the emergency should come between four and eight in the morning, to Anthony Trust's home telephone; failing that, to the CIA Duty Officer.

He turned to Channel 40. *"This is the vessel* Aguila, *the vessel* Aguila *calling Key West. Our Calling Number is Whiskey Able George 9042, Whiskey Able George 9042. We are fifty miles south of Key West. Do you read me, Key West?"*

Silence.

The whole thing repeated again.

Silence.

The whole thing a third time.

Silence; and static. Blackford turned the squelch knob up, to drown out the static.

A fourth try. He was interrupted by a cry from the cockpit:

"There is a ship off our starboard bow, headed for us, approximate distance, six kilometers." It was Eduardo.

One more time, on the radio, never mind Eduardo's ship. No answer.

Blackford was grateful that, by glancing at his log, he was relieved of having to analyze what to do next. He turned the dial to Channel 16, the emergency channel.

"MAYDAY MAYDAY MAYDAY. Extreme emergency. This is the vessel *Aguila*, vessel *Aguila*. I need instant help, instant help. Any coast guard station listening, any coast guard station, or any ship at sea, please respond instantly, OVER."

Silence. From the cockpit Eduardo's voice reached him. Eduardo shouted: *"Estimated distance, three kilometers."*

Blackford heard, on the radio, a woman's faint voice. *"This is Key West Radio, Key West Radio. The yacht—how are you spelling your name?"*

"Able George Uncle Item"—Blackford turned to Cecilio: "What in the hell is the phonetic for L?"—but before getting an answer, he went on, *"Lollipop Able. This is an emergency."*

"What are your call letters, *Aguila?"*

"Whiskey Able George 9042."

Catalina leaned her head through the cockpit cavity. "They are closing fast, Caimán."

"This is an emergency, Key West, a great emergency. Please dial instantly, instantly, the following number in New York: 212-679-7330. OVER."

"Was that 212-679-7730?"

"No, operator, 7330. *Emergency!"*

"How shall we be billing that, sir? OVER."

"Make it collect. OVER."

"They will be alongside within three minutes," Catalina reported.

With his right hand Blackford signaled Catalina to come below. To the radio operator:

"Make it collect. Mr. Oakes is calling."

"How are you spelling that, sir?"

Blackford closed his eyes, while he said in forced rhythm, *"Opal Able Kilo Easy Sugar."*

"Stand by."

A shot was fired from the overtaking vessel. How far overhead it passed Blackford could not reckon. It was while briefly pondering the question that he heard the voice through the bullhorn. Catalina translated:

"He says to stop the engine and head into the wind immediately or the next bullets will be aimed amidships. Eduardo wants to know what to do."

Blackford did not pause: "Direct him to go full speed away from the vessel, head downwind. Give the Cubans as small a target as possible."

Aguila's engine roared to full throttle, and the boat steadied as, mercifully, it went now, after so many contrary hours, downwind: south-southwest.

"Operator, are you ringing that New York number?"

"Please stand by, sir. We are ringing."

The Cuban vessel roared forward in downwind pursuit and was soon abeam, parallel. Another machine-gun shot fired. This one pierced the chest of Eduardo, who fell over the wheel. The Cuban patrol boat slowed its speed to correspond to the ten knots the *Aguila* was now making. It now drew abreast of the boat. Three sailors, on deck, were readying the grappling hooks.

It was then that Cecilio Velasco made his move. He reached for a bundle that had sat in a corner of the after berth, covered with a towel. He bent over it, lighting a match. A fuse spurted out. He bounded onto the cockpit and, in an exuberant gesture as if he were a young Olympic athlete intent on throwing the discus exactly on target, he aimed his aggregation at the center of the patrol boat.

There flew from the cartridge container a cannonade of red and white flares, originally designed to reach one thousand feet into the air to signal a boat's distress. At fifteen feet they hit two of the three surrounding Cuban seamen in various parts of their torsos, causing them to roar with pain and the helmsman of the patrol boat to veer sharply away to windward.

"Yes, who is it?"—the voice on the radio was heard.

"Anthony, this is Blackford. Listen very hard, buddy, can you hear me?"

"Yes. Are you drunk, Blacky?"

"Shut up and listen. We are being attacked right now—right now, Anthony, by a Cuban patrol boat in the Straits of Florida. Now listen hard to every syllable: I have seen with my own eyes not forty-eight hours ago four, repeat four, medium-range Russian ballistic missiles in Havana near San Cristóbal. The intention is to have them and as many as forty more installed with nuclear caps ready to fire within one week or ten days. Did you hear me?"

"I heard you. Are you in danger?"

"Hell yes, but I'll keep talking as long as I can. We are being boarded by the Cubans. We are thirty miles from Key West, approximately at Latitude 24, Longitude 82. Massive Soviet operation under way—"

The radio turned to static. A machine gun had severed the antenna. A second burst of machine-gun fire ripped into the body of Cecilio Velasco, just after he had tossed a can of kerosene-soaked rags onto the deck of the Cuban patrol boat, which looked now to be aflame from its very bowels. A single bullet pierced Blackford through the left shoulder as he leaped into the cockpit to grab Velasco. It was a matter of two or three minutes before the patrol boat's fire extinguishers had doused the flames.

By that time the grappling hooks were firmly on the *Aguila*. A Cuban sailor jumped aboard the targeted prey and throttled down its engine. In seconds he was followed by three other Cuban sailors with machine guns.

Catalina was below, standing by Blackford, taking off his bloody shirt. He drew her to the settee and they both sagged down, close together. The pain of seeing Velasco had immobilized Blackford, who cooperated sluggishly with Catalina's attempt to improvise a bandage.

Brusquely, she was dragged off by two sailors. Two others came for Blackford, one of them with a machine gun pointed at his chest.

It was easier to jump from the Cuban vessel to the level of the fishing boat than to climb back up in a roaring sea. To get their prisoners up to the patrol boat it was necessary to winch them up on a boom.

The officer left aboard the *Aguila* was using a walkie-talkie. The decision was made—on board? in Havana?—to tow the *Aguila* back to Havana. The Cuban sailor would stay aboard and steer her.

"What about the bodies?" he asked the commander.

He heard the orders and proceeded, not without difficulty, to maneuver first Eduardo overboard, then Cecilio Velasco. To make it easier to slide them over the gunwale, he severed the lifelines with his pocket knife. The bodies floated off in the waves, leaving a trail of blood. By the time the line had been rigged, forward from the mooring winch of the *Aguila* to the stern winches of the patrol boat, the sharks had come. Neither Blackford nor Catalina saw this. They were below, handcuffed, in separate, tiny cabins without portholes to let in light. Blackford felt the rising hum of the engine. And he could feel, from the sway of the boat, its direction. South. He lowered his head, and prayed the Lord to keep—*mi querido compañero*, Cecilio Velasco. And wept convulsively at Cecilio's departure, wondering, his focus gone, how ever it would have been feasible to engage in this surrealistic, impossible venture without his *compañero*, the little, cigarette-smoking, Spanish-American who wrote the book of courage.

Thirty-eight

Anthony Trust, after being cut off from Blackford, called the Pentagon. He reached the Duty Officer, identified himself as with the CIA giving the relevant credentials, and said that he had had an emergency report from a fellow agent three minutes before to the effect that Cuban patrol boats were right now firing on, and perhaps at this very moment boarding, the fishing vessel he was on, even though many miles away from territorial Cuban waters. Moreover, the vessel in question was headed for political sanctuary in the United States and returning a U.S. citizen.

He gave the position of the vessel, asked that the information be given instantly to the coast guard and to naval patrol forces, emphasized that if any protective action were to be taken it would need to be within the next hour or two before the Cuban patrol boat reached the safety of home waters, took the officer's name, announced his intention of going directly to Washington on the 7 A.M. shuttle to report the event directly to the Director of the CIA, and hung up.

His intention was to dig out the Director personally. He knew that he had returned from his honeymoon. He did not know that at that moment the Director was in California escorting the body of his young stepson for burial in Seattle. He had been killed in a racing car accident.

So Anthony Trust sought out, and went instantly to see, the Deputy Director.

The atmosphere in Washington was highly charged politically. Four days earlier, Senator Kenneth Keating of New York had said that it was now "fully confirmed" to him by his own sources that missile launching sites were under construction in Cuba, "pads capable of hurling missiles into the heartland of the United States and as far as the Panama Canal Zone."

This charge had been greeted with smiles by the Establishment. The dean of American columnists, as Walter Lippmann was commonly designated, was reputedly the "favorite columnist" of the President (in fact he was not, but it was the fashionable thing for an Establishment figure to declare, much as Reinhold Niebuhr was the "favorite theologian" of any ambitious social-intellectual). Lippmann had written, "The present Cuban military buildup is not only not capable of offensive action, but also it is not capable of defensive action against the United States."

That very morning the New York *Times* had quoted "authoritative sources" to the effect that "the Cuban government has been extremely careful in recent weeks to avoid any chance of conflict with the United States." The source went on to say to the *Times* that "extremely thorough" U.S. reconnaissance had yielded no evidence at all of "illegal arms shipments" to Cuba. And—the nicest touch—that not even a "water pistol, as one official put it," had got through to Cuba. (That man will go far in this administration, Anthony Trust thought, examining the headline in the morning's New York *Times:* "Castro Adopting/ A Cautious Policy. U.S. Notes Extreme Care by Cuba To/ Avoid Incidents That Could/ Bring War."

The troops were out in some concentration to confute the provocative, loose-lipped Republican senator and his fellow alarmists. McGeorge Bundy, assistant to the President for National Security Affairs, was on "Issues and Answers," the ABC televised Sunday show, at noon, and the subject of the discussion was Cuba. Asked whether it wasn't possible that military installations in Cuba might be converted to offensive purposes, he replied, "Well, I don't myself think that there is any present—I *know* there is no present evidence, and I think there is no present likelihood that the Cubans and the Cuban government and the Soviet government would in combination attempt to install a major offensive capability." Sure, there was stuff going into Cuba. But "that is not going to turn an island of six million people with five or six thousand Soviet technicians and specialists into a major threat to the United States, and I believe that most of the American people do not share the views of the few who have acted as if suddenly this kind of military support created a mortal threat to us. It does not."

Anthony Trust reported Oakes's exact words to the Deputy Director, who instantly called his counterpart in the Defense Department. It was quickly ascertained that a Coast Guard vessel had been dispatched to the location given by Anthony Trust to the Duty Officer and had encountered—nothing, save heavy seas. On the broader front, for almost two weeks a U-2 strategic reconnaissance survey of the whole island of Cuba had been scheduled as a matter of routine, but for one reason or another the flights had not happened. But acting on the impulse of Trust's telephone call with his dramatic report on the Soviet missiles, the telegraphic order now went out: go immediately.

And that afternoon, the planes took off.

Two U-2s, manned by veteran pilots. They flew seventy-five thousand feet high, with those miracle cameras which, before needing to reload, can finger inch by inch an area 125 miles wide by three thousand miles long in four thousand paired frames, delivering ten miles of film. In each frame they recorded the latitude and longitude of the entire area, photographed by cameras that could read the headline of a newspaper lying on the ground, special radio-sensitive cameras that could detect the strength of otherwise undetectable radio and radar signals and, even, record variations in land temperatures that betrayed recent movements of any heavy metallic objects.

The order from on high was to dispatch the film *as soon as it was recovered from the U-2s* to Washington by supersonic jet. There every skilled photographic interpreter affiliated with the Central Intelligence Agency, the State Department, or the Defense Department who lived within one hundred miles of Washington was conscripted to duty, and they gathered at the National Photographic Interpretation Center where they worked, in relays, with their magnifying and stereoscopic instruments, around the clock.

Soon after midnight that Sunday night, one photo interpreter said to an associate, "Take a look at this." The photo was of a semiwooded area near San Cristóbal. Indisputably they identified: four erector-launchers for medium-range ballistic missiles, eight medium-range ballistic missiles, trailers loaded with missile fuel, a motor pool of military trucks, and a tent city for about five hundred Russian troops. The tip of one missile was actually visible from under a tarpaulin, and it corresponded exactly with ballistic missiles photographed for the first time in the 1960 May Day Parade in Moscow. A mere two-week hiatus in regularly scheduled U-2 observation flights had protected the Soviet missile installations from visibility right up to the moment when what they were engaged in simply could not be hidden from such shamelessly penetrating eyes as those of the U-2.

By the end of the day the photo analysts had discerned a concentration of intermediate-range missiles near Remedios, and still another near Sagua la Grande. Once activated, the Pentagon analysts quickly calculated, the identified missiles were sufficient in number and in strength to deposit nuclear bombs over every major city in the U.S. save Seattle, where the Director happened at this moment to be, on his unhappy personal mission, and, at the same time, to wipe out fifty percent of U.S. ICBM and bomber bases.

The first team mobilized quickly. There was a problem in catching the attention of the Assistant Secretary of State for Inter-American Affairs because he was irreversibly launched into a speech before the Sigma Delta Chi journalism society at the National Press Club where he was explaining the relative inoffensiveness of the Cuban rearmament. Edwin Martin conceded that Castro had antiaircraft missiles, antiship rockets, rocket-launching torpedo boats, late model MIG fighter planes, and several thousand military technicians. But, smiling, he reassured his audience: "As the President has said, this military buildup is basically defensive in character and would not add more than a few hours to the time required to invade Cuba successfully if that should become necessary." He concluded, ". . . taken together, the present military capabilities in Cuba would not materially increase the Cuban ability to undertake offensive action outside the island." A waiter handed him a message asking that he call a certain number in the State Department, which call, excusing himself, the Assistant Secretary made, only to learn that his verbal assurances were not worth the paper they were written on.

The Secretary of State was giving a dinner for West Germany's Foreign Minister, and in desperation it was finally arranged that, between toasts, a bodyguard should slip him a sealed note. The Secretary, excusing himself as one might on the way to a washroom, reached a telephone, spoke with the State Department official, exchanged circumlocutions ("Are you sure this is it?" "Yes. I am very sure this is it.") and agreed to meet with the top team the first thing the next morning.

The Secretary of Defense was lecturing that evening at what the communicants fondly referred to as "Hickory Hill University," the home of Attorney General and Mrs. Robert Kennedy. His lecture was not easy to interrupt, but in due course this was done, and at about midnight the Secretary of Defense went off to see some photographs.

It was not until the following morning that the Assistant
for National Security Affairs approached the President—in
his bedroom at the White House, where the President was
accustomed to receive the initial daily security briefings.

He was incredulous.

Concerning the missiles, the Assistant reported firmly,
there was simply no ambiguity.

The President thereupon initiated the week-long series
of conferences that would culminate in his television address on the following Monday.

None of this came in time to be of any help to the occupants of the Cuban patrol boat towing the smaller fishing
boat from Latitude 24 degrees, Longitude 82 degrees,
southwest toward Latitude 13 degrees, Longitude 85 degrees, the Bay of Havana.

The United States Coast Guard patrol boat had reached
the designated area within one hour of Trust's telephone
call, encountering, of course, only the six-foot seas and the
hard northerly wind. An airplane stood by and received
orders by radio to search between that point and Havana.
The pilot came on the Cuban patrol boat towing a fishing
boat that rode jauntily down the following seas. A radio to
the Pentagon, giving their position, now only a dozen miles
from Havana, elicited the instruction: Turn around, and
return to the base.

It was, Blackford recognized even in a semidrugged
state, too much to expect that within the three hours necessary to enter Cuban territorial waters the United States
Marines would, so to speak, arrive with their bagpipes. Too
much was needed for such action. Much too much, in the
way of high authoritative direction, to order all of that in
time, even if the logistical resources were there, standing
by at attention. Blackford was certain of only this, that
Anthony Trust would convey the message that mattered
the most, and that in due course there would be action

consistent with the imperatives of the situation: that there were Soviet nuclear missiles in Cuba.

His mind returned yet again to Cecilio Velasco. Cecilio, dead. Blackford had witnessed awful episodes over a period of ten years, and experienced awful losses, casualties of the Cold War. In Budapest he had seen a very young man, an athlete-scholar with whom he had a close friendship, hoisted by a derrick on top of a truck from which a noose had been suspended, which soon held the young man's lifeless body. In Germany he had led a young, inspiring nobleman unsuspecting, trusting, to his execution at the hands of the CIA.

But none had reached him in quite the same way. How would moral historians classify Cecilio Velasco, assuming the unlikely, that they even stumbled across his delible footsteps? Blackford wondered, as he sucked in air in the oppressive closeness of the closed little cabin. He wondered without much interest whether the bleeding in his shoulder had stopped. The boat's movements were, mercifully, smooth by contrast with what it had been like when they were headed against the wind. In his depression these conditions assumed an allegorical meaning, one that grabbed at his spirit as he wondered whether they whom Whittaker Chambers had with such striking melancholy called the winning side had got hold of history's vectors, as indeed Marx had promised they would; so that when the struggle was against the barbarians the going was choppy, while when you ran with them, the seas smiled you along on their course.

He lay down on the little bunk and, closing his eyes, promised Cecilio Velasco that he too, if there were nothing else left, would scrounge for flares with which to hold the barbarians at bay, even if only for moments—crucial moments, it had proved today; and he begged God to give Cecilio peace. And wondered how it would be tolerable in Cuba with the diminutive Cecilio "gone," as his dear mother would unfailingly put it. He would prefer not to think about him, but could think of nothing else while conscious—that and, occasionally, the pain in his shoulder, a very different pain which Blackford eased only when he fell asleep; while asleep, he dreamed of the square at Taxco and Sally at his side, drinking margaritas. Suddenly the young man cavorting about with the bullhorns, chasing the little children and setting off all those firecrackers and Roman candles and flares, went berserk and the flares were soaring, flying up at him and Sally, and he threw himself at her and, sweating, dragged her down on the floor to the protection of the little concrete balcony. *They are everywhere, those dangerous flares.* Blackford was drenched when the cabin door opened and a voice shouted out at him:

"Get up. Get up! Caimán, wash your face"—a pitcher of water, a basin, and a towel had been brought in. "But there is no time to remove and replace your handcuffs. Do you wish to wash, or wait until the medical doctor attends you?"

Blackford motioned toward the towel, and so it was that he emerged with a relatively dry face from the venture that began on the *Aguila.* Down the little gangway of the patrol boat he came, but he stumbled and fell, and they had to lift him into the truck. This time there were two trucks, each of them with independent military escort. He caught sight of Catalina in another truck. He had no chance even to exchange a word with her.

Thirty-nine

It was, yet again, after midnight. The five Cubans were once more together, this time in the room on the top floor of INRA, the Instituto Nacional de Reforma Agraria. Fidel Castro was irritated and irritable.

"You are *absolutely* certain that the transmission from Caimán got through?"

"You have asked me that question eighteen times in two days, Fidel. Let me say it one final time:

"1. I ordered all radio transmissions from within the suspected arc to be monitored.

"2. The transmission to New York was picked up at 5:33: a) recorded in Havana; and b) overheard, though not recorded, on board the *Frank País*, where the stupid lieutenant did not think to prevent it by the simple expedient of talking into the same channel while Caimán was attempting to use it. It is true that there is static in the recording done in Havana, so that some of the replies made by the friend of Caimán, one Anthony T-r-u-s-t as far as I could make it out, were garbled. But aboard the *País* the radio technician said that although he does not speak English, he heard exchanges between the vessel whose line he was monitoring, obviously the *Aguila*, through Radio Key West, and that there followed an exchange that lasted several minutes and was not interrupted by static.

"And c)"—Che turned now to Castro's brother—"Raúl here says that army radar picked up two light airplanes flying at 75,000 feet at slow speeds over both sides of the island on Sunday afternoon. Why our friends the Russians haven't armed our antiaircraft missiles yet I leave it to them to explain.

"It would therefore appear obvious to me that on Sunday, shortly after dawn, Caimán got the message through to his friend in New York. That his friend then alerted the Pentagon. That the Pentagon proceeded to photograph the installations, and from what we all know of the U-2 airplanes, the United States has indubitably blown the cover on our operation."

"But then," Fidel rose and began to stride the length of the room, "how is it that nothing has happened? What about the American invasion? How is that that has not been launched?"

"Isn't it time, Fidel, that we acknowledge that Adzhubei and Khrushchev have put one over on us in the matter of an American invasion? An invasion they said would come in the spring or in the summer."

Raúl interjected. "Of what use to the Soviets was it to suggest an invasion was coming if it was merely a fiction, Che? You have a tendency to downgrade our most faithful friends, the godfathers of international socialism."

"What they stood to get, it seems to me, is obvious: the possibility of advanced nuclear missiles in a forward base, under their command."

Fidel huffed, and chomped on his cigar. "They are under my command."

"Not exactly, Fidel."

Fidel snapped at him. "It is as I say it is, Comandante." Che said nothing.

Fidel resumed his line of inquiry. "Never mind an invasion, what about an air strike? When will that come?"

"I don't know," Che said. "But now something *will* happen. Perhaps at any moment."

They then, each in turn, opined on what was likeliest to happen. Fidel, on hearing from Che Guevara on Sunday morning, instantly communicated with Khrushchev, asking that Moscow publicly declare that any strike by the United States against Cuba would bring instant nuclear retaliatory action from the Soviet Union. But although it was now Wednesday night—Thursday morning, in fact—the Soviet Union had made no direct response to Castro's request. Meanwhile Cuban sources in the United States had picked up nothing. Truly it was as if nothing had happened—as if Caimán's message had disappeared. The Russians had given instant orders to their Cuban military to assign top priority to manning their antiaircraft installations, but the missiles were still ten days away from receiving their nuclear warheads.

"They will of course strike," Raúl said. "They will strike the installations. And a great many people will be killed. Though in fact, most of them will be Russian and that is good, because that will arouse the Russians."

"Are you quite certain," Dorticós came in, "that Cuba has a great deal to gain from a nuclear war between the United States and the Soviet Union, part of it waged here on this island?"

"It would serve the gringos right."

"Serve them right if Russia were to cease to exist, Raúl?"

"Who then would pay our bills?" Ramiro Valdés commented, in disgust.

Fidel was chewing on his cigar and he began to mutter quietly. He then cleared his throat. "One thing we must take elementary precautions about, and that is to guard the —structure of government. Of course I shall need to take extraordinary precautions, but so must you all. Which means most specifically, Raúl, that you are not to go near San Cristóbal, or Sagua la Grande, or Remedios. The strike, when it comes, will be in those three areas." To Raúl: "Is it likely to be a nuclear strike?"

"I would very much doubt it. It would not only offend the Soviet Union and offend world opinion, it is not necessary. Conventional weapons alone would serve."

"Now comrades," Fidel sat down again, "the big question before us . . . before me, is how extensive shall our defense be? There are two possibilities. One is a targeted strike against the missiles. The second is a general strike against Cuba. As far as the second is concerned, we would of course defend ourselves to our utmost, inflicting as much loss of life as possible on the Americans. As to the first, we need to deliberate."

"Doesn't everything depend on the attitude of the Soviet Union?" Valdés asked. "If the Soviet Union stays with us, then we must adopt an appropriate position."

"Which would be?" Fidel raised his eyes at Valdés.

"To fire every bloody thing we have at the Americans. Antiaircraft missiles, the MIG fighters, the works."

"You recognize that these are mostly manned by Russians?"

"Of course. But we are sitting here, are we not, trying to decide what shall be the Cuban response? Surely Cuban authority extends, if not to the firing of the nuclear missiles, to the deployment of the MIGs and the antiaircraft missiles?"

"That is my understanding," Fidel said. "But now: If the Soviet Union does not act? Do we resist the strike at our—at their—missiles?"

"I don't see why we should," Raúl said. "They are Soviet missiles, commanded by Soviet troops, receiving orders from Moscow. What is the point in engaging the United States if to engage them might mean to spread the war beyond the missiles, to an attack on Havana and the loss of much Cuban life?"

"And, conceivably, our government," Che added.

Fidel looked up at Che. "You are responsible for this, you know." He spoke grandly, censoriously.

Che answered, "I made a mistake, Comandante."

There was silence in the room. The other three Cubans had never seen it quite so: a thoroughly chastened Ernesto

Che Guevara. If at that moment Fidel had said, "And I am placing you under arrest," and had pushed the buzzer under his table, summoning his guards, Raúl Castro, Ramiro Valdés, and Osvaldo Dorticós would have been shocked but not surprised. Shocked that it should have come to a break between the two towering figures. Unsurprised that the supreme commander should be taking appropriate action against a subordinate whose carelessness had resulted in the possibility that the entire missile operation would be aborted. Indeed, an act of carelessness that conceivably would lead the United States to interpret the importation of those missiles—as Dorticós had argued—as a *casus belli,* and prompt the Americans to go through, finally, with the invasion Cuba had been told by Aleksei Adzhubei almost a year ago the Kennedy government had decided upon.

The suspense was great. Fidel Castro both knew the moment's gravity and enjoyed it.

To Guevara he said, finally, "Others have made mistakes. You, Raúl, by letting that infernal girl go to San Cristóbal."

Raúl was silent.

"And you, Che, by botching their execution. I warned you explicitly against putting off the executions."

Che did not remind the Comandante that he had specifically approved the delay.

"By the way, have they now been executed?"

"No, Comandante."

"Why in the name of God not? Has Caimán told you he has more government secrets he is willing to give you?"

"There is that primarily, Comandante. But also Caimán has been in high fever, delirious since early on Sunday evening. You will remember he was shot in the shoulder. All in due course."

"And the girl?"

"You will recall, Fidel, that his willingness to give us the secrets depended on her being alive."

"What secrets is he in a position to give us now that matter?"

"I think, Fidel, he might have extremely useful information. Contingency arrangements in particular. He might know the striking plans, the principal targets—that kind of thing."

"Well can't the doctors bring him out of the—delirium?"

"They say his temperature is receding and that by tomorrow morning he should be able to talk."

"Well whether he talks or doesn't talk, I want them both executed."

"Yes, Comandante. But you agree it is worthwhile to wait?"

Castro said nothing, but turned back to the agenda in front of him. That was his way of acquiescing, once again without exactly going on the record.

Forty

For the sake of appearance the President's public schedule was studiedly uninterrupted. It was critical that no one should suspect that the President's Executive Committee, as it had termed itself, was meeting day and night over the crisis. And this included going through with a scheduled meeting on Thursday afternoon with Soviet Foreign Minister Andrei Gromyko. The President had even smiled as they shook hands and Gromyko was ushered out of the Oval Office.

The President went to his rocking chair. No other appointments had been listed for that day, and soon he would be rejoining the Executive Committee downstairs in the Situation Room. Now he wanted to think . . .

What a creep. First, practically all he wants to talk about is Berlin. Berlin is as close to my mind, and as close to his right now, as the Peloponnesian War. But easy does it. I had to be careful not to appear uninterested in Berlin, so we talk about that for a while. Then he—not I—brings up the subject of Cuba. Just wanted to say yet again, he said, what Premier Khrushchev said last month, that Soviet aid has "solely the purpose of contributing to the defense capabilities of Cuba." So that was bad enough, a straight lie. But he wanted to embellish it, so he says, "If it were otherwise, the Soviet Government would never become involved in rendering such assistance." What he does not know, the little creep, is that we've had those photographs since last Sunday.

Speaking of which. My gang has gone on and on about the remarkable speed with which the Soviet Union has got at the business of installing missiles. Not a sign of any missiles or missile sites in the U-2 photos taken on—I can memorize the dates, I've heard them so

*often—August 29, September 5, 17, 24, 28, 29, October 5. So I
said, why not any flights since October 5? And McNamara says there
was a flight scheduled for October 9, but the weather was bad. So I
said how come we didn't fly on the 10th, and he said that was bad
too, bad right up until Sunday. Huh.*

*That's when I pinned McCone down and finally got the story. I
think I was not supposed to know that Blackford Oakes was the guy
who got the message through, that he had managed actually to see
the goddam missiles, and he triggered our Sunday U-2 flight, even
though they were—"regularly flying"—and, I might add, regularly
not seeing what they were supposed to see. Makes me mad that, the
business of nobody telling me about Oakes.*

*And knowing about his message makes a difference, too, because
the chances are that the pursuing vessel monitored Oakes's phone call
to his friend in New York, the way I see it. Which means the Cubans,
from last Sunday on, know that we know. It isn't obvious what,
knowing, they're in a position to do. Presumably they're working full
speed anyway to arm those missiles, but Bob and McCone agree it's a
couple of weeks off. Well, anyway, I can't go to bat for Oakes until the
whole thing goes public. But I'm not going to forget him—*

The President pushed a buzzer under the little side table
by the rocking chair. Mrs. Lincoln walked in.

"Evelyn, until I tell you to stop, every morning when you
and I are alone I want you to say one thing to me."

"Yes, Mr. President."

"Say to me: 'Don't forget about Oakes.' That's all. I will
know what all that means."

"Yes, sir."

"Oh, and Evelyn. Maybe you should also say to me every
morning: 'Mr. President, you are surrounded by idiots.' "

"I couldn't do that, Mr. President."

"And why not?"

"Because," said Mrs. Lincoln, smiling, "I surround you
the most."

The President laughed, rose from his rocker with a difficulty he'd have taken the trouble to conceal from other

than his intimate family, and headed down to resume participation in that conference that never seemed to end.

On Monday, back from his two-day political trip to Ohio and Illinois, fastidiously left on the presidential schedule so as not to arouse suspicion, he found the situation at the White House now quite openly hectic. The announcement had been made that the President would make an important television address that evening, and the congressional leadership having been summoned to come to the White House for a briefing at 5 P.M., Sorensen and others were weaving in and out of the Oval Office with drafts of the speech and of Adlai Stevenson's speech at the UN for the next day. But at exactly 12:08, Mrs. Lincoln found herself quite alone with her dictation pad in front of the President, sitting at his desk editing.

"Mr. President?"

"Yes."

"I didn't see you on Saturday or on Sunday, so I wasn't able to remind you."

"To remind me of what?"

"To remind you not to forget about Oakes."

The President leaned back, his mind departed, for the moment, from the manuscript he had been revising. He lifted the telephone. "Get me the Attorney General," he said to the operator.

"Bobby. You remember Oakes? Blackford Oakes I told you about? The agent we sent to Cuba to talk to Che Guevara? Did you know he was the guy who triggered the search for the missiles? Did I remember to tell you that?

"Well never mind, I'll catch you up later. But now listen. I want a cable drafted to Castro over my signature. No, make it over your signature, come to think of it. Send it via the Swiss in Havana, but not before my speech. Right after. Make it sound as legal as you can. What it ought to say is something like—What? Oh sure, I'll wait. You want to record it or you want Angie to take it on your other phone? You all set? Now? Okay. Something like this: 'The President of the United States wishes the Premier of the Republic of Cuba to know that he holds the Premier personally responsible for the well-being of the American citizen Blackford Oakes who was kidnapped on the high seas on Sunday morning while headed for Key West in Florida. Antecedent circumstances involving Mr. Oakes's visits in Cuba, first under U.S.–Cuban understanding, later at the express invitation of Minister Guevara, have no legal bearing'—Bobby, guff this up as much as you can on the legal front, freedom of the seas, etc. etc. etc.—'on the breach in international law committed by your agents on Sunday. The President desires the safe return of Mr. Oakes to Guantánamo Bay and repeats that he will hold the Prime Minister personally responsible for the well-being of said Oakes.' How's that?"

"Sounds okay. I don't know how much time Castro is going to have to give to the Oakes matter after tonight, or even whether Oakes is alive."

"You've got it wrong, Bobby, remember? Castro isn't going to have anything at all to do for a good while now. Just sit, and wonder what Khrushchev is going to do. He should have time to look after not only Blackford Oakes, but Cuba's sugar harvest."

"How're you coming on the speech?"

"I'm not coming on it at all while I'm talking to you. See you, Bob."

"Good luck, Jack."

Forty-one

Blackford was lifted from his bed in the prison hospital in the special room in which he was being treated—and guarded—onto a stretcher bed. The major in charge of security spoke to an orderly who maneuvered a four-sided curtain that prevented Blackford from seeing anything except the curtain's white material, and kept anyone else from laying eyes on Blackford. The stretcher was then drawn on its coasters through the general population ward to a corridor, down in an elevator, out on what seemed to be the ground floor—Blackford could hear outdoor traffic—and, finally, into a private office outside of which two guards stood. The curtain material was withdrawn and an orderly turned the bed winch, lifting Blackford up to a near-sitting position. His throat felt very dry and he wondered whether all the drugs that had been given him were medicinal. He asked for a glass of water, which was handed to him. He had a little difficulty in focusing his eyes. With his left hand he reconnoitered his right shoulder. The pain was gone, except where he probed. His problem was his weakness, the difficulty in thinking, in concentrating, in focusing. But he knew the voice right away.

And he could understand that the nurses and attendants were leaving the room at the gesture of the man who was now speaking to him.

"You are a soldier, Caimán. And I have always understood soldiers. Your records may reveal, if you have bothered to look at them, that I—and indeed all of us associated with Operation *Granma*—were never vindictive toward the soldiers of Batista."

"Good morning, Che. Or is it afternoon?"

"It is late morning."

"What day?"

"Saturday."

"Am I in good shape?"

"The doctor advises me that you will be able to face the firing squad standing up."

Blackford closed his eyes. He had heard something very unpleasant but didn't have the strength to sort it all out.

"I am prepared to resume the conversation that was interrupted last Saturday."

"You mean, when Velasco came?"

"Yes, that is what I mean."

"What has happened?"

"What has happened where?"

"On the international front."

"Oh, I see what you mean. Nothing has happened. Evidently your friend in New York, Mr. Trust, was not believed in Washington."

Blackford summoned all the energy he could to think through the implications of this. No, it was not possible. Not at all possible.

"I don't think, Che, that I believe you."

Che stepped back and eyed Blackford. He felt he knew Caimán well. Caimán was having genuine difficulty in talking, in thinking. He went to the door and told the major to fetch the doctor. He turned back to Blackford, whose eyes now were closed. In due course there was a light knock on the door. Che went to it and stepped outside to confer with the doctor in a low voice.

"I was under the impression the prisoner would be completely lucid."

"He is lucid, Comandante, but he is still very weak."

"I find he has difficulties in concentrating."

"That is a combination of fatigue and the drugs."

"What drugs?"

"He has been given antibiotics, and they have controlled the infection. He has also been sedated to arrest any unnecessary and inflammatory movement in the wounded area."

"How long do those drugs take to wear off?"

"Eight to twelve hours."

"Was he scheduled to have more drugs?"

"Yes, at noon."

"Cancel that order. Figure out another way to keep his shoulder quiet. I will be back here at eight o'clock and I expect to find him mentally alert." The doctor, without expression, gave instructions to the nurse he summoned, and saluted the Comandante. Che hesitated. Should he go back into the room and tell Caimán he would be back at the end of the day? No. Let Caimán repair the fatigue. If he knew that in a matter of hours they would be conferring again he might not rest. Che Guevara left the hospital.

When he woke in the afternoon, Blackford complained of the binding that strapped him down on his bed. The doctor was summoned. Blackford spoke to him in Spanish and asked that the strap be removed. The doctor said he would order it taken away but that the prisoner was not to exercise his right shoulder. And if he felt he was slipping off to sleep, he was to advise the nurse to strap it on again in case during the night he was restless and did himself damage.

"Tell me, Doctor, when will I be able to leave the hospital?"

"In two or three days," the doctor replied. "If you are careful."

"And when will I be able to use my arm again?"

"It will take two days to three weeks before you reacquire normal use of your right shoulder and arm. The progress will be day-to-day."

"Suddenly I feel quite lively. And even hungry. What am I allowed?"

"You can eat cereals and sugar, and the regular hospital fare."

"Can I have a radio?"

"That is a decision for the military. I shall ask Major Marzo to attend you."

Blackford looked at the little bearded doctor, and wondered whether he was twenty-five years old or maybe twenty-six. He must have spent all twenty-five years studying how to be professional. Absolutely no expression of any kind had crossed his face.

"Thanks, Doctor."

"Para servirle."

Major Marzo was matter-of-fact. No the prisoner could not have a radio. No he could not have a newspaper. No he could not have a magazine. No he could not make a telephone call to the Swiss ambassador. No he could not write out a message for the prisoner Urrutia. No he did not know where the prisoner Urrutia was. Yes he could have something to read.

"Now wait a minute, Major. You know that I am protected by the Geneva Protocols?"

The major was startled. He did not, in fact, know what the Geneva Protocols were, but there was a ring of authority both to the sound of said Protocols, and to the way in which the prisoner referred to them.

"What about the Geneva Protocols?" he asked, cautiously.

"They stipulate that no Western prisoner of war can be made to read anything written by Marx, Lenin, or Castro."

Major Marzo wondered how exactly the Comandante would want him to reply to a jest.

"I will get you something from the prison library."

"Is there anything there by Agatha Christie? I've become accustomed to her."

"I will see."

"Be a good—" good what? If Major Marzo became

known as a "good fellow," they'd probably execute him
too. Be a "good soldier"? No, probably demeaning to a
major. Be a "good sport"? No. He might take that as suggesting he had been bested. "Be a good major, and get me
an Agatha Christie, or if she isn't in the library, any *novela
policiaca*, preferably one that was originally written in English."

The pretty black nurse, who did not hesitate to smile at
the prisoner as she removed the strap, said she would bring
him some cereal, and Blackford suddenly felt preposterously high. Then his mind began to focus. And he
thought back.

He had indeed had a conversation with Che Guevara. He
half closed his eyes and he could visualize Che, beret on,
cigar—unlit, wasn't it?—in his mouth, at the end of the bed.
When would that have been?

And then he had spoken. *They* had spoken. And Che had
said something about—yes. That there was no news on the
international front. And that—yes, yes . . . yes. Che was
obviously rescheduling the session toward which they were
headed when Velasco—Velasco. Blackford clenched his
fists under the covers. Then quickly released the right fist,
because the tautness pained his shoulder . . . When Velasco had picked them up. And now, whether the message
had got through to Washington or whether it had not got
through to Washington (of *course* it had got through. Either
that or the whole government of the United States was bent
on suicide), he and Catalina were under sentence of death.
And what he had put together to tell Che last Saturday—
how would it sound now, with Washington alerted to what
was going on in San Cristóbal, and God knows where else
in Cuba?

He must give them something, enough to spare Catalina.

But wait. Of course. The terms were that he would not
talk with Che *until* he had a paper in his hand commuting
the sentence against Catalina. Right. And that would buy

some time, surely, because it was unlikely that he would bring the paper to the hospital, let alone the paper *and* Catalina.

So tonight they would fence. The next day would be critical. Critical as regards his own life. By tomorrow he should have managed the commutation of the sentence of Catalina. He must rehearse *himself* carefully.

Che Guevara, driving to the prison, reflected on the day's events. Fidel was getting angrier and angrier at the failure of Moscow to say anything publicly designed to brake aggressive action by the Americans or to communicate its intention to do so soon. That was bad enough. But during the past forty-eight hours Castro had not succeeded in getting *anybody* in the Kremlin of any consequence on the other end of the telephone. Castro, by now, was too sensitive to protocol to content himself to speak to just any Soviet menial. He wanted Khrushchev or Mikoyan or Gromyko.

By noon Thursday he had lowered his sights, and told the radio operator he would consent to speak with Aleksei Adzhubei. On being told, twenty minutes later, that Comrade Adzhubei was on vacation in the Crimea and could not be reached, Fidel Castro had had a genuine, uncontrolled, uncontrollable fit of rage and, in the presence of Che and Raúl and Dorticós, had spoken such words about the Soviet Union as had not been heard since, in Wheeling, West Virginia, twelve years earlier, Senator Joseph McCarthy inaugurated the age of McCarthyism. Beyond taking the precautions that had been taken on Wednesday to remove sensitive Cuban personnel from the three areas likeliest to be the targets of an American strike, there was literally nothing to be done; but it was psychologically impossible to address themselves to other problems, even though Cuba was groaning with other problems, from an abrupt scarcity of toilet paper—suddenly, as if at "the ass-end of a providential countdown," as editor Carlos Franqui had put it, there was no toilet paper in all of Cuba—from that to the threatened strike of the fishermen. Castro would show *them* who was running the fishing industry, little kulak Cuban fishing capitalists, or the people.

But nothing, nothing seemed to engage the attention, pending the awful, inscrutable silence from Washington. The only relief Castro could get was to telephone five times a day to the Russian general in charge of the installations. But he always got the identical response, namely that the work was proceeding "on schedule."

On Saturday, Fidel had actually gotten drunk in the middle of the day. Fidel tended to drink only ceremonially, and had no particular taste for the staple of the Cuban spirit, rum. But this afternoon he had sat and drunk daiquiris as though he were Ernest Hemingway. Almost anything to distract him. One of the things that, suddenly, he thought to dwell on was the matter of the American. Caimán. He had sent for Che.

"Did you get any information from him?" Castro asked sarcastically.

"I saw him for the first time this morning. The doctors said there would be no point in seeing him earlier. And even this morning there was no point. He was not lucid."

"Has it occurred to you he might be faking his lack of lucidity?"

"It has, Fidel. That is why I called the doctor and spoke to him, and the doctor said he was still under heavy sedation."

"I suppose he will stay under sedation until after the gringo invasion?"

"I told the doctor to take him off sedation."

"When?"

"Immediately."

"So that you will be questioning him when?"

"Tonight."

"Good. Then we should be able to execute him tomorrow. No. I don't want him executed tomorrow. I don't want him executed until twenty-four hours after he is told that the execution will take place. It hurts more that way." There followed a smile of sorts.

"What if he gives us valuable information?"

"That will make up for the deaths of the prison guards who were ambushed last Saturday."

"Fidel, there is the matter of the girl. You remember that Caimán said he would not talk unless we granted a reprieve of sentence to the girl."

"Grant it, and then execute her. No. Don't execute her right away. Same rule as the American. Let her sweat a day."

Che decided he would make one more pass. "Fidel, when we last spoke about it you agreed that if we gave our word the girl would not be executed, we would have to keep it. Remember that she had nothing to do with the ambush—as a matter of fact, neither did Caimán—so do you think it right that she should then be executed?"

Fidel returned the moral cavil with a stare. It was intended to be withering. "Sometimes you talk like the fucking Jesuits at Belén. 'Do you think it right . . .' Do you, mother of God, Jesus, Mary and Joseph, think it right for *me*, Fidel Castro, to *serve* as *Comandante en Jefe* of this fucking revolution which aims to serve the people of Cuba? Or are you determined to import your mysterious moralities . . . from—from whom? Mao Tse-tung? Who do you really worship, Che? We know that God does not exist. So suppose I tell you that Mao Tse-tung would not ask the question, the *mincing* question"—Fidel Castro was going about as far as one could go with Che Guevara—" '*Do you think it right?*' " Castro imitated a well-known nightclub transvestite of prerevolutionary days. Then with all his might he stamped his fist on the desk. "*Yes, I, Fidel Castro, think it is right to punish our enemies.* Do you understand, Che?"

"I understand, Comandante."

The prison was too near at hand, so Che ordered the driver to take a turn and head for the bay. He did not want to see Caimán until after he had cooled off. He needed very much to cool off, after that session.

It was just eight; the sun had set but the night was bright and warm, and Che drove down the Malecón, past the wharves—busy, as usual, extruding the fruit of Soviet technology. He drove all the way down to the northwest end of the bay, soothing his nerves, and then told the driver to return to the prison. The adjutant, seated next to the driver, signaled the order to the jeep behind, the jeep with the bodyguards, and at 8:35 they drove into the prison courtyard.

Blackford was waiting for them, sitting up in his bed. His eyes were distinctly clearer than they had been that morning.

"Good evening, Caimán."

"That remains to be seen, Che."

Good, Che thought. Caimán sounds normal. He looked at Blackford and suddenly noticed: he had shaved his beard and had got his hair cut. He looked, now, thoroughly American: the well-formed features, blue eyes, the expression of intelligence, acuity; warm, attractive. His prisoner, thought Che, was as poised as if he were preparing, by elfin circumstance, sitting on a stretcher bed, to interrogate an Argentine guerrilla caught in a general's uniform in Cuba.

"You are obviously better, Caimán."

"Your nationalized hospitals are in good hands, Che."

"Well, a lot has happened since we had our original engagement."

"Yes. And a lot, I feel sure, is about to happen."

"Yes." Che thought it appropriate to squirt a little cold water into Caimán's high spirits. "And some of us will live to see it happen."

"Ah, Comandante Che. How differently you speak now from the days—from the weeks and months—when we spoke about the Acuerdo, and what our countries might do for each other."

"That is not on the evening's agenda."

"No. It was very much on the agenda, however, that while I was struggling to bring together an Acuerdo along the general lines you—you, Che—had sketched out in Montevideo, you—you, Che—were busy importing nuclear weapons."

"It is wrong to assume that all Cuban decisions are my decisions." Che reflected for a moment. And quickly added, "It is right to think that all Cuban decisions are decisions that bind me. I too am a soldier."

"Do you believe in the Nuremberg Doctrine?"

"If you are asking me, Would I have obeyed Hitler, the answer is, No, I would not have done so. If you ask me, Is obeying Castro the same thing as obeying Hitler, I have a simple answer: No. Because Castro is not a nazi careerist. He is a revolutionary."

"Seems to me Hitler was something of a revolutionary himself. But never mind, Che, never mind. I don't dispute certain . . . existential things. One of them is that you're in charge here."

"You know why I have come. To hear your secret information."

"And you know that I said that my willingness to talk was based on two things: a reprieve of her death sentence, and the presence of Catalina."

Che paused. He had come prepared for the business of the written pardon. He had forgotten that Catalina's presence in the room had been a part of the package.

"I am prepared on the matter of the commutation of the

capital sentence. I do not see why Catalina need be here. In fact"—Che was extemporizing now, and was pleased he had happened on the tack—"it might be more comfortable for you if you proceeded without her presence."

"Che, the two are not fixed in concrete. I desire her to be here to witness the reprieve of sentence. She need not be here after that, when you and I converse. I am not being unreasonable. I am merely repeating the terms you accepted one week ago."

Che reflected on the alternatives. He knew that Catalina was at that moment being interrogated by the Jiménez in central Havana. It would take at least a half hour to bring her in. And—Che did not like to accuse himself of this, but an accusation it was, given the reputation he had for stamina—Che Guevara was . . . tired. It must have been that hour with Fidel. Moreover, in this room he did not have the facilities of the Intelligence Section, where he had anticipated Caimán's visit the preceding Saturday and where he might more easily have penetrated evasions, or misrepresentations. So he made up his mind.

"All right. We will meet tomorrow at noon. At the—" he broke off. Traditional caution of the guerrilla: Don't tell them ahead of time where the meeting place is to be. "—another location. I shall attend to the transportation. You can come in an ambulance."

"That might not be necessary. I am better . . . Che, a simple request. Can I see Catalina alone tomorrow?"

Che hesitated. "We'll see. We'll see. Much depends on what happens tomorrow. What you have to tell us tomorrow."

"Che, now listen, listen. What I have to tell you impinges very heavily on developments, international developments. If you will let me have in my room tonight a radio that can bring in Miami, I think I can be more helpful to you than otherwise: I mean, I can interpret what I hear, if it has any bearing on Cuba."

Che hesitated. There was burning in him an exasperation with the *Comandante en Jefe*.

So he said. "All right. I will give instructions. *Hasta luego, Caimán.*"

"*Hasta luego, Comandante.*"

Forty-two

Catalina had been kept in solitary confinement from the moment she was led from the truck back to the same prison she and Blackford had left the preceding Saturday, to be rescued by the ambush. Rescued! Yes. Rescued at 9:15 P.M., returned to the same prison at noon the next day having, in between, traveled one hundred miles round trip through turbulent seas, been shot at, seen four Cuban soldiers killed, Cecilio Velasco and Captain Eduardo killed, and Caimán shot through the shoulder.

The security had been heavy, including a soldier posted outside her own cell. No written materials had been permitted, and not until Tuesday, when she complained of the utter pain of her isolation, had she been given a couple of musty volumes which she read with difficulty, using the daylight that came through the small prison window (no electricity in solitary). She hoped only that the Americans would strike, would strike quickly, perhaps causing chaos; perhaps in that chaos something would happen, and she would seize the opportunity.

Meanwhile there was Caimán. He had been wounded, but not, she felt sure, mortally. Another thing: Was the Resistance aware of what had occurred at sea? Were the same people who had banded together under the leadership of Velasco mobilizing for a second attempt? She knew it would be much more difficult now.

Nothing to do, nothing to do. She turned her attention, when she could, to the books. Prescott's *History of the Conquest of Peru.* At least it was long (and, in fact, wonderfully diverting. But then she'd have found almost anything diverting). And on Sunday morning, when informed by the warden that she would be handcuffed and led to another location for a *"conferencia,"* she rejoiced. A conference anywhere, save with an execution squad, would be welcome.

She assumed that Blackford would be there, and Che, almost certainly Che; and so she scrubbed, as best she could, her face, and combed her hair with her fingers, so that she might look as she hoped they remembered her as looking. She asked for, but was denied access to, the tiny bundle of clothes that had been taken from her when she was first imprisoned. No. She would leave the prison in prison yellow.

In the corridor of Hq. Jiménez she sat, handcuffed, on a bench. And saw the doors open and Blackford led in. He was walking, his right arm in a sling. And his beard was gone. He winked at her.

Winked!

"¿Qué tal, Catalina. How're things?"

She smiled, and would happily have thrown her manacled arms about him. The smile did it; and, radiant, they entered the study, contriving to touch shoulders and arms as they passed through the door. They sat down where indicated, at one end of a long table. The guards stayed, and when Blackford began to speak to her, one of them shouted, Silence! And then Che walked in.

Dressed exactly as always, he sat down opposite them. A uniformed, heavy woman secretary-interpreter who wore captain's insignia and no makeup was on his right. She carried papers in a manila folder, a secretary's pad, and a small tape-recording machine.

"Well," Che began, "I see no point in rehearsing old times. These are very tense days. You have both been convicted of high treason against the Cuban state and have been sentenced to death. A deal has been struck the terms of which are that you, Catalina, will have your sentence reprieved and, following this reprieve, Caimán here will talk to me about certain arrangements in the United States of interest to the Cuban government. Have I said it all correctly?"

Blackford spoke. "Yes, you have. On one point, in my message to you a week ago, I was delinquent. I intended to say that Catalina would be reprieved from the death sentence, and that the alternative sentence, if anything at all, would be light. I did not make that plain. Do we have a problem here?"

"You are hardly in a position to change the terms of our arrangement," Che said. "But if you wish from me reassurance that Catalina will not get a life sentence, you have it."

"I hoped for a better assurance than that."

"Ah, you Yanqui bargainers! You begin by stealing Manhattan Island for—was it fourteen dollars?—"

"Twenty-four," Blackford corrected him.

"—And the next thing you want is thirty days in prison for a Cuban since, after all, all she did was reveal to an American espionage agent the deepest Cuban military secret."

There was silence. "We are at your mercy on the matter of the length of the prison sentence, Che."

Catalina now spoke. "Please don't bring it up again, Caimán. I know Che. Comandante Che. And I trust him."

Che looked down at a paper on the table. "Well, shall we begin?

"Here"—he extended his hand to his right, and his aide, perfunctorily introduced as Comrade Eudosia Mestre, handed him an unsealed envelope. Che opened it, brought out a sheet of paper, and handed it to Blackford.

He took it and read it carefully. It was written on the stationery of the Ministry of Industry. It was dated October 20, 1962. And read:

"In recognition of special services rendered to the Cuban state, the sentence of death levied on October 12, 1962, by the Supreme Military Court of Cuba on Catalina

Urrutia Sánchez, state prisoner #322-17788, is hereby commuted. The substitute period of penitentiary service will be handed down by the Supreme Military Court on or about November 1, 1962."

It was signed:

"Ernesto Che Guevara

Minister of Industry."

Blackford handed over the copy to Catalina—not an easy transaction, given the handcuffs.

He was silent while she looked at it.

Blackford knew he was now running a risk. But he decided to run it.

"It is not quite satisfactory, Che."

Che spoke as explosively as Blackford had ever heard him speak. "What do you mean it is not satisfactory!"

"I want Castro's signature."

Che rose, his cheeks red. "I am a Minister of the Republic. I have full legal power to grant reprieves of sentences. I have granted dozens such. In identical form. Would you, if you were in England and received a reprieve from the Home Secretary, demand the signature of the Queen?"

"The easiest way to answer that, Che, is to say that we are not in England, and you are not Home Secretary. Fidel Castro makes the law in Cuba. Nothing is the law that he does not say is the law. You must understand that it is reasonable, under the circumstances, to ask for the signature of the monarch, given that it is after all a matter of life and death."

Che was briefly attracted by the idea of sending them both, there and then, to the firing squad. But he cooled quickly enough to recognize that if he were to do so he would in effect have validated Castro's taunt of eight days ago that Caimán would probably have nothing of interest to say, and that if he did, he was evidently not the type who would say it. And so he decided on a middle course.

He would forge Castro's signature and so avoid the embarrassment of soliciting it.

"Very well, Caimán." This with feigned exasperation. "It happens I will be lunching with Comandante Castro at two-thirty. Will you agree to proceed, on the understanding that at that point I will secure the signature of the Prime Minister?"

"Sorry, Che."

Che rose, spitting out the end of his cigar. He motioned to Comrade Mestre to fetch the guards.

Major Marzo led them in.

"Take them away. Give them lunch. We will resume at 5 P.M."

Blackford looked at Catalina, and she caught his signal. She was to do the petitioning.

"Che," she called as Guevara was on the way out, "might Caimán and I lunch together? Please?"

Che hesitated. Then, over his shoulder to Marzo, he said, "Permission granted. But you, Marzo, must be in the room, and within hearing distance throughout the lunch." He banged the door.

It was an unusual scene. A table was propped up against the wooden wall, under a wide, open window from which the Bay of Havana was visible. A warm breeze flowed in. It was an office, commandeered for a few hours from a junior officer at Jiménez. Chairs were placed side by side. Following the instructions of Major Marzo, two guards unlocked the right handcuff on Catalina's hand and relocked it around the right front leg of the chair where she was seated. Her left hand was then unmanacled and left free.

Corresponding action was taken with Blackford. His right hand was as free as a hand sustained by a sling could be, his left manacled to the leg of the chair. And then, directly behind them, as though his function were that of official interpreter, Major Marzo sat. Plates were put in

front of the prisoners. Rice and beans and an indiscrimi-
nate vegetable, colored green; three bananas, a pot of coffee, and a large bowl of sugar.

The careful plans of the bureaucracy had overlooked
only this, that poor Major Marzo spoke and understood not
a single word of any language other than his own, so that
when Catalina and Blackford burst forth in quiet English he
faced the alternative of trying to find, for immediate duty,
another official who spoke both languages and could substitute for Major Marzo, incidentally drawing attention to
his limited usefulness for any Jiménez functions involving
English-speaking people. That—or simply keeping quiet.

It occurred to him to order them to speak in Spanish, but
if they declined to do so he did not really think he was well
situated to enforce his orders, given that both of them, or
such was his understanding, were under sentence of death.

So he just let them talk. And he let them, after they had
eaten their food—Catalina with some difficulty, handling
her fork with her left hand—let them join hands. They
spoke, it occurred to Major Marzo, without ceasing; in particular the woman spoke, spoke and spoke and spoke, and
the man, Caimán, would utter a word, softly, here and
there, and occasionally a sentence. And their hands, once
joined, never unclasped, and at one point Major Marzo was
wondering whether they were about to lean their heads
toward each other to kiss, and if so whether he should
physically get in the way of such license. He did not need to
act, because although his two charges were inclining
steeply in that direction, suddenly the door swung open,
and even though it was only four o'clock the guard announced that Comandante Guevara had returned and had
summoned the prisoners.

All the careful maneuvers were once again taken: Unlock,
lock. Unlock, lock. They were back in conventional tether,
and were led back to the questioning room. They spoke to
each other again, in English, and Major Marzo felt, through

the alien tongues, the ardor of their communication. They were, quietly, resignedly, on fire, vibrant with the spiritual energy they had generated in each other.

Che Guevara swept the piece of paper across to Blackford, who examined it. Underneath the signature of Ernesto Che Guevara appeared now the scrawl, "Approved. Fidel Castro." Blackford fondled the document. And turned to Catalina. "This is yours," he said. And then, to Guevara, "I am ready. But for this we do not need Catalina."

Che nodded, and Srta. Mestre rose and called the guards, who escorted Catalina, the envelope in her manacled hands, out. She turned her head to Blackford. *"Hasta luego, mi amor."* He waved at her as best he could, his hands manacled, his right arm in a sling.

"All right, Caimán. Business." He motioned to his secretary, who turned on the recorder and sat poised over her dictation pad. In the room, apart from them, were only two guards, one each at the opposite corners, standing at ease, their carbines at their sides.

"Proceed."

"Well," said Blackford, his voice descending to a conspiratorial whisper, "here's the big one." He spoke in Spanish, but occasionally Srta. Mestre would help him, when help was indicated.

"About a year ago," Blackford began languidly, "we got ourselves a very useful asset. Very useful because you thought he was one of yours. He was, once. But we took him on. And for nine months we played a very simple game. Every time we wanted to get somebody out of the way who was particularly . . . nettlesome to us," Blackford turned to Comrade Mestre, "—n-e-t-t-l-e-s-o-m-e. A big bother. An itch. A pain in the behind—we would drop that person's name through our double agent and—wonderful!—that

nettlesome person"—he waved at Srta. Mestre, who handled the English word now with dispatch in her aside to
Comandante Guevara—"simply disappeared. We were using, Che, your man, to get your men!

"Now if *that* isn't worth a pardon, maybe even a parade to
Guantánamo, I swear I don't know what would be."

Che Guevara was pale. But he proceeded cautiously.
"You have not yet been very useful. You have not named
him."

"Oh no, I'm not through. The incredible thing is that
about four months ago, he mysteriously disappeared. We
never found out where. We obviously could do no further
business with him, but maybe he is well entrenched behind
your lines, and is doing business with somebody else.
Frankly, Che, I wouldn't be surprised if there was some foul
play here. Anyway, he would be the biggest catch in Cuban-
Jiménez history."

"Who was he? What was his name?"

"He worked for the Swiss Embassy. His name was Pedro
Nogales—"

If Blackford had intended to say more he couldn't have.
Che Guevara had bolted from his seat and, across the table,
delivered with all his force a blow at Blackford's mouth.
Blackford, his hands tied, unable to seek balance, fell, the
chair with him. He closed his eyes against the pain he felt in
his mouth, and in his shoulder. There were exclamations
and mutterings in Spanish. And he was dragged out, and
strapped down in the ambulance that had brought him in to
Jiménez.

Forty-three

That night at seven, the word having got around that President Kennedy would be speaking to the entire world on the subject of Cuba, prison personnel, the inmates having been meticulously secured under lock and key, gathered at the four or five centers where radios were posted. The simultaneously translated eighteen-minute speech was broadcast live. Major Marzo was the senior officer in his social group, which met in the clerk's office by the armory: six officers, a portable radio, and two bottles of rum.

Fidel Castro gathered his intimates on the top floor of the INRA. He had announced to the media that he would reply to President Kennedy on Cuban television and radio at 10 P.M.

The word had spread rapidly that something of consequence was up, and almost everywhere competing activity had stopped so that all might hear the speech of President Kennedy.

At seven, the Castro party was silent, listening to the translator . . . *"The stationing of the missiles was a belligerent act on the part of Cuba and the Soviet Union . . . Any activity against the United States or its neighbors involving said missiles would be considered by the American government as an act of aggression by the Soviet Union as well as by Cuba . . . There would be a quarantine of the seas surrounding Cuba, and all cargo vessels going in toward Cuba would beginning at dawn tomorrow be hailed, boarded, and passage would be permitted only to those vessels that did not carry arms . . . That situation would continue until the Soviet Union had removed all missiles currently reposing in Cuba, and until a physical inspection of the island confirmed that the missiles had all been removed . . ."*

Castro shouted out his glee. "We have taken them! We have taken them! We have the gringos! They are not coming in for an air strike! And, of course, the Soviet Union will never permit the quarantine!"

He practically danced about the table, and Dorticós, Valdés, and even Raúl and Che caught his enthusiasm. They were dumbfounded that the Americans had not struck, and apparently were not planning to do so. And they shared the conviction of Fidel that nothing, but nothing would prevail upon the Soviet Union to accept the humiliation of removing the missiles, let alone submitting to the boarding of their cargo vessels, steaming in toward Cuba at this very moment, "like dirty little children showing their hands to a teacher," as Castro put it. Castro said he looked forward eagerly to ten o'clock, at which point he would review the record of United States aggression against Cuba, express Cuban gratitude to the Soviet Union for helping Cuba with strategic defensive arms, and reassure the Cuban people that their capacity for self-defense would not be a victim of these tense times. "I can say it all, I am sure, in one hour, it is that simple," Fidel said.

He sat back in his desk chair and turned his thoughts inward, as his associates began to pick at the dishes of fruits and cheese that were brought in, and Dorticós and Valdés and Raúl toasted each other with a rum drink. Suddenly Fidel looked up at Che, and beckoned to him.

Che went over and leaned over the desk. Fidel asked, "What about the American? Caimán? Did he have anything to say?"

"He gave us the name of a double agent, Fidel, I am checking on. The agent was very active while Caimán was in America, and he clearly did us much damage. He has not, in fact, been so active during the past period, but of course

Caimán had no way of knowing this. He has given me clues which I am certain will lead to his apprehension."

"You think he earned commutation of sentence?"

Che Guevara hesitated for just a moment. Then said, "But does that matter, Fidel?"

"No," Castro said, smiling as he looked at the end of his cigar. "No. I wouldn't care if he revealed that we were going to be invaded at midnight. Get rid of him. And the girl. Oh—Che, listen. I was thinking yesterday about it. I want them to suffer. No torture. Just suffer. So I want her executed one day before he is executed. And I want her told she will be executed tomorrow morning, but don't shoot her until Wednesday. Shoot Caimán Thursday. That way she will suffer a full twenty-four hours. He will suffer forty-eight hours, with double intensity the first twenty-four hours. Am I not a born central planner, Che?"

Che decided to hazard one final attempt. "Listen, Fidel—" There was an interruption. A crowd outside, properly stimulated and instructed two hours before the broadcast in what would be the appropriate reaction to whatever President Kennedy said, had gathered and begun to sing the national anthem and to shout, "*Viva Fidel! Viva Fidel!*" Fidel had one ear on the outside noise, another on what Che was saying. "Listen, Fidel, I am really a little embarrassed by my signature's appearing on the instrument that guaranteed remission of the capital sentence on the girl."

"That's simple. Just say I overruled you. Oh yes, and by the way, Che, I place you in charge of the entire operation. You are responsible to me. I shall advise the Minister of the Interior of this. I feel there is poetic justice here; I hope you will agree."

Che drew his breath. "As for Caimán, I quite agree. But I think of him, a CIA spy, as guilty on another level from the girl, Urrutia. And besides, we never promised to remit *his* sentence."

"Did you hear that, Che? Did you catch the words? Listen
. . ." But the crowd did not repeat them; they were extem-
poraneously babbling away. Fidel said exultantly, "They
were singing:

> Fidel, Khrushchev,
> We love 'em both.
> Climb another rung:
> Long live Mao Tse-tung.

"Wonderful! I had not heard that before. Tonight will
prove to be a great night, those dumb Yanquis. Not as
great," he suddenly frowned, "as if we had completed the
installations. But under the circumstances, fine."

Suddenly his mood changed completely. He lowered the
cap on his head and looked Che Guevara directly in the
face. His accents were slow and solemn. "Do not mention
that girl traitor to me one more time."

Che Guevara executed a casual salute. "Understood, Comandante. Now I think I had better leave. There is much to
do, and you will need to think about your address to the
nation. You have less than an hour. You will find me if you
need me."

"Come to me tonight after it is over, and tell me what you
thought of my speech. Bring anyone you like. I think a
modest little celebration is in order."

"I shall come unless duties detain me, Fidel."

En route to El Príncipe he found that his heart was
pounding. That did not usually happen to Che Guevara.
And then it occurred to him, for the first time, to conflate
the speech of Kennedy with the bizarre silence of the Soviet
Union throughout the preceding week. For the first time he
wondered: Could the Soviet Union be planning to back
out? He would greatly hope to be as far away from Fidel
Castro as possible if that were to happen. He wondered
whether he might decide to leave the country on a quick

inspection tour of the Cuban missions in Mexico or Bogotá
. . . But no: there was no way in which someone of his rank
could absent himself from Cuba until after the crisis was
past. He was struggling, he acknowledged to himself, to
avoid what lay immediately ahead.

He made up his mind. It was a risky business, but the
odds were on his side. Because Colonel Gonzalo Citrón,
commander of the military prison El Príncipe, had fought
alongside Che in 1958. Together they had marched into
Havana. And—Che knew—Citrón loathed and distrusted
Aníbal Escalante, the communist opportunist who had displayed cowardice and sadism during the early months of
Castro's ascendancy and was now beginning to exercise
influence on the military command. And Citrón knew that
Che Guevara shared apprehensions about Escalante. On
several occasions they had discussed him and the threat he
posed.

It would, then, not be difficult to talk personally with
Citrón in confidence. There was the single problem that
Citrón tended to take too much rum after working hours.
And it was almost ten. Citrón would feel obliged to listen to
Castro's speech, and perhaps he had brought along mem-
bers of the staff. In that event he would have stayed sober.
But that meant that Che would not be able to talk with him
until God-knows-when—when Castro had finished speak-
ing. Well, he would see.

There was a considerable flurry at the gates when Comandante Guevara arrived, even though for the third time
in three days. The Duty Officer came running from the
adjacent office, saluted, and advised the Comandante that
he would instantly summon the camp commander.

"Where is Colonel Citrón?" Che asked.

"In the officers' common room, Comandante. They plan
to listen to the speech at ten."

It was fifteen minutes before ten. "Take me to the common room."

"Shall I first advise the colonel?"

"No. Just take me there."

The Duty Officer saluted, dived into his own jeep, and led the way to the far end of the building compound. He jumped out and approached a door.

"Permit me, Comandante. Follow me."

Up a staircase.

Coming from the right was much noise and laughter. The Duty Officer did not wish to be the man who intruded on the privacy of the upper echelon of El Príncipe. He indicated to Guevara the appropriate door. Che walked over to it and turned the knob.

The clamor died down only gradually, but came then to dead silence when it transpired who was there. Fifteen men —none of them wearing jackets, most with drinking glasses in their hands—stood at attention. Colonel Citrón walked over to Che and saluted. "My dear friend. What brings us this honor?"

Che let the men continue at attention for a moment or two. "Oh, there are one or two things we need to discuss, Gonzalo. But" he looked rather vaguely about him, "I am interrupting something?"

"No, Che, you could never interrupt anything. We gathered here to listen to the response of Fidel to Kennedy. He will be on in just a minute or two."

Che waved the men to be at ease. Rather self-consciously they resumed conversation, and (quieter) drinking. The boisterousness was gone and one of them turned up the radio. The announcer was talking about reactions against American imperialism in various parts of the world. He then said that word had come down from the Prime Minister's office that the speech of the *Comandante en Jefe*, Fidel Castro, would be delayed by a half hour, pending attention to pressing official business. Che wondered what that was all about; but then Castro often delayed. He had been thirty minutes late in New York City at the reception given in his honor by Nikita Khrushchev. He was just that way about deadlines.

He turned suddenly to Gonzalo. "Let us talk, then, before Fidel's speech."

Gonzalo nodded, poured his glass full (one half Coca-Cola, one half rum), and beckoned to Che, leading him back into the corridor and down three doors. He was now in his own office. Twice the size of the room they had just left, the wall space mostly devoted to photographs of Fidel, of Che, and of other graduates of the Sierra Maestra campaign. Gonzalo beckoned to Che to occupy Gonzalo's own large stuffed chair behind the desk. Che declined, taking a second chair at the side.

"I have on my mind the prisoners Catalina Urrutia and Blackford Oakes."

"Yes. I have the reprieve." He reached into his drawer and pulled it out.

"Let me see it." Che was lighting a cigar.

Gonzalo Citrón reached across the desk and handed it to Che. Che took it with his left hand, moved his cigarette lighter under it, and watched while it slowly caught fire and reduced to ashes over the wooden floor. With his foot he damped the ashes, and shoved them more or less out of the way, under the colonel's desk.

Citrón had said nothing. But now he spoke. "It had Fidel's signature, you know."

"Yes. I have just been with Fidel. He changed his mind."

There was an awkward pause. Gonzalo Citrón was a graduate of the Managua Military Academy. They had been taught there to regard written orders with some solemnity.

"She is to be shot?"

"She is to be shot."

"When?"

"It is this that I wish to speak to you about. In confidence."

"I would treat anything you tell me, my old friend, as a confessor would treat it."

"One day, not very far away, I will explain it all. But Escalante is indirectly involved. What is needed now is an 'abortive' procedural drill. The objective is to effect the execution without the prisoner's foreknowledge that Fidel recalled the reprieve. Advise me. One way would be for an order to be made out to inform her tomorrow morning that she will be executed the next day. Then there could be the confusion. At the time tomorrow when she is scheduled to be told she is to be executed on Wednesday, she should be led to the wall, as though she were being led to an administrative office—and then shot."

Colonel Citrón volunteered instantly that of course it would be as Che desired—Citrón's only concern was simply to achieve that objective without appearing to have been unnecessarily careless about established practices.

"You know of course, Che, that condemned prisoners follow a certain ritual, and that the captain who leads them to the execution wall knows what these rituals are. How are we to advise him to ignore these rituals?"

"What about this . . ." Che was thinking out loud. "Suppose you tell him that you have had a telephone call— do not say who called you. A rumor has been picked up that the Resistencia might attempt an interference, and therefore a different execution site is to be chosen, and no official is to be made aware that an execution is imminent. The squad can be waiting casually for her arrival. She will arrive knowing nothing."

"Will that be the official story of why she was executed one day early?"

Che thought for a moment. It would not work if Castro knew that Che had been involved in any way in the planning. He would need to repose his fullest trust in Citrón.

"Yes. We will do it that way. You will have picked up the rumor about a possible demonstration or effort to interfere with the execution, and you will have decided to counter that plan, if indeed it is real, by proceeding to carry out the sentence along the lines we have discussed. Since Urrutia, along with the American, Oakes, has been made by Fidel my special responsibility, you will telephone my Ministry to secure my consent to the altered plans. But you will not succeed in reaching me. You will then proceed on your own authority. On Tuesday afternoon I will be advised what happened. And I will then make arrangements through Valdés's office to secure an extra guard to surround the prison on Thursday morning, when the American gets executed, to guard against the Resistencia's interfering."

"Understood. My telephone call to you will go out a few minutes before ten."

"A few minutes before ten I shall be unreachable."

"Anything new on Escalante, Che?"

"Yes. But not now, Gonzalo. Not now. You must go now and listen to Fidel's speech. Tell me, is Caimán—the American—still in the hospital?"

"No. He is in his own cell."

"Give me a guard. Make that two guards. I wish to see him."

"Of course."

The area immediately about his upper lip showed traces of blue, and the lip was swollen. But Blackford Oakes, sitting at his primitive desk and writing a fresh letter to Sally, was feeling very much at peace. He yearned to know what it was that President Kennedy had said. The guards, while telling him they were themselves going to listen, did not then come back to say what it was they had heard. Never mind. The missile crisis was now open, official. "It is confrontational," he was writing to Sally, "a word I doubt that Jane Austen ever used. How on earth did she get by without it?" He was interrupted. The clanging of his cell door about to open. He had not expected to see Che Guevara.

The lieutenant said, "Do you wish us to stay, Comandante? If not, shall we handcuff him?"

Che, standing, pondered the tall, strong American, his right arm in a sling. Che's hand moved, not quite unobtrusively, to his pistol holster.

"Never mind. Wait outside. I will knock on the door for you."

The lieutenant and guard left the cell, locking the door.

Che moved to the small upright chair by the bed and sat on it.

"I have come to tell you what is in prospect for you."

"I can guess that. What I can't guess is what Kennedy said tonight. Would you tell me?"

"He said the United States Navy would quarantine the island until the missiles were removed. No arms will be permitted to enter."

A different response from what Blackford had imagined. He felt a surge of disappointment.

"That's all?"

"That's all.

"You will be shot on Thursday morning."

"Why Thursday? Want to wait until my shoulder is better?"

"That is the decision. Remember, Caimán: Your side and my side are at war."

"I will remember. And Catalina?"

"You read the decree. Her new sentence is to be pronounced on or about November 1."

"So, Che, what is there to talk about?"

"You may as well know that as far as it was possible to do, I opposed the substitution in Cuba of tyranny by the Soviet Union for tyranny by the United States."

"Maybe I believe you, maybe I don't. But I hope you'll be around for long enough to distinguish between tyranny under the Soviet Union and their little Stalin Castro, and what tyranny was like under the Chase Manhattan Bank."

"I simply wished you to know this. Have you read Eudocio Ravines?"

"*The Road from Yenan?*"

"Yes. In Spanish we call it *La Gran Estafa.*"

"What does *estafa* mean?"

Che hesitated. "It means deceit, treachery. In English I think it is 'double cross.' Ravines says ours is The Big Double Cross. That is not correct. He is an ex-communist, disillusioned. He does not know that in China Mao Tse-tung is accomplishing miracles for the people."

"He is certainly succeeding in reducing the population problem. When I last heard, Mao was trying to find all hundred of the flowers he sent out to bloom, and was wringing them by the neck until they were quite dead."

"My point is that Ravines may be talking about Stalin's double cross. But the men I have fought with are, most of them, men of the people, true liberators. And in Montevideo I had hoped to contrive an understanding that would permit the best of Fidel Castro, and eliminate the worst of the Soviet Union."

"Well, for the record, Che, you failed."

"I can accept failure. Not dishonor."

"Oh? Well, what about the dishonor you're surrounded by? Every one of Castro's promises is shit. Elections, prosperity, fraternity, justice. Does that not affect your honor?"

"I am not in charge of the Cuban revolution. I had a role in effecting the liberation of Cuba and I am proud of the role I played. I hope to play it elsewhere." Che rose. "I wanted only for you to know that during those quite crucial months, this spring and early this summer, I still held out hope. That is all."

He went to the door and knocked three times on it, and the clanking was heard and the door opened.

He turned to Blackford. "*Hasta luego, Caimán.*"

"No, Che. *Adiós.*"

"Very well. *Adiós, Caimán.*"

"Para servirle," Blackford said, turning back to his letter to Sally before even the door had closed.

The following morning, just before ten, the telephone rang in the office of the Minister of Industry. An urgent call from Colonel Citrón of El Príncipe.

"The Comandante is not in."

"Can he be reached?"

"He has not called in. He may be with the Prime Minister."

"Is there any way I can reach him there?"

"Oh, Colonel, I would not call him there. I would never do that. If you will leave me your number, I shall get to him as soon as I can."

The colonel left his number, and a substantial record of his frustration.

Five minutes later, Catalina was told by a captain she had not seen before that she was wanted for interrogation at the adjutant's office.

Catalina took fifteen seconds to order her hair, and to dig her nails into her cheeks to bring out some color. She smiled at the captain. Why not? She'd also have smiled at him a fortnight ago when she was formally allied with the captain and the whole establishment that supported his authority, against which events had catapulted her.

She followed him out and was not surprised that the handcuffs were put on, though she was slightly surprised that in addition, two guards followed her, the captain leading the way. No doubt since Cecilio Velasco's ambush all her movements, and those of Caimán, were under heavy security.

They walked through the main courtyard over toward the armory building, near the stone quarry, apparently abandoned. Her thoughts were on what it was she would be interrogated about. Anything Caimán had ever told her, she supposed. They rounded a corner and walked out a few yards from the barracks toward an old stone wall, an ancient part of the prison's fortification, about eight feet high. To her right, apparently loitering there, were six soldiers. Suddenly the captain stopped. A large pad eye protruded at waist level from a spot in the wall. He signaled to the guard who removed one of Catalina's handcuffs and refastened it behind her back, through the pad eye to the handcuffs on the other hand. Catalina did not understand, and said to the captain that whatever they had done to her manacles, it was hurting her left wrist.

But the captain was out of immediate earshot she saw as she raised her head from the effort to inspect the manacles behind her.

Then she looked in front of her, and now she knew. "*¡Madre de Dios!*" were her last words.

Forty-four

Tuesday morning in Havana was for official Cuba—the top cadre, really, who quickly assimilated the dimensions of the events made public by Kennedy's broadcast—something of a letdown. The excitement that the night before had confronted them with had substantially dissipated as the consensus grew that it was unlikely the Soviet Union would answer immediately the American challenge. Meanwhile all of Cuba knew, suddenly, that Fidel Castro had made a deal which, if it had succeeded, would in effect have made Cuba into something of a superpower. It was not widely ventilated that Castro had actually ceded to the Soviet Union ownership of the land on which the missiles sat, something Castro later heatedly denied was the case, when confronted with the allegation. The feeling that morning was that the island was safe, for the moment, from any American invasion and that, really, the unresolved issues were now between the Soviet Union and the United States, and it was unlikely that Cuba would suffer directly. Not unless the Soviet Union was defiant. If Soviet submarines began challenging American naval vessels, then presumably there would be war. But since President Kennedy had given the distinct impression that the Soviet missiles were not yet armed, Cuba would not likely be a bloody battleground of a third world war. It all argued, for that part of the population that gave the crisis thought, a kind of tranquillity. There was simply nothing to be done.

Castro's mood was dour, in part because he was rather hung over from the elation of the night before, an elation he had been careful to modulate over television. He did not want to give the impression that he had sat out an entire week in silence while knowing that the United States had three substantial military areas in Cuba between the cross hairs of its mighty air force. Or that he was privately overjoyed that no invasion or bombardment was imminent. He did what he could, without implying any estrangement, publicly to challenge the Soviet Union to prove that it was the true friend of liberation movements everywhere. He had spoken for ninety minutes. And when, the next morning, he asked his press attaché to give him reports from foreign capitals on reactions, he was chagrined to be told that not very much time or attention had been devoted to his speech.

"Not even in Mexico?"

"The radio in Mexico carried an account, and it is of course too early to know what the afternoon newspapers will do." Castro dismissed him.

It was then that Raúl Roa, Castro's Foreign Minister and a longtime member of the Communist Party, telephoned him. He had, he told Castro, just finished receiving the Swiss ambassador, a distinguished old bird who had demanded a personal audience for the purpose of bringing to him a cable from the President of the United States.

"From the President of the United States!" Castro exclaimed.

"Not exactly. But not far from it. The cable is from his brother, the Attorney General. But it might as well have come from the President and there cannot be any doubt that the President himself ordered it to be transmitted."

Castro tensed himself on his chair. "All right, Roa. Read it to me."

The Foreign Minister did so.

Oddly, Castro was glad to have something concrete to do. He instructed Roa to call a meeting for two o'clock at the INRA at which he wished Che Guevara to be present and also Avila Bacarro, the Solicitor General, and of course

Ramiro Valdés, from Interior. He shut down the receiver and put a call in to Che. He was annoyed that he could not find Che until very nearly twelve. "Where on earth have you been?"

"There was trouble down at the bay. Canadian cargo ship with vital spare parts. The captain had a cable from his Toronto office, didn't want to unload until after the crisis was over."

"What happened?"

"I persuaded him. It wasn't hard. But it consumed most of my morning. What's up, Fidel?"

Castro recounted, with some perturbation, the telegram from the U.S. Attorney General. "Your friend Caimán is well connected."

"Well, he came here under high auspices in his own government and, if you will permit me, also here."

"Yes. Have you had a chance to check out the information he gave you yesterday?"

"Fidel! That will take two weeks, at the least."

"In two weeks Caimán will be dead."

"In two weeks he will be rotting. He is scheduled to die on Thursday."

"Yes. Well, I have called a meeting at the INRA for two o'clock—Roa, Valdés, and Bacarro. I want you there. I don't suppose you happen to have the answer to the question of whether our getting Caimán on the high seas makes having him here illegal under international law?"

"I don't. I know we have no legal rights outside the twelve-mile limit."

"How far out were we?"

"Fifty miles."

"I suppose we could say we were only ten miles out."

"We could. We would need to doctor a lot of logbooks. And then there is the possibility that U.S. radar fixed the position of the *Aguila* and the *País*. And then, too, we know that Caimán gave an exact navigational position in his telephone call to New York."

"He could have been lying."

"Imagine!"

At the meeting, Fidel Castro was not in the least hortatory. But he was clearly exercised. He listened to a dry lecture on the law from Bacarro and cut it short by saying he had got rather confused. "I am a qualified lawyer," Castro reminded him, drawing on his cigar. "And it would appear to me that we have a metaphysical problem here. I understand the law says that a tribunal need not concern itself with the means by which a defendant's presence in court was effected. But in our case, 1) the tribunal passed sentence while the American was in Cuba. Now, 2) he escapes, and our forces go out and 3) get him in neutral waters. The question is whether the finding of the tribunal that tried him legally is voided by the subsequent illegal apprehension. If that is so, would it then follow that if he were retried, and the court declined to listen to arguments concerning the illegality of that apprehension, the court could then proceed to find him guilty, and proceed with the execution?"

"That would be a contention we would be prepared to make, Comandante. But there then arises the question of damages: illegal apprehension is an offense under international law. To proceed with an execution following that illegal apprehension would be to make impossible the most appropriate damages, which would be, of course, the return of the person illegally apprehended."

"Thank you, gentlemen." Castro pointed to Bacarro and Roa. This meant that they were to leave. And that Valdés and Che were to remain. They left.

"Forget the law," Castro said. "Let us ask only this: If the President wants Caimán back so badly, what can we get from him? Alternatively, what can he do to us? No, not what *can* he do to us. He could, theoretically, cause the City of Havana to cease to exist. But what is he *likely* to do if we proceed with the execution? Che?"

"Mr. Kennedy is said to have something of a temper."

"On the other hand," Valdés observed, "this is hardly the time for him to be governed by temper. A third world war may be in the offing."

"Taking another approach," Castro said, "what—forgetting the missiles for the moment—would we most usefully have from Washington that Washington would conceivably give us?"

"I have a list I worked up with the prisoner over a period of six months which amounts to one billion dollars worth of industrial items we need very badly."

"He is not going to give us one billion dollars for Caimán. It must not look like blackmail," Castro said. "He would not engage in any exchange of that order. The quid pro quo must have a symbolic value." Fidel looked out of the window, distracted.

"We will think about it. Meanwhile, Che, if we haven't solved the problem by Thursday don't execute him. Every day, just have him told it has been postponed by one day."

"What message will you return via the Swiss Embassy?"

"Nothing," Castro said. "Nothing for the moment. We are presumably very busy. Caught up in our crisis." Suddenly the distraction was over. Fidel pressed on his buzzer and an aide came bounding in. "Anything from Moscow?"

"Not yet, Comandante."

Driving back to his office, it came to Che, slowly but surely. *Fidel is scared. He is scared of what John F. Kennedy might do to him, Fidel Castro, if he does not return Caimán. Therefore Caimán will be returned.*

The change from yesterday! Che Guevara had studied Fidel for over four years. He was at once a brave man and—a coward. Or, perhaps, call it—prudent.

All that had gone on during the past hour, all of it was

sham. Fidel Castro had received a personal ultimatum from the President of the United States. It had not threatened the end of Cuban sovereignty or anything on that order. It involved the life of one miserable young American agent whose involvement in Cuba after all had been impossibly complicated, diplomatically and legally. Yesterday Fidel would gladly have tortured him to death. Today he was resigned to giving him up. What he wants is a face-saver. And—Che reflected—given the sticky background of this mess, *I* had better be the person to come up with it.

That afternoon, Che sent a messenger to the INRA. The envelope, marked "Strictly Personal from Che Guevara," was delivered instantly to Castro.

The covering note read, "Fidel: What would you think of something like this? Here is a draft of a cable Raúl Roa might send back via the embassy:"

Castro began to read:

ATTORNEY GENERAL

THE UNITED STATES OF AMERICA

WASHINGTON DC

THE PRIME MINISTER OF CUBA, HIS EXCELLENCY LICENCIADO FIDEL CASTRO, HAS DIRECTED ME TO REPLY THAT AN INVESTIGATION PRELIMINARILY TENDS TO CONFIRM THE ALLEGATION THAT THE CUBAN PATROL VESSEL FRANK PAÍS INADVERTENTLY STRAYED BEYOND CUBAN WATERS ON SUNDAY OCTOBER 14. THE PRIME MINISTER IS UNDER THE CIRCUMSTANCES DISPOSED TO GRANT THE REQUEST OF THE PRESIDENT OF THE UNITED STATES. BUT THIS ONLY UPON RECEIPT OF A WRITTEN DECLARATION BY THE ATTORNEY GENERAL OF THE UNITED STATES THAT HE WILL GIVE PERSONAL ATTENTION TO THE CLAIMS OF 23 CUBANS IN JAIL IN MIAMI, FLORIDA, WHO HAVE BEEN ILLEGALLY ARRESTED. A LIST OF THESE VICTIMS OF U.S. JUDICIAL INJUSTICE WAS READ OUT AT A PROTEST MEETING HELD IN MANHATTAN BY THE FAIR PLAY FOR CUBA COMMITTEE IN SEPTEMBER 1960 BY THE DISTINGUISHED AT-

TORNEY LEONARD BOUDIN. THE PRIME MINISTER WOULD REQUIRE THAT THE DOCUMENT PROMISING TO GIVE PERSONAL ATTENTION TO THESE CLAIMS BE SIGNED BY THE ATTORNEY GENERAL. THE DOCUMENT WOULD NEED A FURTHER FRANK, TO WIT, "APPROVED:" FOLLOWED BY THE SIGNATURE OF THE PRESIDENT OF THE UNITED STATES. UPON RECEIPT OF SUCH A DOCUMENT AT THE BASE AT GUANTÁNAMO, THE PRISONER OAKES WILL BE TURNED OVER TO U.S. AUTHORITIES.

Following the text of the proposed cable Guevara had written in longhand: "Let me have your reaction, if you feel like it."

The telephone rang.

"It is brilliant, Che. Brilliant! You have succeeded in coming up with something the President is not likely to want to exhibit. But which *we* are free to exhibit at any time we choose. A document that contains the signatures of both the Attorney General and the President! Do you think they will agree?"

"I don't know, Fidel. That business about also requiring the approval of the chief of state is pretty rough stuff. I'd hate to be in a position of having to ask you to write 'Approved' to warrant the authority of one of your own ministers."

"I see your point. But all the more exquisite if they agree, eh, Che? If they draw the line at the President's signature, we can always reconsider. I shall have the message substantially in the form you recommend delivered to the Swiss Embassy this afternoon."

"Any other news, Fidel?"

"No. Well, not quite no. A message from Chomón"— Faure Chomón, the Cuban Ambassador to the Soviet Union, had been bearing the brunt of Castro's displeasure. "Chomón spent a half hour with Gromyko. He reports that the Politburo is in continuous session and that, of course, we will be the first to learn what their response will be. But we are not to expect anything for several days."

"I see. I am at your service, Comandante." Che hung up the telephone.

He had been right about Fidel. Fidel was scared and nervous. That telegram had, in a strange way, got to him.

And he guessed the Americans would comply.

Forty-five

At eight in the morning on Wednesday the usual clanging announced a visitor. Not the guard who brought in breakfast, if that was what he could call one slice of black bread and one glass of water with something orange dropped into it, just enough to spoil the taste of the water. That had come an hour earlier. Blackford was lying on his bed, waiting for the sun to get bright enough to permit him to resume reading his detective story.

It was Major Marzo.

"Sr. Caimán, I have been assigned to . . . supervise . . . you until . . . I am relieved of duty, and therefore it falls to me to advise you—" and he went through the identical routine regarding requests of prisoners to be executed to which Blackford had submitted ten days earlier.

He gave the same answers. And when Major Marzo came to the last question, Did the condemned have any requests? Blackford said, once again, that he would like to visit with Catalina Urrutia.

Major Marzo looked up.

"The prisoner Catalina Urrutia was executed yesterday morning."

Blackford sprang up from his bed, his eyes blazing. He approached to within inches of Major Marzo, who fell back toward the open door.

"What did you say, Marzo?"

Major Marzo repeated that the condemned Urrutia had been executed the preceding day.

"You are crazy, Marzo," Blackford fairly shouted at him.

"*Catalina Urrutia had a pardon from Che Guevara countersigned by Fidel Castro.*"

"The *Comandante en Jefe*," said Major Marzo, behind whom two of the outside guards had rallied, "evidently changed his mind."

Blackford raised his arms, straining the brace on the right shoulder, and lunged at the officer, who ducked to one side, making room for a guard to thrust the butt end of his carbine hard into Blackford's stomach. A second drove the butt of his carbine into Blackford's crotch. The two guards continued their beating until Marzo stopped them.

They left him on the floor, gasping for breath and spitting blood.

When they brought him the lunch tray he was still on the floor, his face only a few inches removed from his vomit.

Comandante Citrón was notified, and made a call to Guevara.

"Hospitalize him," Guevara said.

Blackford Oakes's near-lifeless body was lifted back onto one of those stretchers. His eyes were closed, and he responded to not a word asked of him by prison official, doctor, or nurse.

He didn't know when it was that he was taken from the bed—was he drugged? He supposed so. He remembered nothing, except vague and desultory exertions involved in placing him into an airplane, and becoming airborne. Eventually the engines stopped. He was lifted up and, with one guard on his left shoulder, another managing his right side without putting pressure on the shoulder, he was maneuvered down a gangway into a car. Someone put a cap on his head, tilting down the visor to keep the sun away. There was a pause, an exchange of papers of some sort. He was, all of a sudden, in yet another hospital, except that here they spoke more English.

He woke before dawn, his mind slowly regaining lucidity.

He did not know where he was, but focused his eyes on a bell pinned to the side of the bed. He tried with his right hand to reach up to it, but the pain stopped him. He moved his left hand across his body, reached the button, and depressed it.

A nurse arrived. "And are you feeling better, Mr. Oakes?"

"Where am I?"

"You are at the Naval Hospital at Guantánamo."

"What are they going to do with me?"

"Ah, you will need to ask the doctor that question. He will make his rounds, as usual, at seven. You can talk to him then, and I'm sure he will answer all your questions. Meanwhile you are obviously improving, and that is very good news. Can I get you a glass of milk?"

"No. Nothing. Thank you."

He closed his eyes, and woke when the doctor came in.

Four days later he was in Maryland, sitting, warmly clothed, in a garden. It was noon, and the weather was brilliantly sunny. On the iron table to his right was a glass of iced tea.

"It is a real Indian summer we are having, Blackford. Really quite unusual, and most welcome."

"It is very pretty, Rufus, a very pretty day. And your rose garden looks fine, even in October."

"I think you should stay until May, Blackford. That is when the roses really show off."

Epilogue

Five years later, on October 8, 1967, Blackford Oakes flew into La Paz. He had left Washington for Bolivia the afternoon before with instructions to superintend, to the extent he would be permitted to do so, arrangements involving the debriefing of Ernesto Che Guevara, whose capture was confidently predicted as imminent. "Colonel Zenteno has got them surrounded," the Director advised Blackford. "Tomorrow, or the next day at the latest, they'll have him. Have the lot of them. Che Guevara may have written the classic on guerrilla warfare, but he has certainly made a fiasco of this one. Eleven months in the field and he has exactly twenty-two men, and not one single recruit from the Bolivian peasantry."

"What do they plan to do with him?"

"I talked to General Barrientos' ambassador here. He says he doesn't want another public trial of the kind they went through with Regis Debray. That just gave the whole world one long philippic by Bertrand Russell et al. on the crimes of capitalism. General Barrientos has published the names of over fifty soldiers and civilians killed by Che Guevara and his guerrillas during the past few months. Usually by ambush. My guess is they're going to execute him. But they'll give us access to him if that's possible. I am sure of that."

Arriving at Lima at six to catch the connecting flight to La Paz, Blackford was intercepted by an official from the embassy with a cable.

It said:

GUEVARA WOUNDED AND CAPTURED. BOLIVIAN MILITARY

ARE TAKING HIM FROM QUEBRADA DEL YURO WHERE THE
AMBUSH CLOSED IN TO LA HIGUERA WHERE HE WILL BE
BY THE TIME YOU GET THIS MESSAGE. AT LA PAZ PLANE
WILL BE WAITING TO TAKE YOU TO VALLEGRANDE. THERE
A CAR WILL DRIVE YOU TO LA HIGUERA. COLONEL
ZENTENO EXPECTS YOU.

It was after eight when he put down at La Paz. Blackford
strained for air in the toplofty altitude until he put on his
oxygen mask. The little airplane climbed slowly and
headed southeast to vault the 250 miles to Vallegrande.
The night was clear, and the pilot weaved through the
snowy crags of the Andes. Blackford sat in the copilot's seat
of the Lockheed Lodestar. For some reason he was reminded that this was the same model airplane in which one
of Elizabeth Taylor's husbands—he could not recall his
name; the one who made *Around the World in Eighty Days*—
had been killed. He took the mike and spoke to the pilot,
whose oxygen mask, against the pale moonlight, gave him a
proboscis like an astronaut's. "What do they have at Vallegrande by way of navigation?"

The pilot spoke into the tiny mike that rested on the
protruding end of his headband. "Omni, señor."

"What is the elevation of Vallegrande?"

"It is three thousand one hundred meters."

A hell of an altitude to wage a guerrilla campaign in,
Blackford thought, and looked out at the deep ravines and
canyons that stretched ahead of him.

The flight was uneventful, and Blackford missed the
comfort of the oxygen when he put aside the mask after
they had landed. A station wagon drove up to the aircraft.
Blackford made arrangements with the pilot. "Probably
tomorrow, perhaps not until the next day." The pilot would
wait, he said, and every couple of hours would check with
the airport for messages. "There is usually someone on

duty here, though not between midnight and six," the airport manager said.

They drove off on a macadamized road that became dirt within a few kilometers. La Higuera nestled in a little valley. It was midnight, and the square was empty. The driver took Blackford to a building at the corner. A village cantina, which doubled as a small hostelry. The same man served from the bar and registered guests. He asked Blackford whether he was Mr. Oakes. Blackford nodded, while signing the register. The bartender handed him a letter. "We are closing for the night, señor. Can I give you something to drink?"

Blackford asked for a cold beer. A young man carried his suitcase up the wide wooden staircase to the second floor. His room number was seven. The bath and bathroom were at the end of the hall. It was chilly, but not cold. Blackford tipped the boy and opened the letter.

It was from Colonel Zenteno and said that he would be breakfasting at seven and would brief Sr. Oakes at that time. Blackford opened the bottle of beer, drank half of it, went off toward the bathroom to brush his teeth, and, on opening the door, came head-on up against a large burly man.

"*Perdón,*" Blackford said, closing the door and walking back to his room, where he finished his beer and hoped that the food at La Higuera would not find him spending the midnight hour as the hotel's other guest was spending it.

Colonel Zenteno was a man of few words, as he had established at midnight the night before. While eating a breakfast of steak and eggs and rolls he told Blackford that Che was physically weak, and, in mood, perfectly docile. Zenteno had instructions from General Barrientos of some importance.

The colonel looked about him. There were six other officers breakfasting, but they were in the far corner of the dining room, and the radio on the high shelf above the kitchen door was blaring out the melancholy songs of the area, with twangy guitars providing a percussive accompaniment that made it easy to keep Colonel Zenteno's voice all to himself. The colonel talked and ate at the same time.

"What I am telling you is of course confidential. I had yesterday evening a telephone call from the President. General Barrientos has reaffirmed the decision of the High Command to execute the guerrilla Guevara, even as he would have executed us if he had caught us, and even as he executed the Cuban guerrillas at Escambray when he was in Cuba. I and Colonel Selnich will question him"—he looked at his watch—"beginning at eight. You may sit with us or not as you desire. There are two other guerrilleros captured, in the other room in the schoolhouse. They will be questioned simultaneously, then shot.

"Are there any questions you wish us to ask him?"

"Probably not many you wouldn't be asking him anyway. We've cracked his codes, as you know. But we haven't been able to cross-check all the aliases he has been using. Our records could use an alias key."

"That is on our list."

"Is he that cooperative?"

"Yesterday evening he was not only cooperative, he was talkative. Who knows today?"

"I assume you have not told him he is going to be shot?"

"We have not. When he was captured, he told the soldier who had the rifle aimed at him, 'Don't shoot! Don't shoot! I am Che Guevara, and I am worth much more to you alive than dead.' "

Zenteno laughed. "He is not worth a hundred pesos to us now. His movement is abolished. He was a total failure. He is worth money only to his worshippers. There are no Bolivians among them. Except the two in an adjoining room in the schoolhouse, and they will be late-Che-worshippers by noon." Again he laughed, and lit a cigarette.

"I have four or five questions to put to him that the Agency wants asked. That is why I am here. I have also a personal question to ask him."

"Then you do not wish to sit with us while we interrogate him?"

"No. You are recording your exchange?"

"Of course."

"Where is the schoolhouse?"

The colonel pointed across the square. "It is the second house from the corner, over there. The second house on the right. Opposite is the church."

"You will send for me?"

"I will send for you."

The call came just after eleven.

Wearing corduroy pants and a sweater, and carrying a clipboard, Blackford Oakes set out across the square, led by a lieutenant. He was taken without ceremony to the entrance to a schoolroom.

He opened the door.

On the right, pushed together, were the children's chair-desks, perhaps ten of them. The teacher's desk had been pulled up toward the door, and in the vacated space a cot had been set.

He lay on it, propped up. Not readily recognizable. He was very thin and very yellow, and he wheezed from his asthma. His chestnut hair curled down, reaching to his shoulders. His beard was fuller than it had been, his moustache also; Che Guevara had not shaved recently. He wore an open gray sweater, and a pipe was on the bed table.

"I understand you know Guevara, Sr. Oakes."

"Yes," Blackford said.

"Well," Zenteno signaled to Colonel Selnich. "Come along, Andrés." And to Blackford, "If you need me, there is a guard outside." The two Bolivian colonels walked out.

"So it was not *adiós* after all, Caimán."

"No, Che. My life was saved by President Kennedy."

"I never pretended I had any voice in your liberation."

"I honor that. Your last words to me were that I was to remember we are at war with each other."

"Yes, and our personal circumstances have changed since that day . . . almost exactly five years ago. Yes. The President gave his speech on October 22, 1962, and here we are . . . October 9, 1967—almost *exactly* on the anniversary. Well, I have lost this one. But you will lose the big one, Caimán. You wait and see.

"But you want to question me, I know. You will find me very helpful respecting all questions the answers to which do not matter. Go ahead. This will not take long." He smiled as he reached for his pipe. "Not like the conversations we had about the Acuerdo."

"I want first to ask whether Fidel Castro ordered the assassination of John Kennedy."

"Oh you do, do you? Well, let me first ask you: Did John F. Kennedy order an assassination of Fidel Castro?"

"I am going to answer that question, Che. He acquiesced in the idea. The initiative was not his. Now will you answer my question?"

"No."

"My next question is: Had any of the missiles been armed with a nuclear warhead by October 22 five years ago?"

"No. In ten days, if there had been no interference, half of them would have been armed. In two weeks, all of them."

"My next question: Did Castro initiate the request for the missiles, or did Khrushchev make the suggestion?"

"It was Khrushchev. Via Adzhubei."

"Next question: Are there any nuclear weapons in Cuba?"

"There were none when I left. It has been over two years, you know. That wretched year in the Congo."

"And finally: Is there any approach that might be made

to Castro that would alter his reliance on the Soviet Union?"

Che laughed, and tugged on his pipe. His voice was weak, but he worked into it the old irony. "The only approach you could make to Castro would be through Mao Tse-tung. In short: No. But know this: Among other things, Castro's prominence, his singularity, requires him to be the dominant communist—the *only* communist power in the western hemisphere. He likes it, Caimán."

The door was abruptly opened. It was the same lieutenant who had led him in.

"I am not quite through, Lieutenant."

"Señor, the colonel needs to speak to you immediately. You can return."

Blackford, who had been sitting on the desk section of one of the children's chairs, got up and followed the lieutenant on the three-minute walk to the hotel. He was led to the dining room, which Colonel Zenteno had turned into a provisional office.

The colonel was flustered. "I have just had a message from the President. It was delivered by messenger from Vallegrande—there are no telephones in La Higuera. The President, and I quote him"—he read from the dispatch he held in his hand—" 'wishes to acknowledge his indebtedness to the CIA and to President Johnson for the help you have given us during this campaign. He is prepared to make a very special gesture.' "

Colonel Zenteno looked up solemnly at Blackford. "You may have the prisoner alive if you wish. If you do not want him, we will proceed with the execution. The story to the press will be that he died in the schoolhouse last night from the wounds after the fire fight.

"Well," the colonel paused, "do you want Che Guevara? If so you will have to have a military plane come to La Paz."

Blackford drew breath. "I would need to consult with Washington."

"There is no possibility of that. Before the day is over, one half the journalists in the hemisphere will find La Higuera. He must have died—or have been turned over to the United States."

"He is not guilty of any crime committed on American territory."

"Please, Sr. Oakes. Do not go into questions of American law. Return to finish your questions—how much longer do you want?"

"Three minutes."

"And then you tell us. He is your prisoner—or our corpse. We will be waiting."

The altitude made it no easier for Blackford. He was short of breath when ushered back into the schoolroom. He began to talk, but was interrupted by the shots. Four of them. In the adjacent schoolroom.

"Well," Che remarked, drawing on his pipe. "There go Willy and Aniceto."

Blackford paled. "Che, I want to ask you now a personal question. What happened to the reprieve of execution you and Castro signed for Catalina?"

"Castro never signed it. I forged his signature."

Blackford's eyes narrowed. "What then happened to the reprieve?"

"I burned it"—he drew his pipe under his left hand, simulating a match burning a piece of paper.

"Why did you do that?"

Che shrugged his shoulders. "Castro wanted her killed."

"Did you know that at the time you signed the reprieve?"

"Yes."

There was silence.

"Her execution—" Che began. But stopped. He decided not to tell what little he had in fact done for Catalina, sparing her preknowledge of the firing squad. It would have had a supplicatory feel, unmanly, under the circumstances.

"—Nothing. Never mind."

Blackford had remained standing ever since his return from the meeting with the colonel. He was leaning against the door. He paused a long moment.

"Well. I guess it's goodbye, Che."

"*Adiós, Caimán.*"

There was a slight wave of the hand.

Blackford walked out into the sun. Colonel Zenteno was there, also a sergeant with a carbine rifle, and the two guards. Blackford looked up at the colonel.

"He is your prisoner, Colonel."

Colonel Zenteno acknowledged the communication and its meaning with a decisive nod of his head.

Blackford started off toward the hostelry, breathing deeply the rarefied spring air. He had gone only a few steps when he heard the two shots.

ACKNOWLEDGMENTS

I am indebted to a number of sources, but most particularly to *Family Portrait With Fidel* (1984) by Carlos Franqui. This revealing narrative, by a sometime friend and colleague of Fidel Castro, is a singular feat of portraiture. I owe a great deal to Mr. Franqui, with whom I also visited. Richard Goodwin recounted his experiences with Che Guevara following the Punta del Este conference in 1961 in *The New Yorker* (May 25, 1968). Two biographies of Che Guevara were helpful, both titled *Che Guevara*, the first by Daniel James (1969), the second by Andrew Sinclair (1970). And a most informative book on the missile crisis is *Strike in the West* (1963) by James Daniel and John G. Hubbell. Once again I found *A Thousand Days*, by Arthur M. Schlesinger, Jr., useful; perhaps more useful than Professor Schlesinger might have wished.

I am most particularly grateful to Antonio Navarro, a Cuban-American New York business executive who in 1981 wrote *Tocayo*, an account of his own experiences under Castro until his flight from Cuba in 1961. He gave me one hundred useful details about Havana and otherwise guided me, relying on his knowledge of Cuban terrain, manners, and history. There are anomalies in the book and one or two anachronisms for which he is not responsible.

Dorothy McCartney, the research director of *National Review*, was once again invaluable. She hopes that future books, if there are to be any, will happen in European countries, access to whose urban features is ever so much easier. I am grateful to Miss McCartney; as also to the indispensable Frances Bronson, whose editorial coordination and drive make life possible.

Samuel S. Vaughan of Doubleday once again acted as my editor. It is inconceivable that anyone alive could have given better advice, or taken greater care. I am profoundly grateful to him. I record also, with gratitude, the criticisms of Christopher Buckley, my son; of Patricia Buckley, my wife; of Priscilla Buckley and Reid Buckley, siblings; of Lois Wallace, Thomas Wendel, Charles Wallen, Jr., and Sophie Wilkins. Dear Sophie couldn't stand the book's title, and I think the world should know how heavily she labored to persuade me to change it.

Alfred Aya, Jr., who is my personal Aberdeen Proving Ground, this time around coached me on how to get a bomb to explode at a predetermined altitude. For the benefit of all, I elected to leave out one crucial detail, *pax vobiscum.*

Chaucy Bennetts of Doubleday once again did her splendid job of copy editing. I am bound to profess that in my lifetime I have never come across anyone with her combination of taste and knowledge in editorial detail. And, of course, I would not publish a book Joseph Isola had not copy read. My thanks to them both.

W.F.B.
Stamford, Connecticut
July 26, 1984